Nothing's as sexy as a boy in uniform,
especially if he's one of the

Raw
Recruits
the second edition

A Collection of Stories
and two Erotic Novellas,
Edited by
JOHN PATRICK

STARbooks Press
Sarasota, FL

Other Books by STARbooks Press

First Edition Published in the U.S. in August, 1998
Second Edition Published in the U.S. in December, 2002

ISBN No. 1-891855-41-7

Contents

Editor's Note

Most of the stories appearing in this book take place prior to the years of The Plague; the editor and each of the authors represented herein advocate the practice of safe sex at all times. And, because these stories trespass the boundaries of fiction and non-fiction, to respect the privacy of those involved, we've changed all of the names and other identifying details.

"In Italy young men live with their families,
have girlfriends and get married. The idea of the
family remains intact, and the power of the Church
has seen to it. However, most Italian boys lead
bisexual lives, particularly in the brief time they are
away from their families doing national service.
Soldiers give themselves for a good meal or an
evening's drinking. The encounters are brief and
forgotten in the morning. Sexuality has a value,
and 'bellafigura' its price."
- Derek Jarman,

INTRODUCTION:
A TASTE FOR SEAFOOD
by John Patrick

Having a yen for sex with men in uniform cuts across all classes. Celebrities, however, can indulge their fantasies more often than most it seems, especially as it relates to gay-for-pay scenes with otherwise closeted studs.

Jean Cocteau, for instance, enjoyed affairs with sailors and rough trade. In his unsigned autobiography *Le livre blanc*, acknowledged that he recognized his love of youths when at a very young age he first saw a fresh farm boy bathing naked, and fainted in an ecstasy of joy and fear at the sight of his penis in the midst of its dark patch of pubic hair. In his book *My Dear Boy*, Rictor Norton notes, "At the Grand Condorcet school in 1903 Cocteau fell in love with Pierre Dargelos, the thirteen-year-old school vamp, who had 'the beauty of an animal... that insolent beauty that is only heightened by filth.' Shortly afterwards, Cocteau was expelled for 'disciplinary reasons.' He was sent to another school, but absconded for the port of Marseilles, where he indulged in drugs (he was a life-long opium eater) and sexual affairs with sailors and rough trade."

Another famed celebrity, George Cukor, usually fulfilled his desire for sailors and rough trade on trips overseas, but when he was in Hollywood, his tricks of this type were usually brought to his mansion by his friends. In his book about the director, *A Double Life*, Patrick McGilligan says, "By the 1930s, he pursued sexual gratification with the same fervor he applied to his career. ...There were plenty of young men in and around the fringes of the motion-picture industry, in and around Los Angeles. He and his friends made forays to the beach, to the desert communities—especially to Long Beach, where sailors roamed the streets—to pick up their sexual tricks. Cukor rarely went alone. The group not only afforded security but facilitated the approaches, at which Cukor was notoriously clumsy.

"Part of the function of the group—informally, but a function—was to pass the tricks around, and to keep Cukor supplied with sexual partners. Andy Lawler, for example, was notorious in the circle for cruising practically every night, and for being Cukor's procurer—passing on tricks to Cukor, who had no compunction about passing on his tricks afterward to someone else. One of the legendary tricks was Bob Seiter, a would-be actor, the brother of director William Seiter, as much a 'cockhound' as his brother was a cocksman. Seiter, from St. Petersburg, Florida, is spoken of fifty years later as one of the all-time legendary lookers. Everyone in the circle had a chance at him. After Cukor, Seiter went up to Santa Barbara for a fling with Alex Tiers. Seiter was so well liked, quite apart from his being so handsome, that he was one of the few tricks that graduated into the circle itself. This was rare. Even the popular tricks had a transient appeal. But Seiter stayed in Hollywood as a film editor, and became everyone's friend—no longer a trick. Cukor himself preferred heterosexual, masculine men. He did not like his lovers to be effeminate or blatantly homosexual. He could discover beauty in all types of women in his films, but his ideal of male pulchritude was a strict one: young men who were invariably tallish, muscular, with broad shoulders and sculpted faces. Never Jewish. The guardsman type—preferably in a uniform of any kind.

"Cukor had a predilection for young sailors, whom his friends, in amusement, dubbed 'seafood.' Most of the young men were anonymous, just passing through. They never stayed in his life very long—a week, a month. After a while, a new boyfriend bored him, he said. According to close friends, there was never any emotional intimacy between Cukor and his partners—never any confidences—just sex, usually paid sex.

"The director of some of the screen's most stirring love stories relinquished the idea of true love in his own life. He didn't harbor any romantic illusions. For one thing, Cukor couldn't help but suspect that his pickups were attracted to him only because of his status as an important director. For another, Cukor's friends were, if not leading men, then handsome, dashing, and (unlike him) athletic, as well as wealthy. All things considered, they were among the most desirable homosexual men in Hollywood. By comparison, Cukor had to feel, more than ever, fattish and ugly.

"'He was the mecca' is how one longtime Cukor friend put it. 'You met everybody through Cukor.' Invitations were screened, of course—for a long time James Vincent was an informal majordomo in charge of Cukor's parties—because Cukor had to be concerned about the possible theft of valuables from his house. However, there was also a lot of 'Who do you know?' and 'Just bring him along.' There was sometimes a sprinkling of hustlers and hopefuls, dubious characters, and tricks at the Sunday parties. '...Some people were there for the purpose of getting tricks for George,' said a friend, 'because George wouldn't and couldn't go to bars.' In this secret society, it was an act of friendship to take someone to meet Cukor— someone who might appeal to him—because everyone close to the director knew he was afraid to go out and look for people, and that he had a fear of being recognized. People also knew that Cukor was notoriously inept—a notoriously poor judge of tricks—when picking people up. 'There was always a little sharing here and there,' said Bob Raison. 'It was the least someone could do, after all his (Cukor's) entertaining, to bring up a cute thing once in a while, reciprocally.'

"'If George liked someone, he might have them back and sleep with them himself,' explained Cukor pal Bob Wheaton. 'A very nice operation all around, and I met some very nice people that way myself.' The Sunday parties helped provide a turnover in sex partners.

"'George was mainly interested in 'trade,' noted another Cukor pal,

Michael Garman, 'someone he knew he wouldn't have to put up with.'

"'The boys were always given a few dollars and a lovely dinner,' said long-time Cukor aide Bob Raison.

"...In the years after World War II, a Hollywood rivalry began to develop between Cukor's circle and another clique of homosexual men that gathered, also on Sundays, at the home of the celebrated composer and songwriter Cole Porter.

"Cukor and Cole Porter were not intimate, but professionally they were best of friends. ...An unspoken competition went on between these two world-class egos with their magnificent houses and friends in common, however, for each saw himself as the center of this unique homosexual universe. Behind their backs (no one would have dared say it to Cukor's face), some referred to them as the rival Queens of Hollywood. There was some competition, especially, over the handsome young soldiers and sailors who were abundant in postwar Hollywood...

"Cukor usually had some professional excuse to scout foreign locales and write off expenses. ...Wheaton remembered the long, stimulating conversations they would have while driving between cities. Friends have commented on how different Cukor could seem overseas, how relaxed and open. He would behave differently, do things in Europe he wouldn't do in the United States, where he carried the weight of his importance. One of Cukor's favorite stories for intimates was of the times he and Somerset Maugham cruised sailor boys in Nice. Cukor wouldn't have dared to be so flagrant in Hollywood in the 1940s. 'In Europe he (Cukor) could be an ordinary person, not a great and famous man,' said Wheaton. 'There was a bit of sex mixed in with it all,' continued Wheaton. 'For example, he was always afraid to do things in an automobile. That was too frightening for him. That didn't inhibit me, if I happened to meet someone in the Italian Navy. George wouldn't do anything himself. But he was relaxed enough to drive the car while I did.' Another reason why Wheaton was Cukor's ideal companion is that he was good at making introductions to men. 'George wasn't great at picking up. That's why he liked traveling with me, or someone else.' ...Once, outside Palermo, Wheaton remembered, they picked up two stunning men—Wheaton had an Adonis tennis player, and Cukor a sailor from New Zealand just off the boat. The sailor happened to be married. For twenty years afterward, Wheaton recalled, Cukor stayed in touch with this particular sailor and sent him letters and toys for his children. 'Whenever I came to visit (Cukor),' said Wheaton, 'he would always show me the Christmas card from (him).'"

Famed literary lions also loved seafood. Henry James, starved of love all his life, was warmed by vitality and youth, especially the splendid frame, the simplicity, even the so-called "unletteredness" of the artist Hendrik Andersen, thirty years his junior, which often has a piquant appeal for the sophisticated. A. L. Rowse in *Homosexuals in History* says, "James did not respond like this to intellectuals: too much of that already in his own life' he felt happier with simpler types: that was why he felt comfortable with the sailors and the lifeguards.

"There followed the usual symptoms, the aching void of absence. 'Since then I have missed you out of all proportion to the three meager little days (for it seems strange they were only that) that we had together,' he said. The Master remembered the young giant at every turning, every corner of the road they had bicycled together. Weeks later, 'I walked up from the station that soft summer morning of your departure, much more lonely than I should have thought three days of companionship could, in their extinction, have made me.' At this time the Master shaved his beard: it succeeded in making him look years younger. Very exceptionally, the letters of this intellectual devious man to Andersen take to physical expressions. 'I hold you close', 'I feel, my dear boy, my arms around you', 'I meanwhile pat you affectionately on the back, across the Alps and Apennines, I draw you close, I hold you long'.

"A year or two later: 'The sense that I can't *help you,* see you, talk to you, touch you, hold you close and long, or do anything to make you rest on me—this torments me, dearest boy, makes me ache for you, and for myself. I wish I could go to Rome and put my hands on you (oh, how lovingly I should lay them)'... And so on.

"The Master tried to lure Hendrik to stay for good with him, offering him the studio next door, evidently wishing to set up the master-pupil relationship he so readily assumed with writers. Hendrik was very sparing of his visits and his physical charms; he saw in the Master a useful promoter of his career, but remained obstinately in Rome. About this same time that James woke up, so belatedly, to life's possibilities he fell for a far more attractive personality: Jocelyn Persse, of old Anglo-Irish family and of a 'constituted aura of fine gold and rose-color.' There was an easy, intuitive rapport between the older and younger man in this case, though in later years Persse said: 'Why he liked me so much I cannot say.'"

Another literary lion who liked men in uniform was the novelist Hart Crane. "In Washington," Rowse says, "Crane went in for drunken orgies; soldiers and sailors were always available. He did not care for the professionalism of accredited homosexual circles, rather deploring a well-known painter and a poet whom I recognize as an acquaintance of D.H.Lawrence. Crane found the willingness of sailors on the sea-front and in the bars somehow more authentic and more rewarding: they had a physical need, so had he. With one of these, a steward away on eight-week cruises, Crane had a more permanent relationship, which entered into his imagination.

"His lusts, however, were not his ruin, but drink: he was becoming an alcoholic. Often enough his waterfront sessions would end in a drunken fracas, and a beating up. Everywhere provided experiences freely. In the Isle of Pines he had met a young Cuban sailor 'in Park Central. Immaculate, ardent and delicately restrained, I have learned much about love that I did not think existed. What delicate revelations may bloom from the humble! It is hard to exaggerate'. 'Though a sailor could give Hart a week of happiness during Christmas of 1929 and during a few days of May 1930 when, back from Cuba, he spent his leave at Hart's apartment, most of Crane's relaxed moments were often of shorter duration.' These were wilder, more dangerous evenings with drinking companions. Crane's last phase in Mexico yielded even freer and easier experiences, more varied than ever before, 'it would take a book to describe it'. He had never cared for the professionals of Greenwich Village and Hollywood; he fell for the happy and spontaneous sexuality of the Mexicans, whether heterosexual or homosexual, it did not seem to matter. 'Ambidexterity is all in the fullest masculine tradition. I assure you from many trials and observations. The pure Indian type is decidedly the most beautiful animal imaginable, including the Polynesian, to which he often bears a close resemblance. Even Lawrence couldn't resist some lavish descriptions of their fine proportions.'"

You didn't have to be a literary lion or a celebrity to indulge your taste for seafood, especially during the war. Many boys had their first homosexual encounters and formed their earliest queer alliances as a direct result of their participation in the service of the wartime labor market. Allan Sherman (a heterosexual) described this culture shock dramatically in his 1973 book, *The Rape of the A*P*E**, "There were 13 million of us drafted to fight for God and country, and every one a full-fledged, clean-cut, wholesome, decent, interchangeable American boy. We all kissed Mom and Dad good-bye at the railroad station." Then they were shipped out and whipped into shape by foul-mouthed, intimidating superiors. Soon the realization hit: "It was almost too good to be true. *Everything* in the army was obscene or pornographic." With fifty men sharing a latrine, toilet taboos vanished "in a symphony of grunts and smells and flushing noises." Privacy was nonexistent. "Answering nature's call meant subjecting yourself to loud and detailed criticism—perceptive and merciless descriptions of your sex organs, ranging from ridicule to glowing admiration." This became a game for many men, and a challenge for others. Soldiers soon learned to flaunt their genitals and brag about their toilet mannerisms.

"Anyone who was modest about these was immediately and forever labeled a homosexual. (In those days, that was an insult.)"

"Suddenly," Bill Brent said in *Black Sheets*, "a generation of servicemen raised under the oppressively genteel mantle of American Victorianism were forced into an awareness of one another's most intimate body parts and bodily functions. San Francisco was the point of departure and reentry for many men involved in the war. Those searching for the growing number of gay bars and restaurants in this port town got an unknowing assist from the armed services themselves, who routinely posted lists of off-limits bars. Rather than returning home, many soldiers (and particularly those dishonorably discharged for homosexuality) stayed or settled in San

Francisco after their service ended. After the war, masculine gay men began to seek out each other in rough waterfront bars, cruising areas, and other venues. Eventually, the S/M-oriented ones coalesced into two factions: those who enjoyed sexual power play modeled on the military system of rank they knew so well, and a group of more free-spirited others who formed the prototype of the gay biker image."

One of those who enjoyed the sex available during the war—and profited richly from it—was John Barrington, notorious photographer of the male nude from the '40s to the '60s, who deliberately distanced himself from obvious queers and their soft, effeminate ways. He contrasted his own healthy bisexuality with their soft, pink homosexuality. "At the time, though," Rupert Smith reveals in the delightful biography *Physique*, that John "enjoyed the gay clubs with their sexually charged atmosphere that spilled out on to the darkened streets. It was at this time that he started enjoying 'trade,' a term he learnt from his friends to describe the servicemen and other hustlers who frequented the clubs and streets."

Barrington himself described these wonderful days: "Uninhibited, open queerness was acceptable as long as one didn't go 'too far'. What 'too far' meant was never clear to me; it certainly didn't include propositioning attractive bobbies on the beat. London was becoming decadent, said some. It was certainly very gay. There were so many clubs: the Boeuf sur le Toit in Panton Street, The A&B in Wardour Street, The Starlight opposite, Jimmy's in Denmark Street, Lady Molly Howard's in Newport Street, the Burlington, the Rockingham and half a dozen piano-music-filled establishments discreetly catering to members and their forces guests. From June 1940 there were a lot of Free French, Free Polish, Free Belgian, Dutch, Norwegian and Swedish young men in uniform, at loose in the West End. A certain section of Londoners had never had it so good. The authorities turned a blind eye; the police, especially, had other things to do."

Barrington was always afraid of girls who might steal away his boyfriends. These vixens would spend the night with a good-looking serviceman, would take presents of cash or nylons from the officers, and would even allow themselves to be kept in rented flats by well-to-do admirers. Smith comments: "They had polished to a fine point the business of being a whore without standing on a street corner. They never actually charged, they never made bargains, there were no financial transactions, they just said hello and laughed with the boys who took their fancy and kept them company till the morning, extracting as much as they could in the way of gifts, meals and drinks. Leicester Square was a seething mass of young men in uniform. The ones that were moving around were heterosexual, looking for girls. The ones that were leaning against the railings were trade, looking for men because they wanted to get paid.

"All the girls loved John, the eccentric, attractive young man who encouraged them in their exploits, told them all how talented they were, advised them on their dress and was available for double dating if there were enough sailors to go around. It didn't take him long to realize that the easiest way of picking up the good-looking, masculine men that he preferred was not by cruising the gay bars, but rather by frequenting the places that a serviceman on leave would go looking for female company. There the boys would drink, flirt and allow themselves to be seduced by a man if they were feeling curious enough. It was a fantastically successful ploy, as much of John's wartime correspondence testified. 'My dear John,' wrote a sailor named Bobby, 'What a pleasant surprise to hear from you again —and many thanks for the enclosed. Came at a very opportune moment I must say. Well, I can always do with some anytime... Anyhow I'm looking forward very much to seeing you agai,n John, as we have got a lot to make up for haven't we? Will you save one of those 'grand mysteries' for me when I get leave again John?

"John had perfected his routine. He picked Bobby up in the Cafe Royal, introduced him to the girls, plied him with drinks and took him back to one of the West End flats and offices that were his overnight stops. There he photographed him (some portraits, some nudes), had sex with him and sent him back to his ship with his horizons considerably broadened (and, as Bobby's letter shows, with a few extra pounds in his pocket).

"Many faces came and went in John's wartime circle of girlfriends— some of them got married and gave up the West End life, some of them were killed in air raids. There were always plenty of new girls in town to take their place... There was one more layer to John's London life during the Blitz. While not pulling dead bodies out of smoldering buildings or living it up in the clubs, John could be found relaxing in one of the city's steam baths. He had started going to the Central London YMCA on the corner of Great Russell Street to clean up after his ARP shifts, and had immediately discovered to his delight that the hot showers were crowded every afternoon with servicemen eager for relief, who wouldn't even cost him a few shillings in drinks and cab fares. Some of them he would take away to photograph; others he would quickly enjoy and move on. From the YMCA, he explored further: the Imperial Baths in Bloomsbury Square, the Turkish Baths in Regent Street, bath houses as far afield as Bermondsey and the Elephant and Castle. Some of the boys in the baths were interested in a bit of casual whoring, but rarely charged more than a meal and a bed for the night."

Interestingly, Barrington would share the wealth, especially if he thought it would do him some good. For instance, one notable whose life he enhanced was the esteemed theater critic, James Agate, the scourge of the *Sunday Times* and a prolific autobiographer, author of the multi-volumed *Ego* series. ...By 1942, they were on cordial terms. Smith reports, "'You do seem to have the most delightful young friends,' remarked Agate one night to John, who proceeded to show him photographs of some of the sailors and soldiers he had admired. 'Agate has captured my nice Welsh soldier!' he complained to his diary. ...At first they would have drinks together, then

Agate started taking John to first nights and taught him the grand manner, of which he was a fine exponent. ...If John saw in Agate a mentor, Agate found John endlessly amusing, an eccentric type as well as a good source of soldiers. One night over whiskeys in the Cafe Royal, they decided to concoct a dialogue between the critic and a 'Young Man' for inclusion in the forthcoming volume of *Ego*. ...John teased Agate with stories of his sexual conquests, showed him photographs and letters from his favorite sailor friends, among them the permanently randy Bobby...."

At war's end, Barrington celebrated like everyone else. He wrote, "Impossible to get into Corner House, crowds too great. So pick up superb sailor, take him to office and fuck him 'silly', an exceptional activity for both of us. Give him a bottle of whisky and ,5. ...At 3 a.m. tiredness crept over London. People just sat down and talked. A few made love. Young men with girls. And I also saw in dark doorways and in phone boxes sailors and kneeling men. ...Nice lonely sailor, never learnt his name, at same table. Big, tall, very masculine. Dark hair, blue eyes, olive skin, perfect teeth. Half an hour's chat. Established that he never had. Couldn't. Nothing a man could do would make him come, so what's the point. A real challenge. Took him—without much protest—to my office and persuaded him to show me his body. And then a rapid erection as he assumed poses. A little more persuasion and he lay on the divan, posing as a sleeping god. A jaw-aching, tongue-tiring hour resulted in his sheepish, grudging admission that everything is possible given the right time place, incentive and partner. I'd like to have seen him again, but he wouldn't even join me for breakfast. Half a tumbler of whisky, a refusal to let me kiss his cheek, and he was gone into the now- depleted crowds. Before he disappeared he raised his arm with a clenched fist, but he didn't look back."

After the war, the sex scene in the U.S. had changed appreciably. In *Lonely Hunters*, James T. Sears recalled the sex scene in Charleston in the '50s and '60s: "Navy and air force men could be readily picked up along the Battery, in the town square, or at the Meeting Street bus stop. African-American homosexuals could also be found walking down Meeting Street. 'Cruising was easy,' our respondent Billy Camden recalled. 'Sex was easy in the fifties and sixties! They were just horny soldiers. If they had had a choice—a man or a woman—most would have taken the woman; but the choice, at the moment, was a man—so they took it! Of course, some of these men would want money before or after, and a lot of gay people got into trouble.'

"As in all cities during the homophile era, the life of the homosexual posed dangers. Unlike cities such as Miami, where police ruthlessly raided bars and patrons' names appeared in the morning newspaper, Charleston was more refined. Care and discretion though, as Billy pointed out, were paramount: 'For people who were in the military, teachers, government and state workers—if they found out you were gay, then they would lose their jobs. So these people were very careful not to be seen in a place known as a 'gay bar', which is why a lot of the bars were mixed. Those are the places where people went. Even if you were a civilian working for a private company but were hanging around military or government employees, the navy would investigate you. They'd go in and question you and your employers trying to get people fired.'

"He vividly recalls one visit from naval intelligence officers: 'They came in with a whole photo book of marines, navy, and air force men they suspected of being homosexuals. They wanted to see if I could identify any. Well, I wouldn't let them interview me at my business. I made them come to my house, making it as inconvenient as possible for them. But I was cordial, and of course I did not recognize any as homosexuals.' (Laughs) 'Sure are some good-looking men,' I commented to one of the investigators, "'but I don't know any of them.'"

In his book *Monsters in the Closet*, Harry M. Benshoff talks about "secret societies and shadowy sailors at RKO" in Hollywood during its Golden Age, the time during which Cukor began his career. But Benshoff notes things changed radically after World War II: "One of the biggest changes… was the ever-increasing number of individuals and communities specifically identified as homosexual. As one historian puts it: 'World War II created a substantially new 'erotic situation' conducive both to the articulation of a homosexual identity and to the more rapid evolution of a gay subculture.

"Richard Dyer expands upon this: 'The war involved mass mobilization, throwing men together with men in the military and women together with women in both the military and on the home front. It created conditions in which homosexual experience became almost commonplace and in which people might easily realize they were gay and well known to be so.'

"In other words, despite the Armed Services' determination to 'weed out' homosexuals during the recruiting process, such attempts regularly failed and many gay men and lesbians found themselves (and others like them) in uniform. For those who could 'pass' as straight, or for those whose deviances were overlooked, tentative communities of homosexuals arose within the hetero-centrist world of the Armed Services. Many were hunted out and expelled. Some of these less fortunate men and women received the infamous 'blue' discharge, which effectively denied them their GI honors and benefits.

"Lesbian historian Lillian Faderman notes how these men and women were loaded on 'queer ships' and sent… to the nearest U.S. port. Many of them believed that they could not go home again. They simply stayed where they were disembarked, and their numbers helped to form the large homosexual enclaves that were beginning to develop in port cites such as New York, San Francisco, Los Angeles, and Boston.

"Paradoxically, institutionalized government discrimination may have helped to solidify the urban gay and lesbian community and its emerging sense of identity. The idea of homosexuals forming secret societies and coteries was prevalent during the pre-Stonewall decades. While this notion would develop into the idea of homosexuals forming almost communist cell-type structures during the 1950s, other commentators understood that the 'secret society' of homosexuals was necessary as a means of survival...

"Sailors have especially figured in gay erotic tradition... for a number of possible reasons: longer enforced periods spent in enclosed single-sex environments suggest they may have greater homosexual experience; their rootlessness accords with the anonymity and fleetingness of much gay sexual contact... Even their clothing, perhaps by association, seems more erotic—open-necked tops suggesting broad chests; trousers worn tight at the crotch and made of molding serge; the flap fly; bell bottoms, which emphasize, by their oddity, naval costume as costume.

"As is appropriate for a sailor's tale with homoerotic undercurrents, *The Ghost Ship* does indulge in a bit of visual beefcake surrounding bare torsos and tight T-shirts. Interestingly, the one port at which the ghost ship docks is named 'San Sebastian,' a name linked repeatedly throughout history with male queers and immortalized by homosexual artists including Caravaggio, Tennessee Williams, Yukio Mishima, and Derek Jarman. *The Ghost Ship is* also filled to the brim with overdetermined phallic signifiers. Gleaming knives are featured prominently, first seen (in the film's opening shot) in the window of 'Rubin's Seamen's Outfitting Co.,' and eventually in the climactic knife-fight. Other phallic signifiers foregrounded by the text include hypodermic needles, scalpels, guns, spikes, and cigars. One of the film's most striking sequences involves a large cargo-hook that swings out of control during a storm at sea: it serves as an apt metaphor for untethered and uncontrolled phallic power, and as such comes to represent the obsessed Captain Stone's monomania."

During the war, "soldiers and sailors swarmed through this teeming crossroads, and gay men pursued them with abandon," Charles Kaiser notes in *The Gay Metropolis*. "Tennessee Williams loved to cruise Times Square with Donald Windham in the forties. Williams recalled making 'very abrupt and candid overtures, phrased so bluntly that it's a wonder they didn't slaughter me on the spot.' First the soldiers stared in astonishment; then they usually burst into laughter. Finally, after a brief conference, 'as often as not, they would accept' the playwright's invitation."

Franklin Macfie was the son of a merchant seaman and he became enamored of all his sisters' soldier-boyfriends during the war. He looked like a Highlander, with vivid green eyes. By his fourteenth birthday, in 1951, he had already had sex with several men. But he marks Memorial Day weekend of that year as the moment when he "officially came out."

"I met a man in Rockefeller Center who took me home," Macfie remembered. "The space around the skating rink used to be a big cruising ground. He was an actor. I remember he picked me up—literally—when we got home. He carried me across the threshold like I was Irene Dunne. It was the first time I knew, the minute I started talking to the guy in Rockefeller

Center, that I was going to go home with him, and I knew we'd fuck."

Soldier sex has become one of the turn-ons these days for gay writer Edmund White, who says, "If you're 57 like me, and overweight, and your hair's turning white... I couldn't get into the bars in Paris, but I pick up a lot of sex sort of peripherally, with people who think they're straight, or working class people, or soldiers, or hustlers or trade. And by and large, I've had a lot more fun than I did when I was on the A-list."

Sometimes it's enough if an object of your affection happens to *look* as if he belongs in uniform. Tim Miller recounts in his marvelous book *Shirts&Skin* the time he was serving on a panel once in England, when he noticed a boy in row four who was "so pretty. He had that wonderful, slightly shocked Scots-Irish nineteenth-century look, like those old daguerreotype photos of the fresh-faced Civil War soldiers of both sides, so optimistic about their big adventure before they got slaughtered at Antietam or Chickamauga. This look on the alternative-styled queer boy in row four made him exactly the kind of young man Walt Whitman would favor on his shifts as a nurse back at the Civil War hospital. Old Walt would have given many lingering thigh massages to such a youth. Row Four and I kept looking at each other. I felt both foolish and daring to be flirting in so public an arena. Remembering that I was on a public panel, I thought I'd better say something intelligent and earn my keep. I suppose I needed to show off for Row Four. Fortunately, I hadn't been talking too much, so I wouldn't be a panel hog if I spoke up now. I couldn't have this young man... thinking I'm a dumb faggot.

"...I was hoping my comments would have impressed the Celtic beauty. He kept looking up shyly at me under his beach-umbrella-size eyelashes. I tried to pay attention to what was happening on-stage, but I felt weirdly drawn to this man in the audience. I had a fateful feeling of a pressure cooker building up steam. It wasn't just the shirt, though the shirt was a big tip-off. There was a feeling inside me of a camera lens focusing for a close-up shot of my heart. With the flair of a computer graphic, the eye of the camera went right through skin and bone to gaze on the rhythm of my bellowing aorta. Everything else in the room started to recede, and I was left in the theater at the ICA, where I had performed many times in my life, with just a spotlight on me and this guy in Row Four."

Later, Miller said he finally met the youth. "'I saw you in the audience at the panel,' I said. He looked nervous for a second. It was a look I would come to recognize later as that of a man who is close enough to his actual feelings to find it difficult to be anything but honest. He had the alertness and the terror of a sleek animal during hunting season. It seemed like he didn't know what to say next. 'Well, thanks for coming,' I said. 'I'm Tim.' 'I'm Alistair.' He pronounced the last syllable of his name so that it rhymed with *hair*. ...It seemed like he was still learning to occupy the man's body he had suddenly found himself in. His chest and arms bore vivid hints of the grownup strength that was going to arrive as soon as he shook off the final terrors of adolescence. We shook hands. A buzz moved through me, like sticking a fork in a light socket. Our hands held each other and saw the future. I saw a kiss in a bus station in Scotland. I saw his asshole squeezing my dick dry a thousand times. ...I saw hearts that might open to each other. I saw the impossibility of the situation becoming possible. Then the room came back into view."

MY BOY
by Jack Ricardo

I made an effort to be at Man's Land Sunday for their first- ever Underwear Night, with half-price drinks to men sporting skivvies. I've never been to any public event wearing just my briefs, but I warmed at the idea of a roomful of vigorous men swilling bargain beer and cruising around in their shorts. I did have second thoughts, though, when I pulled into the lot. Few cars were there. I was hoping for a crowd to help disguise my apprehension. But what the hell! I gulped up my courage, struggled out of my Levi's, retied my boots, and tucked ten bucks in my sock. I got out of the car and sprinted to the windowless Man's Land. I flung open the door, rushed inside, and was flabbergasted. I was the only man in white. The odd assortment of men standing around were geared up in their usual, denim and leather. I felt a fool. But it was too late. I'd be more of a fool if I scurried out with my tail between my legs. All eyes were on me when I sauntered up to the bar. I have a toned body built by hard work, I have short, dark hair on my head, the same splattered on my chest and webbing into my shorts, and my equipment was well-packed inside my pouch.

My unease was relieved when I eyed the bartender. At least he was wearing skivvies, a pair of gray briefs with the fly and legs outlined in white stripes. He gave me a welcoming grin. "You're lookin' hot, man. What'll you have?" I paid half-price for my beer and ambled to the bench at the side, hoping I didn't look as awkward as I felt.

Then I thought again, Fuck It. Those bastards are gutless. I lifted a leg to the bench, rested my elbow on my knee and looked around. Every man caught my eye and just as quickly left it. Then I spotted him coming from the door behind the bar. I'd seen him at Man's Land before, but not in a jockstrap. And that's all he was wearing now, not counting the laced work boots. He was small and bulky, but not fat by any means, and the muscles of his body only made his bulk more alluring. You could not only sense but also see power there, in his movements, in his stance. He had free rein to come and go behind the bar. I assumed he was the manager. He also had a military bearing about him, in part because of an unusual crew cut that made the hair atop his head spike up about an inch while the sides were shaved to his scalp. That jock he was wearing, that unique, lusty accessory of manhood, added to his soldierly bearing. When he set one foot atop the rail and leaned over to whisper to the bartender, my nuts gave out a spiny tingle. His bare ass was framed by two thin straps of elastic outlining two bold mounds of solid flesh broken by a taunting streak of hair that crawled into his crack.

He turned around, eyed me, and didn't turn away. Neither did I. When he walked towards me, I had an eagle-eye view of a teeming sack holding two balls crowding the mesh and pushing up an outline of a conspicuous cut dickhead. I almost drooled at the sight.

"They ain't got a hair on their asses," he said, sneering at the clothed men. "You got balls, buddy."

I smiled. "I could say the same for you," I replied, flagrantly admiring both his hair and his balls. "But I thought this was Underwear Night, not Jockstrap Night."

"Hey, this is my underwear," he said, lifting his leg to join mine on the bench and snapping the elastic waist band. "Never wear no other kind. Don't hardly ever wash 'em, neither," he added. "Wanna smell?" The idea sent wafts of manful aroma careening into my brain. "Can't wait," I told him. He nodded thoughtfully and said, "Then don't." I sensed rather than saw a playful smile on his face when he added, "I got my boy with me. Wanna meet him?" I hadn't planned on a threesome, but I was game. "I'll follow you."

He turned. I left my can on the rail. The backroom was a storehouse of beer kegs, cardboard cartons, and stacks of soda and beer cases piled haphazardly. A bare bulb hung from the ceiling. I didn't see his boy. And at the moment it didn't matter. He faced me and I cupped my hands over his chest, massaging the hard flesh of his pecs, pricking his nipples.

He reached out, one hand gently petting his fingers over the outline of the cock in my shorts. My dick awakened like a GI at reveille, swift and strong and ready for action.

I swept my hands from his chest to his arms, kneading his hardy biceps, grasping him under the arms. The sweat of his concave pits, the dank hairs crowding them, sparked a fire over my skin. I nestled my face into his neck, gnawing the thick jugular vein with my lips while almost lifting him from his feet as I trailed my mouth over his shoulder, slobbered over his chest, and lifted both arms.

I licked my way under one armpit, spurred on by an arousal accentuated by the potent grip he had on my dick. I opened my mouth and slurped up the raw perspiration.

He snarled in a heavy satisfying undertone, dropped his fist from my shorts, used both hands to cup my ears, and scraped my face over his chest until I lifted his other arm and feasted there, opening my mouth full wide to gobble at, to inhale, to savor the moistened and hairy stench of a hardy soldier's workday. "Go to it, buddy," he ordered, his voice the harsh force of a hurricane. His hands left my head.

I crushed his rib cage with the strength of both hands as I sank down, licking over and biting at the trail of hair that led to the wide jock band. I lashed my tongue over the band, tasted the label, gnawed and snapped the elastic with my teeth. My chin was brushing against a hard cock pulsing inside his pouch. I held his hips, lifted my head, and looked up to see this resolute military man glaring down at me. His hands were overhead and clutching the bare pipes on the wall. The hairs from his armpits were

shining, plastered to his skin by his sweat and my saliva. I
The thickened rod inside his pouch was leaning to the sid
strength of mesh; a dark splotch of juice almost covered th
my nose against the slimy material and inhaled poter
aromatic jock, compelling me to open my mouth and smoth
with my lips. He slammed it into my mouth and a gratifying
his lips like a ball from a cannon.

I wanted more. In one rapid movement that surprised and almost spun
him from his feet, I turned him around until I was faced with the cheeks of
his ass and that enticing chassis of elastic straps. He leaned forward on the
cases with both arms upraised, and spread his legs. I lifted a hand between
his legs and grabbed his pouch from behind, wrenching the contents until he
snapped his head around and emitted a moan that was half-pain and half-
pleasure.

I was aiming for all pleasure. Holding fast to a crowded fist of hard cock
and sweaty balls molded in mesh, I licked my tongue ever so slowly and
carefully down the crack of his ass. His moans suggested more pleasure
than pain. The hairs of his ass strafed over my tongue like flames. I
siphoned up the salty moisture of his crack like a thirsty man in the Arizona
desert. But it was only a taste. I wanted the full meal. I released his pouch
and slipped both hands under the slender straps of his jock, dug my
fingertips into the hard flesh of his cheeks, pulled them apart, briefly eyed
the singular male beauty of hair and pucker, then tickled the ridge of his
asshole with my tongue, scarfing up his smell with my nose. He humped his
ass back with a savage snarl of, "Eat that fucking soldier's asshole, buddy."

I wrapped my wrists around his straps and pinched his ass until he
yelped in his own private pleasure, arrowed my tongue, and plunged it deep
into his hole. My nose was buried in the hairs between his crack while I
flicked my tongue around and around the mushy insides of his asshole,
melting into the soothing sensation of the man. My mind was soaring, my
tongue was alive and snaking every corner it could reach while I yanked his
cheeks apart and rammed my face up his ass.

Again, with a movement he didn't expect, I pulled his body around until
he faced me again, tore down his jock until it dangled at his knees, and was
rewarded with a powerful rod that sprang up like a recruit saluting his
sergeant, its capped head leaking at the hole and as large and as a ripe as an
overgrown cherry tomato. Perhaps it was the biting flavor of the inside of
his ass that made me long for another tongue to taste the inside of mine.

And even though I was damn near breathless, my mind did a sudden spin
and I asked, "Where's your boy?" This time it was his turn to surprise me.
He stepped aside, just out of reach, and left me panting. His legs were still
spread, his chest was heaving and shining with pellets of sweat. He wrapped
the strong fingers of his fist around his cock, peered down at me with
shaded eyes that gave off a wicked smile, and said, "This is my boy, this is
my lover. We live together."

...ughed and he waved his cock in front of me like a staff on the bow ... ip. "I call him Boy," he said. "Open wide and show Boy how much ...u like him." With that be grabbed he by the hair, slipped Boy between my lips, and plugged my throat with the thick, hard flesh of his cock. I damn near choked. But I wasn't about to let this fucker know it. I inhaled from my nose and was rewarded with a hearty whiff of acrid wet cockhairs that made me shiver. I ached to have a gutful of creamy juice to join that tangy aroma. I could almost taste his cum already. I latched onto his hips and started to fuck my face with his cock.

But he pulled out with a vengeance and said, "Boy ain't ready yet. He ain't dressed." He added, "Back off, buddy."

It was a command from a topkick sergeant. But he didn't wait for me to comply. He pushed me onto my back, kicked off his jock, knelt between my legs, shoved his hand in the fly of my briefs, and plucked out my cock. My cut cockhead was stringing with thick, oozing fluid. He shoved his hand down into the waistband of my shorts, snatched at my cockhairs, and rammed his mouth down on my cock. I groaned loudly and clutched at the spikes of his hair while he ravaged my cock and twisted my cockhairs until I thought they'd be plucked from the roots. I lifted my hips and slammed my cock in and out of his throat. He slid his other hand into the back of my shorts and started fingering my ass. When his finger scraped over the tender wrinkles of my asshole, he hit paydirt. My body quivered. I snarled incomprehensibly, mashed his mouth to my cock, forced it to stay while gripping his ears, shot my hips to the ceiling, and blasted off. At the first spurt, he savagely tore his hands from my shorts, pulled my hands from his head, lifted his face, and kept only the globe of my dickhead between his lips while it gushed my seed into his mouth.

I lay there on the cement floor with my eyes closed, gasping for air. The room was quiet, I wondered if he was still there. I opened my eyes. He was sitting on a stack of cases, one foot on the floor, the other lifted onto another case. He was stroking his stiff cock, the head gleaming, due mainly to the covering: a cloudy rubber that molded around the shaft like a second skin. His balls were looped down beneath, as hairy as his ass and just as enticing. Even though I had just dropped a load, I could feel an awakening tingle in my balls when I dug my hand into my shorts and swept my palm over the sagging flesh of my balls. The warm moisture lingered on my hand like dew on a rose. I lifted my hand to my nose, inhaling the well-earned sweat. He watched keenly, a sneaky smile lifting one corner of his lips, then stood up. He walked to where I lay. From my point of view, he was a giant G.I. fisting his cock like a weapon ready for battle. He planted one foot on each side of my chest. His balls waved in the air like two hot air balloons. He knelt down and cautiously swiped his dickhead over my lips. His balls grazed my chin. My nuts gave out more than a tingle this time. He parted my lips with his dickhead. I tasted rubber and flesh, an odd combination. I had never sucked a cock covered with rubber. Maybe he sensed my discomfort. He eased his cock out.

"Take off the rubber," I muttered. "I wanna blow that fucking gun until it shoots down my gut. Take it off," I ordered.

He grumbled something I couldn't understand, then slapped me in the face with his cock. The wallop was as powerful as it was sensual. While he worked his cock over my cheeks, my eyes, my lips, I started to swipe it with my tongue, slobbering it with my spit, the newly-discovered sensation of thin rubber and hard dick awakening new thrills inside me. I wanted more. But I didn't get it.

He stole the treat away and snaked his body down between my legs until he was kneeling on the floor. He tore off my shorts, grabbed my thighs, and lifted my ass. His biceps bulged with the exertion, which only made his robust virility more imposing. He was looking in the eye of my asshole when he leaned over and opened his mouth. Slimy dribbles of cum slopped over his lips and onto my asshole. It was my own cum. It was warm, my ass was hot. He pressed his face down on my ass and began sopping the slimy cum around the hole with his tongue, teasing my hole and starting a grumble in my stomach that rapidly turned to a boil. He lifted his face and dropped one hand from my leg. He reached out, snatched at his jockstrap on the floor, and threw it on my face. He again utilized both hands to grab my ankles and spread me wide. The pouch of the soggy jock was on my lips. I bit down and succored choice unwashed sweat that seeped through the cotton and swept through me like a storm at sea. I gnawed the jock and peered up at him. His hair was blazing strands of electric wire; his mouth was sloppy with spit and cum. His eyes were bright, yet as dark as pissholes in the snow. "Boy is ready now," he said.

He inched his hips forward and positioned my legs until his quivering and dribbling dickhead was pulsing at the door. I let it in. He let it in. His cockhead widened my asshole and plopped inside, a white hot iron spike molding into a warm pot of butter. I snapped my head from side to side, the palms of both hands trying to grip cement, and groaned. "Meet Boy," he said, his voice a hush, yet vibrating inside the room like an echo in a rock canyon. And he rammed Boy home.

One masculine man with his cock speared up the ass of another masculine man. I yelped and gasped and was drowning in a sensation of unqualified power that lifted me and spread me wide while he pounded my ass, while his cock continually plugged me deep and hard and left me craving for more.

"Boy, Boy, Boy," I kept repeating, gulping down air and spouting out, "Boy, Boy, Boy." Each word a grunt, a plea.

"Here's your fucking Boy," he yelled, ramming Boy home, pulling Boy out then plugging him so deep I thought Boy's head would sprout from my mouth.

The sweat from my brow was searing my eyes. The sweat from his chest combined with the sweat of mine as he slammed his body atop me, my ass full of his Boy, Boy pulsating and spitting inside my guts, bringing with it intense and unbridled pleasure, as he clamped his mouth to my face.

His jockstrap was smashed between and scraping both our faces. We both chewed it, snarling at the reeking elastic like two matched wolves in a fair fight while he emptied the cream of his balls into my ass.

Again, I lay on the floor, carefully forcing air into my lungs, the weight of his body now released from mine. Minutes passed before I had the energy to open my eyelids. He was sitting on the floor, eyes wide open, a sated grin on his face. His softening cock was still covered with rubber. He caressed his cock and the rubber with a tenderness that was all the more surprising because it was so endearing.

He said quietly, "I love the feel of rubber on Boy." He slid a finger around the rim of his head, squishing the cum and coating the fleshy knob. His face seemed to turn a slight shade of red. He added, almost apologetically, "I miss it when I'm not wearing it."

"You wear it well," I told him as I grunted to lift myself to my elbows. "You ever wear it on the inside?"

SEAMAN'S REUNION
by Peter Eros

I'm lying here, listening to the sounds of morning, and thinking about the strange course of my life, cradled in the arms of the most gorgeous guy I've ever seen. He's gently snoring, his little puffs of exhaled air warming my shoulder. I just can't believe my good fortune, after a twenty-year search.

My parents' marriage confirmed the vulnerability of youthful alliances. Pop claimed he married in an alcoholic bout of amnesia. He was an error-prone and often tipsy Greek patriarch who was emotionally abusive. He set up a system in which I could never manage to *earn* his love. Mom was his door-mat. Their relationship was a misery. They split when I was fourteen. My only refuge was the local boxing gym, where I sparred around, but with no serious intent.

I realized I was truly gay, with no interest in girls, when I was about fifteen. I soon learned I could earn a few dollars, and relieve my sexual itch, by hanging around flop-house hotels and letting older guys suck me off. They paid even more if I fucked their asses for them. If I liked their looks I sucked them too and learnt to deep-throat cock and swallow jiz. But I never let anyone fuck me. I was no longer adolescent but not yet a man. I guess I alternated between being a child and a man. I was both the seducer and the seduced. The guys I picked up taught me a lot about sex and gave me a little of the masculine affection that I'd lacked and which I craved. But I can't say my activities added to my self-esteem.

Being the only Greek kid, and named Diogenes besides, in a predominantly Hispanic part of the Bronx didn't help. I'd been made to feel unworthy of respect, unworthy of friendship, unworthy of love and protection. And that's when Sly Stallone saved my life. Just before Bicentennial Christmas I saw *Rocky*. He was irresistible as the movie's no-name palooka with a heart of gold who, full of hope and drive, beats all the odds. I was turned on by his hot bod and inspired by his television interviews about his "roaches to riches" story.

I knew I couldn't write a screenplay, and I couldn't really box, though I'd had plenty of fights. But I could build my body with dedicated zeal, and I decided to see the world. I dropped out of school, joined the navy and adopted my second name, Peter. When I think of my service the sorrow is sweet. We Greeks coined a word for it: nostalgia.

In 1977, a lanky sailor from Kansas City taught this chunky sailor from New York all about the right hook. We first met as raw recruits aboard the first ship we were assigned to, a carrier. I was boxing in a tryout match and my opponent slipped me the right hook. It was finesse that I had not encountered before. I started to go down. But then this tall guy, Luke, jumped in and picked me up before I hit the ground. He told me that the punch was not fair, that the guy was not supposed to knock me out. And then he showed me all about the right hook, how to pivot, how to move my feet and how to deliver the devastating punch against other young U.S. navy fighters. He taught me a few other things as well. We soon cottoned that we shared some predilections.

Despite his favored sexuality, Luke was married with a wife and son in Kansas. He had a bronzed, aquiline face, that seemed chiseled out of bone and leather, large, gleeful eyes, black as a shark's, wavy black hair, and a slim but well-muscled frame. He claimed he was part Indian. His arms were like anchor ropes, his hands large and shapely. We became best pals. Luke was only a month older than me but he acted much more mature. He was my protector and though we didn't have much opportunity for intimacy aboard ship, we got together just occasionally to suck or masturbate, and more often to furtively kiss and fondle.

After six months at sea we were wild men. We wanted booze and passion. Those are times I can't forget. My primary objective was to surrender my virgin ass to Luke. I'd been secretly stretching my asshole for months with anything I could safely grease and stick up there, mostly larger and larger bananas. We had a forty-eight hour liberty in Okinawa and Luke took me to a Japanese bathhouse. I didn't realize at first that it was a bathhouse called Palace of Fantasies. It was run like a *ryokan*, a traditional inn, combining the amenities of a sauna, social club, restaurant, hotel and bar.

After paying our money to a grinning Geisha-dressed male, we had to remove our shoes and strip. In return we were given slippers and a *yukata*, the long, flowing kimono, which promises everything yet reveals nothing. We had to explore the building for ourselves, walking through passageways and sliding open doors at random to see what they concealed.

The second floor was the bath area, where we had to switch to special bath slippers made for Thumbelina. We washed down with buckets of water and soap before stepping into the large communal bath where, dewy-eyed and hungry for love, we gave each other exploratory gropes. The Japanese preserved their modesty through this process by use of small towels that doubled as wash-cloths. After that, and a quick visit to the adjoining sauna, we found ourselves in the television lounge and my first experience of eye-popping porn flicks. It didn't take much viewing for my pecker to become hard and bouncing against the fabric of my gown as I viewed possibilities I'd never thought of.

Each of the seven floors above catered for a special interest. There were rooms for sadomasochism, transvestitism, private bedrooms, and that holiest-of-holies, the mixed room. This was a large chamber, spotlessly clean like the rest of the building, but with a pervasive odor of spent sperm. It had a traditional Japanese floor of woven straw mats. On it were many thin mattress beds with head pillows and quilts. In some of them couples were writhing in every kind of sexual activity, oblivious to the little circles of watchers sitting cross-legged in their gowns, paying great attention, like judo students at a lesson.

The very latest American disco-beat records were playing quite loudly. As the Village People's anthem *In the Navy* belted out its sex-charged message, Luke pulled me onto a futon and said: "Let's us *gaijin* give the Nips something to remember, kid."

We shucked our robes, kicked aside the quilt, and fell into a clinch. I'd never done anything like this in public before and I felt extraordinarily licentious and voluptuous. We cavorted, eating each other's mouth, crushed in a suffocating embrace, then explored every crevice of each other with mouth and fingers. The sense of unbridled, irrepressible liberation was amazing, and the avid grins and excited and approving murmurs of the intent spectators gave an added compulsion to our wanton and completely shameless carnal exhibitionism.

But I didn't want to be fucked for the first time with an audience. I didn't need to worry, Luke took the initiative. Straddling my head he slowly ran his tongue along my distended; glistening member, sucking gently on the head, tonguing my cum slit. My big knob slid beyond his soft palate and into his throat, all eight inches, and the contractions of those soft, warm, swallowing tissues about my glans drove me wild. My balls were tightening with every stroke of my prick through those greedy lips. I felt his stubble rubbing my pubics. Up and down his mouth went, his tongue wrapping around my dick, squeezing it, caressing it.

I latched onto his waving stalk, bobbing in my face, and he began fucking my mouth. I worked my way up and down his throat-opener. The thick shaft of meat throbbed and jerked yet larger. My taste-buds were savoring the tangy precum percolating from his ample piss-slit.

Needing air Luke withdrew, took a deep breath and said, "Suck my ass, Pete. Get me ready to be fucked."

He slewed around into a shoulder stand and I knelt reverently, his feet on my shoulders, imagining myself an initiate of some primitive, magical tribe, conscious of, yet unconcerned by the eager eyes glued to our antics. Anticipation and desire electrified the air.

I lathered his rosy pucker with my hot tongue, happily licking and lapping, wanting to taste his tangy hole. His cock-starved, funky crack twitched as I probed his crevice, burrowing deeper with each plunge. I cupped his muscular butt in my hands and pulled him onto my face. His smell was intoxicating. I slurped his manhole as he rotated his ass in my face, bathing it with my own spit.

"Oh yeah, lick that ass. Wet me with that tongue."

I pressed into him insistently as his overwhelmingly aroused prick bounced uncontrollably. Luke sighed deeply and fell to his hands and knees, thrusting his ass up. I kept eating him out until he was open and dripping.

"Oh, shit, fuck me, Pete. Screw it! Let me have it!"

I gave his asshole a few more swabs with my tongue before sliding a couple of lubed fingers inside. Luke beckoned a bold young Japanese, who'd shucked his robe and masturbating, to fuck his mouth, while I attended to his rear passage.

Luke opened his mouth and the muscular hunk inched his rod past his lips and over his tongue. Suddenly he stiffened and let out a muffled gasp, as I spread his buttcheeks and entered his tight, nearly virginal ass, my large dick stretching his internal muscles to their limits.

Even though I slid in slowly, my delicacy didn't lessen the initial pain. I stopped momentarily, then eased in even slower until my pubic hair brushed against his buttcheeks. The dick-filled mouth gurgled with pleasure.

He relaxed and began massaging me with his colon walls. He thrust his hips back and forth, sucking my dick in and out of his gut as I pumped. He picked up my pace, rocking back and forth, humping, as he relinquished the cock in his mouth to take a breath.

"Oh, yes! Fuck my ass, Pete, fuck it! C'mon."

Grasping his waist, I fucked him harder now, as Luke resumed sucking the hunky Jap. He writhed beneath me as the ecstasy radiated through his body. He reached beneath his legs and began to pull at his swollen cock, working himself into an even greater state of lusty pleasure, as his ass-muscles milked my dick.

A slim young Jap threw off his robe and lay underneath Luke, sucking his bobbing prick. Our collective grunts and groans became more insistent as another caressed me from behind, pinching my love knobs, his waving prick bobbing between my thighs. My body shuddered and convulsed as jets of my cum exploded deep inside Luke's spasming ass. At the same time Luke's gusher of hot cum erupted all over the diminutive figure beneath him as Luke gulped down a huge discharge from the guy in his mouth.

As we uncoupled and stretched out our satiated flesh on the futon, our bodies pressed against one another, the Village People were belting out *YMCA*. We were convulsed with hysterical giggles, a result of the emotional release and sense of overwhelming freedom: our months of camouflage blown away.

It turned out the muscular young guy was our *maid*, just coming on duty. Tomichi spoke good English and happily showed us to our private room, which was equipped with video. He produced our bedding, tissues and a tube of lubricant from a wall closet, assuring us that if we needed anything at all we were to call him. He'd be nearby in the passage.

Luke pushed me down, spread my legs and began licking and sucking, thoroughly cleaning my sweaty rosebud. Then his tongue eased inside my hot, clasping tunnel.

"Oh, yes," I murmured, twisting gently, rotating my ass in small circles, as his tongue slid in and out of my throbbing rectum. His tongue circled and slurped as my ass muscles relaxed. He sucked furiously, burying his face between my trim buns, pushing his stiffened tongue deep into me, tasting my inner core.

It seemed like a minor transition from his tongue to his slippery cock entering my wet hole. He was very gentle at first, the dark, bulging cockhead, partly capped with delicate foreskin, teasing me with flirtatious stabs. But soon he was pushing in, relentless in his desire to have it all in me.

"Oh, it's soooooo tight."

"Yeah, I love the feel of you up there. Ooooh! Yeees! Oh fuck meee!"

He started to thrust harder, faster, while I circled my own hard cock with lubricated fingers. Our eyes locked as glistening pre-cum moistened my bulging cockhead. Luke's eyes were intense and searching. His pendulous balls slapped against my ass. I grinned as his thrusting brought even greater urgency to the growing demands of my cock throbbing in my grip.

Mutual excitement swelled as we grinned at each other, our breathing taking on a spasmodic quality. We were on a mutual excursion to a known but mysterious place. We had never been there before, not like this, not together. He hugged me to him and kissed me, probing with his tongue, as he accelerated his pounding.

"Oh God, I'm gonna...."

"Yeah...." I muffled my voice in his mouth as a massive orgasm twisted through me, my cock shooting hot globs of cum the length of my torso. He grabbed my hips and slammed into me two, three, four times, his pulsing cock spurting hot cum into my depths. We lay still, panting, feeling the tidal pounding in our bodies, waiting for our vision to un-blur.

Okinawa set the pattern for our shore leave, from Sydney to Naples, wherever we were in the world, until a couple of years later. We were on patrol in the Persian Gulf and Luke was one of the ill-fated crews of an aborted helicopter attempt to rescue American Embassy hostages in Iran. He was hit by a grenade explosion, thirty-plus holes in his back and legs, one in the head, two in an arm. Most were superficial but one, astride his left kidney, was very bad and hemorrhaging. Medics gave him an industrial-strength hit of morphine.

When I rushed up to the ship's hospital he lay on a stretcher outside the operating theater. I held his uninjured hand, but I don't think he recognized me. His coal-black eyes seemed to absorb the dawn sunlight but gave back little of its warmth.

Luke was shipped back to the States. I wrote to the address he'd given me but never received a reply. For a while I thought he might be dead. I got out of the service soon after that and became a commercial sailor with a Marine Science, deep-sea exploratory company, based in San Diego. My work is pretty strenuous and I've kept myself buffed with regular workouts and a lot of surf-boarding.

I didn't, I couldn't bring myself to hook-up with anyone else on an emotional level, assuaging my still-raging hormones with casual and anonymous encounters in gay bars and venues wherever I happened to be working in the world, fucking and being fucked, always with a condom, and never sucking since the discovery of AIDS. But I couldn't get Luke out of my mind, or the remembered feel of him up my ass.

As I grew older, I had an increasing desire to make contact with him. I needed closure. I tried libraries and phone books. Then I tried a trace service. They supplied me with a list of forty-three people with the same name. I wrote to the first ten addresses and got a reply last week. I got this call from an operator. She said, 'Someone wants to talk to you, but he can't hear you.' I asked myself, 'Now what in the hell is this all about?'

It was Luke, deaf from the battle injury, using a telephone-relay service in which a special operator types into a computer what the hearing person says and transmits it over the phone line to the deaf person. Luke said, "Hey, Pete. How come the Bronx kid isn't welterweight champion of the world?"

I knew it had to be him. I told him, "I've been looking for you for nearly twenty years."

Then I just choked up. Tears were rolling down my cheeks. There was so much I wanted to say. I told him he'd better come out and visit before something happens to us and it's too late.

"I tried to find you too, Pete. I could never forget you, but by the time I got out of the hospital, my wife and kid had moved to Connecticut and you seemed to have vanished. And then today I got this letter and I let out a shout."

I took some leave and he arranged a flight to arrive last evening. I waited impatiently at the disembark gate. I nearly collapsed with shock when a young man in a sailor suit, looking like I remembered Luke, but younger and stunningly handsome came marching forward, dropped his duffel bag and embraced me.

"Hi, Pete." He looked me in the eyes with those same liquid black eyes and very deliberately kissed me full on the lips.

"I'm Luke's son, Danny. Dad's not able to travel these days, but he didn't want you to be disappointed any more. He wanted for us to meet. You know, you don't look too much different from the photo he has of you, only more mature, more handsome. I've been fantasizing about that picture for years."

I blushed at the thought.

He picked up the bag and we headed for the exit. Suddenly he grabbed my arm and said, "I guess I'm the consolation prize."

"What do you mean?"

"I'm a bit of a phony, I'm afraid. This is Dad's old uniform I'm wearing and it's a bit tight. I hope I didn't give you too much of a shock."

"No, nothing shocks me anymore," I said, although I was lying.

The drive back to my condo is a bit hazy. Danny's serge-covered thigh touched my denim one, magnetized. He massaged my inner thigh till he could feel my raging hard-on, then deftly unzipped me and swallowed my boner to the hilt. He set my senses reeling, and copious precum dripped from my twitching prick. He slurped and suckled till I almost shot my load. I whimpered and jerked so sharply, my knees twitching, that my driving must have been erratic. I'm just grateful no cop saw me and pulled me over.

Safely parked, I zipped up and headed for my place with my humpy sailor close behind.

Inside the door he swiftly stripped, and so did I. I pulled him toward the bed and he thrust me down on it. He straddled my head, his huge cock swaying in my face as he dipped his head down to my crotch, darting his tongue along my swollen dick and sucked the pearl of precum from my slit. He fingered my pubic hairs and massaged my balls. Then his lips latched onto my slicked probe, sucking hard.

I took his long, bronze cock in my mouth, gripped the young, firm buttocks in both callused hands and pulled him close, forcing his whole prick down my throat with a hunger born of pent-up desire. His huge balls bobbed on my nose, filling me with his spunky scent. We both felt the need to express and accept love, sucking and being sucked, our hot pricks throbbing and thrusting.

We came quickly and together, filling each other with the essence of lust, spurt after spurt of rich cum flooding and soothing our parched throats, each drop a promise of joy and release and a commitment to each other, though we'd hardly talked.

Danny screwed his body around and embraced me, pushing his tongue into my mouth and I tasted who I was. I gently pushed him off me. He agreed to just lay back and let me examine him. He was a fraction taller than his father and more muscular. His nipples were huge, very inviting. The hands were heavily veined, strong. The mouth was a little wider and the lips fuller, but the eyes were identical. I gazed into their depth and nearly wept with happiness.

In the afterglow of our sex, we talked a little, grinned a lot, but I could tell Danny was fatigued. He yawned and said he'd had a long day of travel. Languidly he kissed me, then, with a contented smile on his face, fell asleep in my embrace.

As I lay there, still recovering from the jolts of everything that had just happened, all I could think of was the Village People singing, *I did not choose the way I am / To love is not a sin.*

LOOKING FOR IT
by Mario Solano

My parents signed me up for the New York National Guard; they thought it would make a man of me. I consider myself *try*-sexual; I'll try anything! The night mother and father made the big decision, I eavesdropped and heard them discussing my sexuality. Mom told Dad, "He goes looking for it."

So what do they do? They enlist me in the service! Thanks Mother, I don't have to look too far here.

My first night at the Kingbridge Armory in the Bronx, this guy with olive skin and a large, not unattractive nose asks me to join him for a cigarette break. He leads the way. I follow behind and check him out like he's a new suit. He's large and thick, maybe nineteen or twenty, beefy thighs, wide back and shoulders. His ass cheeks strain against his khaki pants, which are tucked into his highly polished boots. His hat tilts forward leaving a thick, bullish neck from his shaved head to inside his highly starched collar. The prevalent appendages on this sauntering lion leading me to the slaughter are his hands. They're huge! His right hand wraps around his rifle like it's a toothpick. His left hand is animated as he explains the importance of keeping the place he's taking me to a secret.

We just met and he's showing me a secret place. I know what's coming and I wonder, what's wrong with me? Do I exude sex? I console myself with the fact that at least it's never boring.

"By the way, I'm Duke." He stops walking and shakes my hand. One of his hazel eyes is slightly crossed. My head reaches his shoulder. "And I think you're pretty cute."

I'm five-five, 130 pounds, blond hair (which they make me cut real short), and blue eyes. I've been called cute before.

"My name is Vincent, but my friends call me Vince."

We climb a bunch of stairs and crawl into a tunnel which leads to a dungeon. Duke is right! This is a dark, dank, secret place. Why would anyone want to come here?

He stretches out on the cold stone floor, takes a pack of Camels from his shirt pocket, taps a couple of cigs halfway out, puts the pack to his lips and removes one with his teeth. At the same time he bends a match with one hand and lights it on the striker. He holds the lit cigarette toward me. When I reach for it, he jerks it away and holds it toward his crotch. It's dark in the dungeon but the embers create enough glow for me to see his hard-on straining his zipper.

"Sit down here," he says, patting the ground next to him. He places the cig between my lips. His thumb and forefinger caress my mouth. I take a deep drag, swallow the smoke, lean my head against a bumpy stone wall, and let the smoke gush out. Duke puts his fingers back on my lips and maneuvers them so they pry my mouth open. He uses my saliva to moisten my mouth, inside and out. Before I know it he has five fingers in and he's trying to fist fuck my mouth. I oblige as much as I can. This is kinky but erotic. I never sucked off a hand before. His forefinger tickles my tonsils.

He rolls toward me and presses the bottom half of his body against the bottom half of mine. I feel his hard prick on my thigh. He buries his head in the space between my neck and shoulder, and he puts his big hand on my cock and balls. He massages in a circular motion while he humps my leg. At this moment, for some reason, I think of my parents and wonder what they would think of this development. After all, they signed me up to get me away from this.

His big fingers wrap around my groin and his middle finger reaches under and finds its way to my anal opening, which he's able to probe at the same time. I lift my ass to let him. "We're gonna have a good time during these breaks," he rasps into my ear, followed by a big wet tongue that makes me lose my equilibrium and become dizzy. "But now we're in a hurry. We don't want them to miss us on the first day."

Duke unzips my fly, then his. He lowers our pants to our knees. He climbs on top of me and sticks his hand back in my mouth. I take his hand in mine and suck it like it's a big dick. He rolls over and I'm on top. He guides my mouth down to his big, uncut prick. As soon as I'm on it, he flips us into sixty-nine position and swallows my cock and both my balls like a vacuum cleaner. He nibbles, bites, slurps and sucks. My mouth wraps around the bulbous head of his massive prick. He fucks my face and sucks my dick like no one has ever done before.

Soon, too soon, it's time for us to cum. He shoves his finger up my asshole and keeps rhythm with my spurts. As wads shoot out of my dick hole, he frigs me with his fingers. He swallows every drop of my cum and keeps sucking.

I'm spent and sore, and I want him to stop, but he hasn't cum yet. He rolls me on my back and straddles my face. His huge, hairy balls rest on my mouth. I open my mouth wide and lick him. His balls bounce on my eyes, nose and cheeks. Whenever they get close to my mouth I gnaw, chew and lick. Right above my eyes, Duke pounds his prick and I get a clear view of his foreskin sliding back and forth over the head of his prick. Both his massive hands are wrapped around the shaft and the entire head still protrudes.

He gasps and spreads his legs. My tongue slips into his asshole. He thrusts down on my face. He grunts, and groans. Stifled screams echo through the dungeon. "Oh my fucking god," he says as his body relaxes. He lies down, backwards, on top of me. I'm under him, his hairy ass in my face, my boots by his shoulders. He licks them the same way he licked my cock.

"Careful!" he says. "We don't wanna get cum on our uniforms." He carefully inches his way off me and stands up. Cum drips from his pee hole.

He reaches out his hand to help me up. As I rise, I lick the cum from his prick. He squeezes out one more large wad. I take my finger and wipe it off, then lick it. He watches me suck his cum off my finger with lust in his eyes. He'd like to do it again, and so would I.

"I came a gallon," he says, pointing to the wall that is dripping with gobs of cum. "You didn't do so bad yourself." He milks my dick one more time, then bends over to suck out the last drop.

Now I'm looking forward to going on bivouac for a weekend in Oswego, New York, and then two whole weeks in Camp Drum. No, I don't have to "go looking for it" anymore!

THE MEAN MARINE
by Anonymous

Adapted by John Patrick

Even when I was just a kid, I'd thought of myself as one mean dude, a big bully, lifting weights and picking fights with the toughest guys, just to show how bad I was. I joined the Marines when I got kicked out of high school. The discipline did me good and helped straighten me out. But on leave, I was still a wild shit. Me and five other guys would get shit-faced, then go faggot-hunting in the park. We'd go deep into the park. I'd walk off alone, my buddies keeping close eyes on who I talked to and where I went. Sure enough, no less than five minutes in the park, some sweet-ass sucker was eyeing me from his perch on a park bench. I went up to him, a cute smile on my face, swishing my hips a little. I sat next to him and he couldn't take his eyes off the huge bulge in the pants of my uniform.

He offered me a cigarette and I took it, thanking him in a real raspy voice, as my hand accidentally fell onto his thigh. I felt him tense up, almost ready to shoot his wad right there, but he tried to hide it and calmly lit my cigarette with trembling fingers. I took a drag off the cigarette and settled back, letting my fingers tickle his thigh. Pretty soon his pecker was busting out of his chinos. His throat was dry and he coughed. He leaned over and whispered, "Can I see it?"

"Sure, boy," I said, slowly nodding my head. He smiled. We got off the bench and walked into the bushes to fuck. I turned him around and ripped off his pants, letting the material fall in shreds about his ankles. He was squealing in terror now, because I had also got an arm grip around his waist. I undid my fly, hauled out my nine inches of cut meat, rubbed it between his ass cheeks, listened to his breath come in desperate gasps. I leaned over his back, my mouth close to his ear so he could hear me plain. Then I rammed my cock straight up his hole, not caring about his pain or cries but relishing the tight clasp of his asshole.

I beat my huge prick into him, talking nasty to him all the time, my breath beery and hot. "This is what you wanted, baby. You wanted my cock up you."

He tried to answer but he couldn't, he was crying so hard.

I stabbed my hot weapon deeper inside him as I neared orgasm. My hands ran up over his bare, hairless belly and half-developed chest, pinching and twisting his erect nipples and then over his hard cock. "Yeah, you love it," I growled, squeezing his cock as hard as I could.

When I started to come, I held his shoulders and thrust up until my balls ground into his; an overflow of my cum foamed out into my pubic hair. I dropped over him, then dragged my damp, deflated cock out of him.

I looked up and all my buddies were there, erect dicks in hand, ready smiles on their faces. I laughed a little and stepped aside, letting the next guy in. I loved watching the dainty-assed, red-faced kid when he saw what he was in.

"No, no!" he screamed, but Sarge shoved his cock in his mouth to quiet him. The look of shock and fear was inspiring and my dick was soon throbbing again. It was great watching those hard, brown cocks pulse outside the bleached blue uniforms. None of them took mercy on their victim, but beat ass like wild dogs. I stood to the side, slowly smoking a cig, watching my buddies wham this silly little queer.

My cock stood out in all its glory, glowing with a coating of cum. As Sarge left the kid's mouth to finish in his ass, I stepped over. "Suck me down to my balls," I ordered. I pushed my weapon in and out of his quivering, rosebud mouth, pressing to the hilt, feeling the cockhead graze the back of his throat until he gagged. I dragged it out, only to slam it in deeper. I pumped his face, as Sarge jabbed his ass, our rhythm matching, me feeling as though my next haul would crush this boy, bend and break him in half.

We came together, Sarge's mouth gaping and shouting out wild cries as we released, loud as cavemen, crazed as lunatics. Cum was spurting out of the boy from both holes as we drew away. Once done, we kicked the punk over and laughed at him. We walked off to piss in the tall grass and get back to base before listed AWOL.

We weren't faggots—none of us. We just liked bashing them. It's what they wanted—being worked over by six husky Marines in the park. Once back with the troop, we wouldn't mention what happened, but sometimes smile at each other, knowing what he was thinking.

Nowadays I'm no longer a Marine. I'm still in uniform, however, working as a security guard. I'm fucking two chicks a week, but I've never had much of relationship with a girl. Even when I was a kid, my best times spent were with other guys. The boys and me, we had things in common. Women make me feel good, but they mess up my mind. Guys don't.

One of the guys I used to bash fags with was named Lonnie. He and I were close. Mighty close. I'd see him everyday—practically lived with him. He lived off base and I used to go to his room and lift weights and drink beers. When we were good and shit-faced, we'd cruise the park and bash some sissy-ass. It was better than our girls because a guy's just as strong as you. Lonnie loved it best watching me fuck, rooting me on as I jumped some ass. We'd kick him a couple times and then go back to base, have a few more beers, Lonnie telling me how great it was. He even once said how great it would be if we could live together all the time. I'd laugh and tell him yeah and fall asleep on the floor. He was the closest thing to a brother I ever had and if I loved anybody, it would have been Lonnie.

Lonnie left the service and moved to California to get a job in the movies. I never saw him again, but every day I'd check the credits on the television shows to see if his name was there, but it never was. I decided to take a vacation in Southern California, look up Lonnie.

"Shit," I sputtered when I saw where he was living. It was a gay ghetto if I ever saw one. I wanted to rape every ass I saw walk by. Lonnie didn't seem to be very happy about seeing me. He was cool, distant. We talked about old times and the beer flowed. Finally, I asked, "Why the hell do you live here?"

"Here?"

"In queer city. God, I never saw so many of 'em!"

He chuckled. "Yeah, that's what I like about it. I don't have to go far to get one."

"Yeah, just reach out the door and yank one in! But do you still do that? Really?"

"Oh, I've changed a lot. Well, really not changed. I mean, I've worked things out."

"Oh?"

"Yeah. See, I've decided I like guys better than girls."

I was stunned, stopped drinking my brew. "You mean—?"

He nodded.

"I'd better go."

"Don't go, Dave."

I stood, but I'd had too much to drink and I fell back down again. I was dizzy. This had been too much after a long flight from Pensacola.

His hands were soon wandering over me. He had taken control. Before long, he was pulling at my prick. He sucked me for a few moments, and I was ready to come. I looked into his sun-tanned, beautiful face. He opened his mouth and our kiss was tentative, me pulling back at first, scared to death. His tongue slipped in and out of my mouth like a wild darting fish. My hand slid from about his thick throat to behind his head, our bodies pushing closer. In one movement, his head was down, continuing the delicious bobbings of his hand. His tongue was racing over the veiny shaft now, my back pressed against the sofa. He pulled my pants fully off, and I closed my eyes to permit my brain to swim in the delight of my buddy's practiced touches. He rotated my body, without missing a beat on my hard-on, and raised his cock so it swung above my head, brown, even more thickly veined than my own, a dagger over my face. I stared, then slowly rose to grab the smooth shaft, fingering the balls. Something snapped in me. I still felt dizzy—but I was alive. I wanted Lonnie. Maybe I had wanted Lonnie all along. I ran a hand up through the dense pubic hair to the fur of his slate-flat stomach. I wanted his cock in my mouth. I wanted it. Pulling on his cock, one hand grasping his muscular ass, his flesh slowly entered until all of it was encased between my lips. I gagged at first on the heavy smell. But I quickened to his pace, wrapping my tongue down the whole meaty shaft. It was like pure ivory filling my mouth, my whole body. I grasped his ass-cheeks, clenched them and forced his cock into my mouth again and again.

He spasmed; his cock quivered. Cum pounded forth in streams, a river of milk filling my mouth, spilling over my lips. I lay back, stunned, while he worked on my cock, but it was useless. I was hard, but I couldn't come. This had all been too much. I pulled him off my cock and lifted him up. We kissed. It was the most passionate kiss of my life.

Lonnie told me it was crazy for me to go to a hotel so I got my bag out of my rental car and started to unpack in his bedroom. He came in, held me. "I'm so glad you came," he said.

"I didn't come, but you sure did."

"I've been saving it for you," he joked.

We decided to go out to dinner, and we took my little rental car. Everywhere I looked there were queers. *Obvious* queers. They were asking for it, in my opinion. It made me sick. Even Lonnie began to look queer to me in this place. "You gotta get outta here," I told him over dinner. He just didn't get it.

When we came out of the restaurant, it was dark. We had a long walk to the car and when we got there, the guys who had been following us down the hill from Sunset Boulevard were right on top of us. These guys were prime bull and we both knew it. Lonnie ran. But not me. I stood firm. But then I saw the baseball bat. I wasn't going to hurt them; he was going to hurt me. There was no place to hide. He grabbed me under the arms, hoisted me up easily and leaned me against the car. He leaned close, his breath hot and moist in my face. He was chewing a mint; I guess there's always something to be thankful for, if you just look for it.

He jammed his knee in my crotch. That didn't feel too good, either, but I couldn't work up enough breath to tell him. "You shitty faggot, you been jacking off too much. We gotta teach ya—" He nodded at his buddy, who was only slightly smaller than he was, who grabbed my wrist before I had a chance to resist. He yanked my hand out and held it on the hood of my rental car while the bull brought the baseball bat down on it. I screamed as the pain shot halfway up my arm to my elbow, then I slid down the side of the car. All I could do was cradle the hand and rock back and forth in the dirt as the bull hovered over me and spat, "That'll teach ya." An ugly laugh, then. A laugh of mean merriment. And then they were gone.

My hand felt as if it were full of broken glass. I watched their taillights recede down the road as I stood up. A cold, damp fog had begun to roll in from the ocean, chilling the sweat on my face and making me shiver. Maybe it would numb my swelling hand. I took a deep breath. Where Lonnie had been all this time I had no idea, but now he came running up; he sounded shocked. "My God. Are you all right?"

"I think they broke my hand. They said I was jacking off too much." I knew they were just administering an object lesson.

I woke up groggy from the pain pills the E.R. doctor had given me. I also had a headache, which got worse when I reached up and smacked myself with the cast I'd forgotten about that was holding my two broken metacarpals in place. I swore and rubbed my head with my good hand, then got up and made coffee. I made extra noise doing that, mad as hell, thinking about how I owed those guys and how I would more than likely never get the chance to repay them. After three cups of coffee, I'd cleared enough cobwebs to go back to bed, to Lonnie.

Lonnie kept saying how sorry he was until I had to shut him up—the only way I knew. And he didn't learn to suck dick like that in the Marine Corps. Now it was my turn to come. I was ready, with the java levelling out the effects of the drugs. He licked up the beads of pre-cum, then kissed the full length of the shaft, then lapped at my balls. He returned to the head of my prick, nibbled at it, then plunged his mouth over it, nearly taking all of it down his throat. Weaving my fingers between the wet strands of his hair, I began thrusting my pelvis in time with Lonnie's efforts and my body contorted in ecstasy as I started to come.

"Aaaahhhh!" I shrieked, my body thrashing against Lonnie's.

Lonnie let the cock loose and it slapped backward across my flat stomach, still pulsing, squirting what remained of my load onto my chest. Lonnie leaned down and licked away the last drops of cum, then attended to my nipples in the process, sucking them with lingering passion. My first orgasm at Lonnie's—and somehow I knew it wasn't going to be my last.

- Adapted by the editor from an account which originally appeared in Blueboy magazine.

DRILL SERGEANT
by B. L. Peterson

I joined the Marine Corps because I love men. I like being around them and living with them. I like giving them orders and teaching them how to take them. That's why I joined the service. It's the right place for me, the place I want to be. A military paradise, filled with hordes of young men to serve my monstrous cock.

I'm six-four, two-hundred-forty pounds of muscle, and my cock matches the rest of me. For sure I've been blessed with a butt-pleaser. I love to use it—especially for breaking in some young recruit who hadn't even known he wanted it until I was ramming it into him. I love to get these grunts beggin' for it. There's nothing like watching my huge hog disappearing up some kid's cherry butt while he beats the mattress and screams for more. I drive 'em crazy. The room that doubles as my bedroom and office is located at the end of the barracks where forty or more young men sleep, shower and perform their military duties.

From my office I can see the entire barracks, including the shower stalls, and watch their every move. Polishing boots, making beds, shooting the bull, running around in their skivvies, stripping to take a shower, grab-assing and, late in the night, jacking off. I noticed that one young guy would hide under the stairs so he could watch the other guys shower without being seen. His name was Marino, Joe Marino, a stocky Italian about five-foot eleven. His dark features and muscular body gave him a sexy, masculine look you wouldn't find on most men of eighteen. I had watched Joe for some time now...he was on my list.

I remember thinking the first time I saw him stripped for a shower that he had one of the most fuckable asses in the company. It was beautifully formed, with the smallest traces of hair running under his plump balls to disappear in the dark crevice of his muscular asscheeks. My cock would strain against my underwear just watching him walk to the showers, contemplating the Speedo tan line that marked his muscular buns. I knew he was a virgin, at least to man-sex; I also knew that he wanted cock but was too afraid to admit it to anyone. I would change all that—in due time. I noticed also that Joe would particularly wait around for a muscular guy named Rod. Joe would try and see this guy naked any chance he got—and who could blame him? Rod was the perfect Marine. Short-cropped blond hair, six feet tall and a lean, muscular body. He passed all inspections, kept his nose clean on and off base, and performed each of his duties well. At 19, he had that all-American look like a young Robert Redford. Since Rod wrote his girlfriend almost every night, I took it he was straight and didn't go for man-sex.

Each time Rod dropped his towel to get into the showers, I would see the interest Joe had in him. With his well-developed chest, tapered waist and firm, hard buttocks, it was easy to see why. But I think it was the eight-incher that swung between Rod's legs that had Joe in hiding just to get a peek at it.

Uncut and thick, Rod's cock was truly beautiful. It always seemed half-swollen, as if just waiting for an excuse to shoot out thick globs of scum. His ass was smooth, lightly downed with blond hair that darkened as it disappeared between his small, tight asscheeks. Joe's eyes would widen as he watched Rod scrub himself in the showers, soaping his cock and balls, spreading his legs to clean his virgin ass. Joe would stand there wide-eyed, rubbing the stiffness between his own legs.

Joe would practically step on his tongue, watching Rod dry his tight body, running the towel between his legs, up the crack of his ass and back to his reddening cock. As soon as Rod would leave, Joe would come out of hiding, trying to ad- just his hard-on so the guys wouldn't see it. Rod would dress and go about his business, never guessing he had a secret admirer who longed to service him but who was too inexperienced and scared.

But one night, Joe got over his fear.

I sometimes would get up in the wee hours to see if I could catch any of the boys jacking off in the open toilet stalls. I was on such a mission when I spied Joe getting out of bed. I ducked into a space between two lockers, and watched. But Joe didn't go toward the bathroom. Instead he walked over to Rod's bed and, careful not to wake him, slowly pulled the blanket down his sleeping body until the handsome Marine lay fully uncovered, clad only in his boxers.

Then Joe gingerly tugged Rod's shorts down to his knees. Rod squirmed a bit, but didn't open his eyes. He knew what was coming. His beautiful cock rested across his thigh, and as Joe (and I) watched, Rod's cock began to rise, until it was snapped up hard against his stomach. Fully erect, it must have measured almost nine inches.

After all these weeks of waiting, Joe could resist no longer. Gently he took the thick organ in his hand. Rod grunted but didn't wake up as Joe took the cock into his mouth and began sucking it down his throat. I watched him make love to Rod's fuckpole, licking the bulbous head and sucking the shaft with his mouth. Rod seemed to be dreaming, spreading his legs in his sleep as Joe caressed his full balls.

Joe began to suck harder. Up and down he went on the big cock, his spit making it glisten in the dark night. He could hardly get the fat organ into his mouth, but he worked on it faster and faster till Rod was moaning low in his sleep, his cock twitching and jerking. Just as it seemed that he was about to cum, he woke up. To his surprise, he found Joe sucking the life out of his cock.

"Hey, what the fuck you doing?" he said, mad as hell. Joe let go of the surging cock in his mouth and looked at Rod in embarrassment. "I couldn't help it," he whispered, "Don't hurt me. I'm sorry, it's just that you're so sexy." Joe tried to make a quick exit before Rod could hit him. But Rod pulled him back to his bunk with a strong tug. In a commanding whisper Rod told him, "You got me all hot and horny, you cocksucker—and you're gonna finish what you started!"

Rod made the kid go back down on his throbbing cock, gripping him by the hair and brutally face-fucking him. He pushed and pulled at his head, forcing him up and down the long length of his cock, being as quiet as he could so as not to wake the other guys. Joe sucked the best he could, but Rod was boiling over in a heated lust. He didn't care that he was choking the punk with his cock as long as he got off. His strong hands moved Joe's head up and down like a jackhammer, ramming his gullet with fat cock, pulling out and jabbing back, again and again. His thighs tensed as his straining balls began to rise.

"Oh God, I'm gonna cum!" Rod rasped. After a few more powerful strokes, Rod pushed Joe's head so far down on his stiff rod that his pubes were in the recruit's nose. Joe was fighting for his breath, Rod's cock stuffed so far down his throat that he couldn't breathe. But Rod didn't care. He bucked his hips powerfully into Joe's face till I thought the kid would choke on the massive tool. Rod lifted his ass into the air as he let out a small cry and his cum erupted in Joe's throat.

It seemed like a gallon of cum oozed from the kid's lips as Rod climaxed again and again. He held Joe's face down in his groin, spurting cum from his rigid cock until I thought the punk was gonna pass out from lack of air. Finally Rod let go of his head and he gasped, coughing and gagging, trying to get air back in his lungs. Rod pulled his boxers up over his cum-covered thighs, his cock making a long wet mark in his shorts as it softened.

"Good. Now if you tell anyone what happened I'll beat the shit out of you, you got it?" Joe nodded his head again. "Good, 'cause I ain't no faggot, and I don't go for that kind of stuff. If you hadn't made me so horny I would have kicked your ass." The kid cowered before Rod, not able to look up at him. "Now buzz off, I've got to take a shower, I'm a *mess!*" Joe started to get up. "Hey," Rod said. The kid turned around, looking him in the eye for the first time. "You're one hell of a cocksucker." Rod smiled. Joe smiled back and hurried off before he got into more trouble.

It was time for me to make my move.

Early the next morning I informed Joe that I had to go pick up supplies in a town that was a six-hour drive from the base, and that I wanted him to go with me to learn the routine. Since the trip was a long one, I told him we'd stay in a hotel in town and come back the next day. I think Joe responded so eagerly because it meant he wouldn't have to face Rod that day.

When we got a few miles from the base, I turned and looked the kid square in the eyes.

"You're a virgin, aren't you?" I said as we drove along. He denied it, telling me he had fucked plenty of girls. I just smiled.   By the time we got to the hotel that night, I was hot. Hot from what I'd seen the night before, and hot from watching Joe's butt muscles flex all day as he loaded supplies. It was hard for me not to just jump his young bones, but I didn't want to freak him out. I ordered some rum and Coke from room service, and the more the kid drank the less nervous he was and the more he stared at my crotch. I could tell he was waiting for me to get undressed, but I just sat in the chair, legs spread so that he could get a real good look at me. He couldn't pull his gaze from between my legs. "Like what you see?" I asked as I grabbed my crotch.

Joe nodded his head, embarrassed to lift it up.

"You know? Did Rod tell you?" Joe asked guiltily. "I didn't mean to do it. I couldn't help myself!"

"Don't worry about it, Private. Relax. It's okay." I knew it was time for me to take command. "Now get out of those clothes!" He obeyed, and soon he was standing butt-naked in front of me, trying to hide his stiff six-and-a-half-inch cock. "Don't be embarrassed, kid. You have a great body." I walked over to him and pulled him to me.

"Damn, I want it," he said, "but I'm so afraid."

"Don't be," I said. I rubbed his shoulders to relax him and began to kiss his neck. I moved down to one of his erect nipples and sucked the dark red flesh into my mouth. He moaned and almost went limp in my arms. I licked a trail down his hairless chest to his rippled stomach. The kid grabbed my shoulders as I bent down and began sucking on his balls. He was moaning continually as I made love to his body. I grabbed his cock with my lips and swallowed it. As I sucked him forcefully, Joe was getting hotter and hotter, his head thrown back as he gave himself to me. When I knew that he was ready, I told him to show me his hard, muscular ass.

To my surprise, Joe turned around and bent over onto the dresser, spreading his big thighs, his tiny butthole winking at me in anticipation of being penetrated by my awesome dick. He had a big, round butt; not a sissified bubble-butt, but a rock-hard, chiseled ass with a butthole so small you could hardly see it amidst the few dark hairs that surrounded it. When I got on my knees and pierced his manhole with my tongue, the kid nearly went through the roof. I attacked his bunghole savagely, working my tongue deep into his bowels. I licked on it and sucked it and nipped at it with my tongue, getting it loose and slimy. Soon Joe was moaning as if he was gonna cum. Spit was running out of his hole and down his balls. I stuck a finger in, then two, then three and finger-fucked him till his hole was wet and pliable. The punk loved it as he gave his ass up to me.

I pulled my fingers out of his asshole and started to undress. Soon Joe was staring wide-eyed at the bulge in my boxers.

When I pulled my shorts off, my tool must have already reached nine inches. By the time it was rigidly sticking up in the air and ready for fucking it was showing its full eleven-plus.

"My god, that can't be real!"

"If you're afraid—"

"Hell, no, Sergeant. Drill me." This guy had more guts than I thought.

I straddled his ass and greased up his hole with good old Vaseline, applied some more to my cockhead, then positioned it at his cherry-red hole. Slowly I began to ease my prick into him. I waited as his asshole adjusted to the log that was pushing into it. When I knew he was past the initial fear and his hole had relaxed as much as possible, I drove my shaft deep in his quivering ass.

Joe's whole body knotted up as I rammed him with my full length. His cherry hole clamped my dick like a vise and I held still, giving him a chance to get used to it, fearing that if I moved suddenly I might rip him apart. When he let out a dazed moan and began to squirm beneath me I knew he was ready, and I slowly began to withdraw my cock and thrust it back, pulling out a little farther with each stroke. His muscles quivered from the steel-hard pole going into his virgin ass, and soon he was twisting his head from side to side, groaning incoherently and humping his butt back for more. Joe's little fuckhole was stretched to the limit around my cock, and I rotated my hips to loosen him up more. He gripped the dresser as I began to plow his tender ass faster and faster, giving him longer and longer strokes. I grabbed his hips and shoved into him so deep I thought my cock must be reaching his stomach.

His hot hole was now a dark, angry pink, and with my cock still inside him, I carried him over to the bed and laid him on his back, spreading his legs in the air. I began fucking him faster, pulling my cock almost all the way out before shoving it back into him, feeling his taut asshole grip my cock, spreading and squeezing it. The kid was clawing my back and ass, flailing his arms and drooling, as I pistoned into his fiery aperture till he screamed that he was going to cum, and he didn't even have his hand near his cock. Soon he was shooting cum high into the air. I twisted and ground up his ass as his fuckhole sucked the cream from my cock. We were tangled together, and I was so deep in the punk's ass that I touched erogenous zones in him that he never even knew existed.

As the head of my cock popped out, Joe's butthole still gaped, spilling cum down the crack of his ass. He just lay there, gasping for air.

"Don't worry, it'll close up by morning," I told him. I turned out the lights and got in bed with the still-dazed recruit.

"Damn," he said in the dark. "I've never felt anything that fuckin' good!"

I put my arms around him and licked his ear. But already I was thinking about Rod's tight little ass again—after all, they didn't call me the Drill Sergeant for nothing.

SOLDIERS' REUNION
by William Cozad

The phone ringing jolted me out of a deep sleep. It was Jake, and hearing his voice again threw me for a loop. We'd been in the service together, and I'd always wanted to do him, but I never made the move. Now, he was calling me, asking me if I remembered him!

"I'm passing through town," he said, "staying overnight at the Hilton. Thought maybe we could get together for a drink or something."

"Hey, yeah!"

"When can you meet me?"

"Give me about an hour," I said, looking at the late hour on my clock. I frantically took a shower to shake the cobwebs out of my head and got dressed.

I wouldn't lose sleep over just anybody. Just thinking about Jake, I got a hard-on and was tempted to beat off, but decided to save it. Did I remember him? Like it was yesterday. The short soldier in khakis. Brown hair that was parted in the middle and crowned his head. Perfectly chiseled features. Bright brown eyes. And God, those bee-stung lips. And then I'd seen him naked in the showers. A patch of hair between his small nipples. The hair fanned out around his belly and completely covered his solid trunk. That cock was a beauty, fat and uncut, hanging over hefty and hairy balls.

Once I swore I spotted him whacking off in the latrine. Lots of horny soldiers did that on the sly. He was breathing heavy but when I barged in he jumped up off the crapper and stuffed his fat cock into his uniform pants. No way he could conceal that bloated meat. He had a shit-eating grin on his face as he moved past me.

After that, when I jacked off, I often thought of Jake. His image got me off every time as I fantasized about fooling around with him.

And now, that's the effect Jake still had on me after all these years. I grew hard just remembering him.

Of course I had wondered whatever happened to him. He never wrote, he wasn't the type, but I later heard from another Army buddy that Jake had gotten married. That didn't change things; I still had the hots for him. Arriving at the Hilton, I spotted him in the lobby sitting in an overstuffed chair. He hadn't changed much. His hair was longer, kind of sassy, like he could shake his head and it would fall in place. His skin was a bit more leathery. He'd grown a thin mustache which only served to make him look more macho.

He jumped up when he saw me and we pumped each other's hand and embraced. "Let's go to my room and have a drink," he said, turning toward the elevators. "It's great to see you. Looking good, old buddy."

"Hey, you too."

In his room in the tower on the fourteenth floor, overlooking the bright lights of the city, we drank whiskey with beer chasers, boilermakers, his way of drinking.

"How's the wife?" I finally got around to asking.

"Decided to call it quits. No kids, thank goodness. We got married too young. Neither of us was ready to settle down."

That surprised me. How could a bitch give up a guy who looked like Jake?

He was gulping the whiskey while I sipped mine. He'd be shitfaced in no time at that rate, I thought.

"Yeah, she started running around on me. I don't blame her. We had problems. I was tired. Too much pressure, working for her old man. So I'm on my way to Nevada. I've got an older brother who has a ranch there."

"I'm sorry things didn't work out for you."

"Well, that's history." He poured himself another shot. "Hey, you remember Sergeant Jackson?"

"Who could forget him?" Not me. He was my first sexual experience.

"Yeah, you got all those weekend liberty passes. Everyone said you were his pet. Of course, I didn't believe them at first. Then when the sarge hit on me I realized the truth."

"You had sex with him?"

"Hell no. I wasn't no queer. But I never forgot about it. And I always wondered about you."

"Well, there's no use denying it. I gave the man what he wanted. Sometimes you gotta do that in life, you know?" Now I was gulping down the whiskey. What the hell was I saying? I never thought I'd admit it to anybody, let alone Jake.

Jake was quiet for a few moments, finishing his beer. Finally, he said, "I always wondered what it would be like, you know, doing it with another guy."

"You know the old saying, 'Don't knock it if you never tried it.'"

"I've even thought about it, you know, when I saw a really cute guy. I wondered about him. But I never did anything."

I moved closer to him. He was trembling. I touched his arm, squeezed. "Let you in on a little secret. I whacked off over you dozens of times, maybe hundreds."

"What?"

"It's true. When I was doing it with the sarge, I'd be thinkin' of you."

"You're shittin' me."

"No. It's the truth."

He sat back in his chair and grinned. He got a kick out of my confession. "Maybe I'm too old for you now. We ain't little soldier boys no more."

"I think you're even hotter looking. I dig men, not boys, now." Now I was getting worked up by his cock-teasing. He leaned back and rubbed his crotch.

"You still want me?"

"God, do I ever!"

Jake stood up, stumbled a bit, then started to strip right in front of me. His body was even better, more muscular than before. I was too blown away to move. He took my hand and placed it on his cock, which was semi-hard. Having it in my hand at long last almost sobered me up.

I squeezed his cock, not wanting to give too much too soon. Quickly I stripped out of my clothes. The lights were still on and I was glad that Jake wasn't repelled by my body. I wasn't a fat wreck or anything like that, but I wasn't the real trim stud I used to be when I went to the gym all the time.

I turned around to see Jake had stroked himself to a nearly full erection. I obviously didn't turn him off.

As much as I wanted to start sucking on that cock, strange as it sounds, I wanted to kiss those sensuous, thick lips almost as much. Pressing my lips against his, I felt the tickle of his mustache. He wrapped his strong, muscular arms around me. I felt his cock rub against my belly, like mine did against his.

I couldn't hold back any longer. I dove right in. To his pits, that is. I don't think he realized how sensitive his body was. He giggled and squirmed but I wasn't about to be denied. I nuzzled in his pits individually, lapping the tufts of chestnut hair. His nipples were dime-sized but I tweaked and sucked on them till they became erect. I laved the patch of fuzz between them. Heading south, I licked his washboard belly. Even rimmed his inner bellybutton. Spreading those sinewy, hairy thighs, I ignored his cock which now showed signs of life. I mean the rosy cockhead was peeking out of the folds of foreskin. His low-hangers heaved and tightened up against the base of his prick as the spongy tissue became engorged with blood.

I licked his hairy thighs, pasting the hair against the skin, tasting the salty skin.

"Oh, please suck my dick."

I ignored him; this was my party and I wasn't about to rush things. Three years I'd waited for what was for me one of the great wonders of the modern world: Jake's cock. Attacking his genitals, I lapped at his ballsac, coating it with spit. I licked down the cord below his balls to his butthole, despite the forest of hair. I even sniffed his musky hole and blew my hot breath on it. I licked his balls like a cat taking a bath. He squirmed some more. I gobbled up those suckers separately, then together, swishing the hard nuts around in my mouth.

"Oh shit, I never felt nothing like that."

His cock was fully engorged after the ballsucking. It was even bigger than I expected. Might have been only seven inches or so but it was really thick, veiny and pulsing. It looked enormous on his compact frame. Meat for the poor and cock-hungry. His cock throbbed. The bulbous head with the wide slit had turned from rosy red to a purplish hue. It was glossy, coated with precum. I held the thick base of his cock and licked the prickhead.

"Oh God, God, God," he groaned.

It was a divine worship service on my part as I did a quick butterfly flick on the shaft.

"Eat me. Eat my dick."

I took the plunge. Just dove down on that stiff prick which bore into my throat tunnel.

Beyond redemption now, Jake pulled my hair. I thought he'd snatch me bald He had his fat cock in a masturbation rhythm now and wasn't about to stop. He thrust and pumped his randy prick down my throat, battering my tonsils. I drooled spit down his cock until his dense bush glistened with dew. He held my nose in the wet hair. He throttled my throat. I felt like I was being choked but I didn't care. All that mattered was that hard meat sliding down my gullet, getting closer to exploding.

"Oh shit!"

Suddenly I heard him groan. I felt his cock throb wildly and it gushed what had to be the thickest and sweetest cum I ever tasted. As steely hard as his cock had been, it deflated like a pricked balloon after he blasted his wad. I swirled the soft meat around in my mouth and licked off the spunk until he pulled his prick out.

I had a diamond-cutter boner to say the least after having sucked off my idol and tasted his precious cum. His brown eyes were glazed and he reached out and touched my cock. He slowly masturbated it. I didn't have an overhang like him and my rosy mushroom crown pulsed and oozed.

"Want me to jerk you off, buddy?"

"No way. No how. Can do that better myself."

"But you're horny. You wanna get off, don't you?"

"Oh yeah. Just sit there and let me look at you will I get off."

He leaned back on the couch and parted his thighs so I could get a beautiful view of the full package. I dropped to my knees and jacked off while I worshipped his beautiful body. I ran my hands over his thighs, his balls, his sopping cock. After a few moments, I spread his cheeks and dove into his fur-lined crevice. I lapped up a storm. His pucker was cherry and protested it but I darted my tongue right up into his brownie. His crack was steamy and I could feel the heat from his guts. "Stop."

I ignored him. As I tongued him, I noticed he was getting hard again. Still, he kept protesting, his eyes closed.

I held his thighs wide apart and I pointed my muscle on target and it slowly penetrated the soft membranes of his cherry asshole. "What are you doing?"

"If you thought my tongue was good, wait'll you feel this."

"No, no," he protested, but weakly.

I had the head and a couple inches in him.

"It hurts, buddy."

"You can take it. You were a soldier. A good soldier. Hang in there."

I felt his assring expand and clamp around my cock. This was the hottest, tightest hole I'd ever penetrated. Not only that, it was the butthole of my soldier idol. I was at the gates of paradise for sure.

I was overheated and sweating heavily as I began fucking him, ever so slowly, ever so gently.

Before long he opened his eyes and looked down. "Look at it! I can't believe it's in me. Bill's prick! I can't believe it!"

"Yeah, it's in you all right." Once my tool was firmly entrenched in his hole and I was sure that he could handle the assault, I started to really fuck him. I was sure now that this is what he'd been wanting all along. Better late than never. I pounded his butthole relentlessly. My heavy cum-laden balls slammed against his hairy cheeks. I could even feel his crack hairs tickle my cock. "Now it's all the way in."

"Oh, yeah, fuck me. Fuck me in the ass."

I crammed his butthole, hammering inside his guts until my cock got harder than I could ever remember it.

"Oh, Bill!"

I lunged my meat balls-deep in his hole and shot off with wild abandon, spurting gobs and gobs of fiery jism deep into his assguts. I held my cock in him until it softened and slid out.

Jake showed his mettle. I expected as much, now. I mean I'd fucked and rimmed him into a brand-new hard-on. In a quick maneuver he scooted out from under and told me to get on the couch myself. I did as I was told and he assumed the position I had been in. I spread my cheeks for him, saying, "Spit in that hole if you're going to fuck it."

A glob of cold saliva dripped into my ass. Showing no mercy to my slutty ass, he rammed his cock into it and rode me like I'd never been ridden before. He prodded lustily, born to do this.

"Fuck me!" I begged him.

That he did. He pumped away until my asshole was on fire, then he filled me with his hot cum. Even when his cock finally softened he didn't pull out for some time, just plugged my hole as he kissed me.

Later, we polished off the bottle of whiskey and lots of beer between more bouts of my cocksucking and mutual assfucking. At gray dawn I reluctantly pulled my ass out of bed and got dressed. Jake was sleeping like a baby. I took a long look at his hunky body, the hairy lower half and his fat jewels in repose. I kissed him gently on the cheek. He stirred but didn't waken.

I had to get my ass in gear. My sore ass. It was another work day for me but I had a smile on my face. I tried to call him at the Hilton around noon but he'd already checked out. I never heard from him again but I still feel blessed for the late, last chance to spend the night with him. Wet dreams can come true.

ME AND THE COLONEL
by William Cozad

Through my living room window I watched the men move the furniture and appliances into the house next door. There was a light rain falling.

I wondered about our new neighbors. Mom had heard that the man was an Army officer. I wondered why he didn't live on the local base.

I spent the summer after my eighteenth birthday working the late afternoon shift at a fast food place. So I slept late while my folks got up early to go to work. My room was upstairs and I heard their chatter while they drank coffee and got ready to go to work. I lay in bed with a morning hard-on, but I waited until I heard the car pull out of the driveway before I got down to business.

Tossing back the sheet (I sleep in the raw), I took matters into my own hand, wrapping my fingers around my straining hard-on. Images of men I'd served food to at the burger joint flashed into my mind. I didn't care much for young guys with their skinny bodies. I lusted after mature men. I'd had a secret crush on our football coach, but I wasn't a jock and the man didn't even know that I existed. That didn't stop me from fantasizing about him. The image of the beefy middle-aged coach never failed to get me off. Nor the images of the daddy types who patronized the burger joint. From older construction workers in dirty clothes to businessmen in short-sleeved white shirts and ties, I stored up images that were grist for my jack-off mill.

I tugged on my balls while I stroked my dick. Beard stubble, a hairy arm, a bulging crotch I'd seen; all of them added fuel to the fire in my loins. I pulled down the pants of the older man wearing the hard hat and inhaled his musky stench while I gobbled up his soft cock, which got hard in my mouth.

I beat my meat faster and faster until I felt the cum churn in my balls and surge up through my aching dick. Splat! Thick white cum drops rained on my chest. I rubbed my finger in some of the cum and licked it. The rest I contentedly smeared into my skin. I liked the smell and feel of cum caked on my body. After a while I got up.

Having the house to myself, I shoved a cassette into the deck of my stereo and turned it up full blast (something that drove my folks crazy and I wasn't allowed to do when they were home). Jacking off made me hungry, so I ate some breakfast and then rinsed off the dishes and stacked them in the washer. I puttered around in my room.

When I heard someone pull into the driveway of the house next door, I glanced out the window. I was greeted by the sight of a man getting out of a car. He was fortysomething, medium height but muscular. He wore a summer khaki Army uniform with a silver eagle insignia on the cap and the shirt collar. He was a full colonel. I was impressed.

The sight of the hunky military officer made my dick stir in my pants.

He was getting a bag of groceries out of the car. I was basically shy but I'd learned to be outgoing and friendly at my job.

I summoned up some of the courage I'd gained at work and decided to make a move. This guy was too hot. I had to at least get an up-close look.

The sight of the slender, handsome colonel made my cock start to ooze. Seeing the mailman approach gave me the excuse I was looking for to go outside.

Opening the front door, I greeted the mailman like he was a long-lost friend. He gave me a funny look but smiled. Then he crossed the street.

When I glanced over at the new neighbor, I looked right into his clear blue eyes.

"Hello there," I said.

"Hi," he nodded.

I sauntered over to him. I introduced myself and he grasped my extended hand.

"I'm Colonel Foster. Nice to meet you."

He held my hand for what seemed a second too long. I felt extra nervous. My palm was sweaty.

"Welcome to the neighborhood." That sounded dumb, I thought.

"Thank you. Billy was it?"

"Uh, Bill."

"Okay. I was just going to have a cold drink. Care to join me?" His deep bass made my balls rumble in their sac.

"Sure," I agreed eagerly.

I tailed the colonel into his house.

"It's a mess in here. My wife's staying with her mother, who's sick, so the moving chores fell on me."

The colonel put the groceries in the fridge and popped open the tabs of two soda cans. He handed me one.

"Cheers," he said.

I smiled.

He took off his cap. I was surprised that he was bald. It made him look really tough and macho.

We sat at the table. Cardboard boxes were stacked on the counter by the cupboards.

"You still in school, son?"

"Well, I'm going to college this fall. I got a summer job at a burger joint."

"Hmm." His eyes were drilling into my head.

"What do you do in the Army?"

"I'm a finance officer."

"You keep the books."

"Something like that. What about you, Billy? What do you wanna do?"

"I'm not sure. My dad's a lawyer, so maybe—"

"Well, you've got time to decide."

I polished off the soda. "Thanks for the drink," I said.

"Hey, it was my pleasure, Billy."

For some reason I extended my hand. He clasped it. Then he pulled me toward him. I was shocked. There was an embarrassed silence.

"Are you this friendly to your troops?" I didn't know what the hell I was saying.

He chuckled. "No way. It's just that I felt something strange when I touched your hand." He was carefully studying my eyes.

I started to wrap my arms around him. I was afraid he'd reject me, maybe call me a fag, or one of those queer names. But he didn't.

"You're a cute kid," he said. I could feel something stiff pressing against my leg, and I let go of my reservations. "And lonely, I'll bet in this place."

"And horny," I said, panting.

"That's normal at your age. Have you ever been with a man before?"

"In this town? Are you serious? You probably think I'm weird."

"No, indeed. I have the same feelings sometimes. It's nothing to worry about. Are you a virgin?"

"If you don't count jacking off."

"Every guy does that. But there are better things to do." He moved in real close.

My voice trembled. "Show me."

The colonel took a deep breath. "This is highly unusual. But delightful. Step into my bedroom."

The colonel clasped my shoulder as he led me into the bedroom. The bed was made and there were several cardboard boxes stacked around the room. He closed the drapes.

"Go ahead. Take off your clothes," he said.

"Is that an order?"

A scary grin formed on his face. "Oh, so you want fun and games? You got it, little Billy."

"It's Bill."

He snickered. "Billy. Do as you're told." I caught on fast, and decided not to make this too easy.

"I'm no soldier you can boss around."

"We'll see about that. Strip out of those clothes."

"Yes, Sir." I saluted the colonel over-dramatically. He slapped me.

"Careful, smart-ass! Respect this uniform."

The colonel's eyes were bright blue flames. Excitement ran through me like a high voltage wire.

Standing in front of him while he sat on the edge of the bed, I peeled off my shirt. I was no muscle boy but I was in good shape and proud of my hard body.

"Oh, yeah, not a feather on you."

I unfastened my belt and slid off my low-hanging, baggy jeans. All I wore was a pair of white cotton briefs.

"Nice legs," he said.

His admiration made my heart thud in my chest.

"Take everything off, young man."

I noticed the sweat bead his brow when I kicked off my hightop sneakers. I left on my tube socks. Hooking my fingers in my briefs, I peeled them down and flashed the colonel my dick, which was semi-hard.

Gripping my cock, I stroked it. It was fully hard, all fat eight inches of it, in seconds.

"God, what a great cock, and what a great little ass! You've been blessed!"

By now my dick was oozing clear pre-cum. Stepping up in front of the colonel, I waved my dick towards his face.

"Stroke that dick."

I masturbated lewdly in the colonel's face.

"Stick your finger up your butthole while you jack off."

"What?"

"You heard me."

I poked my middle finger in between my cheeks and up into my tight hole. I'd only done that once before.

"Lick your finger off," barked the colonel, sweating hard.

"That's gross," I said, half-heartedly.

"Do it now."

I licked the tangy ass-juices on my finger, something I'd never done before. The smell and taste really turned me on.

"Beat your meat for me, boy. Yeah, that's it. Tug on those nuts. Your dick's so red. So hard." There was an earthquake in my nuts.

"Oh, shit, I'm gonna blow!"

"I didn't give you permission to come, boy!"

"Oh, god, I just can't stop it, sir!"

Just in the nick of time the colonel leaned forward and wrapped his wet, warm lips around my dickhead, pulling it down his throat.

I groaned and rewarded him with an incredible gush of cum. The old boy didn't spill a drop. I was shaking and squirting at the same time. It felt so good.

When he let go of my dick he licked his lips. I took a moment to catch my breath. Suddenly the colonel spoke. "Turn around. Show me that cherry butt of yours."

Turning around, I kicked off my shorts and mooned the colonel. I glanced over my shoulder.

"Perfect. A gorgeous bubblebutt. It needs to be fucked," he stated.

"No, no! I can't do that!" I panicked.

Whack! He slapped me across the butt. "Address me as *Sir*, understand?"

"Yes, Sir."

He spread my buttcheeks. I thought I'd died and gone to heaven when he stuck his tongue up into my asshole. I rubbed my butt in his face as he darted his tongue up my chute.

"Your ass tastes like peanut butter. It's delicious."

"Wanna fuck me, don't you, Sir?" I could feel my ass muscles relaxing.

"Yes! An ass like yours was made to be fucked, and fucked good!"

I watched over my shoulder while the colonel unzipped the fly of his khaki uniform pants and freed his dick. It was soft, fat and uncut.

"Get down on your knees."

Turning around, I kneeled in front of the colonel.

"Suck it. Get it hard, bitch."

I licked his dick. I gobbled it up and chewed on it until it grew hard. It must have been nine inches. I wasn't sure I could handle such a monster on my first try. I bobbed my head up and down on it, dripping spit all over.

"Watch the teeth, now. Cover 'em. Yeah, that's it. Get my dick ready to fuck that cherry butt of yours."

I loved the salty taste, the spongy feel of his cockhead and the rubbery feel of his veiny shaft as I sucked on it.

"Oh, yeah. Got it ready. Get belly-down on that bed."

I plopped down spread-eagled on the bed and watched him over my shoulder. The colonel unhooked his belt and dropped his trousers, then his boxers. I gasped at the size of his pecker. I was going to enjoy this!

Grinning, he straddled my legs. "God, I can't remember the last time my dick was so hard."

He slapped his big boner on my buttcheeks. I could feel the sticky pre-cum ooze out of it.

"Tell me how big it is and how bad you want it, boy."

"Oh, yeah. It's a monster, Colonel. I want it up my virgin butt."

"Beg for it. Beg for my dick."

"Oh, please fuck me, sir! I want you to be the first one. Stick it up my ass. I gotta have it!"

"Yeah, that's the spirit." I had to beg the colonel to screw me but it was worth it.

When he popped his crown into my asshole I bit into the pillow. The pain was incredible. "Aw fuck, I can't take it."

"Relax that ass. Let it slide in. Yeah, that's it."

"Sir. I can't take it, Sir."

"Yessss, Sir!" I felt my assring grip his dick as he inched the shaft inside me, stuffing my hole. The pain of penetration disappeared and it suddenly felt real good. I bucked back.

"Yeah, that's it!"

"Fuck me, Sir. Fuck my ass."

"You got it."

He punched my butthole slowly at first. Then he reared up and began to hammer my ass with his bullnuts banging against my buttcheeks.

I moaned, "Harder, Sir!"

The colonel tore up my ass and I loved it.

"Oh, Jesus, it's so fucking hard. Oh, yeah. Shoot it, Sir. Squirt it up my hole!"

The colonel crammed his cock a mile up my ass and let out a grunt. His hose sprayed his fiery wad deep into my guts.

At the same time I felt my balls buzz. The second dose of cum blasted up my shaft and squirted out onto the bed. I was shaking.

The stud collapsed on top of me, sweating and breathing hard. I clamped my ass muscles around his cock and drained his nuts until his soft dick slithered out.

To show the colonel my appreciation for his gift up my ass, I turned around and grabbed hold of his jewels and cleaned them off with my tongue.

I kissed the colonel on the mouth and he kissed me back, roughly. We sounded like a couple of marathon runners, the way we were panting. "Oh, Sir," I cried.

That summer passed a lot faster than I had hoped and, fortunately, my folks never caught onto my lust for Colonel Foster. They thought I might want a career in the Army. But they were wrong. All I wanted was to have sex with the colonel.

THE DRAFT
by Peter Gilbert

"You won't find it so bad," said my dad. "Everybody has to go. I did; your uncles did and, when you think of it, your father did."

My mom laughed. "It's all over in three days," she said, "and you'll come back with a number. Just think of that!"

"And a sore back and backside," I said.

"The pain soon fades," said my dad. "Why, I was at the swimming pool showing off my number just a day after I got home."

We'd just had breakfast when my dad switched on the monitor and there it was; the dreaded draft notice. I was to report to the collection center in three days' time. I guess it's funny, really. We knew we had to go.

We had learned recent history in eighth grade. The war had contaminated the world. Billions of people had died. Billions were too badly affected to be allowed to breed. It was our job—our privilege, they said, to help in re-population. We all knew we'd have to go soon after our sixteenth birthday but the arrival of the notice was still a shock. It was frightening too. We all knew about sterilization. If they discovered that you'd been contaminated you were snipped. It didn't hurt, they said, and nobody would ever know. You still got a number and there was no need to tell anyone. It didn't impair pleasure. Only the little chip implanted in your backside contained the information and only the medics at the centers could read it.

I felt happier the next day. Rick, my buddy of long standing, had received his notice on the same day and his center was the same as mine. Rick was a great guy; a great sportsman, a real good looker and, need I say, highly popular at the Rec. When we were little kids there was always a gang of girls round him. After we'd gotten to "the age" that was out of the question of course but he was still pretty popular. There were rumors that he still had leanings in that direction. I don't think there was any truth in them and, hell, most kids go through weird stages. At the time I'm writing about he was going out with a really nice guy; a scientist of some sort. His dad, I heard, was not terribly happy about the relationship but it carried on.

With Rick next to me on the transport, I felt better. There were over a thousand of us from our conurbation alone, which gives you some idea of the success of the program. It had only started twenty years before!

They called it the Spunk Factory or the Milking Parlor. Its proper title was Donation Center 485. It consisted of a group of low, white buildings, set in the middle of the desert.

The first day was devoted to medical examinations. That was a bore. They probed and prodded. They listened and they looked and they stuck needles into us to pull out all sorts of samples. Painful? Only relatively. The numbering came first and when your back feels like someone's stuck a thousand red hot pins in it, a needle in the spine; even a needle in your balls is tolerable. They use anesthetics for those. As far as I know, they don't for the numbering. Maybe that's part of the plan. "Hurt 'em like hell in the first ten minutes and they won't yell so loud next time." We hadn't been in the place for more than an hour when, undressed and showered, they lined us up and took us to the numbering bureau. Up onto the benches. Hold onto the handles. The machine was lowered onto the area between your shoulder blades. For a second, it felt cold. Then "Buzz, buzz" and the noise was deafening. I think we all screamed out in unison. I was two, two, seven, eight, three, five, three. Rick read it for me. He was two numbers before me.

It didn't hurt quite so much on day two but I was glad I didn't have to wear any clothes. That day was all intelligence and aptitude tests and interviews. Again, a bore.

Then came the third and final day. They woke us up early. We'd slept in what they called "sleeping units." They were more like tubes really, about four feet wide and seven feet long, sealed with a hatch with a circular inspection window. They took some getting used to. The worse part was having your wrists anchored to the walls. Mustn't yield to temptation, see? After two nights like that the average sixteen-year-old is a very randy creature indeed and guaranteed to fill his tube nicely. There was even a guy who peered in every few minutes to make sure you hadn't invented a new way of jacking off!

I first saw Bob when we were having breakfast. A white-coated young guy kept smiling at me. Most of the staff there seemed to have forgotten how to smile. I guess when you have to deal with several hundred naked teenage boys every day, your sense of humor gets a bit frayed. I finished the compulsory vegetable juice and protein-enriched biscuit, slung the cartons in the recycling can, and walked out. He followed me.

"I spotted you when you were being numbered," he said. I said I hadn't seen him which, when you're lying on your front, is not surprising.

"You've got a fine body," he said. That, in all honesty, was nonsense. Quite apart from Rick there must have been hundreds of boys there with better builds than mine. I said so. He said something about the eye of the beholder. I suppose I should have realized what he was after then but I didn't. I guess that, like all the other guys, my balls were full of the reason for being there and my mind was full of the thought of going home.

The batch Rick and I were in was number eleven on the list. That gave us at least an hour of free time before we were sent for.

"Got anything planned before your time?" said my new acquaintance. I said something about a game of chess. Violent exercise wasn't allowed.

"My room's in this building," he said. "Care to come up there?" He bent his head forward slightly. "There's coffee," he whispered. Coffee! In those days coffee was the number one adults-only drink. Just about the fastest way for an under- eighteen to land up in a rehabilitation center was to be caught drinking coffee.

"They'd know, wouldn't they?" I asked.

"No. You've done all your tests."

"And it won't affect—?"

"Don't worry about that. It might make it feel even better."

I said, "Yes." Who wouldn't?

His name was Bob.

"What do you do here, Bob?" I asked as we stood on the walkway.

"I'm a castrator."

For a moment I was panic stricken. Was this the way they did it? Invite the guy for coffee and then snip him? I almost turned round and ran back. Then common sense took over. We were going in the wrong direction. The center was arranged on a flow principle. Guys got unloaded from the transports at one end and moved through the station. The clothes you'd last seen when you got undressed were waiting for you at the other end. We were going back in the direction of the reception area as witness the batches of guys on the opposite walkway. Guys with electrodes stuck on them going to the medical block; guys still shaking from the shock of being numbered. Everybody else on our walkway was white-coated—except me. If they wondered what a naked boy was doing on that one, they said nothing. Maybe they thought I was going to repeat a test or something.

"Here we are," said Bob. "In here." We stepped off the walkway. He opened the door. It was a nice room. There were chairs, a divan bed, a holovision, the usual things. "We sometimes have to work late or early in the morning," he said, explaining the bed. "My living accommodation is over there next to the CA's." He pointed out of the window to a group of living blocks. "Maybe that's where we'll meet next time," he added.

I laughed. The chances of me being a CA were nil. CA stood (in everyday speech) for Come Again. They were the guys who were so special that they were held on reserve and were called upon to provide the very best sperm for very special purposes. Top athletes, government ministers and scientists were all descended from CAs. I had only met one in my life. He told me about the luxury they enjoyed. No lining up with a load of other guys for CAs. They had their own luxury suites and were waited on hand and foot. Cock too. The guy actually came to you with the tube.

The coffee machine was hidden in a cupboard. He switched it on. It burbled in the background as we talked.

I said that I didn't envy him his job. It was, he explained, a sabbatical. He'd taken a year off his studies to do it and earn money. I made a weak joke about his getting a testimonial for his knowledge of testicles. He laughed. "I guess I've seen more than most people," he said.

"I just hope I'm not on your list for today," I said.

"No chance." He picked up a print out. "You missed out by two digits," he said. "Three five one in your batch is on the list."

I couldn't believe my ears. "No. There's some mistake there," I said "I

- 52 -

know the guy. He's from our conurbation."

"Then I shouldn't have said anything. Forget it."

I couldn't of course. I told him about Rick, and his superb exam results and his sports successes.

"Be that as it may," he said, "he leaves here without his balls. Wait a moment." He went to a computer console and tapped in Rick's number.

"Radioactive contamination," he read. "Not lethal but it's there. Cells are already beginning to misform."

"But our conurbation is clean!" I protested. "It's impossible."

"He could have got it through a contact," said Bob. "That sometimes happens."

I knew straight away. It had to be the scientist Rick was going out with.

"The idiot!" I muttered. I told Bob all about it. I suppose I was hoping that, knowing the full story, he might be able to save Rick. "His parents let it go on," I said, "although the guy's about forty-five."

"I don't see anything wrong with that, personally," he said. "I guess I'm a bit of a rebel. I'd rather see a young guy in the arms of someone who really cares for him than screwing right, left and center with other youngsters. What about you? What's your social life like?"

It was non-existent at that time. I'd just packed up with a really nice guy whom I had gotten to know at the Rec. We'd never gone all the way, though. I had never done that. My dad would have gone spare if he knew about our cock-fondling sessions in the changing rooms.

Bob nodded and said something about the right guy coming along, went to the coffee machine, and returned with two cups of the stuff. I sipped it. The truth is that I had drunk it once before and hadn't much liked it then. Bob's tasted better.

"How is it actually done?" I asked, trying to change the subject away from myself.

"Your buddy? It'll all be over in a second or two. His legs are lifted up in stirrups. A couple of quick snips, out with the originals, in with the prostheses, two stitches and he's done. Bob's your uncle, as they used to say in the old days, though this Bob isn't anybody's uncle."

It was something of a relief to hear that he wasn't a rebel in every respect. My folks were very conservative. My dad had two boyfriends, both of whom were officially registered as my uncles. I got on well with them both.

"But you live with somebody?" I said.

"No. This Bob is all alone."

It was difficult to believe. I mean, he was a real good-looking guy. I guessed his age to be about thirty. (In fact, he was twenty-six. We've laughed a lot about that.)

"I guess someone will come along," I said, repeating his own advice to me.

"I rather hoped he had," he said.

"How. You mean...you mean me?"

He nodded. I was shattered. I honestly didn't know what to do or say. What do you say when you are sixteen, stark naked, and you've been given a cup of a forbidden stimulant and a good-looking grown-up guy, a potential doctor, says something like that to you?

He sat on the bed and made a beckoning movement with his finger. Like a robot, I drank the last drops of coffee, put the cup down, and went over to join him. He kissed me. I remember that. I also remember him playing with my nipples and saying nice things about them. I had to ask him to stop. I didn't want to but, of course, to have come then would have been a disaster. I had never seen the veins in my cock so distended. It looked like a purple-headed lighthouse that had been overgrown by some weird climbing plant. He wanted to suck it. I wanted him to but we both knew it had to be off-limits. My spunk was destined for a deep freeze, not a deep throat! He hoisted my legs into the air. I had another moment of blind panic. Was he going to get his knife out? I guess it was his experience that made him concentrate on that region and my lack of experience that made it feel so great. He stroked and tickled round my balls and my asshole. He talked all the time; talked in a low, husky voice about what he'd like to do.

"You'd be lying on your back," he said, "and I'd lick you all over, like you were made of sugar. Like this. I felt his tongue on my nipples, in my navel, on my cock and balls. Again I had to ask him to stop, and lay there panting for breath. Then, when relative equanimity had been restored, he started off again about my sweet ass. I wouldn't have called it sweet myself, but he sure enjoyed licking it out. So did I. Once again, we had to stop. I was too far gone that time to speak. I had to push his head away.

"I guess you're right," he said, ruefully and he fetched me another coffee. I sat there drinking it with a hard-on such as I had never had before. He asked me to stay over for a few days. That was impossible of course.

"I have to see you again," he said.

"I'd like to see you again too," I said.

He said he would think of something. I didn't really expect anything to come of it. I think we both felt frustrated at that moment. My balls were aching. Fortunately my target time was getting nearer. His seemed impossible to achieve. Center 485 was a hell of a long way from our conurbation. Rick's people might turn a blind eye to an age difference. Mine certainly wouldn't—even though the difference was less. We were both feeling more and more miserable when the console pinged.

"Time for work," said Bob. I protested that there was no way I could go down the walkway with a raging hard on. In fact I needn't have worried. Of the others in our batch waiting by the doors, quite a few were in the same state. Rick's was enormous, standing out from his middle like the branch of a tree. I heard later that it's quite usual for that to happen.

They let us in. Our chips were laid out on a table, each in a numbered pack. We lay face-down on the tables. They put the leg supports under us and strapped us down. I felt the guy roll the sleeve over my cock. Then came a strange, mechanical noise like someone breathing in their sleep. The feeling was amazing. I felt it contracting and relaxing. I thought of Bob. A weekend with him would be great. No need to tell him to stop. He could do what he liked, as often as he liked. I would be his boy. The thought became a fantasy. I was swimming in his pool and he was watching me. He beckoned. I climbed out. "What do you want?" I asked. He smiled and led me, wet and dripping, into the house and into his bedroom. He laid me on the bed. I felt him licking down my back, along the furrow between my asscheeks. Then his tongue touched it. I spread my legs to make it easy for him. I felt his cock on my anus, and there was long, drawn-out pressure. I knew I had to yield. I wanted to yield. His hands went underneath me, squeezing my cock. The ache in my balls was getting really painful. My head began to swim. There was a strange illusion of black flags and bright lights dancing in front of my eyes. I wanted so much to admit Bob and release the pent-up spunk.

I felt a hand on the small of my back. Bob's voice, whispering, cajoling. "Lovely. Give it all you've got. That's right. Good boy." I lay still. The picture of a boy over Bob's bed faded into a white tiled wall. All around me I heard the gasps and moans of the other guys as the juice was sucked out of them.

"You did real good," said Bob's voice. I couldn't turn round.

"Is that really you?" I asked.

"Sure is. You don't think I'd leave you at a time like this, do you?"

He continued to talk to me whilst they put the chip in. I felt so happy that I hardly felt it. Just a pin-prick, a feeling like someone was drawing something on my ass and it was over. The technician unfastened the straps and peeled the sleeve off.

"A very quick word," said Bob as I went to the shower room. "That chip in your butt is the real thing. I can't play around with chips but I can play around with the computers here. Not a word to anyone about that, or me, or about your buddy. Understand?"

I nodded and went into the showers feeling happy and relieved. My heart thumped a bit when Rick and four others were called out.

"Guess there's something wrong with their records," one guy shouted over the sound of cascading water. Somebody else suggested that they might be going to be snipped. I was one of many who trashed that idea.

I saw Rick briefly as we got dressed. He looked a bit pale. I grinned and he grinned back. On the transport going home he told me why he'd been sent for. His spunk was of such amazingly high quality that they had to double analyze it. He couldn't wait to tell his friend.

I guess he did. He certainly told everyone in the Rec. We went there every day showing off our numbers and telling the younger kids frightening stories of what would happen to them when it was their turn. There was one kid. I guess he was about fourteen or fifteen. I had always thought him pretty before I went to the center and had been planning to date him. After I got back I noticed the acne on his chin. "I've heard there are guys at those places who want to get it off with young kids," he said. "That's why they work there." Young kids indeed! I turned my back on him, just to let him have a real good luck at the number!

The second day of Month Six, 3501. Breakfast. Lecture from dad about my solitary status. All my friends were dating, why not me? Could it be? "Please be honest, son...." Didn't I fancy girls? If so, there was no problem. They would send me off to a private rehabilitation center. My Uncle Ned had the same problem when he was sixteen. As for my friend Rick, well, he'd had problems in the past. It was probably as well that the man who seemed to take such an unhealthy interest in him was dying but dad had seen Rick recently with another boy and it was pretty obvious that Rick was normal enough. I sat through it without saying a word. Dad switched on the monitor.

It had come through in the night. In accordance with the Central Government Decree Donor Reservists, two seven eight three five three was required at Center 458 for a six-day stopover. Departure in three days time. Thereafter at monthly intervals. Private transport had been arranged.

Neither mom, dad or my uncles believed it at first. I had to strip to the waist so they could check the number. Dad called someone and got told by a grea-haired bureaucrat not to question Central Government communications.

Three days of partying followed, the aim of which seemed to be to allow everyone we knew to congratulate mom and dad! I failed to see why. Like everyone else of my age group, I was the product of a sperm and an egg, neither of which came from them but I let them have their three days of pleasure. They were nothing compared to my six!

Bob was there to meet me. We went straight to his house, passing several of the real CAs, enjoying the sunshine under their protective screens.

"They look pretty good," I said.

"Not as good as you," said Bob. He hugged me.

There really was a swimming pool. A good one. The oddest thing, though, was the picture above the bed. It was a picture of a boy—exactly as I had imagined it. I guess I saw that picture from every conceivable angle during those first six days. I saw it from a kneeling position; from below when I was on my back with my legs in the air and once from above when the bed banged so hard against the wall that it fell down.

They were six of the best days of my life. Bob was so good, loving and considerate. I, of course, was in a position to shoot as much as I wanted—in several positions, actually. Bob liked to go to sleep with it in his mouth. So did I—and his was quite a mouthful! I was an ass—full too! With that throbbing inside you, you don't feel much like sleeping!

Well, six years have gone past. Flown past. Bob is now a doctor and specializes in vasectomies and prosthetic testicles! All that training and back to square one. He likes it though. The present crazes for big balls and boy sopranos have been a great boon. As I write this, the waiting room is full of potential Hercules and small boys wanting to be stars!

Hey! I'd better stop and get a meal ready. Not for much longer, fortunately. Bob's arranged for an impregnated female and he reckons that I'm going to recognize the little sprag when he's born. I wonder.

RAW RECRUITS
by Ken Smith

A Diary of Days—and Nights—in the Navy

Monday: How did they expect us to eat this crap at 6 a.m. Jim, the junior chef, was brilliant at blow-jobs but frying a fucking egg was beyond him. I offered him a seductive smile and scooped a couple of the limp liquid cackle berries onto my plate. They looked about as appetizing as Twiggy's tits and I sleepily led them to a table where a stocky butch stoker sat, scoffing a bowl of cornflakes. The greasy rashers of bacon I'd collected enroute helped cheer the sorry sight and I arranged them into a happy face before slamming the lot between rounds of bread, in an attempt to create something that looked edible. The stocky stoker's eyes never left his bowl but he was aware I was searching his every expression; searching for sexual clues. It was a must for me.

Sex on board a Royal Navy ship was usually hard to come by and you couldn't afford to be wrong if you were going to proposition someone. As far as I was concerned, everyone dropped their pants, until proven otherwise!

Beneath the table, I let my leg brush against his but he pulled quickly away and remained transfixed by his Wheaty-pop breakfast. Shame really because he was quite a Wheaty-pop himself. Anyway, the day was just developing and he looked like he'd just come off watch and was heading for his bunk. I hung around until he'd finished eating, just to glimpse his butt and absorb the rest of his features as he left the dining room.

I liked stokers—they were a bit of a turn-on for me and had the reputation of being "goers" if you got one. I reckoned it was the boiler-suits, usually unbuttoned to the navel, and the inevitable line of sweat trickling down a smooth, bare chest, and knowing that they were completely naked beneath the greasy, blue material.

I'd been below decks into the boiler room many times - to deliver signals to the Commander or Engineering - and watched the young lads dipping oily rags beneath their boiler-suits and into their crotches, mopping up the liquid as they exuded sweat in the hundred-degree temperatures. I often wondered how that would smell—steamy, sweaty crotch and oil. I reckoned it would smell just fine, especially if the legs were parted over my feasting face. But, as yet, I hadn't poked a stoker.

I thanked Jim for his wonderful creation and gave him a wink, signalling I'd see him during the week for one of his haute cuisine blow-jobs.

The Communications Office was somewhat silent for a change, just a printer chattering away in the corner and the telephone buzzing. Tim was bent over the printer reading an incoming signal. We were alone, so I trotted over and pinched his butt.

Tim was a great fuck and a fun guy. I was privileged to know he liked being screwed and obliged him whenever he was on heat. But with his butch manner and manly voice, which didn't suit his young age and features, nobody knew of his tendency to swing—unless he was two-timing me.

One peculiar aspect of Navy life: guys seldom told each other if they were having it away with other guys. It was added protection. The least amount of people who knew of one's sexual leanings, the better. The guys who usually got rumbled —for rumbling each other—were those who formed threesomes or more. Two was the safest number and there were ample hideouts in which to perform. Also, a couple of guys knocking around together was less suspicious.

Tim spun around and I grabbed his cock. It was semi-hard and protruded just enough to make it look appetizing. I grabbed his golden-haired head and planted my lips onto his, giving him a good morning kiss, or good night in his case as he was going off watch. He pushed me away but managed a half smile. I guessed it had been a hectic night and he was tired. He called me a tart in that masculine manner and I wondered how he could make such a feminine word sound so butch. I wrapped my arms around his waist and squeezed his cock, but he butted me away with his backside. Well, I had to try! I even offered to return to his mess-deck and tuck him in but he grabbed his cock and muttered something about sitting on it. That's precisely what I had in mind—well, him sitting on mine. I guessed we didn't have a date.

I didn't know if it was just me but I was constantly thinking about sex. I didn't join the Navy with getting laid in mind, but there were so many good-looking guys, it was impossible not to constantly think about it. Also, there was so much groping or guys strutting around naked; and in the mornings, so many stiff cocks on parade, it was difficult not to drool at the sight of them—many of which were still dribbling from an early morning shake. Had there been a post of Early Morning Cocksucker, mine would have been the first application on the Captain's table. That said, not every guy was edible. Some were gross, grotty and even gut-heaving. But a good few of the baby sailors possessed beautiful bouncy bollocks, buttocks and bonnie boners—all requiring a friend. And by God, I was in the befriending business!

Tim went to bed—alone. I went to work on the incoming signals. Within thirty minutes, the office had filled with its complement of watch-keepers, so I shot off to my own office on the deck above. This was a real hush-hush place and only two of us were allowed access, which was a real bonus as some of the things I did there were pretty hush-hush as well. The thought that one day I'd get caught filled my mind many times, but when you have a mouthful of Marine, it's difficult to let it materialize into a real fear. In fact, often the size of the Marine's cock manifesting in my mouth was more frightening. No wonder they were such good fighters. No need to threaten the enemy with a bayonet; just show them your dick, darling!

It felt like it was going to be a dull day. No War Games. No enemy to investigate. Nothing much to do except fire up my equipment and check that it was in working order. (Sorry, wrong equipment. You're disgusting!) Which is what I did. Well, what would you know? Blank screens. Not a green dot in sight. Just like the contents of East 17's underpants—or was it their heads!

Surprised? I'll say I was. For a million quid you'd at least expect the batteries to work. At least my day wasn't going to be spent alone.

I needed an electrician. To be honest, I needed a shag! But an electrician would be a start. My favorite, Sparks, one that I hadn't shagged, informed me they were snowed under with problems and could only spare a Baby Sparks—a Sparkler, I supposed. Desperate, I agreed.

In a flash, Sparkler was thumping my door. It was the sweetest little voice that asked, "Do you have a problem?"

Well, I did. But now I had an even bigger one, thanks to the vision before me. That was no one-and-a-half-volt-battery bulging in my briefs, but a pylon of power promising to protrude! Christ! A boy simply could not be *that* beautiful. It was criminal. Cruel. And I cried, "Come inside."

My little sparkler set about stripping the machinery and I set about doing a mental version of the same thing to him. Usually, Naval working clothes did little to enhance a body— even a beautiful one—but this Power Pack must have had a buddy or lustful admirer in the stores, because he'd set a pair of working trousers upon him so tight they might have been painted on.

Together we searched for the goblin in the works, but there was only one goblin I was interested in. And my mind worked overtime, thinking of a way I could use some paint-stripper on those pants!

"I think it's up," he cheerfully chirped, giving me a grin the length of his flies. Did he mean what I thought he meant, or was he referring to my dick?

"Up?" I repeated, looking lustfully straight at his crotch, then at my own.

"Yes. The mast," he clarified.

"Oh!" I sighed, disappointed, and tried to produce a grin of similar length.

He'd have to go aloft to sort it out, but couldn't do it alone— safety and all that. Now, when it came to heights, climbing over a locked toilet door was about my limit, but my mixed-up mind told me that at some point up there, there would come a moment when I might have to grab this little Sparkler—for safety reasons, you understand—so I agreed to assist. Trouble was, this Sparkler looked too hot to handle, and I could see myself getting burnt.

A fair swell rocked the mast back and forth as we climbed the hollow centre. There was a ladder on the outside, but even if he had told me I could fuck him when we reached the top, I don't think I could have climbed it.

He opened the hatch to the pretty blue sky above and as I watched his buttocks when he climbed through, somehow I managed not to bite them. But when we stepped out onto the platform, the only thing I was biting was my lip. Sixty feet doesn't look high from ground level, but up there in the breeze and four-way sway of the mast, certainly put lie to that notion, and to my erection.

He soon found the offending aerial and the cable that had freed itself but it was just beyond his reach. He was a brave little bugger and without hesitation began to climb the guardrails, in order to reach the broken cable. Then it happened. My premonition came true and he asked me to hold him. I don't think I leapt on him, over quickly—but it was panther-like, and I stuffed my eager hand down the back of his pants so far, my fingers delved between the crease of his buttocks. He looked quizzically over his shoulder. I guessed I'd gone too deep. Reluctantly, I withdrew and grasped the back of his belt and he gave me a look that said, "That's better," and resumed his climb. But it was no good, and I stopped him.

"It's no use. You'll have to put your arms around my thighs and hold onto me tightly," he ordered, rather masterfully for a youngster.

I don't recall saying, "Oh, thank you. Yes, please. Thank you, God." But I sure as hell thought it.

He resumed his climb and as he reached the danger point, precariously balancing on the top handrail, I threw my arms around his young muscles. With both my arms wrapped tightly around my treasure, he eased himself up the final inches. Miraculously, he made it and his nimble fingers began their task of teasing wires together. However, my nasty little digits, unexpectedly, but delightedly, had discovered his crotch. I could just make out the shape of his bell-end against the tip of my index finger.

Gently I moved my dexterous digit from beneath the supple sausage and slid it over the top. My strokes were minuscule, micro-dot movements, making out the shape of the bell-end's ridge. His pert little buttocks were in my face, so I daringly let my teeth take the slightest nip. His meat jarred beneath my fondling friend. I was in fear of dropping him as my excitement increased and was just about to strengthen my hold, when down he jumped.

"Finished," he gleefully announced.

Well, I wasn't! And I looked hard at the masterpiece I'd created with one finger, and like the tart that I was, questioned, "Don't you think you'd better make sure?"

He gave me another grin—the length of both our flies—and planted his sexy eyes onto my stiff prick, then told me he'd pop down to the office and check if my equipment was working, and then he'd be right back.

Well, nobody looks at my dick like that and gets away with it!

I watched him bolt down the hatch like a sexy rabbit, but what this bunny didn't know was that I had a plan.

I waited until I heard the clink-clank of him ascending the inside of the mast, then popped down the hatch, pulling it shut above me. In total darkness, I waited to snare him. It was a gamble; I might be wrong.

The sounds became louder as he approached and my crotch expanded in sympathy. Perched on a rung, legs wide apart, feet pressed against the bulkhead for support, I waited.

His head came between my thighs and into my crotch and he released a surprised yelp.

Placing my hand at the back of his head, I gently teased his face into my bulging groin. He didn't pull away but edged slightly higher and simply told me my equipment was working. And it certainly was!

He sounded nervous and I wondered if I'd finally made that fatal mistake, but eased his head into my cock. This time I slipped my other hand between my crotch and his face, sliding my fingers over his moist lips, then pushing them into his wet mouth.

He didn't pull away or warn me off. So, freeing my erect dick, I pushed it against his lips. He began to move his head from side to side, as if trying to avoid contact but his movements were not convincing. I persisted, not forcefully, just teasingly—indicating it was up for grabs if he wanted. Moments later his lips parted and his mouth carefully covered the head. It was sensationally hot and I wanted to push deep but knew he had not done this before, and let him work the head at his own pace. Slowly but surely, little by little, more of my meat began to penetrate his soft palate.

As I caressed his face with loving strokes, his movements became more eager, more lusting, deeper, and then his young face began to work frantically, sucking my cock from the tip to the base.

I lifted the hatch, allowing the light to shine down on his black hair, and excitedly watched as he lavished my length.

Stopping him before I came, I raised his body until his boyish bulge was level with my face. Greedily, I pulled his shirt from his pants and lifted it to his pin-sized nipples. My tongue licked at the soft flesh and firming studs, then around his navel. Reaching inside his pants, I released him from his clothing. A consumable cock with a foreskin sprang into view and I rolled the loose flesh back and forth over the head before consuming the whole length with the passion of a starving child.

Whilst we crazily kissed and darted tongues into mouths, we finished each other with our hands. He came first, his white cum splattering all over me, mine falling to the depths of the deck below.

It was a brilliant start to my week. And what a place to have sex. I couldn't say that I now belonged to the Mile High Club, but sixty feet was a start.

One thing was certain: I was a mile high all day!

* * *

Tuesday: I knew something big was going down, besides my erection. It wasn't often I was dragged from my bunk at three in the morning. Well, not by a big butch Bootneck, unfortunately.

I felt the ship shudder as the skipper rolled-on-the-revs, sticking 35 knots onto the speedometer as I climbed topside into the gale-force winds, in an attempt to blast the cobwebs from my bewildered brain, before it was bombarded with ultrasonic sounds. Electronic Warfare was my game.

The stern churned a funnel of white foam and it shone in the moonlight like a train on a wedding dress as the props dug deep into the ocean, slicing our bows through the stormy sea. I thought of Wheaty-pop, dipping his oily rag into his crotch as he beefed up the engines, but before I had time to let that voluptuous vision reach my dick, a mountain of Marine tugged at my arm, insisting I hurry.

When something like this happened, I was entrusted with an armed Marine as protector, who would guard me in my office whilst I worked. In these situations, everyone was the enemy.

We had six studly Marines on board. All straight? Except one, who relished being sucked. He was with me now as we ran to my office, me following him, naturally. I wouldn't have missed a view of that backside for anything.

Zak was his name. Well, it would be, wouldn't it? It was the kind of name you would give an Android, and Zak fitted that description admirably. His muscles were like metal, and if you had any notion of parting his solid steel buttocks, forget it. You'd need a dick like a can opener. Zak did not get fucked! But he did get sucked, and had a pit-bull in his pants. And, if everything went according to plan, it would be parting my lips when things calmed down.

I got the jist of what was going down from the Communications Officer. No need to go into details, safe to say one of our boys was in trouble.

Zak and I entered my office and I began firing up various pieces of electronic wizardry. Zak bolted the door and stood solid in its entrance. I told him there was no need, he could sit if he wished. But I got the feeling he loved the butch pose: legs apart, arms behind his back, rigid as a post, pistol swinging from his hip.

Jesus. He looked gorgeous!

Soon the office was buzzing and lights were flashing. I sat before my console, headphones on head, miniature mike at my mouth, and began twiddling various knobs—scanning the relevant frequencies. Meanwhile, the jammers were warming up, in case they were needed.

Zak stood like a chiselled stone statue behind me. I could see his reflection in one of my screens and was able to distinguish the outline of his pit bull. I'm sure I saw it move, growing and growling in his pants, and glanced over my shoulder, giving him a brief smile. He acknowledged with one of his own but didn't speak. You'd have thought we were total strangers rather than suck buddies, but duty was duty to this Marine.

"For Christ's sake, Zak. Take your bloody cap off!" I suggested, giving him another smile.

He thought for a moment. It seemed like a big decision, so I let him ponder it over. I suppose it was more of a sexual request, really. Well, if I couldn't see his dick just yet, at least I could relish his shaven head. Jesus, I just loved running my hands over the sharp spikes, and thoughts of shaving it whilst he gave me a blow-job filled my mind many times. But, alas, Zak didn't do that, either. He only received sex—the bitch!

I made contact with our boy in trouble and set the tape rolling, in case of cock-ups and to refer back to at a later date. Then he informed the captain on the hot line. I heard a clunk beside me, and jumped. I suppose I was a little tense. These situations certainly sent the adrenalin surging. It was Zak's cap, not a terrorist attack, and I shot a quick glance at his shaven head. Zak grinned. He knew what I was thinking and gave me a look that suggested I get on with my work.

I grinned back, and muttered, "You tormenting bitch," beneath my breath.

Zak shouldn't have distracted me because I lost contact with our boy whilst playing with my hormones instead of my hardware, then had five minutes of pulse-racing panic trying to regain it.

Concentration back on course, I resumed my job with the skill of an artist—delving into code-books, decoding, recoding, switching frequencies, jamming and unjamming. It was frantic, but I loved it. All the while, Zak stood silently watching me. Sometimes I wondered whether he was overwhelmed by the technicality of it all.

Without warning, two pieces of equipment went Pop! and their screens blanked. "Fuck!" I screamed, thumping the console, and frantically flew around the office, desperately trying to regain contact and retain the information I already had.

"Zak, get an Electrician!" I yelled.

Zak, pleased to be involved in a crisis, jumped to the task and was on the phone in a flash.

"He's coming," grinned Zak, excited by the trauma I was in.

"You slut, Zak!" I shouted. "Did you have to say 'coming' like that?"

Minutes later, a couple of heavy thuds echoed through the door. Zak released his pistol, placing his meaty hand around the butt. I knew it wasn't a terrorist. Zak must have known also. But he had a job to do and was more than likely doing it to the best of his ability.

Zak threw the iron bolts back, pulling his pistol from its leather holster, only to be greeted by the smiling face of my Baby Sparkler. Well, if you could have seen Zak's face, and mine, to be honest.

I was right, he was a slut and I wanted to slap him but simply asked if he was going to let my Sparkler in, then whispered, "Whilst you're at it, stop dribbling!"

Brad, that was Sparkler's name, gave me one of his fly-length grins, totally ignoring Zak, and that pleased me immensely. And I gave Zak a look that said, "Serves you right, you bitch." But Zak was totally besotted and began telling Brad my problem. I was just about to say, "Whose bloody office is this?" when Brad charged straight through Zak and asked about my predicament, which at the moment appeared to be Zak.

Speedily, Brad worked his nimble fingers at the wiring, temporarily regaining contact with our lost buddy long enough for me to complete my task. Panic over, I made coffee whilst Brad began a more permanent job. Zak had seated himself—at last! I think he was in a state of sexual shock, and I had to ask him, several times, if he wanted a cup.

Zak and I drank our coffee in virtual silence, both observing Brad's tight buns as he bent over, soldering wires. It was an awesome sight and I began to bulge in my bell-bottoms. A quick glance between Zak's legs confirmed his thoughts were on a similar wavelength.

Now, remember what I said about threesomes or more? Well, I could see that that rule was just about to fly through the port- hole. I wanted sex. Zak wanted sex. And Brad? I doubted if he'd refuse. So, my dilemma: Should I have sex with Zak, or Brad, or both? Or should I let them both go? In which case I was sure they would end up shagging somewhere. So why not?

Decision made, I delved into Zak's pants and pulled out his prick, parting my lips over the enormous, pulsating head. Zak was speechless, but was so engrossed with Brad's backside, he didn't bat an eye.

Zak stood, releasing more of his manhood, enabling me to get most of his meat into my mouth. And as I moved down its length, I kept one eye on Brad, waiting for him to turn around.

Brad spun to face me and was just about to inform me everything was back on line, but on seeing us his mouth simply dropped open and not a word left it. His eyes began to sparkle, and as I gazed between his thighs, he unconsciously caressed his cock.

Finally I stopped sucking Zak and nodded for Brad to join us. Zak's dick gained an inch as Brad moved forward, unzipping his fly and pushing his incredible tool tantalizingly through the opening.

Eagerly I went down on the mouthwatering morsel when Brad reached me. His was such a perfect prick and I pushed my mouth hard into the base, bringing it to its full potential. All the while, my left hand rolled Zak's foreskin back and forth over the head of his cock, keeping it firm.

Bringing their dicks head to head, I licked along both lengths, then devoured each in turn—first Brad's then Zak's, and continued the sequence whilst they kissed and tongued each other's throats. In my lustful state, I wanted to lavish both and made an attempt to get two cocks into my mouth, but Zak had enough dick for the three of us and I couldn't manage it. Pulling my prick from my pants, I began to work on myself.

Zak was awestruck by Brad's boyish body and began stripping the clothes from his smooth skin. And when Brad's trousers and briefs came down, I almost came at the sight of the black moustache above his dick and totally forgot about Zak's, and began to mouth hungrily at Brad's uncut cock, eager to tease his teenage juices onto my lavishing tongue. My mouth consumed all of him—lips pushing hard against the soft, black hair.

Standing up, I pushed Brad down. Instantly his young mouth began working on our cocks, repeating what I had been doing. He was a fast learner. An ecstatic Zak sank his tongue deep into my throat. It was almost as big as his dick and I sucked on it with just as much passion. Meanwhile, Brad went so deep on me, my balls disappeared and I nearly shot my load.

A sudden urge to screw Brad surged through my groin. He was a virgin for sure and might not be ready for it. But with my brain being bombarded by hormones and testosterone, I left Brad sucking on Zak's massive monster and went to my safe. Excitedly I spun the combination—69 69 69—well, it was easy to remember—and returned with condoms and lube.

Standing behind Brad, I glanced briefly at Zak, who looked as if he were about to come, and watched them perform. I'd seen porn before, but this was electrifying and exotic beyond belief and I could see how threesomes could easily become the norm for me.

Raising Brad's buttocks, I tore open a sachet of lube, my fingers trembling with excitement, and smeared the slippery liquid into his hairless crevice, then slowly began to tease my fingers into the tight opening. Brad moaned with pleasure and mouthed ever faster on Zak's dick. I guessed I'd got the green light and eased a condom over my dick and lubed it with two sachets. I reckoned it was going to be pretty painful for Brad.

Ever so gently, I eased myself between Brad's muscular, young buttocks, and he released a yelp as they flexed tightly. Once he'd relaxed, I teased a little more into his tight opening.

The head of my cock vanished.

I'd gone deep enough to make movement and began to ride him more robustly. And with each forward thrust, more and more of my dick disappeared into the dark depths of his trembling buttocks. Suddenly, I was all the way.

Desperately I began to thrust and withdraw, thrust and withdraw, Brad responding by pushing hard against my pelvis. Soon we were in unison. Brad was loving it!

Almost immediately, Zak released an almighty, manly gasp as he shot his load. Brad pulled his head away. The jet of creamy, white cum sailed through the air in a single stream and landed on his bare back, sliding towards his parted cheeks. I guessed the sight of me fucking Brad was too much for Zak.

I was absolutely stunned. It was unthinkable. Brad must have pushed some sexual button of Zak's because Zak raised Brad from the kneeling position—me still attached—and went down on him, sucking furiously on the teenager and pumping himself hard. There was no doubt Zak could come again. He had an automatic weapon. There was always another round in the barrel. And whilst Zak worked on Brad's big bone, I pushed deep and hard into his rear. Brad's legs buckled in excitement.

Zak's spunk slid between our bodies as my chest rubbed over Brad's bare back. Placing my hands around Brad, I grasped Zak's shaven head and rubbed the spiky hair. I was ready to come. At the crucial moment, I pulled Zak's head deep onto Brad's cock, forcing him to swallow the whole length. Then, with a trio of gasps, the three of us came. Brad folded between us.

I made another round of coffee and we sat silently, each pondering our own thoughts. I wondered if Zak and Brad would get it off at a later date, or if we would repeat this some day. Or if Brad and I would make out.

The telephone buzzed. Brad and Zak were called back to their bases, and with a kiss for each, I reluctantly released them.

The afternoon dragged and I was bored. All I could think about was Brad. I made another coffee and fired up my equipment, giving it a final check before going below decks.

Opening one of the panels, I began to study the multi-coloured wiring. Taking a pair of wire cutters, I selected a green one.

SNIP!

"Hello, Brad. It's Matt. Yes, number two's gone on the blink again. OK. See you in a few minutes."

* * *

Brad returned to my office and I told him straightaway what I had done, pointing out the wire I had deliberately cut. He laughed, and played, "Pretend I don't know why you did it."   In no time, the fold-away bunk I had in my office was sprung open and we were humping furiously. We sucked and fucked, fucked and sucked, until our balls were desert dry. I didn't ask whether he fancied Zak and if he was going to hump him. I'd rather not know. Trouble was, I had a feeling Brad and I could easily fall in love, and that, unfortunately, was a dangerous thing. I'd seen many a guy crack when a lover was quickly dispatched to another ship after an officer had become suspicious. I was determined I wouldn't go through that, or let Brad go through it either. We agreed to give it a rest—if we could manage it—and also agreed that if we wanted to bonk another guy, we could.

* * *

Today, because we had all been good boys (if only he knew!) the captain had granted the ship a Make and Mend. In layman's language, time to repair kit and catch up with washing clothes and so forth. Or, to put it more bluntly, have a bloody good rest!

I wasn't feeling at all horny and cruised to the canteen for some grub. Jim was there slopping slop on plates and gave me one of his "Do you want to play with my sausage?" looks. I tried desperately not to appear interested but somehow he got the opposite vibes and ran his tongue and lips erotically over the wooden spoon he was using. So much for hygiene! I walked beside the counter, searching for something that resembled food, Jim cruising me on the other side, continuing to suck suggestively on the spoon. He could see I wasn't impressed by what was on offer—discounting him—and giving me a smile, delved into a hot cupboard below. The hugest of rump steaks was quickly produced and plopped onto my plate, accompanied by a sexy smile and a wink from those swooning eyes. I returned his smile with a thanks and blew him a kiss. I guessed it was his own dinner, the love.

Our brief bout of flirting was soon halted by the entrance of the head chef. He was a horrible, fat bastard with a face that only a mother could love. I quickly shuffled away, tossing potatoes and veg around the steak, then soaked the lot with gruesome gooey gravy. I chose Spotted Dick for sweet. No, not for that reason. I happened to like it. Then I searched for someone more edible than my dinner to sit beside. My rump steak was prettier than most things filling their faces, so I took it to an empty table and began to slice a piece off. It was only then that I remembered something Jim had told me some time back—and I wished I hadn't. Jim had said it was not unusual for a boy to get really horny at four in the morning when preparing breakfasts, and as most of the chefs were big, fat, overfed farts, who he wouldn't stick my cock inside, let alone his, he needed a way of freeing his frustration.

"Now, a wank is fine," he had said, "but it's a long way down the line from a blow-job or a fuck." So, what was the next best thing? Well, he got his dick nice and firm, then, selecting a couple of juicy, uncooked, blood-red steaks, he wrapped them around his dick and pumped away like hell. "It is nearly as good as the real thing," he had said.

And with that thought fixed firmly in my mind, rump steak took on a new dimension. If I could have been sure that Jim was the only person who had fucked my dinner, I reckoned I could have handled that—I expect he washed it afterwards. But the thought of the head chef sliding his meat around my meal was not mouthwatering. The Spotted Dick I ate. It was scrumptious. But try as I did, I could not stop wondering what they stirred the mixture with and, indeed, if those little black bits were truly currants.

I had a real soft spot, or should I say "hard spot" for Jim. He was great sex, and his main forte was blow-jobs. As yet he hadn't dropped his pants and let me screw that main meal of a bum, but I expect the time would come. I was in no hurry. But what I like most about him was his sense of humor. It was wicked.

I remember one time we were trolling around a floral park, pissed as penguins on pot, when we came across a notice pinned to a tree. It read: Lost duck. Blue and green. Family pet. Dearly loved and sorely missed. Jim produced a pen and wrote: Thanks. It was delicious! It was something only a chef could write. Further along we came across a similar notice about a cat. But I stopped him writing: Made a lovely pair of slippers. Well, I loved cats.

I continued to sit in the dining room, drinking coffee and contemplating whether I really did want Jim's mouth around my meat, when in walked Wheaty-pop. I felt that unmistakable tingle in my togger as I observed him cruise the counter, placing grub on his plate. Eventually having so much, I thought he planned on climbing it rather than eating it. Well, he was a growing lad and, after a quick glance between my legs, so was I!

His boiler-suit was unbuttoned lower than before and I could make out a line of fine hair creeping from his navel to whatever treat lay hidden below and, no doubt, soaked in oil. I shot him a penetrating glance, which he held for a moment, then averted his eyes. Yes, he knew what I was up to. Suddenly, from nowhere, the campiest, slim black number came rushing up behind him, and I swear he pinched his butt. Wheaty-pop gave him a wide grin and a wink.

So, he was into Shirley Bassey look-a-likes. I must remember to buy some brown boot polish, I thought.

Jim caught my eye, distracting me from thoughts of Wheaty-pop with a big, black dick sliding into his bottom. Yes, I know it's stereotyping, but all young black guys appeared to have dicks as big as a Doberman's. I nodded to Jim, confirming the session was on and deliberately walking past the black and white minstrels, gave them a 'threesomes are fun' flirting glance. Shirley giggled. Wheaty-pop changed color. I was definitely a possibility, I guessed.

I had a shower before venturing to the cable locker, which is where Jim and I had our humps. It was in the bows of the ship and deep in its depths, and would only be busy when we were anchoring.

Jim changed into working clothes, otherwise it would be suspicious to see a chef in his whites in that part of the ship.

Lifting the metal, circular hatch, I descended into the dank- smelling room with its huge, rusting cables. It was the kind of place guys into a little slap and slap would love, with its various-sized cables, ropes and wires hanging about. That wasn't really my scene, but I expect I'd have a dabble with someone I could trust.

The familiar sound of someone descending an iron ladder echoed around the vast room. My heart began to pound. It was always a nervous moment, because if it happened to be a Seaman, I had no reason to be there.

I recognized Jim's butt as it came into view and grabbed his hips, lifting his lightweight body from the rungs. Back in the canteen I hadn't thought I was horny but the sight of that boy bum and the smell of his young body, soon had me fired up. In a flash, I was nibbling the nape of his neck and eating his ears.

Jim remained still, allowing me to work on his neck and shove my hand into his pants and fondle him. I found the fleshy quite a feast and freed it from his pants. His was a cut cock, the only one I knew. I found that disappointing at first because I loved a foreskin—if it worked properly—but I soon got used to it. I mean, the dick was attached to a really ravishable guy.

I released my own cock whilst his hands groped me from behind his back. He swiftly spun around, dropped to his knees and began sucking. In a flash my pants and knickers were down and both my balls were rolling around his massive mouth. I cannot say I enjoyed having them sucked because it was far too sensitive but I seldom stopped him. I also had huge nuts, and marvelled as to how he could get both them and my cock in there. I suspected he practised on a couple of new potatoes and a courgette.

Very little Jim did surprised me. So when he asked if he could tie me to the anchor cable, I simply said, "Why not?"

Jim tied my hands and then my ankles against the metal links. Already I became excited by this new experience. But, hell, if someone should discover us, this was going to take some explaining.

The cable was bloody cold against my bare bum and my white cheeks were soon brown with rust. I prayed that the anchor wouldn't suddenly be released with me shooting through the hole in the deck-head and out onto the upper-deck.

Well, what can I say? Not having any control whatsoever whilst Jim did the business—like he'd done it all his life—soon I was begging him to finish the job. He teased me to coming, then stopped, then teased again. And when I did come, it was with such force it nearly knocked his bloody head off. Being sucked and restrained was some experience!

Jim had dropped his pants and had been working his own dick whilst he worked on mine, but hadn't come yet. He released me from my bondage and I was just about to return the pleasure when he unexpectedly said, "Look what I've got!" And produced a massive carrot.

I looked at him quizzically.

"Shove it up my bum," he begged, handing me some lube.

Well, this time he did surprise me. What with the bondage and now this, I guessed he'd been reading some naughty books. Naturally, I obliged. I mean, if he was prepared to let a carrot fuck him, then at some stage he would let me.

I bent his beautiful buttocks before my face, pulling the cheeks wide apart, then sank my tongue deep into the hole. I reckoned he was stunned by how electrifying that was, because he yelped with pleasure as I worked his cock with one hand and tongued his rear. Soon he was writhing in ecstasy, begging for the vegetable.

I lubed the edible dildo and began to ease it between his parted cheeks. He'd chosen rather a large one for a beginner, but I controlled the entry so as not to hurt him. Moments later, I was pumping it powerfully into his passage, fearful not to lose my grip as it became slippery.

With squeals of pleasure so loud I thought the whole ship must have heard his orgasm, he shot a gallon of cum clean across the cables and through one of the links.

What a session. The best we had ever had!

I allowed Jim to leave the Cable Locker first, watching his biteable bum bounce up the ladder, thinking, "I'll soon be shagging that!" Five minutes later, I followed.

Happily, I strolled along the main passage humming a tune but when I reached Jim's galley, I stopped and suddenly thought, "I must remember not to have carrots for supper!"

* * *

Thursday was a pig of a day. Gale force winds and high seas. The ship was going up and down more times than my knickers. But I didn't mind the rough weather—rough anything, really! Perhaps the worst thing that could happen when it was rough was having some sailor throw up over your dinner, but even that could look more appetizing than what was on your plate.

I'd never known a week like this. So much sex, my dick was in danger of dropping off, and I think my foreskin was wearing out fast. I thought of going to the doc with my red, raw knob but that would have certainly raised his eyebrows. Unless I told him I'd been tossing every minute of the day. Which wasn't far from the truth because after I'd had a session, I like to run it through my mind again before sleep. God, my sheets were disgusting!

A good few of the sailors were heaving their hearts up - poor dears. But I was one of the lucky ones. Not many things would make me heave. Well, seeing a couple of 'hetties' humping, probably would.

It was on a day like this that I wouldn't mind being a medic, up in sick bay nursing all those pretty baby sailors who hadn't found their sea legs. But I looked like crap in a nurse's outfit! Then again, drag was something I could never get my head around. I mean - if you are a guy and you want to attract guys who like guys, then dressing as a bird defeats the object, doesn't it? It gets so complicated. Like - you're a guy who likes guys who likes birds but doesn't mind guys, so you dress as a bird so he can screw you, knowing you're really a guy. Give me a break. I mean, does it work the other way? Birds dress up as guys because the guy fancies a guy who is really a bird?

The weather was getting nasty now and we had more water inside the ship than out and every few yards some spew to slide around in. The Captain ordered Nuclear State Zulu, which is a little tricky to explain but basically meant, "Shut all the bloody doors before we sink!"

Oh, I forgot to tell you. I was living in a bath tub built from old cola cans, Pollyfilla and discarded plastic bottles. It was a shagged-out ship with a little gun on the front in case of air attacks. We'd have had more success filling condoms with petrol and throwing them at the aircraft. Molotov condoms. They sound like fun.

"Here, slip one of these on darling."

BANG!

"Wow. That was fantastic. Can you take my balls off the ceiling!"

But seriously. This foul weather was screwing up my screwing. All the trade was either mopping gallons of water from decks or dying in some darkened corner. But I did find a cherub on the upper-deck, having the contents of his stomach thrown back into his face as he bent his body—buttocks, beautiful and beckoning—over the guardrails. I did the decent thing and left his butt alone, easing him below decks and into the sick bay. I helped undress him and put him to bed, but even in his sickened state, he had enough wits about him to stop me nicking his knickers. Polka-dot boxers—not my favourite, but they outlined his youthful leg muscles and 'love' muscle, perfectly.

I left the sick bay before a baby sailor got knocked up and I got locked up and did a tour of the ship, searching for a shag. Tim was at work in the communications office. I departed swiftly before I was asked to help but managed a word with him, asking when he got off watch and if he was on heat. I think he muttered something about me getting a vasectomy. I guessed we still didn't have a date!

Jim was in the galley, turning perfectly good food into crap. I noticed a pot of carrots bubbling away on the stove and wondered which one was his lover from yesterday. He glimpsed me and gave a girlish giggle, dangling a jumbo sausage from his fly.

"Oh, Jim. You haven't been practicing with that," I mouthed, but departed when he received a bollocking from the head chef. At least Jim was on the right track, using something closer to my dick. No, I'm not bragging. I meant the texture, not the size!

I thought of searching out Wheaty-pop in the boiler room but had no reason to go down there. But visions of embracing him tightly, sucking in that smell of sweat, grease and oil, whilst my tongue slid down his throat and my hands dived inside his boiler suit, feasting on his firm buttocks and youthful cock was, quite frankly, disgusting, but oh for the opportunity.

After that disgusting thought, tossing myself looked more than a probability, so I headed toward the forward heads.

About halfway through the ship, who should appear? Shirley Bassey! Jesus, she wasn't camp. She was CAMP! How the hell did she manage to get recruited?

Swish. Swish. Swish. She floated past. Screeching, "Hi!" in a pitch any choirboy would have been proud of.

Well, if that wasn't a shag then I was a butch dyke. Watch it!

I watched her buttocks swish from side to side as she did her cat-walk number down the corridor, each cheek almost striking both bulkheads in turn. She glanced over her shoulder, giving me a smouldering smile. If ever there was a look which said, "I bet you would love to shag me!" then that certainly was.

Adjusting my crotch, I increased my pace toward the heads before I started tossing on the spot. I had almost reached the toilet when Zak popped up from the deck below. My eyes lit up. "Sex!" I thought.

Zak was in a hurry, marching straight through my body, and blurted something about the boss looking for me. Reluctantly, I ventured to the main office to enquire what was up. Just my luck. The forward heads were wrecked and I had become the chosen skivvy to clean them. What was a professional guy like me doing with his head down a toilet, you may ask? My thoughts precisely. Not that it would be the first time my head had been in such a place.

Well, it so happens that in this lovely Navy of ours, we were not only obliged to do our professional jobs but also mundane tasks like teasing turds around a U-bend. Marigolds on hand, I began exploring the unsavoury contents of each bowl— unblocking and scrubbing, unblocking and scrubbing. No doubt a few bad-mouthers would say I was exactly where I belonged. But, joy! And I hummed happily away, ramming my rod into every orifice and sprinkling Vim and bleach with joyful abandon.

I had nearly finished fist-fucking the final bowl when the door burst open, almost pushing me down the pan. "We're closed!" I yelled, not wanting another baby sailor bombarding me with bits of regurgitated carrot.

"Oops. Sorreeeeee!" came the triple soprano voice that I recognized instantly.

I spun about. There she stood—Shirley Bassey—panting and pouting, pinching her prick. Looking brown, beautiful, begging and by God, I think my banana just burst.

What could I say? For once in my life I was almost speechless but managed to mouth, "Use the end urinal."

Now then, I'm not a nosy bitch or a cottage queen but if the opportunity is there....

Shirley unzipped her fly and began pissing. In a flash, I was kneeling beside her, Marigold fist foraging around the adjoining urinal, head level with her line of fire. Her hand was cupped around his cock, hiding it from view. Don't you just hate that! What a tart!

Without warning, she pulled her hand away, turned toward me, grabbed my head and pulled my face into her crotch, spraying droplets of pee around my flushed cheeks and parted lips. What a bitch! Didn't she know I wasn't into yellow?

Talk about fast black! This girl was well above the speed limit and by the look of it, eager to take me on the ride of a lifetime! In seconds she was flinging her wardrobe across the deck and standing naked, except for a skimpy, black leather jock. Well, that wasn't Navy issue!

I managed to stick my sensible head on and reached for a notice, warning the crew that this place was out-of-bounds—on Captain's orders— and hung it on the outer door. Sucking in a breath of bleachy air, part excitement, part relief that no one had entered whilst she did her strip, I began sweating excitedly. This bitch was on heat and I was going into melt down.

Protected by the notice, I allowed the panther to paw me. And what paws! She was.... well, what wasn't she? I managed to erase the image of her dressed in a slinky outfit and wearing an Afro wig. But who was I to criticize? I still had my Marigolds on.

We chose the third cubicle—my lucky number. My mouth was soon biting into her leather pouch, tongue sliding between her brown thighs and into the expanding material. In an instant it was off and my second cut cock sprang into view and slid into my palate. It was a delightful, delicate dick with smooth balls the size of grapes, hanging beneath. Like a Roman emperor, I devoured the succulent pair as they hung over me.

Shirley moaned and groaned, squealed and sighed, yanking at my head and ears. I bit hard into those tight, wiry curls as she ripped my shirt clean from my back, her nails furrowing eight deep channels into my shoulders.

"Shit!" I shrieked. How was I going to explain that to my mates? Yes, we did have a cat on board, and another by the looks of things. And I shrieked again as its large, luscious tongue lassoed my dick and balls.

Shirley began devouring me to an unbelievable depth, her ravishing passion sending cum pumping from my cock in uncontrollable bursts. Shaking and exhausted, I plonked my butt onto the bowl.

Shirley straddled me in seconds, her rounded, brown buttocks pressing onto my cock, her thighs gripping my waist. "Fuck me! Fuck me! Fuck me!" she begged and pleaded, rubbing her buttocks into my crotch, bringing me firm again.

"Calm down, dear," I thought. "You only have to ask me once." But this cat was wild and was looking for a taxidermist. Sadly, I had no condoms. My raunchy mind raced, desperately trying to think of an alternative. I glanced at my Marigolds. I could cut one of the rubber fingers off. But would it fit over my cock? Watch it! I'm not that small.

I resigned myself to the fact that I'd missed a shag. No protection, no poking. But I worked hard and fast on Shirley's dick, sucking on her small, brown nipples and licking all over her brown skin. Then I shoved a Marigold finger deep into her butt.

"I love you. Marry me! Marry me!" she squealed, sucking a love bite the size of an orange onto my neck.

"Oh, you dizzy queen," I thought. Yes, we did have a cat on board but I'm sure it didn't do love bites.

With an ear-splitting scream, as I shoved three fingers deep inside her, she came, sending cum cascading down my chest and over my cheeks. But as much as she begged and pleaded, I didn't come a second time. I was also sure that I wouldn't have sex with her again. She was the type of boy who would want my babies and I was no good with kids. I mean, after you've washed them, do you hang them up to dry by their fingers or their toes?

* * *

Last evening we popped briefly into port to collect one of our communications staff who had got married, then popped out again.

The weather had changed, to the relief of many a baby sailor, but the task of clearing up continued. It was one of the worst storms I'd known and, unfortunately, one poor seaman had suffered a broken leg. He was dropped off when we were in port.

Rumor had it that next week we were going to troll across to Amsterdam. But it was only a rumour and we would most likely end up in Scotland, shagging sheep.

My sparkler, Brad, hadn't ventured to my office since his last visit and, Zak, too, had not been required—there being no traumatic incidents to investigate. I wondered if they'd managed to get together for a bonk, but doubted it. Although Zak was big and butch, he was a big girl's blouse when it came to propositioning guys. Brad, however, was a brash bugger and wouldn't be backward in coming forward with his boner. Anyway, I hadn't had sex since yesterday. What the heck. I wasn't trying for the Penis Book of Records. And my dick was still as sore as hell. Germolene really stings. I'll kill the sod who suggested it. It's like sticking your cock in a kettle of boiling water. One of my mates suggested Iodine. Yea, right. Walk around with a purple cock for a week.

I wondered why Tim had stopped spreading his legs. He used to be up for it at least once a month, but he did swing. Perhaps it was breasts and not balls at present. Wheaty-pop, too, was still a mystery but I'd bet a pound to a pinch of puff he was stuffing Shirley. And should I be lucky enough to get that boiler suit from his sexy skin, his back would resemble a ploughed field. Mine was still pretty painful and I'd resorted to wearing a crew neck vest under my shirt, which, thankfully, also hid the love bite.

We spent several hours of today scanning the sea for a sailor who was lost overboard from another ship. A good many of the crew were on the upper deck looking out for him. We had no luck. It was a sad time but life went on. The sea, like sailors, can be a real bitch!

I'd nearly gone overboard once—in a mini-huricane—but luckily I managed to get my legs around something and save myself. Well, I'd had a lot of practice. After that incident, I'd learnt my lesson and stayed away from topside when it was too rough. But the only place I was in danger of falling into now was some sailor's backside. I mean, a carrot was nothing to some sailors. You could get a fruit and veg stall up some arses! My arse? Passing a pip was painful. But I was in love and when you get into that dizzy state, a lot of self-made rules fly out the window.

It was one of those moments that you never forget. He was a scrumptious Indian youth about the same age. A civilian I'd met whilst ashore in Singapore. Beautiful would not be a compliment in his case.

I'd got well bevied on shore one night—sins of being a sailor —and had got chatting to him in a straight bar. Sometimes, in this strange life of ours, you can become besotted in a nanosecond. This happened to me.

I'd never seduced a brown boy before and my whole being tingled with excitement at the prospect.

Back at his hotel, we entwined on his bed, fully clothed, kissing and caressing for what seemed an eternity before he finally allowed me to disrobe him. In childlike wonderment, I removed each item of clothing from his satin smooth skin, kissing and licking every inch of his flesh before removing the next.

He lay before me in all his splendid nakedness. An adorable, edible, brown beauty. He had the blackest hair I'd ever seen. Even his eyes were dark. His pupils matched the iris, making them appear even larger. I lost my soul into their darkness. His name was Minish. I would have done anything for him!

Minish had been a virgin in every respect and I had been one, in one. Our bodies and souls meshed as he glided over me. Moving his head between my thighs, he slid his mouth so tenderly around my balls and over my cock.

And then it happened. He raised my legs, kneeling between them whilst working with his magnificent mouth. His chest met mine as our tongues searched. Then, without me realizing, he entered my body, sliding his dick deep between my buttocks. His movements were slow and sensational. My head swam in a sea of sexual sublimity as he seduced me. And gripping his boy buttocks, I pulled him deep. Pulled him into a part of my being I never knew existed.

When I made love to him, it was even more meaningful. His youthful, muscular thighs gripped me like a vise, pulling every last centimetre of my youthfulness into the darkest depths of his body.

He came. Not with squeals and screams but with a sigh of deep satisfaction—as if I had given him the universe! And the sensation when I came was similar—nothing like I have ever experienced. A zillion nerves erupting in ecstatic empathy. It wasn't greedy and lustful sex, but delicate and loving. To be honest, I doubt I could ever find the words to describe those hours. And for the brief time that we were together, I thought I'd gone to heaven.

Perhaps it was the only time I could say that I had truly made love. The following day our ship sailed. I never saw or heard from him again.

At one in the morning, I was called to my office. Routine stuff, so Zak wasn't required—shame—but I did need assistance and another communicator was loaned to me. It was Paul, the baby sailor who had just got married, silly boy! Paul was a smashing lad, very quiet, and good looking.

Whilst working at my console, I shot a few glances in his direction. Nothing sexual or seductive. But Paul did have a decent packet and I couldn't resist running my eyes over it. Whether or not he noticed, I wasn't sure. But one thing I was sure about and what Paul probably didn't know: I had watched him skylark with another sailor. They were well into each other. But what was apparent to me and must have been to both, each had a hard cock as they grappled and groped. Now then, a stiff prick said to me that this kind of fun had slightly more meaning than a friendly frolic. Naturally, I began to wonder at the possibility of a raunchy wrestle of my own.

Can I first tell you about straight lads? They don't exist! Only if you have lived on a ship with five hundred sex-starved sailors will you be able to understand this. You see, when you have been at sea for months, and you're straight, you need a shag. Then "hide the sausage in a female" becomes "hide it in any hole that will accept it." Now, I'm not saying that all straight sailors run around shagging all the gay sailors—dream on! But a good old face-fuck is that grey area that straight lads are able to cope with without thinking they've turned queer. So, with this in mind, what was hidden inside Paul's pants looked a pleasing possibility. After all, he only had time to get married—no honeymoon. Consequently, no shag. How sad. And I was banking he was sick to death of wanking.

Our mission accomplished, I set about my mission. First I did some serious chat about his wife and sex. Then in true Navy skylark fashion, I began to arm-wrestle, tickle and hug this humpable hettie. And as sure as there are no gay virgins, up popped his pecker.

I allowed Paul to wrestle me to the deck and get his thighs around my head, the rough, serge material of his bell-bottoms rubbing my face. And when I felt that he was beyond the fun stage, I bit hard into his erect cock. He made the slightest attempt to pull my head away and giggled something that sounded like, "Stop it." But I needed "Stop it" in writing before I'd let go of a succulent, stiff dick. Anyway, I did a quick anagram of 'Stop it' and it came out as 'Suck me' - I suffer from sexual dyslexia, you see. I pried his prick from his pants. His was one of those strange cocks, about as thick as it was long, and I was worried about stretch marks around my mouth. But, shit, I swallowed it anyway.

Sex-starved or sex crazy, I don't know, but he rammed away at my mouth, so powerfully, I hardly had time to breathe. All lights green, I popped out my own prick and offered it up for consumption. And consume he did!

For me, blow-jobs were one of the best sex acts to perform and we had the rhythm in no time. A sexual metronome. No head movements, just buttock thrusting. Him then me. Him then me. Him and him. Me and me. Together we created "Symphony 69"—Mozart, eat your heart out—and with sexual symbols slamming in my head, cum went simultaneously from him to me and me to him.

I reckoned it was the best wedding present he'd received and I was really pleased for his wife. She'd married a right little fuck bunny and I was delighted for her.

Paul left my office at a little before three in the morning. I decided I would stay and crash for the night. I ventured to the forward heads to bathe before turning in. At this time of day the ship was quiet, only sailors on watch floating about. And I didn't want anyone to see my love trophies when I showered.

On reaching the heads, I was baffled to see a notice saying they were out of bounds and was just about to troll down aft, when I thought, "Sod it." and entered. Unexpectedly, I heard a shower running and gently closed the door and tiptoed toward it. Well, you could have knocked me out with a strawberry condom! The beauty being shagged was unmistakable, but who was shagging him? I moved closer, not wanting to disturb them but eager to gain a good vantage point. Brad was in total bliss, bless him. And the butch boy body that was bonking him was beyond the bounds of beauty. The pair of white buttocks looked delicious against Brad as he bumped and ground, thrust and withdrew, all the while pumping Brad's dick with one hand and stroking his balls with the other.

I was stiff in seconds and, withdrawing my cock, playfully pumped my playmate.

The beefy boy bounced vigorously against Brad's buttocks, pushing him hard into the wet bulkhead, his mouth eating eagerly on Brad's unblemished back and neck. A fine spray of water cascaded over them like confetti. Brad was releasing gasps of delight as the boy's dick delved deep into the desirous flesh. All the while, water ran over their faces and between their passionate bodies.

These two were in love. A couple of married boys. Of that, I was certain. I knew. I'd been there.

I continued my surveillance, mesmerized by the sheer pleasure passing between them. Painfully, I watched as the boy pumped Brad's youthful prick, rolling his foreskin back and forth and filling his buttocks with what I can only describe as a "mountain of meat."

I put my dick away. Somehow it seemed wrong. But I continued to be voyeur and protector. For I would stop anyone entering and disturbing this beautiful union.

Brad caught my eye. I felt embarrassed, as if I had intruded on some sacred ceremony. But he was in another blissful world and simply smiled, knowing that he was safe. His seducer spun around, able to pick up on Brad's every expression, and paused for the briefest moment, but couldn't stop shafting him because both were close to climax.

I was right about Wheaty-pop's back. It resembled a ploughed field. Shirley had definitely been there. So it was Brad and Wheaty-pop. I felt slightly sad because I had lost Brad, and somewhat envious that he was the one to suck in that oily scent and wash the grease and grime from Wheaty-pop's groin.

Both came in bursts of frenzied excitement, holding back the screams of delight they dearly wished to release.

I closed the door silently behind me and walked toward the aft heads. Come morning we would be back in port and I had the weekend off. I thought I should give sex a miss for a couple of days and allow my dick to repair.

But, then again, I desperately need a haircut and there was this really cute, civilian barber who did a brilliant cut and blow-job!

SHORE LEAVE
by Richie Brooks

Greece, 1949.

In most countries around the world, oil refineries are situated well away from towns and cities, the one in Pireas being no exception. You have to take a twenty-minute taxi ride to get to the town; a forty-minute one to Athens.

I was an officer's mess steward on a small tanker on this particular occasion. We were late tying up; the evening meal had been delayed, and by the time I got away, all my mates had already gone ashore. But I wasn't the only one who finished late; an engineer named Brian caught up with me as I walked through the refinery, and we arrived at the main gate just in time to see the last taxi disappearing up the dusty road, which meant a good half hour wait until one returned.

Although early evening, it was still hot and humid, and when Brian suggested that we pass the time with an ice cold beer in the bar just up the road, I didn't demur. My own thoughts had been straying in that direction too.

The bar was busy, full of refinery workers just off the day shift. All the tables were occupied by garrulous Greeks, except one, at which sat a young blond with a crew cut, a golden tan and bright blue eyes. I figured he was a seaman from the Yankee tanker berthed astern of our own, so while Brian went to get the beers, I walked over to the blond to ask if we might share the table with him. He spoke excellent English, but his accent was German, his nationality confirmed when he told me he was from the World Enterprise, a super-tanker moored opposite to us, registered in Hamburg. Its officers were all German; we had once had some of them aboard for lunch, in Kuwait.

By the time he had introduced himself as Kurt, giving me a warm smile as he shook my hand, Brian had joined us. Learning that Kurt was from the Enterprise and also an engineer, Brian began to ply him with questions about the technology involved with these super-tankers. The pair proceeded to get carried away in technical details that I couldn't begin to understand. The Enterprise was certainly huge, at least three times as long as our own H Class tanker; three times as high out of the water, even laden, and with five times the tonnage, so Brian was ecstatic at the chance to talk to a fellow engineer who actually worked aboard her; I barely got a word in edgeways, although Kurt did attempt to change the topic of conversation from time to time, asking about myself and my job. His bright blue eyes twinkled at me in a way that held a hidden interest, which I found intriguing.

Kurt was an attractive guy, filling his well-scrubbed jeans and snow-white T-shirt to perfection. His well-muscled arms were covered in silky blond hair, right down to his wrists and over the back of his hands, causing me to wonder if the rest of him was so hairy, the very speculation giving me a hard-on, which I also suspect he noticed, much as I tried to hide it by pulling my chair nearer the table.

He had been drinking Retzina, and after we had all drained our glasses, he went up to the bar and got a whole bottle of the stuff, with three more clean glasses, insisting that we join him. By the time the bottle was empty and I had replaced it with another, all thoughts of going to Pireas had been abandoned, especially after Kurt had promised that he would show us around the Enterprise. Brian just couldn't wait to get down into that engine room, but my thoughts had taken a different path.

After one more bottle of the fiery liquor we made our way back to the jetty, me having great difficulty in walking straight, much to the amusement of the other two, who seemed to be able to hold their liquor much better than I could. That was just as well, for it was high tide and the gangway of the World Enterprise was almost vertical; but between them they managed to get me to the top. We were then given a quick tour of the ship, ending up with a long sojourn in the engine room, which like everything else, was huge. Brian was impressed.

Eventually we arrived back in Kurt's cabin, which was enormous compared with our own. Kurt had all the mod/cons; a king-sized bed, a built-in dressing table, walk-in wardrobe, a writing desk, a comfortable three-piece suite, and his very own bathroom with shower and toilet! Sheer luxury. Both Brian and I were envious.

Kurt also had a bar, and right away the glasses came out, this time with a bottle of Schnapps, which he placed on the coffee table. He took one of the armchairs, Brian the other, leaving me with the settee all to myself.

Liquor affects different people in different ways: Some get all maudlin and miserable; some get over lively and want to sing and dance; others get aggressive and want to fight. I just get sleepy and tend to doze off if my attention isn't suitably held. So with the other two rabbiting on about by-pass feed-backs and negative roll-back systems, etc., of which I hadn't a clue, it was inevitable that my head would start to loll sideways as the drone of their voices, together with the curling tobacco smoke, gently sent me into the land of nod.

I don't know just how long I was out, but I roused to hear Kurt saying, "Yes, you are right, I do not think that we can get him down the gangway in this state," as he shook my arm and went on to ask me, "Now, my young friend, what time do you have to be on duty in the morning?"

I liked the way he called me "my young friend." Most people got the impression that I was about nineteen or twenty, when in actual fact I was no more than a year younger than either of them. He was obviously unaware of this, just as the two of them were unaware that I wasn't half as sloshed as they thought. Playing along, I deliberately slurred my words and said drowsily, "Don't have to start work until mid-morning, the other steward does breakfast tomorrow, I did it today."

"Then I think that he should stay here overnight and sleep it off," Kurt told Brian thoughtfully. "I will make sure that he is sober before he leaves, and by then the gangway will be easier for him to negotiate, do you not agree?"

"Yeah, I reckon you're right," Brian told him, and shaking my arm, went on, "D'you hear that, mate? Kurt here says you can stay aboard tonight, we don't want you risking a broken neck trying to get down the gangway at the moment, it will be easier tomorrow morning, is that okay by you?"

"Yeah, yeah, whatever," I mumbled, curling up on the settee, and a few minutes later I heard them leave, Kurt saying he would see Brian to the gangway and make sure that he also got down safely.

By the time he returned, I was feeling much perkier. The snooze, together with the anticipation of spending the night with this enigmatic guy, had quickly sobered me up, but I kept my eyes shut tight as he picked me up effortlessly and carried me over to the bed, saying as he did so, "Time for bed, my young friend." As he lowered me onto the mattress, I opened my eyes just in time to catch the mischievous gleam in his eye. As he started to undress me, the thought of having to share his bed already turning me on. His nimble hands expertly removed my T-shirt, then my jeans. His hands stroked my thighs as he murmured, "Mmmm, you have a beautiful body." This gave me an instant erection, which caused him to chuckle as he tugged off my boxers. He took it in his hand and stroked it gently for a while. Then he quickly stripped off and climbed on the bed alongside me.

Getting a close-up view now, I was amazed to see just how hairy he was. His whole body was covered in thick blond hair, reminding me of a teddy bear I once had, except that it didn't have a whopping big penis! Now it was my turn to be impressed.

Running his hands over my body once again, he said, quite softly and sweetly, "You really do have a beautiful body, and such a smooth skin, just like a baby."

"And you have a beautiful hairy one, just like a teddy I once had, except my teddy didn't have a cock like this!"

Giving me a wicked grin back, he replied with a chuckle, "Well then, this big bear is now going to have a picnic, my young friend. What do you say to that?"

Before I could think of a suitable answer he had opened wide my legs, knelt between them and gone down on me like a starving dingo. First he was teasing my prick with his tongue, then sucking it like there was no tomorrow. At the same time he began kneading my buttocks with his strong fingers, one of which he covered in saliva. Then he began to work it slowly into my anus. God, it felt good, especially as he started to screw me, first with one, then two, and finally three fingers, stretching me to the limit. My prick was jerking each time he touched my prostate, causing me to moan with delight, and unable to hold out any longer, I shouted, "Oh yes! God,

I'm coming." Soon I was shooting my spunk halfway down his throat. He swallowed hungrily, licking up every drop before padding over to the bathroom and returning with a warm soapy cloth. He washed and dried me, then lay down beside me again. A moment later, he opened his legs and told me, "Now it is your turn."

Just holding that long, thick prick in my hand gave me another instant erection. I could barely wait to get my tongue working on that eight inches of manhood standing up between his thighs. Covering my middle fingers with saliva as he had done, I gradually worked them up inside him. He moaned in ecstacy as I took the whole eight inches down my throat in a series of long slow motions. I slid my mouth up and down it, teasing it with my tongue each time I reached the tip.

After he had let me enjoy myself for a few minutes, he suddenly stopped me. "Okay, now let's try something else. Come up and sit on it."

Closing his legs as I straddled his hips, he began working a couple of fingers coated with Vaseline up inside me before positioning his prick at the entrance. "Now slide down on it."

I nervously lowered myself down. He was so big, but I knew how to handle it. Instead of tightening my sphincter muscles, as some guys do, I pushed outward against it, relieved to feel that swollen knob slide in. This was followed by the rest of the shaft, and, once used to the size, I began to work myself up and down it, gripping his shoulders with my hands, his thighs with my knees. Kurt began matching my movements with his own upward thrusts, while at the same time masturbating me; a lazy grin on his face.

But once again I was unable to hold out for long. Breathing a drawn out, "Oh, yes, yes," I started to come.

I shot my load all over his hairy stomach and chest, his grin turning into a chuckle as he milked every drop from my throbbing prick. Then he told me, "Now let's *really* fuck," and motioning me to ease off his rampant flagpole.

"What?"

"You heard me."

He turned me over onto my back, opened my legs, knelt down between them, and, after putting a pillow underneath my ass, raised my feet so that they rested on his broad shoulders. Then he entered me again, pushing that prick in as far as it would go before sprawling out on me, his hairy arms taking me in a bear hug. As he started to fuck me again with long slow strokes, I became hard again.

Gradually his strokes began to quicken and I knew he was coming up to his climax. He began to breathe heavily, and with a final thrust which I felt sure would force his prick out of my bellybutton, I felt a warm glow spreading out inside me as the sperm shot from his prick.

After another long, drawn-out kiss, where our tongues played tag for a while, he finally pulled out of me, relaxing on his back. As I cleaned us both up, then he surprised me by saying, "Now you can fuck me."

"What?"

"You heard me." Smiling, he turned over obligingly, and the sight of those hairy buttocks once again gave me a hard-on. I eagerly knelt astride him, got a couple of fingers full of Vaseline, and began to work them between the cheeks and up inside him.

Savoring every moment, I entered him slowly, then began to fuck him with long steady strokes. I loved the feeling, a thrill of togetherness, as he gripped me tight with his strong sphincter muscles each time I drew back. Gradually increasing the momentum, I was spurred on by his cries of, "Go on, fuck me harder, do it harder," until I could no longer hold back. With a final savage thrust, I came high up inside him, my body rigid for a few seconds as I came. Relaxing slowly, all energy spent, I lay there on top of him, my arms wound around him. My cheek against his cheek, our mouths sought each other for a long kiss. Finally we drifted off into a deep, satisfying sleep.

From force of habit, Kurt awoke at his usual time, then roused me, saying, "Come, my young friend. Let's shower together."

I followed him, sleepy-eyed, to the bathroom, where once again he fucked me. This time we did it standing under the sharp needles of a hot shower. He masturbated me with a soapy fist while his cock was being thrusted up inside me until we both came to a glorious climax within seconds of each other.

After that there was just enough time to get dressed and say a tearful farewell before he escorted me down the gangway. We shook hands formally as we parted, me walking across to my own gangway, Kurt returning aboard the World Enterprise to go on duty. The two of us paused on the deck to give a last sad farewell wave.

Sydney, 1969

There is a certain irony in the way that fate guides our footsteps along a pre-destined path, for after spending twenty years in the British Merchant Navy, I had barely settled down ashore when something happened that certainly changed the direction of mine. Doing crossword puzzles and entering competitions had become a hobby of mine, and one day, out of the blue, I was suddenly informed that I had won first prize in a competition run by a well-known travel agency. And the prize? Yes, you've guessed it: a luxury stateroom on a newly launched Italian cruise ship, due to start her maiden voyage around the world, plus a thousand pounds pocket money to spend as I chose. I could have taken a lump sum and skipped the cruise, but I was already missing the sea, so decided to take just one more nostalgic trip, especially after I saw that one of my favorite cities, Sydney, was on the itinerary. The ship was due to sail from Genoa and call at Naples, Tangier,

Tenerife, Dakar, Capetown, Durban, Freematle, Melbourne and Sydney, before taking a month to cruise round the New Zealand coast, then return to Sydney to start the last leg of her voyage, via Brisbane, Jakarta, Singapore and Colombo, through the Suez Canal and back to Naples and her home port of Genoa. It would be four months of fun and sun before returning to the cold and rain of England in the spring.

The stateroom was sumptuous, the food great, and it felt good to be looked after and waited on for a change. I was enjoying every aspect of the voyage, and in particular, Guido, a dishy young deckhand who would slip into my stateroom after midnight, two or three times a week!

Guido was quite a stud, although inclined to be a bit of a "bang bang, thank you ma'am" type, with very little foreplay or imagination; he was too darn horny for that. But I couldn't grumble, for he was a real handsome hunk, with dark soulful eyes and black curly hair, plus the eight inches of uncut Italian manhood dangling between his legs! I could have done much worse, and he did prefer older men.

However, by the time we reached Sydney I had come to another decision. Noting that the ship would be returning to Sydney after the New Zealand cruise, I planned to leave, then join it again in a month's time for the return voyage. The company making no objections. Since the stateroom was already paid for, they could re-let it for a month, and I would be free to look up old friends and perhaps see a bit more of Aussie.

There was a delightful motel just down the Edgecliffe Road. I had once stayed there before. The place consisted of a couple of dozen chalets dotted around well-landscaped grounds. Each chalet had its own carport and secluded patio. The main building housed a cafeteria, launderette and indoor swimming pool, besides a shop and hire car facilities.

After I had showered and had a meal, I picked up a car and headed for Kings Cross, fun centre of the city, deciding to spend the rest of the evening in my favourite pub.

Any seaman or sailor who has tied up at Wooloomooloo Docks, Sydney, will no doubt recall that some ten minutes walk away, on the Darlinghurst Road, just along from the Cross, was a pub known as Murphy's, a real seaman's drinking place.

A noisy, sleazy, barn of a pub with a circular bar, sawdust on the floor, spitoons, dim lighting and a jukebox that belted out top ten tunes endlessly. Here seamen, sailors, pimps, prostitutes, rent boys, drug pushers, petty criminals, long-distance truckers, and a sprinkling of locals and construction workers all rubbed shoulders in the smoky area around the bar, or sat on rickety chairs at rickety tables around the walls.

There were no openly gay bars in Sydney in the sixties. Aussie men have always guarded their macho image diligently, and still do (male bonding originated there), but Murphy's had the reputation of being able to supply whatever you fancied. Male or female, you could always get a pick up there, but it had to be done discreetly. You had to know whom to approach. The only alternative was to go cruising in Hyde Park or the Domain, both of them dangerous, especially after dark.

Murphy's had a great atmosphere and it was only the really noisy, obnoxious drunks who got thrown out by the tough- looking bouncers, who doubled as table clearers most of the time. Usually it was a case of live and let live. If you behaved yourself, you had no worries.

After pushing my way to the bar, I saw that one of the barmen was an old queen named Tansey, with whom I had sailed on a couple of occasions. She had a droll sense of humor and a face like the back of a beat-up old jalopy. She was delighted to see me and we were chatting away about old times when a young guy slid onto the stool next to mine. The youth pulled out a handful of small change which he started to count methodically on the bar. Then he pushed it over to Tansey and ordered a schooner.

"You been robbing some poor bastard's piggy bank, Charlie?" Tansey asked him sarcastically, throwing the money in the till without bothering to count it.

Charlie's freckled face broke into a grin as he replied cheekily, "Some rob piggy banks, others suck cock!" Giving me a nudge and a wink as he inclined his head toward Tansey, who flounced over to the other side of the bar, shouting over her shoulder, "At least I don't do it for money, like some I could name."

This caused Charlie to retaliate with a string of obscenities, followed by a really wicked grin directed at me.

Taking stock of him, I saw that he was slim and good looking, with warm hazel eyes and auburn hair swept back like a lion's mane to his shoulders, the current fashion for guys in the sixties, and despite the fact that he was valiantly trying to grow a moustache, it was obvious that he was under age, no more than nineteen at most, which surprised me, although it didn't seem to bother Tansey; I guess that if the barmen had challenged every young guy who was in there about their age, the place would have been half empty.

Turning back to me, the grin still lingering on his face, Charlie said with a chuckle, "That put the old fart in her place, she likes to take the piss out of people, but don't like it when someone does the same to her," and before I could answer, went on to ask, "You off a ship, sport? I ain't seen you in here before."

After I had explained that I used to be in the Merchant Navy, but was now on holiday, he began to ply me with questions about life at sea, and all the places I had visited, saying wistfully that he would have liked to have gone to sea himself, but didn't think he could take the rough weather. "I get queasy just going over to Manley on the ferry," he told me ruefully.

By this time I had finished my beer, but it was obvious that he was making his last as long as possible, so I told him to drink up and I'd buy him another.

"Look, I'll be honest with you sport, I can't shout you one back, I'm skint until Friday," he told me with a "have pity on poor little me," kind of look.

"That's okay, mate," I said. "No worries," and got him another one.

After that he kept the conversation going with question after question, the difference in our ages didn't seem to bother him, even though I was old enough to be his dad, but didn't look it by any means, and it wasn't until much later that I realized I had practically told him my life story, yet learned very little about him.

After I had insisted in buying him a second beer, he said he had to go to the john, and while he was away, Tansey came over and said confidentially, "Watch yourself with that one, mate, I suppose you know he's rent?"

I hadn't given it a thought, but wasn't going to admit that, so giving a shrug, said indifferently, "Isn't everyone in here on the make?"

It was a good fifteen minutes before Charlie returned. He downed the rest of his beer and, putting a twenty-dollar bill on the counter, ordered another round, much to my astonishment. I was tempted to ask where the money had suddenly sprung from, but didn't—one didn't ask leading questions like that in Murphy's! What the hell, I told myself, what he gets up to in the john is his business,

Five minutes after time had been called, I drained my glass and said, "Time to be heading home."

Charlie said, "Yeah, I guess so, sport," and followed me out the door.

It was raining heavily, and when it rains in Sydney, which is not often, it really pisses down, and as Charlie was wearing only thin cotton jeans and a skimpy T-shirt, I told him to wait there in the pub doorway, I had a car parked just round the corner and would pick him up and run him home, no point in both of us getting soaked, then sprinted off without waiting for an answer.

Moments later he was scrambling in, saying, "Thanks sport, you're a true blue," then he sat there combing his hair, after flashing me a grin.

"Which way then?" I asked, only to get a blank stare in return. Thinking he hadn't heard my question, asked it another way, "Where d'you live, Charlie? Which direction do I take?"

After hesitating, then giving me a rather sheepish glance, he replied, "Well, to be honest, sport, I don't live anywhere, me old man threw me out a few days ago, I don't have a place to go."

"But that's terrible," I said, really concerned, "How are you managing?"

"Aw, I been kipping down at a mate's place, but his wife don't like me and cut up a stink, she don't want me back there again."

"Don't you have another mate you can stay with?" I asked, having the feeling that I already knew the answer to that question. Shrugging his shoulders, he told me, "Naw, can't think of anyone, they don't wanna know you when you're down."

Giving a deep sigh, I said, "Well, look, mate, you can come back with me, just for one night," stressing the "just for one night" bit as I remembered

Tansey's dire warning, and wondered what I was letting myself in for.

"Jeez, thanks sport. I won't be no trouble, I'll be gone early, I start work at seven."

"That's early, what do you do?"

"Didn't I tell you, sport? I do a cleaning job until nine, then I work part-time for a mate two or three days a week, but he don't pay much, which is why I'm always skint."

Just before we turned off the Bayswater Road I spotted a late night take-away place, and asked, "You hungry, Charlie?"

"Like a pregnant dingo, I ain't eaten since morning," he told me, so I stopped and got us two burgers. Charlie wolfed his down and half of mine when I said I couldn't finish it, having eaten earlier.

Back in the chalet, I switched on the television for him, then heading for the bedroom. I got out of my damp clothes, had a shower. After putting on my bathrobe, I got a blanket and a pillow from the bed and dumped them beside him, saying, "Here you are mate, this settee should be quite comfy to sleep on, so you can watch the end of the film. I'm turning in now. I'll wake you in the morning early, okay?"

Once again I got that blank puzzled stare, then he said in a disbelieving voice, "You mean you don't want me to sleep with you?"

"What makes you think I wanted that?" I queried.

"Well, you bought me a few drinks, and a burger, and said I could stay the night, so w-e-e-ll, you know, I just naturally thought—" and he tailed off, giving me a grin and a knowing glance.

"Look, mate, I bought you drinks because I was enjoying your company. I bought you a burger because you said you were starving. And I couldn't let you spend the night sleeping rough in this weather, so here you are. You don't owe me. I don't take advantage of a guy when he's down." Seeing the "pity poor little me" look back on his face, I added hastily, "Not that I don't fancy you, Charlie, I do, you're a very attractive guy, but I've had a long day. I have to be up early in the morning, so if you don't mind, I'd prefer just turning in, okay?"

"Yeah, okay, sport. Whatever," he said with a shrug, and went back to watching T.V. so after a hasty "goodnight" I retreated to the bedroom and shut the door.

Being a night person, Charlie had very little to say the next morning, he was still bleary-eyed and yawning as I dropped him off close to where he did his cleaning job.

But he thanked me sincerely for letting him stay the night, and was very reluctant to take the money I offered him, even though I told him it was to help him find some digs. However, he took it in the end, and as I drove back I was fairly confident that provided I kept away from Murphy's, that was the last I would see of him.

I spent a pleasant day visiting some old friends, and was just about to go out to meet some more for a meal, when there was a knock at the door.

When I opened it, I saw Charlie standing there.

"Can I kip down here for another couple of nights, sport?" he asked plaintively. "I got a place lined up, but I can't move in till Saturday."

What could I say but, "Yes, okay, Charlie. But just until Saturday." After explaining that I was about to go out for the evening to meet some friends, I gave him the spare key, told him that he could get a meal over at the cafe, and that I would be back about eleven. Then I left him to it, wondering all night if I had done the right thing, or if I would regret it.

When I returned he was watching the television. He was wearing my bathrobe, and his hair still wet from a recent shower. After chatting to him for a few minutes, I decided to take a shower myself, but turned down his offer to give back the bathrobe, suspecting that he had nothing on under it and might opt to remain sprawled out naked on the settee. I just didn't need that sort of temptation.

Locking the bathroom door, I had stripped right off before noticing that the shower curtain was missing, but managed by hanging up one of the big bath towels. After a quick sluice. I tied the other towel firmly around my waist and joined Charlie. Before I could ask him what had happened to the curtain, he said, "Oh, I nearly forgot, sport. I got us a couple cartons of chocolate mousse, you did say it was your favorite, didn't you?" He flashed me a mischievous grin.

"Yes it is," I told him, "but I couldn't eat any at the moment. I just had a big meal out with my friends. It'll keep in the fridge for a while."

The mischievous grin turned positively wicked then as he chuckled, "Oh, it ain't for eating, sport. It's so I can thank you properly for being so good to me!" And before I could protest, he had leaned over, taken my face in his hands and given me a long lingering kiss full on the mouth. His probing tongue playing tag with my own. Then he sent tingles running up and down my spine as he opened the towel and took me in his hand, giving me an instant erection.

Pulling me to my feet, he then opened the bathrobe to reveal his own hard-on. Pressing it against me, he wound his strong arms around me and kissed me again.

By this time of course, Tansey's warning and all my good intentions had flown out the window. I wanted him and he knew it. Steering me into the bedroom, hepulled off the duvet to reveal the shower curtain spread out on the mattress. After pressing me down onto it, he took out a carton of mousse from a pocket of the bathrobe, which he now discarded, and without as much as a by your leave, began to smear the mousse all over my penis and genitals. It reminded me of a guy I met in Jamaica who had used a similar method to turn me on, which certainly worked again because I became hard as a rock. Then handed me the tub, lay down beside me, and told me, "Now put some on me," accompanied by another mischievous grin which made him so attractive.

It was without doubt one of the most satisfying sixty-niners I have ever had. Charlie really knew his stuff. The two of us practically ate each other in a feverish attempt to lick off that delicious mousse. Our questing tongues probing every nook and cranny. When Charlie finally got round to sucking it off my penis, I was so turned on that I came halfway down his throat. He swallowed without protest, still licking up every drop. The two of us squirmed around on the shower curtain, bodies streaked with mousse and giggling like a pair of naughty schoolboys let loose in a chocolate factory.

After I had sucked him off, we took a short breather. Then he turned me over and began to work some of the mousse up between my buttocks, giving me a sensuous finger fuck before kneeling astride me, his own well muscled buttocks resting on the back of my thighs as he slowly pushed in his hard shaft and started to fuck me.

Although not as long as Guido, who was uncircumcised, Charlie had about seven inches of cock, and knew how to use it to give maximum pleasure. His long, slow strokes gradually increased as his urges grew stronger. His sweaty chest slapped against my back, his laboring breath hot on my neck as he came to a climax, shooting his sperm high up into me in that final spasmodic thrust.

Finally his lean body went rigid for a moment or two, then limp and heavy as he lay there until his breathing had subsided. He then rolled off with a sigh of contentment. He flashed me another wicked grin. "So, how was it for you, sport?"

"Oh, you're the best, Charlie," I replied, and I meant it.

Giving me another mischievous grin, he said, "And it ain't over yet, sport, I reckon it's your turn now," then turned over on his stomach, obligingly.

It was a night to remember, with Charlie giving and taking as his mood dictated. He never did move out; he was still sharing my bed right up to the day I was due to rejoin the ship.

Fortunately, by then, I had found him some cheap, clean digs to move into. He had already found himself a better paying job, and he could now afford to live on his own without supplementing his income by doing nasty things in the john at Murphy's.

Nevertheless, it was a painful parting. Charlie didn't want me to go; he really didn't. He did his best to persuade me to stay. I was tempted. However, I knew that the longer I stayed, the harder it would be in the end, especially for Charlie. He already regarded me as the dad he had always wanted. I guess, in a way, he was the kind of son that I knew I could never have. There were tears in both our eyes when we said our goodbyes on the quay.

Epilogue

I still write to Charlie once or twice a year, and always send him a present for his birthday and a card at Christmas, but he never writes back, partly, I suspect, because he is not very good at letter writing, or spelling, and partly because it is to punish me for deserting him. Charlie is a Leo, they have to be in command at all times, and don't take kindly to having their wishes thwarted.

But to be fair, he does ring me from time to time, preferring voice contact, and he is forever urging me to go down and visit him, always ending his calls with, "Oh, and don't forget the chocolate mousse, sport!"

However, Charlie is married now, as I knew he would be, needing someone to take care of him and cook him some nourishing meals. I am loath to disturb the new relationship now that he is trying to make something of his life, even though I do get the impression that all is not running smoothly at times. More and more I find myself picking up holiday brochures for down under, telling myself that they are just to reminisce over, or find new pictures of Sydney for my scrap-book.

But who am I kidding? Let's face it, whenever I go out to dinner and see there is chocolate mousse on the menu, I am tempted to order it, but I know it wouldn't taste the same without Charlie.

DÉJÀ VU
by Ken Anderson

Chunky, red-haired, hard, you held me
in your eyes. I reflected your stare
like glass. But then you turned away—
a handsome blind man lost
in a bar, someone who simply
couldn't remember
just what he'd been looking for.
So I played a little game—I talked
with a friend—and won. You said,
"I'm tired of cruisin' you." We turned
into some great pornography. In the morning
I dozed. You collected your clothes.

I didn't know what to say.

The dark-blue candle, the bottle
of amyl, the dented tube
with its little sailor's cap—these
were the props
in the bedtime story
we told each other once more
last night. But you forgot
we had played the scene. I phoned you
in the next. I had to be someone else,
I guess, before you could swallow me twice,
my friend, before you could take me in
again, some other place and time.

THE SEMENSHED OF BOYS
by Antler

We've heard tales of terrible bloodshed
for thousands of years,
How so many innocent people were butchered
rivers ran red with blood,
Why don't we hear
How so many boys were jacked off
rivers ran white with come?
Think of all the streets on earth
which've flowed with the gore of massacres—
How many orgies of love so great
semen flowed down the street?
Bloodshed vs. Semenshed—
Which is more relevant?
Which is more revelatory?
Which more revolutionary?
Hot wild white cum
from myriad shy balls of boys
spurting from iridescent cocks
in exquisite shocks of joy—
Don't we want to see that
more than bloody guts, bursting
from exploded bellies?
More than gushes of dark red blood
from bullet-riddled backs?
More than spurts of blood from bloody stumps
where heads or arms or legs just were?
Shouldn't auditoriums be built
where devotees flock to watch boys jack off—
free binoculars for the farthest rows?
(Or must there be so many seats to accommodate pilgrims
the farthest rows must be supplied
with telescopes?)
The semenshed of boys should be looked forward to
rather than bullfights or gladiators,
rather than guillotines or firing squads.
The semenshed of boys should be looked forward to
as much as the first robin in spring,
as much as the first violet in spring.
In the future old men and women
will enjoy telling their grandchildren

how they can still remember when the streets first flowed with cum.

"Life is fuckin' good..."

MILITARY MANEUVERS
by
Rick Jackson

The Collected
Uncensored
Sex Diaries of a
Horny Dog

STARbooks Press
Sarasota, Florida

BASIC TRAINING

You might think it would be fun living in an open barracks bay with nearly a hundred other youths, all in their prime and oozing hard, sweaty sexuality. You'd be wrong, though. It's hell. I know because I enlisted thinking that being around lean Marine bodies 36 hours a day would be like one long Chippendale's show.

I was right there. One of the first elements of basic training is to break down individual hang-ups. Marines must ask permission to piss or shit — and then do it with others lined up, watching them as they wait for their turns at the porcelain. Guys lounge around the barracks bay in shorts or less, hard muscles popping out in rippling knots from their thick necks down to their meaty calves.

It says something about the cruelty of fate that the biggest tease of the bunch ended up in the rack right across from mine. The guy made the average Calvin Klein model look like the dog's lunch. During those first three weeks of boot camp, I would lie in my rack, exhausted from the day's drills and marches and PT, desperate for sleep, only to have young Brad MacGregor stretched out naked as a glutton's prayer not four feet away.

The barracks were always dark after Taps, but moonlight had a nasty habit of streaming through a window to glisten across his hard recruit body, usually draped across the loins only by the corner of a sheet like a Michelangelo marble. The easy rise and fall of his broad, hairless pecs nearly drove me crazy — but they were nothing compared with the early-morning woodies that made his sheet stand tall and tasty.

Some nights I spent more time in the head spanking off than I did in my rack, but I was sure nothing short of a lobotomy could banish the waking and sleeping dreams of MacGregor's taut Marine body that made my life such a nightmare. I was wrong. Just when I was sure my lack of sleep and frazzled nerves were going to get me washed out of boot camp in disgrace, some passing god must have taken pity on me.

I woke up about 0330 to find MacGregor's rack empty and my bladder full enough to rupture. As I shambled into the pisser to drain, the back of my mind registered the noise of a shower running. I'd seen Mac showering before, of course — I showered with him every chance I got. For obvious reasons, though, I could never really *watch* him shower — admire the steamy water streaming down his muscled torso, watch him flex and twist in animal pleasure as the gushing torrent licked the soap from his naked flesh, or take careful note of the tight joy of his powerful glutes grinding against the lucky hand that soaped his shithole. That night I finally had a chance to stand outside the shower and watch his reflection in a well-placed mirror to see all I had been missing.

As I stood there in the darkness, looking into the brightly lighted shower, I saw more than any randy young voyeur deserves in a cosmic cycle of lifetimes. For the first few seconds I was too taken with his perfect beauty to notice what he was doing, but the way he was going at it soon left little doubt. His right hand was frothing soap, stroking rabidly along something half the size of M. Eiffel's erection and infinitely more appealing. Mac's head was back, eyes shut and mouth agape as he worked, oblivious to anything but answering the ancient call of man's fiercest need.

The water boiled off the back of his head like a steamy nimbus, splashing down onto his shoulders and cascading in frantic ripples down towards the firm ass he had planted against the tile. His tits were stiff with pleasure and his belly and hips answered every cue to fuck hard up into the tight Marine fist that was then the essence of his destiny. For a few seconds, his beaver-brown eyes opened and looked out past the blond lashes that helped make my dreams such torment. I worried for a passing moment of sanity that he might catch me watching him, but I was well hidden by the darkness and my own timidity and his eyes were focused far beyond any mortal realm.

How long did I stand watching him work, agonized more by my own limitations than by the unattainable perfection of his body? Time had ceased to function except in answer to the pounding of his fist and the heaving of his chest. All I know is that when I found my balls at last, my dick felt ready to split along the seams and I saw the world as though for the first time. In a very real sense in that instant, when my priggish fears dropped away and the lush landscape of certainty opened up before me, I became a man.

I left the darkness and padded into the shower to help my warrior brother complete his mission. I ignored the risk to my military career. I ignored the sodden shorts that soon disappeared anyway. I even ignored what Mac might think when I reached out and took his thick dick away from him. Just then, I didn't care about anything but busting the nut of my young life.

Mac pretended to be shocked and offended for a moment, but, looking back, I think he must have wanted me as much as I needed him. He certainly didn't run screaming naked into the night. Instead of outraged virtue, those big brown eyes smoldered momentarily with the heat of the ages and then slipped silently shut as his hips picked up their rhythm again, fucking this time up into my soapy paw. The sizzle of the shower almost drowned out the low moans of pleasure that echoed every thrust and taunted me to whip him harder.

He must have worked my shorts off. I was too busy to notice until he hefted my poor overworked balls and took me firmly in hand to return the favor. He was awkward at first because of the unfamiliar angle, but soon learned his craft and set seriously to work. The feel of his powerful hands jacking me off seemed suddenly to snap me out of a magical spell and dropped me into an even more enraptured reality — a reality of stiff dicks and hard muscle and tight ass that replaced all the steamy zephyrs and idealized forms of my romantic enchantment.

I kept my hand on station for him to fuck but leaned forward to show each of his tits in turn what the dangerous edge of a man's teeth could do. Mac's helpless body convulsed in building rapture as my mouth moved north to lap his pits and then up towards his ears for a tongue-fuck he could write home about. His jack-hand spazzed, but I didn't care. I was more interested in licking and touching and possessing every inch of his perfect young body than I was in having him spank me off. If there was one thing I'd had enough of in the last month it was hand jobs.

When my lips finally met Mac's, I think he was startled for a moment, but maybe it was the way I'd finally let his dick slap down against my belly as my hands reached around to grab his full-flaring Marine butt. His hips didn't miss a stroke as he switched to fucking upwards hard against my belly, but his ass was soon the center of my affection. His powerful Corps-built glutes ground against my palms, filling them to overflowing as I wriggled my fingers deep down into his hairless crack in search of the secret wonder I knew lay hidden there.

I had to compete with the gushing stream of steamy water, but the rigid rules of fluid dynamics were nothing compared to my determination to show Mac's tight recruit shithole how good one Marine can feel. By the time my fuckfingers found their target and sliced across his tender, parboiled asshole, I had spread his glutes wide and almost lifted him off his feet. His body ground and writhed against mine as our lips locked tight until the pressure of the moment and the unfamiliar feel of a man's hands up his ass exploded his heavy balls into a storm of flying sperm that blew up between our bellies and seemed suddenly to envelop his body in a swirling cyclone of creamy white Corps-cum.

Mac's head slammed back so hard against the tile that he'd have knocked himself senseless if we hadn't already gotten him that way. He jerked and twisted and bucked and heaved against me, spewing and spurting like the honoree at an exorcism until even his massive Marine body passed its limits and collapsed into my arm, a helpless hulk of his former glory. Above the sizzle of the water, all I could hear were his gasps for air and his punctuated mantra: Oh, God—Oh, God—Oh, God—Oh, God—Oh, God—Oh, God… "

I knew that if we were both to see the face of the infinite, there was no time like the present. In one fluid motion, I pulled my fingers out of his ass, dropped his body face-first against the tiled wall, rubbered up, and shoved my desperate nine inches of Marine recruit training against his shithole to start my Marine career with a *semper fi* flourish.

Mac was born a virgin and had stayed that way until I found his ass that night in the shower. The poor gorgeous bastard had no clue what to expect, but he knew soul-deep and gut-sure that he needed to be fucked more than he needed anything else in his military life. I'd had my fingers up his ass, but they did no more than tickle his fancy. My baton-sized dick was about to do the same thing boot camp does on a different scale: break him down absolutely and then rebuild a new, improved Marine on the ruins of his former self.

Looking back on the pain a needledick named David caused me the first time I was boned, I can only imagine what my swollen Marine member must have done to Mac's nervous system. He somehow managed to keep from screaming out and waking everyone in southern California, but his body held nothing else back.

Muscle knotted on muscle as his hands clawed helplessly at the tile and his guts plunged irretrievably down my dick. By the time my pubes were shredding what little was left of his shithole, his liver was already scratching away at my swollen knob, teasing me with the possibility of dislocating his pancreas if he were a bad Marine. Nine inches of slick jarhead guts waved and rippled along as many inches of swollen Marine dick in an instinctive timeless tango that knew both violent conquest and transcendent surrender.

My hands on his pecs pulled him closer to me, harder down my dick. His hands echoed my need, reaching back to grab my butt and force my way even farther up into his helpless body, begging me to fuck him hard and fast and deep enough that we would both know he could take anything Nature had to throw against him.

By then, I needed more than to bust a nut. I even needed more than to posses Mac's hard Marine body. I needed him. I needed to prove myself and accept his surrender. I needed to be his brother, to share his strafing fire and take him into my foxhole. In a subtle, unspoken way no one outside the military can possibly understand, I needed to seal our Marine bond by fusing our flesh and flushing part of me far enough up into his core that it would remain there until his final hour.

Bonding and warrior nobility aside, on a baser level I also needed to fuck his ass until my heads came off—and Mac needed it even more. His hands had stopped clawing at the wall by then, but, as he braced his forearms against the tile and clenched his jaw and whimpered with each brutally reaming fuckthrust up into his vitals, I saw his body surrender as his soul had done. In the magic of a man's most sublime moment, his powerful warrior body began confusing pain and pleasure, reaping rapture where only agony had been sown. Then his whimpers died away and a low, almost subsonic groan of ecstasy took their place—a sound that grew and matured with every slicing stroke of my plow along his firm, fertile furrow.

Our soapy, jism-covered bodies slammed helplessly together and fucked Mac forward into the wall until we were both lucky just to be standing. My mortal mistake was taking my teeth from his neck and leaning back to watch my dick drill up through his powerful mounds of Marine man-muscle and slide snicker-snack into his asshole. I've always liked seeing my work up close and personal, but that night Mac was too much of a good thing to endure. The instant my brain realized what my dick had known — that the Marine body wrapped around my reaming unit was studly, perfect, boy-next-door Mac, I lost my load quicker than a Texas dope smuggler caught in a speed trap.

My whole universe exploded up Mac's once-tight ass and kept on exploding until my nuts ached with over-achievement and I was half drowned by the boiling water we'd somehow stumbled into. We ended up on the deck, a mess of arms and legs and still-stiff dicks that knew neither of us was finished for the night. By dawn, we limped back to our racks and, for once I was able to sleep—for all of about four minutes before the lights went on and a new Marine day began.

I haven't gotten any more sleep the last several weeks than I got before, but even our drill instructor has noticed how my outlook on life is much improved. Several other recruits in our company have joined our late-night workouts lately, but Mac and I always come back where we belong in the end.

LONG, HARD & OFTEN

The first thing a Marine officer learns in OCS is that he is responsible for his men. Lieutenants must make sure their sergeants have the plan before they can kick back; sergeants see their corporals get chow before they break out their own MREs, and so on down the line. The other services generally use men either as beasts of burden or sacrificial lambs to be fucked hard up the ass the first time disaster strikes and someone needs to burn. The Corps does have defects, but its officers carry their own packs, take their own blame, and help everyone else do the same. We are a family first and a government organization second. Long before the Corps, warriors knew each other as brothers—long and hard and often.

We also listen. We officers are the big brothers that set our Marines straight and keep them humping their way through history. Marines in my company come to me all the time with problems, and I listen—even if there isn't much I can do to help. Often the young Marines just want to talk about home or their hopes for the future. Sometimes they are little more than kids who want a clue about the way the works. I always do what I can, even when the answers are anything but easy. The PFC who came to my stateroom one night several years ago is a perfect case in point.

We had been deployed off Somalia for five months, doing nothing but floating around forever as we waited to be needed ashore, when Anabasis knocked on my door and asked if I could spare a moment. The name Olaf Anabasis probably conjures up a different image for you than the Marine did for me. Olaf's mother loved old Viking movies. Her father had been a Blackfoot Sioux, but most of Olaf's other relations were Italian. I will have to ask sometime where the name *Anabasis* came from. In any event, Anabasis stands five-seven and has a solid, bantam build that looks puny but has muscles out the ass—every one developed and ready for action. His hazel eyes and Mediterranean-olive skin seem as incongruous as his name.

As he sat across from me and tried to get to the point, I had other things to worry about—and I wasn't feeling the least bit like a traditional big brother. Marines underway usually wear T-shirts and UDTs (khaki-colored dive shorts that live up to their name). They're so short some guys call them Daisy Dukes because they barely cover ass when a Marine is standing up. We freeball with UDTs so when a Marine sits, his nuts and dick generally fall out through the legs and lie in the chair in front of him, like some primitive tribal token of good will. Sailing to freedom's frontier with hundreds of other men for months on end, a Marine sees a lot of dicks and balls. We train ourselves to pretend not to notice; but with Olaf's gear on display, it was hard.

His balls were so swollen with jism, he couldn't have jacked in a month;

but the main attraction was his cute little uncut dick. It was just a shy little nubbin, hiding inside the leg of his shorts, looking all coy and shrivelled and soft behind the tastiest-looking foreskin I'd seen in years.

When I snapped my mind back to what he was saying, I discovered I hadn't missed much. He was having feelings that bothered him, but he didn't want to discuss them with anyone officially for fear they might kick him out of the Corps. All he ever wanted to be was a Marine—besides, he had car payments to make. He asked if I could advise him what to do, man to man and strictly off the record. I'm sure you have guessed what he was about to confess with that wide-eyed innocent look of his, but I was clueless, assuming he was worried whether he had the stones to measure up in battle. For one thing, the kid had wasted fifteen minutes circling the wagons before he staggered up to the point. For another, his cute little wrinkled wee-wee had spent that quarter hour peeking out at me and making it hard for me to concentrate.

He finally stammered that he was "afraid" he was gay. He had always looked up to me as a man and a Marine. Could I help him out? I tried to stop looking at his dick long enough to tell him that was like being "afraid" he was Italian or had a goofy name. He was what he was. His job wasn't to wish he were someone else, but to make the most of who he was. When I gave him my usual "Just play the game and don't get caught" speech, he dropped the real bombshell. He wasn't just gay. He had a crush on someone he shouldn't: me.

I didn't say anything for about two minutes, trying to sort my duty to the Corps and to Olaf from what I needed. In the end, I decided there was no conflict. The best thing I could do for him was to give him the self-respect that would come from seeing he wasn't a freak, and, incidentally, blowing the biggest nut of my military career up that tight jarhead butt of his. Finally, I stopped his blushing by telling him I'd be happy to help him—and myself—out. So long as he understood what happened between us was man to man, one warrior brother to another. I thought he was cute as a bug's ear and would fuck him as senseless as he wanted. All he had to do to cross our personal Rubicon was reach over and click my door locked.

He looked first at the knob as though it were a grenade with a missing pin and then down in my lap to see my nine inches of leadership material growing stiffer by the second. A trembling finger reached out for the button and snapped it in with a click that echoed like Doom around the stateroom. Then his hand drifted along my shank as though it were a holy relic. He knelt onto the deck and put his face into my crotch, breathing in my musky scent and cooing low all the while. I slipped my hand around my dickhead to keep him from going too far, but let him lick the base of my shaft and suck at my balls for a few moments before I suggested he might want to get more comfortable.

Shorts and T-shirts don't take long to lose. We left our boots on, just in case. I took a moment to admire his Marine-issue body as he stood before me, good to go. It was hairless except for the pubes and pits, but toned and tanned and tender enough to make any man's mouth water. One over-developed muscle wrapped across another like a Michelangelo drawing.

I pulled him up onto my rack and held him in my lap as I leaned against the bulkhead. My lips met his, tenderly at first and then with the fierceness I knew he needed. Our lips and tongues tangled forever as my hands did recon down his hard back and firm flanks until I'd cupped his Corps-built ass and found heaven. I spread wide his cheeks and let my throbbing nine inches slide up to lie along the very bottom of his crack, teasing his tender asshole with my shaft as his body scraped along my shank. His tight glutes jacked at my joint as my tongue moved to his ear then down to his huge, hairless tits.

He clung like a horseleech when I pried him loose to get at those tits, but the sacrifice was worth it. His every nerve seemed set to explode with a lifetime of pent-up sexuality suddenly gushing free. As I lifted his ass off my dick to elevate his tits, he hung on for dear life. He was so fresh and tender, I was determined to take my time, tonguing and sucking and chewing his hard nipples until they started to bore me before I did him up the ass. Since all this would take forever, I kept my hands on station, working their way deeper between his glutes until I found his quivering asshole.

As my tongue circled and raided his tits, my fingers did the same with his butthole. The gungy little bastard went crazy, squirming and thrashing about and moaning so loudly I had to wad my shorts into a ball and shove them into his mouth to keep him quiet. By the time I was ready to use my teeth on his left tit, his shithole was years past ready to wrangle. I slipped in with my first nip and felt young Olaf go off like an earthquake in a crystal factory. His overdeveloped pecs slammed tit into my teeth at the same time his spine arched backwards, driving his ass up my fuckfingers.

I splayed my fingers wide so I wouldn't lose touch with his powerful cheeks as one finger slipped down his ass-crack from his tailbone while my main anal intruder rode deep from below. As his body jerked and twitched with my finger up his ass and my teeth gnawing away like a beaver with fresh aspen, his huge, man-sized nuts jiggled across my wrist. While I worked that young Marine body as though it were my own dick, his face spent most of its time pressed hard against my shoulder, trying to come to terms with the meaning of bliss incarnate.

His ass knew just what it wanted. I had no sooner adjusted to the wicked thrill of Olaf's balls rolling across my wrist than I noticed he was using my fuckfinger to scratch his prostate. It barely reached, but when I spared his tits for a time and pressed him back against my upraised knees, my finger tore into his buttnut like a Tomahawk missile hitting a fireworks factory. His twitching and gagged moaning went into super-hyper-overdrive. Olaf opened his eyes to relish the experience for a moment, and I was touched to find tears there.

My index finger slid in next. I used it to stretch his tight little jarhead shithole wide while my fuckfinger gave his prostate the abuse it craved so much. Since his body had convulsed off the other hand I'd had in his ass-crack, I decided to put it to better use: playing with the gorgeous little muzzle cover that now bobbed along between us. I slipped my little finger into his mouth to soak up some spit and then down into his `skin-clad cock. Even swollen hard and purple, his meat was only a little over four inches long and no wider than the average broom handle, but the way his little vertical purple smile grinned out from inside that wrinkled cock-cowl was worth a world of inches.

I pressed deeper, easing my little finger into his foreskin, pressing down and around his tender head just the way I'd have done with my tongue in another time. His body didn't know whether to rub buttnut against my finger or gyrate his jarhead joint so it took turns doing both until his hips seemed stuck in some new-age frolic only a tripped-out raver could master. Within seconds, his cum-slit was awash in a clear, sweet ooze that bubbled up from his very soul to prove he was ready for anything. The soft heat of his cocksock around my finger and the silken flow of dick-lube were even more delicious than the feel of his hands on my tits or drifting across my shoulders or wrapped tight around my flanks.

I burrowed deep down into his foreskin and then slipped my finger back into his mouth so the taste of his sweet syrup could put him into the mood for my thick nine inches up his tight, meat-starved ass. His tongue and lips used that finger almost as frantically as his joy-nut used the one sunk up his ass. Olaf slipped a hand down to his shank to give his foreskin a tight squeeze, milking up about a Texas gallon of pre-cum to slather all across my own swollen knob. His hand kept busy stroking and twisting and jacking at my Marine joint until I began to know how fine he felt.

We let time cut loose and drift free as Olaf jacked and twitched and moaned like a muffled, misbegotten fiend of hell. My finger made more trips into his cocksock as I coaxed one new feeling after another from his unit and carried the leavings up to his eager lips. When I couldn't put Christmas morning off for another moment, I wrapped a firm hand around his shank and jacked down hard, stretching the skin on his shaft as tight as it was tender. His purple head popped into view—a throbbing, shiny knob I knew I had to have up my ass. It wouldn't set any records for length, but I don't think I've ever wanted dick half as much as I did in that instant.

Since Olaf's asshole was still locked tight around my right fuckfinger, I had no choice but to use my left to jack what he had. First slowly and then with a speed born more of desperate need than finesse, I slipped that sloppy foreskin up and down his shank, capping his cock and then stripping it clean. His pre-cum flow had reached runaway proportions, but I didn't mind. The stuff was splattering down across his balls and onto my lap, but enough was lubing my hand so that every yank of his crank was a slicker, more delicious treat.

Once I found my rhythm, my lips eased down to do Olaf's ear for a time. He was grunting and moaning and convulsing enough without having my tongue tickling his brain, so I eased off and concentrated on my handiwork. It must have been good enough, for suddenly I felt his grip on my crank lock up tight. Olaf's whole body had been thrashing for half an hour, but somehow it cranked up the shaking and shivering another twenty notches until I had to drop my jack hand just to hold his shoulder down.

By that time, he didn't need any help from me. His first-class privates erupted on their own, spraying one blast after another of slick, frothy ball-cream up into the air and onto my chest and belly. Some landed as far up as my shoulder; some landed on Olaf himself as he tried to shit my whole hand up into his ass. Mostly, though, his cute little Marine weapon turned into a savage RPG, launching one jism-grenade after another up to splash into my commissioned chest.

Shortly after blast-off, I was busy twisting my hand up his ass to maximize his satisfaction; but when I got a minute, I reached back down to his dick and jacked away at his uncut jarhead weapon like a monkey on Benzedrine. I was too busy stroking away with both hands to dodge the incoming rounds, but even Olaf's Cold War sperm arsenal eventually ran dry.

When peace descended upon the field of glory, I was a mess. I suddenly realized Olaf had gone slack and was leaning forward against my shoulder again. I managed to pry my fingers from ass and eased his head back so I could give him a comradely kiss of thanks before I set him to policing the area. As his head came up, I got my next major surprise of the evening. The kid had tears streaming down his face as though he'd just seen his dog die. These tears weren't the glisten in the corner of the eyes I'd noticed before, but a ceaseless, heart-breaking sob that gushed up from some private cataclysm of the spirit.

Ever the romantic, I pulled my shorts out of his mouth and stroked his sweat-streaked hair with my hand and held him close for a moment, neither of us much caring I was smearing his face and chest with great globs of melting jism. After a few quiet moments, he got control of himself enough to gurgle, "Oh, Sir. I didn't know it could. Thank you, Sir."

I like having my work admired as much as the next guy, but what he needed was to get on with his life. I tossed his ass down the bed and stretched out onto my back so the PFC could lick his load off my face and chest and belly. It took him about ten very sloppy minutes, but I was in no hurry. Then I sent him over to my desk for some rubbers. I'd been thinking the whole time his ass was clawing at my fingers how much fun it would be to see him riding my joint as I lay quiet and let him do all the work. Then I was going to have him use that untrimmed meat on me until he knew how fine a man could really feel.

Once I had the chance, though, I changed my mind. He was still going to get up my ass all right—even if I had to tie the rubber on his little pecker—

but first I was going to lay him onto his back, spread his legs until he threatened to snap, and then I was going to fuck that tight little jarhead ass of his until I needed a whole team of corpsmen to resuscitate me. I thought I'd come just watching his expression as my overgrown shank slammed down his virgin hole, but that was just the beginning. In a way, I guess that's our story in a nutshell.

Olaf needed my help with his personal problem. I'm his superior—his big brother in a warrior fraternity stretching back past antiquity, so I gave it to him. What's more, I kept on giving it to him every time he showed up. Marine officers live the motto *Semper Fi* and always try to see their hard, hot, tight-assed little brothers get the most out of their service.

HOOKING GANGBANG

The absolute worst thing about Navy life is having to roll out of a nice warm rack to go on watch at screwy hours. Doing wake-ups, on the other hand, always gives me a warm, gushy feeling deep down.

I should explain for those of you who don't live on Navy ships that one man from the off-going watch section goes around waking up the reliefs. When a watch is due to be relieved at 0330, the wake-up messenger will usually amble down to berthing around 0300 and make sure the poor bastards who are on-coming will have plenty of time to pull themselves together before they come up for watch. The reason I usually like doing wake-ups so much is that I get to roust out the no-loads who have been sleeping while I was on watch—and savor the realization that they'll be taking my place so I can roll into my rack where I really belong.

Now and again we have to wake up one of the officers to stand a bridge watch. Rousting them out in the middle of the night and dooming them to suffer the myriad horrors of pre-dawn consciousness underway is even more fun—but not usually as much of an experience as it is with Ensign Morgan.

He sleeps in a stateroom with another junior officer so the first time I was assigned to roll him out, I tried to be as quiet as I could. I was new to the watch section that night so I needed awhile just to decide which rack was his. Once I was sure, I reached a hand through the curtains that gave him the minimal privacy a man gets aboard a ship and shook his leg. I was just about to whisper that it was time for his watch when his leg shook me.

Curtains or not, most of the officers sleep in shorts. Morgan obviously wasn't most officers. I had no sooner grabbed hold of his upper thigh than the thing heaved around and shoved my hand right into his balls. Before I could even begin to react, I found myself with a handful of dick—stiff, hard, commissioned dick that was positively determined to have a good time at my expense.

Finding my hand wrapped around an officer's dick at 0300 was surprise enough. Finding the dick hard and hot and already thrusting away was a shock. What really decked me, though, was that the thing was already rubbered up. At first, I couldn't believe what I felt. Then I decided maybe I had caught him secretly beating off. Maybe he was just using the rubber to keep from spunking his sheets. Officers are an odd bunch so a guy never knows what to think. An instant later, I found out the real reason for that rubber—when Morgan's hand snapped through the curtains and pulled my head into his rack.

The bastard had his big dick in my mouth and his hands locked around my head to hold it in place before I could do a fucking thing about it—even if I'd wanted to. He had me in a delicate position in more ways than one.

Not only was I trying to avoid gagging on his monster dick as it kept busy trying to tear off the back of my head, but Lt. Jensen was asleep in the upper rack. Just about the last thing I needed in my military career was to make enough noise choking down Morgan's stiff dick to wake Jensen up and have my enlisted ass hauled off to the brig.

Don't get me wrong—I've swallowed my share of Navy bone over the years, but it was usually a quick latex-driven kneel-and-knob job in a fan room or a longer, more relaxed bout of slurpy 69 in some foreign hotel room on liberty where I could take my time and savor the upward curve of stiff Navy dick meating the downward arc of my gullet. This business of sucking a dick as long and hard as Morgan's was bad enough —but doing it sideways, on his terms, in the dark, and without making a sound was more than even a veteran bonehound like me could manage.

At first, he didn't seem to mind a little awkwardness, perhaps thinking he was breaking in some lame-assed little bootcamp cherry boy. After a minute or so, though, his hands pressed down harder on my head, wedging his dick sideways against the opening to my throat. Instead of managing to work it deep, all the crazy bastard was able to achieve was to make me gag. I tried to keep it down—both the noise and the dick— but had no joy with either. Finally, with what I read as a snort of disgust, he pulled my face off his dick and slammed it down onto his big, hairy balls.

His dick immediately slammed against his furry belly and set about keeping time with his pulse like some Neanderthal's metronome. The savagery of his need, however, was strictly hard *Homo erectus*. His hands ground my mouth into his sweaty crotch as his hips arched upwards until I had no choice but to open wide and give his balls the rough sucking they craved. I even slid a paw up to give his dick a hand, holding it in place as his hips reamed upwards against my face and drove his dick up into my fist.

I'd noticed Morgan plenty in the three months he'd been aboard. A guy couldn't help noticing him. Most of the other officers were complete shitbags, for starters. He was anything but. With his curly black hair and omnipresent five-o'clock shadow, his hunky body was enough man to make any amount of semen proud. He had another side, though—a cute little nose and blazing blue eyes and full, cock-suckable lips that gave him the virginal aura of a high school freshman that seemed both very much at odds with and oddly complementary to his role as one of America's finest surface warriors.

A few times I had been lucky enough to follow him up a ladder, watching that full, hard ass he packed around wriggle and grind relentlessly away inside its khaki prison. I would wonder how it would feel stretched tight around my angry enlisted dick until that fine piece of commissioned ass gave me dreams. The dreams, though, were nothing nearly as complicated as reality.

His hands were back on my head for starters, smearing my face into his toothsome nuts as his hips humped harder upward into my hand with every passing moment. The glorious musky scent of his crotch filled my lungs and consciousness until I knew how pallid my poor dreams of reaming out his ass had been. I tried to teach him to slow down by jerking down between his legs with a mouthful of testicle, but the more abuse I gave him, the more he obviously needed. I licked and slurped away at those hairy commissioned nuts like a country dog with a world of time—but both of us needed even more. When he felt my nose prodding into his asscrack, Morgan spread his legs as wide as the narrow confines of his rack would allow so I could snarf him deep and happy while my mouth kept his balls busy.

There was just no way, though, that I could get my nose against his asshole leaning into his rack the way I was. Besides, for the longest time I'd had my own troubles. My dick had swollen to record proportions all crunched and cramped up inside my dungarees. I was just about to ease back for a second so I could drop trou and give my lizard some room to breathe when I felt his hands at my belt and zipper. I don't think it was until I felt his hands planted firmly on my hips and lifting my ass upwards that I realized his hands were also still grinding my head down into his crotch. Either the gorgeous bastard had more hands than Shiva, or I was about to be the main meat at a tail-hooking gang bang.

I tried to pull my head out of Morgan's crotch, but his legs first held me tight down where I belonged and then pivoted about to throw us both out of his rack and onto the deck. Before I could even begin to get my balance, he and his buddy Lt. Jensen were using me to maximum advantage. Morgan shoved his latexed dick far enough down my throat to rupture a tonsil even as Jensen stabbed me up the ass with enough dick to make a Marine gunnery sergeant bawl like a boot recruit.

I found out much later that Jensen had rubbered up, too—probably so he wouldn't get enlisted shit on his dick. Jensen's angry joint ripped through my outraged asshole with the fury of a panzer division through a parson's tea party. Who did the bastard think he was, anyway? I was the one who was supposed to be doing the fucking, yet there I was—swinging helplessly back and forth between Morgan's furry belly and the unseen brutality of Jensen's thick bone.

Even worse than the wounds to my macho pride was the pain up my ass. Unlike so many men in the service, I'd never been into having my ass broken open and my guts churned to tapioca just so some shipmate could shoot his load. Jensen hadn't bothered with lube or even a quick feel-up to open me up first. He had seen my ass sticking out of Morgan's rack and decided to use me like his own personal enlisted fuck-toy.

I hadn't been fucked in almost a year—and that was by a needle-dicked kid at a supply depot who could barely keep it hard. I had felt so sorry for the kid after I reamed him for an hour that I hunkered down and let him have his fun—and regretted it for days. He was nothing, though, compared with Jensen. Even if I'd just finished a tour of Turkish prisons, Jensen's dick would have done me in. The minute the thing rammed up my ass, I knew I was done for.

Wave after blinding wave of red-hot torment surged up every nerve ending I had until they all crested together in a paroxysm of such surreal horror that, even as the last fragments of consciousness were being fucked brutally away from me, some quiet corner of my brain couldn't help being impressed with the totality of the destruction that dick was wreaking up my ass. It was at once devastating and majestic—like witnessing the air burst of a hydrogen bomb or surfing Krakatoa.

My guts were ripped relentlessly from their supports and cascaded backwards to engulf the invader within. Oddly enough, my shithole didn't hurt after the first few strokes. I was fucked too numb for that. All I felt up my ass was the seething fire of creation packed deeper and tighter with every reaming fuckthrust. Trapped the way I was between two dicks, each more eager than the other to use me hard, I tried to give that bone up my butt the room it needed, but it had already taken every inch I had and kept coming after more.

I couldn't even scream out. Morgan's dick down my throat saw to that. If he'd had trouble reaching my throat before, now that he was standing tall, slamming his shank down my gullet was second nature. Soon the two of them had worked out a perfect rhythm, reaming me one way and then the other, bouncing my butt and nose off their bodies like a nuclear-powered shuttlecock. The more I tried to breathe and scream and beg for a break, the farther down my throat Morgan drove my dick until I was sure he was going to bump boners with his buddy.

As they got theirs, though, a funny thing happened. Almost before I realized it, the agony up my ass had moved over enough to invite ecstasy in for a visit. My butt still hurt like hell, but it hurt in a nice way—rather like a chipped tooth your tongue just cannot leave alone. The more man-inches of dick I had thrust upon me, the more I liked it and the more I needed it—and the more I wanted it.

My hands had found their way to Morgan's butt to help me hang on to something solid amidst the pounding waves of man-muscle, but as the searing fire up my ass turned to a welcome glow, my fingers dug deeper until they found his fuck-hole. Whether it was my prime-quality dick-sucking or the sight of his buddy reaming my ass or the feel of my fingers prying his shithole wide, something suddenly made Morgan mighty happy.

He had been grunting and talking dirty ever since Jensen joined in, but all at once Morgan let out the kind of gurgle and gasp that proves a man is about to make his mark. His hands wrapped tighter around my head while his ass gobbled my fingers for breakfast.

Then, suddenly, his bone started slamming upwards as though Morgan were determined to fuck my head off altogether. The rhythmic reaming thrusts slipped slowly into history as his swollen knob ground away down my throat, spewing up every drop of commission jism he could so much as borrow. I couldn't feel it, of course; the rubber saw to that. Nothing could keep me from feeling the underside of his dick pulse with life, though—or from hearing his savage growls and animal grunts as he bred my face so hard his bone threatened to break off at the base.

Morgan nutted and spunked and spewed sperm until I was sure he intended to keep going until he had my air-starved carcass pumped full—whether I was left alive to enjoy the party or not. Just about the time the lack of oxygen and pain up my ass was making me terminally goofy, his body seemed suddenly to deflate with a long, almost subsonic sigh, almost as though he had lost his mettle along with his load. He collapsed atop me and into Jensen's arms for a moment to gather his wits and then dragged from my throat first his dick and then the load it had left deep.

Jensen, of course, had been busy all the while—getting meaner by the moment as Morgan did his worst down my gullet. Once I got the bone out of my craw, I was willing togive up Morgan's ass, too— mainly so I could concentrate on saving any fragments of mine that might be left. Oddly enough, though, Morgan had other ideas. Before I noticed what he was doing, he had slipped a rubber up my shank and was draped over Jensen's rack, ass-up and just begging me to fuck him. He didn't have to beg very long.

I had to pull Jensen forward a little, but he didn't seem to mind. Within seconds, I was up Ensign Morgan's tight commissioned tail and the morning was definitely looking up.

His ass was as hungry as his dick had been desperate. I'd have liked to use him long and slow and hard, but with Jensen slamming forty feet of dick a minute up my tail, I knew I didn't have long in the saddle.

I made do with what I had, locking my teeth into Morgan's shoulder and reaching low to grab his tits as Jensen pounded into me and I ricocheted on up his ass. Morgan's guts grabbed at me, worshiping my every jolt with jubilation and begging for an enlisted-quality boning.

I tried my damnedest, but at 0300 after a twenty-hour day, a guy can do only so much. The thick dick grating away the ruins of my prostate, the firm feel of Morgan's furry pecs, the smell of his man-sweat, and the lingering damage his dick had done to my throat all swept me over the edge until I felt myself falling forward, pushed from behind to explode up into his ass.

I was at once the perfect engine of my own fulfillment and a cum-conduit to focus the energy of Jensen's spewing jism upwards through my body to swirl together with my seed in a whirlwind of semen's delight.

The dual raptures of giving and taking, of using and being used, of reaming butt and being reamed all numbed what little was left of my brain and sent me clawing mindlessly away at the hard body wrapped around my dick.

By the time my wits had started to coalesce again, Morgan had pried himself off my shank and was halfway dressed—and Jensen had dropped his jism-packed rubber into the garbage and was crawling, naked and happy, back between his sheets.

You'd think that the two of them would have thanked me for a good time, wouldn't you? If so, that just shows how little you know about the Navy. Just before he went out the door, Morgan looked at his watch and growled.

It was already 0340, and he was ten minutes late for watch. He glared at me and said that if I knew what was good for me, I wouldn't wait until 0300 next time to wake him up—I had made him late.

Tomorrow night, I'll be down there at 0200 and we'll see whether he doesn't sing a different tune. Now that I know what he and Jensen like, I'm going to fuck them both so hard they'll have to be carried to the fucking bridge to stand watch. We'll see how much they bitch about late wake-ups then.

LIBERTY DOWN UNDER

From my very first days as a Marine, I had heard stories about what a party place Australia is—and what can happen to a young Marine on liberty there if he isn't careful. During the six months we floated around the Arabian Gulf, sweating our balls off aboard *Tarawa* and waiting for Saddam to do something even more goofy than usual, I looked forward plenty to our port visit in Fremantle. Marines talk so much shit, though, that I knew 95% of the stories I heard about liberty down under were impossible. For once, though, my doubting conventional military wisdom was dead wrong. I barely got off the ship before I ran into enough adventure to make a gunnery sergeant howl for mercy—and pray he wouldn't get it.

Tarawa tied up just across from the local train station so I ambled in that direction to catch the first train to Perth. I stopped by a public toilet to splash some piss first, and wasn't there ten seconds before a gorgeous young stud sidled up beside me at the pisser and asked if I'd like to have my dick sucked. His accent was as adorable as he was, but I was still trying to convince myself he'd actually said, "Hey, Yank— how'd ya like yer cock sucked off proper?" when he leaned over for a peek at what I had in my hand and gave a low whistle of admiration. He looked me up and down and up again and changed his mind: "I take it back, mate—we'll just have to shove that beauty tight up me freckle."

Even playing that last bit over in my mind, I wasn't sure what he was saying, exactly, but the look on his face came through loud and clear. In a way, I can see why he was getting all excited. Aussies get their dicks hard when they hear American accents almost as much as we do when we hear what they pretend is English. Shane obviously knew I was off the ship because I was standing there with my dick hanging out of my Charlies—the olive uniform that makes a Marine's hard young body savory enough to lick raw even when he isn't hanging low with his advantages on parade. The Corps builds a man's body to perfection and then keeps it that way through constant abuse, so I might have expected Shane would drool at me.

I hadn't been ready for how fucking cute he was, though. Everyone had said that Australian men are supposed generally to look like the dog's lunch, but that was the rankest of calumnies. Shane was good enough to have me hard in a heartbeat. He was about 19 and big-boned for starters—and had thick, shaggy curls hanging low over a strong brow and big, brown, jumbuck eyes that just plain refused to leave me alone. His lips were full and fuckable, and his perky little nose just begged to have my pubes grind them down. His strong jaw and thick neck, his broad shoulders and narrow hips continued the theme just fine. Because of the sweltering February heat, he was barefoot, wearing only a tight T-shirt and tighter shorts— but they stretched across his washboard abs and stiff tits until I was the one who broke out in a sweat. When he reached into his shorts and pried out the thickest, stiffest Aussie dick I'd ever seen, I knew for sure how true all those sea stories had been—and what a good time I could have if only I could break through the language barrier.

For maybe two or three minutes, I stood there at the pisser, stunned by his blatant beauty and watching him slowly slide his floppy foreskin up and down across the throbbing, silky-smooth head that had my mouth watering and my tongue twitching away on overtime. It was so fucking flawless and good-to-go gorgeous that I couldn't take my eyes off the thing, but finally he broke the spell for me, reaching over to grab my hand and slip it inside his shorts to cup his balls.

They were huge and hairy and sweaty in the afternoon heat, but they leaped magically about in my hand as though capering in carefree counterpoint to the driving rhythms of his dick and the salaciously slow striptease of his foreskin. Shane left my hand holding his balls and reached out to pull me closer against him. I smelled the musk of his sweat and the slightly gamey scent that makes untrimmed meat such a treat. Then he mumbled something by way of warning about what sounded like "Raingers" and pulled me after him into a crapper stall.

In a flash, he had his T-shirt and shorts on the deck and was kneeling on them, tearing at my trou like the starving young dick-dingo he was. Fortunately for him, I had come out free-balling because of the heat, so he had no trouble getting a faceful of my Marine nuts. I hadn't been bad in days, so my load was hanging low and heavy—and ready for just what young Shane had in mind. He licked the salt off my balls and moved quickly on to the thighs that flanked them, flicking his tongue about like a shameless adder even as his hands cupped my butt in overflowing worship.

The yearning desperation of his touch, the sweltering heat, the scribbled graffiti on the back of the stall door, and the feel of his brown curls between my clenching fingers all seemed at once surreal and the living definition of perfection. I looked down to prove to myself that Shane was no ephemeral delusion sucking at my nuts, but the real flesh-and-bone man I needed to start my liberty off just right.

Looking past his bobbing head, I couldn't see his bone, but I found plenty of tanned Australian flesh, stretched tight and hard across muscles that seemed sculpted in living marble by a whole committee of Renaissance masters. One muscle rippled deliciously into the next, tightening down to disappear at his hips and then flare back to life in a butt that ground and wriggled and thrashed about below me like a rudderless schooner in a typhoon.

As Shane stripped the trou down off my ass so his prying fingers could get seriously to work, I managed to ease my right shoe up between his thighs to rub his balls the right way and give his ass something hard to hump against. He made the most of getting the boot even as I used his curls to grind his face harder against my nuts with every self-satisfying slurp.

Good as his beard stubble felt grating along my thighs and fine as his mouth felt wrapped relentlessly around my aching nuts, my nasty little mind couldn't avoid the picture of his ass grating along the top of my shoe. I knew I had to give that tight Australian ass more to think about before it rubbed its way to a frazzle on my shoelaces and I exploded from pure horniness.

I stripped off my shirt and pulled Shane up off his knees so I could savor his lips and the lingering taste of my own crotch. As my tongue slipped between his full lips and met his, a helpless shiver coursed down his naked young body and seemed to ricochet through his loins. His big Australian dick throbbed against my belly as his hands tried to decide whether to worship my ass or the wide expanse of my back and ended up splitting the difference.

Shane's broad pecs were as hairless as they were perfect and as hard as his tits were swollen with promised pleasure. In the fullness of time, I let my lips and teeth drift low to caress the one and torment the other. Shane proved himself a slut by moaning low and loud at the first brutal touch of my teeth around his nipples. His body seemed almost to wilt in submission, yielding himself into my arms as I went to work sucking and scraping and chewing rapture out of his throbbing tits. When he could stand the abuse no longer, his hands guided my face into his left pit to fill my mouth and lungs with the lusty taste of aged man-musk. The harder I sucked and lapped and snorted up his savory scent, the louder he moaned and the more he thrashed and ground against my face like the trapped wild animal he had become.

Ages before I was ready, he broke loose and assumed the position against the back wall of the stall. He lifted his left foot and parked it onto the crapper to give me more room to work and then waited for the dick he knew was about to come his way. I was rubbered up in an antipodean flash but took a long, slow minute to admire the sweep and scope of his tight ass. Up close and personal, my lips blew against his quivering pink pucker, daring it to leap out and give me the kiss I deserved. His gorgeous glutes clamped shut and then flexed wide, at once desperate for dick and fearful his ass might not be man enough to handle all I had to give.

I didn't have any lube to fingerfuck him open, but he didn't need any. The instant my fuck-finger darted across his shithole, Shane turned his guts inside out to grab a good time and hold on tight. His tail wriggled and flailed around on my finger as goose bumps surged across his body and he growled something about "Bloody fucking yessssss." The whore kept on growling and cursing and grinding his shithole farther up my hand with every finger I slid his way. Soon I could feel the hard slickness of his prostate as well as the desperate determination of his sphincters never to let go. His whole body pumped up and down against my paw and promised that if only I would dick him deep enough, he would show me the best fucking liberty any young Marine could want Down Under.

I remember reaching around and jacking his dick for a moment or three—and relishing the slick hot streams of pre-cum that gushed out past the wrinkled lips of his foreskin to coat my hand until I might as well have been pumping away on a prize bull's pizzle. Shane gurgled something that may have meant for me to hurry up—or may have meant anything. Just then, I didn't much care what he felt or wanted or said. I knew enough for both of us: that it was time I fucked him like a stray dog in heat.

Getting my fingers out of his ass took determination, but his shithole wasn't empty for long. I gave his ass-crack a quick swipe of my dick hand to coat that tight tail with enough of his hot love-honey to lubricate a Panzer division. Then I slammed my big Marine dick between his slick glutes where it belonged and got busy.

Shane had thought he was ready. Shane was wrong. His body lurched forward towards the wall, half to regain his balance and half to escape the reaming my jumbo-sized joint was giving his guts. Even before my hands reached up to snag his shoulders and jerk him back down my dick where he needed to be, the gorgeous guy's body transformed itself. What had been tight, rippled muscle clenched up in uncontrollable agony knots of outraged anguish that cobbled his back and flanks even as my cruel Marine unit finished its brutal attack on his rear guard.

Almost at the same time my short curlies found his asshole and began to grind at them in the triumph of possession, Shane fell backwards off the crapper, impaling himself against my hips and ripping nine inches of rampant ruin upwards through his guts. My teeth dug hard into his shoulder to keep him in position as my hands moved to his pecs and my butt pulled backwards, jerking seven inches of meat out of his ass, only to put it back with a vengeance.

I'm usually a mean fucker, but Shane was so prime and foxy that I outdid even myself. From the first thrust up his ass, I started to lose control and was soon reaming and fucking and slamming away up his ass, banging his head into the far wall of the stall, and twisting his shitchute so tightly around my rampaging shank it's a wonder I didn't gut him like an elk. One sensation blended into the next, all more perfect than the others combined, until only a mingled maelstrom of delirium was left lurching through addled memory: the slick, sweaty smack of my brutal hips against his butt; the glorious stench of man-musk and sweat; the tight feel of his ass wrapped around my rod and his hands clutching desperately backwards at my butt; the flop of my aching balls against his; and the moans and jungle groans of men at rut.

Time seemed to fold in on itself even as our bodies shared a singularity of space-time and life lurched from paroxysm to convulsion and thence into seizures so sublime as to be beyond mortal ken. The next thing I knew, my teeth were grinding harder into the knotted muscle of Shane's sweat-soaked shoulders and my hips were still pounding dick up his ass even though my load had long since blown. I'd nutted so hard and long that my rubber was back-flushing, pumping my own thick Marine jism backwards onto my balls with every bone-bursting, butt-crunching thrust. I kept on humping that jism-hungry Australian shithole until my balls threatened to drop off and seek political asylum if I didn't show them some mercy. Even then I had to think thrice about giving up Shane's hole.

When I finally did pull out, he licked the lingering pre-cum from my hand and then lapped up the sweat streaming off my chest. He'd have done more if I had let him, but I needed a bit of a rest. I was on liberty, after all, not some Tara field hand trying to break some cotton-picking world record. I pushed Shane back onto the crapper and dropped my overflowing rubber between his legs into the drink. Then I wiped my dick across his bare, sweaty chest and licked up the leavings.

When Shane eventually pulled on his shorts, I figured he was ready to get on with his life—but I underestimated an Aussie's party potential. The kid hauled my ass up to Northbridge and then from one end of Perth to another. At every stop he found more of his friends for us to fuck until, a couple of days later, I had to come back down to Fremantle to haul some of my jarhead buddies off *Tarawa* to help me out. If you ever hear outrageous stories of what can happen on liberty in Australia, believe them. You won't understand a word you hear, mind; but that's okay. Conversation isn't always necessary to have a good time. Just don't expect to get any rest on your liberty Down Under. That's the one fucking thing you're *not* going to find.

MY NEW BUDDY

Marines on liberty want three things in more or less equal measure: to seem cool, to drink until they pass out, and to be fucked hard up the ass by a tougher Marine than themselves. If they can work a good bar fight in somewhere along the way, so much the better. Everyone in the Corps knows what his brother jarheads want. Most Marines' idea of heaven would be to be staked out and taken hard by every man in their company. The problem is that because they have to seem tough and cool and gungy, they can't let on how much they want to put out. My new buddy is a perfect case in point.

You'd think that a guy with a pansy-assed name like PFC Kensington J. Pottersworthy, USMC, would be grateful just to have a buddy to hang with on liberty. Maybe he was, but the first time we went out on libbo together, the bastard sure as shit didn't show it. He spent the first half of the night swilling enough pitchers of mojo to embalm a mastodon and then bitched for hours about how horny he was. In my 18 months in, I'd seen the story enough to know what was going on. The bastard wanted dick, but couldn't admit it. He would drink until he was nearly unconscious and then confess he'd fuck anything—even another guy. My part of the drama would be to take offense at being his bitch and then take my revenge up his ass.

Potts was definitely Grade-A meat, but I wasn't about to dance around his hang-ups all fucking night. Libbo time is just too precious to waste. By about midnight, I'd had enough of his whining and just said, "OK, boot. I don't mind giving it to you, but you fucking pay for the room and supplies." His jaw dropped almost to the table, but he trailed my ass out of the club faster than an Apache scout on a fresh mount.

We stopped by a 7-11 for a case of beer, a box of rubbers, and a can of whipped cream on the way to the motel. Potts paid for the works, but I don't think the horny bastard said a word the whole time. He acted drunker than he was, but I could see he was more excited than anything. His tight 501s got tighter by the second as his Marine unit eased its way farther down his left thigh and started to stand at attention.

I guess going in, I should confess that I'd planned to do Potts all along. He was new to the platoon, but I make it my business to spend quality shower time checking out all the new guys. I usually go for studly types so Potts' face with its brown eyes and delicate features was a little prettier than normally rings my chime, but his Marine-built body was strictly a Disneyland quality ride.

A guy expects his Marine meat to be in good shape, but Potts was something chronic. For starters, he had a thick thatch of blond hair across his massive chest and down the flattest belly in Pendleton. Standing tall through all those blond curls, his tits were always stiff and ready to wrangle and his ass was pumped with enough hard Marine muscle to shag out the Seventh Fleet. His dick wasn't as thick as mine, but was almost my nine inches long and looked postcard perfect and ready to mail. In short, Potts had all the other muscle you'd expect from a kid who spends his whole day on PT and more besides.

Aside from that big meaty ass of his—which you just can't say too much about—what really got me going was the contrast between his boy-next-door cute looks and the hardened-killer body it was attached to. From the day he reported, I tried to decide whether he'd be the kind of fuck that makes little squirrel noises the whole time my dick was reaming him raw or whether he'd fight back like a rabid Klingon with a bad attitude. In the end—where it all counts—he was a healthy blend of both.

He started out as squirrelly as they come, standing headlight still as I tossed our party pack onto the bed and got naked and ready for business. His big Bambi-brown eyes darted around the room as though looking for a bolthole or a clue. His dick was almost ripping through its denim prison by then, so I shoved the shit on the bed to one side and shoved Potts down onto the other. I wasn't gentle as I stripped him, but a few rips in his shirt and lost buttons would soon be the least of his problems.

He finally opened his mouth to give voice to his outraged virtue, but I put a quick stop to that—by shoving my hairy nuts into his face. I hadn't done anyone in four days by that point so my nuts were swollen hard and swinging low with enough sweet jarhead jism to satisfy a truckload of boot Marine PFCs like him. Potts sputtered and gurgled for a minute as I straddled his face and then knelt down, sitting on his face and pushing one nut at a time into his mouth whether he liked it or not.

He liked it plenty. At first he tried to lick the sweat from my nuts and chew on them at the same time, but he soon had his mouth so full that he was lucky to breathe now and again. I rocked slowly back and forth, grinding the rough beard stubble of his chin into my asscrack even as his nose played dodge with the base of my dick. My legs locked his head in position and kept it where it belonged—wrapped around my big, heavy Marine balls.

If his face was locked down, his hands were all over me from the get-go—sliding up my flanks and reaching up to pump away at my dick and, finally, spreading my asscrack wider so his fingers could slide in and play a naughty game of chicken with my shithole. He obviously hoped I'd let him slip a quick fingerfuck my way, but was too tame to do more than polish the outside of my poke-hole and pray for divine intervention.

His face felt so fine wrapped around my `nads that I was in no hurry to move. As the minutes passed, Potts' suction picked up and pried my load loose to start the long trip up into firing position. When, at last, his gagging started getting on my nerves, I kicked back beside him and let fly with the whipping cream, leaving a thick trail of that sweet, cool cream across my chest, over into my left armpit, and up my neck. The goof looked a little lost when I ordered him to lick me clean, but got with the program big time once his tongue skidded across my hard right tit on a slick layer of non-dairy love.

I didn't do much for the next five minutes or so but wriggle as his tongue and lips first cleaned me up and then sucked me dry. Potts couldn't keep his hands off me, but as he hoovered his face across my body, it was the way his dick always seemed to find somewhere new to fuck that felt really good. He poked that stiff jarhead joint into my belly and side the most, but also managed to rub my arm and legs the right way, leaving a trail of glossy dick-honey behind like some overgrown and undertrained snail.

Once that first trail of store-bought cream was history, I lunged at him and pinned his shoulders to the bed. When my lips first met his, he didn't seem much to mind; but as my tongue tore through to slide deep inside his mouth, he remembered his bearing and tried to object to anything uncool or the least bit faggoty. I just reached low to grab a fistful of his balls and squeezed him into line. He took turns whimpering from pain and whickering from pleasure as my tongue raped his mouth and showed him what kind of abuse a boot Marine on liberty could expect from a buddy.

His hard young body thrashed beneath mine as I turned up the tongue. When I changed holes and moved to his right ear to tongue-fuck his brain, the bastard went ballistic, squeaking and bucking and screaming and tearing fecklessly at my body with his hands, trying to desperately pry me off and hoping all over that he couldn't manage it.

I got gradually rougher as he deserved it, reaching back for his balls and twisting them with one hand while I pinned his shoulders with the other elbow—and, for good measure, sank my teeth into his left tit to teach it some manners. My big-tailed Marine gave more of his frightened little woodland squeaks and tried to scamper out from under me to prove what a timid little spermophile he was.

I grabbed his head and slammed my rubbered dick down deep, forcing his lips wide and ramming my bone home. He gagged and gurgled and thrashed about while I fucked his face hard, reaming my dick back into his throat and reveling in the chin stubble grating against my balls. I kept at him, prying his teeth wider and twisting my swollen knob deeper into his wet hole until I couldn't work his cocksucking face any farther up my shank. Then I let fly with the verbal abuse Marines crave as foreplay: He was worthless. He couldn't even suck dick without screwing the fucking pooch. No wonder the rest of the troops wouldn't hang with his ass—and speaking of ass . . . .

I reached down and lifted one leg up towards my shoulder and had my dick between his glutes before the boot knew which way the worm had turned. I hated to pass up a slow, quiet in-depth inspection of his ass, but that could come later —after it was mine. With one leg over my shoulder and his other stretched out, I was able to fuck his ass sideways and watch the show while I did it. I couldn't see his shithole, of course, but I didn't need to. My dick knows how to point towards tight jarhead tail the way a born bird dog locks on to quail. What I was interested in was Potts' pretty-boy face and how it would look when love struck.

I wanted to see those full, kissable lips curl back against his teeth in the classic rictus of the mute Marine scream as my dick slammed through his shithole and tore the living glory out of the first nine inches of his guts. I wanted to see those brown eyes of his twirl and bug as his brain shut down and his body discovered the depths a man can suffer. I wanted to watch each wriggle and grind of my grunt dick against his liver echo across his face in abject submission as I mastered his ass and made him my bitch and my fuck-toy.

I got what I wanted—and what Potts needed more than anything. If anything, reality was better than the past week of waking fantasies where I'd imagined his quivering butthole stretching taut as my knob and shaft rammed through into the secret refuge of his soul.

Things happened so quickly that they're hard to separate, but impossible to forget. I didn't dally as I dicked his ass open, but reamed right through, ground my shaft across his prostate, and pulled almost out again. The pressure changes as my thick pole-piston slammed up and down through his hole tore little kiss-like noises from his ass as the thick presence of my bone shoving his guts aside ripped first gasps of horror and then screams of delicious torment from his lips.

Potts' hands tore at my back, neither meaning nor wanting to push me away and lessen his pain, but desperately needing to stuff my whole body up his ass as though that were the only way we could become one being. His pain was intense. The beast filled every dark corner of his being and twisted relentlessly through his consciousness like a savage predator seeking the weakest of the herd so it could pounce and slash and destroy.

After the first couple dozen fuck-thrusts ripped wide his ass, agony was everywhere; but Potts' Marine mind captured it and made it his own. The searing, twisting, all-consuming firestorm up his butt slowly became his friend, a test of manhood to be welcomed in a modern tribal initiation that allowed him to prove to himself he really was Marine material. The more brutal and savage the torture that held him hostage, the faster he fell under the thrall of that terrible torment until the prisoner of pain became his tormentor's most frantic lover, caressing each ceaseless rolling wave of agony and lusting only for more.

Potts' mortal body shuddered in almost demonic hunger with every slashing stroke of my dick up through his shattered hole. Mindless moans of rapture and greedy prayers to half-forgotten gods alternated as his body tried at once to wrap itself around my surging shank and yet survive another slashing stroke. His slick guts were greediest of all, caressing my pounding dick and ripping loose the sweet fruit of anguish as my hips slammed harder against Potts' glorious glutes with every bucking, mind-numbing thrust.

I must have closed my eyes for a time as my body surged forever into his and let true consciousness evaporate into the haze of breeding bones and clenching muscle. Whether I ripped that tight ass wide for ten minutes or ten millennia, I know only that when my eyes opened to savor the tormented rapture scrawled large across Potts' fresh young face, the ecstasy written on those features was too majestic a story for any mortal mind. Like Lot's silly wife or the Gorgons' myriad victims, I could not endure the sight of my Marine buddy doing the timeless dance of love along my dick. My guts ruptured wide, spewing blast after soul-shattering blast of hot jarhead jism up through my breeder bone and out into the secret depths of that warrior brother's soul.

My body was as helpless and wracked as Potts' as we clung each to the other, desperate that our union never end and knowing well that we must savor the passing moment to the fullest. Inevitably, my balls eventually flushed dry and even our hard Marine bodies temporarily lost the strength and the will to rut on. We fell together in each other's arms, awash in sweat and exhausted by our brush with the infinite. We may even have slept for a few minutes before our bodies remembered their strength and we moved into the shower to clean up and start on our case of brews.

I used Potts four more times before we had to get back to base for morning formation. Just as dawn was threatening to happen, I slid my ass down Potts' dick and rolled back to let him tarnish my virtue at will. Like most Marines, Potts likes getting the dick better than giving it, but he needed relief so I was willing to help out a buddy in need, even if it was a pain in the ass. Fortunately for both of us, Potts was the quickest, happiest fuck I had ever seen—and I've seen a buttload.

By the time we went together back into the world, I think we'd accomplished enough for a first date. I'd nutted enough to make my balls burn. I'd proven to Potts that he was my little jarhead bitch. I had begun to teach him what being a man can mean. Most of all, though, I had shown him why there was no way our first date could be our last. If I'd enjoyed the living fuck out of Potts' ass, he found my dick the dictionary illustration of habit forming. For a first date, it had been a good beginning.

HARD MARINE TRAINING

When most civilians think of Marines, they picture us charging ashore on Guadalcanal or up Pork Chop Hill. Sometimes they have the idea we spend our duty time standing in front of the White House or *Marine One,* looking pretty, but doing very little of substance. The truth, as always, lies somewhere in between; but given the choice between throwing myself headlong onto the flaming altar of liberty and scoring duty where my prime job is to look nice, you can call me pretty-boy any time. Even in the rear, Marines can make a real difference. I think my duty billet during the Gulf War is a good illustration of what I mean.

While my brothers in the Corps were sweating their feckless asses off out in the Saudi desert, I was stationed at the US embassy in Bahrain. Because the Administrative Support Unit in Bahrain is also the headquarters of SouthWest Asia Command, my job involved a lot of fairly significant contributions to the national defense—of Kuwait—as well as air-conditioned duty with a weight room, two pools, and four separate bars. ASU and the embassy are both hidden away in a residential neighborhood called Juffair, presumably to confuse terrorists into thinking the compounds are kindergartens or something. Most other countries have big, flashy embassies in the Diplomatic Quarter or along the coast road downtown. Western diplomatic staff sometimes showed up in our weight room at ASU, though, or stretched out around one of our pools. Ever the good diplomat, I tried to make them feel welcome, even it if meant inviting them back to my room for a short, cool drink and a long, grand fuck.

I'd seen Jean-Pierre around before. He was hard to miss. One day around Christmas as the political situation was heating to a boil, I stopped to take his measure in the weight room and liked what I saw. We worked out together and ambled into the shower, talking about international relations and the other affairs of the day. Once he was naked and soapy, I slowly took his measure again and invited him back to my room at the Gulf Hotel. Since then, the government has built a BOQ, but until `93, Uncle Sam spent huge sums renting hotel rooms around town. I liked the hotel arrangement. In the new BOQ at Manai Plaza, you can't make a guy howl too loud or you'll attract a crowd. Hotel rooms in the Gulf are well enough insulated you could hump virgin camel triplets without anyone noticing except the bellboys—but how I kept the bellboys happy is a different story entirely.

I won't bother you too much with the patter I laid out for JP. If you've been in the service, you probably know the line: "Are you married? It must be hard to be here without access to women! We have to make do." By the time we were finished with our first beers, my palms were coasting across JP's T-shirt- clad pecs to encourage his rapidly rising tits—and his paw was wrapped hard around my basket. He gave me a long, slow smile and said, "I hear American Marines like to be hard fucked. What do you think?"

Still the diplomat, I pretended to misunderstand, telling him I didn't think that was true. Most of my buddies do, of course; but since I'm a top, that's as it should be. I certainly wasn't going to let some Frog civilian tarnish the Corps' golden image, however fucking foxy he was. We went back and forth, each trying to cap on the other. I explained that everyone knew Frenchmen were all raving queens; he came back with the news that Marines wouldn't know what to do if they stumbled across a real man. The more shit we talked, the stiffer our dicks stood until we both knew no sperm would leave the room unspewed.

Given the shape I was in and that I am paid to kill foreigners for a living, I was surprised—and obviously excited—when he turned rough. I love nothing better than a good fight to work myself into the mood. JP lunged at me, trying to pin me to the bed so he could sink his tongue down my throat. The silly bastard ought to have known better—perhaps he did and just liked being taken hard. In any event, I let him have his way with me for a long moment, just to make him overconfident, you understand. Then I rolled over and ripped the shirt from his chest and hooked a foot under his shorts to get them down. Once the battle was well and truly on, we wrestled like Greek Olympians—and probably with much the same prize in view.

After about ten minutes, JP began to flag. We had long since crashed to the floor amid overturned tables and chairs and were both sweaty enough to be slippery, but eager enough to be caught. JP thought he had me at last, but I reversed out of his Nelson and slammed the bastard to the deck, pinning him face-down and vulnerable as a recruit in a gunny's shower. After ten long, sweaty minutes of rolling about with a blond Gallic stud like JP, I had no trouble keeping my Marine unit standing tall and good-to-go. I kicked my leg over JP's thighs, took the briefest of seconds to admire his full, muscular ass and the balls splayed out between his legs, and then hove to.

His asscrack was so sweaty that even my thick nine inches had no problem prying him wide. He said something insulting in French and tried a bucking rear-guard action to throw me, but just ended up backing his tail up my Marine unit as I slammed it downward through his tight shithole and into the very center of his being.

Jean-Pierre was not a good loser, but he was one outstanding fuck. He howled like a Highland regiment facing a pay cut and pounded the deck in mock fury. As he called me every insulting English name he knew, he twisted and arched his body and did everything but send out for the Foreign Legion. I had him hooked like a carp, though. We both knew it—and both knew he was exactly where we wanted him. Once my throbbing dick was plowing through his tight furrow and twisting away up his guts for all it was worth, I pressed my hands into the small of his back and lifted my body far enough off his for a really good view of the action.

I hadn't noticed in the weight room how well-defined JP's back and lats really were. His broad, tanned shoulders tapered from one knotted muscle to another down to a waist dwarfed by the huge mounds of firm, flexing muscle I was busy spearing with all my martial might. I've always gotten off watching my thick dick slam in and out of another man's straining hole, but the view down JP's asscrack was a special rush—because I'd won him by brute strength and seasoned skill, because he was the single most gorgeous thing I'd done in months, because his ass responded like a Stradivarius to every stroke of my bow, and, yes, because I had fallen in love with his huge uncut dick and knew, once he had a buttload of my sweet *creme de marine* sprayed deep, I would show him how well a man could take what he dished out.

As I watched my swollen shank pound its smacking, slurping way through that eager French fuckhole, I gave him my full repertoire of strokes and angles and cadences. JP met every change in the program with a tightly clenched hole, slick guts that rippled along my rod like all the tongues of heaven's houris, and a greedy wriggle of his ass against my hips to breed deep-seated satisfaction. There were plenty of brutish growling howls and insults to my manhood, doubtless designed to make me use him all the harder, but I'd fucked so far into his French diplomatic channel that his every *cri de coeur* was Greek to me.

Once we were bucking together so fast that my bone was a mere blur of satisfaction, I eased my hands off his back to give him more room to meat my onslaught. My right elbow snaked around his neck and pulled his head back towards me so I could tongue-fuck his ear or nip at his neck at leisure. That brought him up off the deck enough for me to slam his body up onto my bed—both to spare my knees a bit and to use the mirrors along the wall. If anything, the rabid look of sheer, animal pleasure on his face as I rode him ragged was even finer than the sight of my bone reaming wide his studly, shuddering hole. His blue eyes shone like reflected beacons of satisfied lust, his long blond hair hung in sweat-matted tatters over his strong brow, and the full lips that had tried to kiss me were stretched wide in the most primitive, most abject, most sublime possible agonecstasy of the rut.

I kicked his thighs wider to give myself more room to ream and reached forward for a fistful of hair. As I roughly jerked it backwards, his chest rose into reflected glory, strong and broad, glistening with well-earned sweat and tipped by tits of iron that begged for my teeth. I used his hair like reins and my throbbing cock like a brutal crop to urge him forward, ever faster and harder and tighter. Soon, his mirrored image faded into the mist of rapture that enveloped us both as we charged forward, man and mount, heedless as a Cherrypicker at Balaclava of the shot and explosions all round about. The harder I rode, the thicker the smoke of battle grew until my breath stopped dead and all I could do was fuck. My very soul answered the bugle call to charge and half a billion little whip-tailed Marine rounds exploded upwards through my cannon to conquer that fine French ass and make its depths forever mine.

I would like to say I was taking careful notes of what JP and I had to say just then, but I don't think either of us was thinking clearly. I know I wasn't. By the time I was breathing again and had stopped my own lupine growling, Jean-Pierre's torso had collapsed onto the bed, though his ass was still wrapped around my dick where it belonged. I administered a few last fierce fuckstrokes and a savage male grind to put the seal on my conquest before I reached down to his leg and heaved it onto the bed.

That popped my dick out of his hole with a loud *thud*, followed at once by the wettest possible *smack* as it snapped up against my furry belly. I didn't mind the mess. I'd upheld the honor of the Corps—and had JP's gorgeous French horn quivering away, ready to play, just inches from my lips.

He was busy trying to suck up all the oxygen on the planet, so he didn't mind my casting an admiring hand across his firm, sweat-soaked chest and belly. His huge low-slung balls also dripped from our workout and smelled savory as the musk of Samarkand. In a way, I was sorry time hadn't stopped after all. I could have joyfully spent any number of eternities caressing and licking and sucking at that magnificent body. As it was, since I knew he would recover soon enough to give me trouble, I centered my attention on the glorious slab of Gallic glory throbbing away before me.

It was only about eight inches to my nine and had a smaller shank, but was blessed by the gods with a head almost half again the size of mine. More to the point, of course, was the huge French foreskin covering all but the very tip of his knob. His purple cum-slit smiled shyly out at me to say "Bon jour!" but I was long past the niceties of diplomatic small-talk.

I grabbed that lizard in a low chokehold and squeezed until his head was about ready to rupture. My nose went first, inhaling nature's greatest fragrance: the sublime scent brewed only in an active man's hot cocksock. He had overlooked stripping and cleaning his weapon during our shower, so there was at least a day's treasure laid by for me to loot: musk and sweat and a perhaps the merest dribble of some carelessly shaken piss aged together to make my heads swim. Jean-Pierre had recovered enough to start making noises, but I was too busy to give a shit. I liked him well enough, but I wasn't about to let him distract me from a more intimate companion.

When my tongue tip darted between those tender wrinkles and wormed its salacious way south, prying soft skin from the hard, smooth, purple pride that lay below, I felt his body stir seriously to action. Every flick of my tongue engulfed my taste buds with stingless honey even as the gossamer of his `skin seemed to dissolve into liquid sugar that made my ravenous mouth water all the more. That huge, sweet dick was a triumph of nature and deserved slow, reverent consideration.

JP's hand on my Corps-cropped head shoved downward, hoping to grind my face down his crank for a quick fix to his need. I wrapped a firm fist around his nuts, warning him that the Marines were still in charge. He eased up and let me have my way as I maneuvered atop him so I could slowly swallow his shank. I tried absent-mindedly shoving my dick down his throat by way of reciprocity, but he apparently couldn't be bothered to lick his own shit off a man's dick. Instead, while I eased myself millimeter by glorious millimeter down his savory shaft, he licked and tongued my asshole the way only a seasoned diplomat can.

By the time his knob was spit-polished and ready for inspection, my ass was awash in drool and something long and bumpy was teasing the living fuck out of my hole. I ignored that diplomatic maneuvering in favor of a frontal assault down JP's defenseless column. When I reached the bottom of that throbbing knob, I slammed my fist down into his soft, blond pubes, ripping his `skin from its station and leaving every tender nerve open to the brutal tongue-lashing he knew he deserved.

I went at him with my wet lips and cat-like tongue, careful not to spare the rod. Then I cranked up the suction and moved farther south, keeping his knob busy on the top of my mouth or in my throat until my nose was nested deep in his golden down and I could just hang tight for a moment to enjoy life.

We ebbed and flowed like the tide, back and forth, my face twisting along his throbbing tool, his tongue teaching my ass advanced French. Nothing shuts down my brain faster than a good ass-licking—unless it's the tangy taste and firm texture of uncut dick. What chance did I have when both of them came at me at once and caught me in a classic pincer action right out of Clausewitz?

If JP hadn't started moaning and thrashing around, he would have caught me off-guard again and shot his load to waste down my throat. Don't get me wrong. I wanted to sample some of his fresh French vintage—and intended to as soon as was convenient. I thought it only fair, though, that his first gusher be up my ass. Even as I was licking his dick, I relished the image of my hot Marine load frothing the inside of his guts, coating his shitchute with the kind of creamy good time only my USMC spooge can provide. Taking a man is fine, but having him carry your spoor around is icing on the cake. If that doesn't make sense to you, call me a pervert. I just thought I owed JP some turn-about and fair play before I slammed him into a coma.

I wasn't about to let him get the wrong idea, though. When I pulled myself off his dick and shit his face out my ass, I held him where he lay and worked his impossible dick up my tight hole myself. I hadn't been fucked in months and knew JP's monster madness would hurt like hell. Oddly, it wasn't all that bad. By the time I was easing up and down his shank and ready to let him bowl me over so he could actually make himself useful for a change, my Marine-built body had adapted once again and I was stroking along like the satisfied slut of creation.

Looking up at Jean-Pierre's face as he reamed me wide, I felt really good. The clenched jaw and brutal eyes told me he was having a fine time pretending that he'd tamed himself a United States Marine. We would show him otherwise very shortly, but just lying there taking everything the gorgeous stud could slam my way was relaxing in a knock-down, drag-out, no-holes-barred, bone-crunching buttfuck kind of way that is hard to explain unless you've been there. As he grunted and swore away in French, his sweat splashed down onto me, and I realized from the muskiness of his pits that he wisely didn't bother with deodorant.

I stopped playing with his tits long enough to sweep his hair out of his face and spread his butt with my heels. I had obviously primed his pump before he ever came aboard, so I wasn't surprised to see the earth move for old JP long before I had to call for corpsmen to patch my ass back together. I wasn't sure JP wouldn't need them, though. He huffed and puffed and spewed my ass full, crying out to *Jesus* and *Mon Dieu* and a whole wagonload of other French religious folk I didn't recognize. I bore down with every muscle up my butt and even reached up to give him a healthy cat-bite on the neck to keep him interested; but from the way he was twitching and howling and carrying on, I expect Jean-Pierre didn't much need my input. He was busy enough giving me his.

He kept charging away longer than the French have done since Napoleon's time, but when he finally unclenched his jaw and opened his eyes, I saw right away he was going to say something cocky and get himself into trouble. I picked his ass up and carried it into my shower. Ever the perfect host, I didn't want to shove anything down his throat he wasn't ready for, but if he thought I was going to let him fuck and run, he didn't know dick.

Sure enough, before either of us was clean all over, I was having to slam his head back against the title and wash his mouth out with my soapy dick. Once I added some protein to make the suds go down easier, Jean-Pierre just licked his chops and said, "Yes, Sir." Now if the rest of the diplomatic corps would be so pliable, international relations would be worlds easier. In the end, I worked out with Jean-Pierre about twice a week until Desert Storm wound down and I was transferred to my next assignment. We would almost always start at the ASU racquetball court for a couple of hard games and then go back to my hotel to make the loser's life interesting. Looking back, I'm sure Jean-Pierre must have thrown those games—both in and out of the sack. Nobody could be so bad at ball games and so good in the clenches. Obviously, he just craved all the hard Marine training I had to give.

DEAR JAKE

For the first four months of the *TARAWA's* deployment, I heard nothing from my roommate but how great his fiancee was and how happy he was going to be once we got back to civilization and they could marry. Personally, I thought Suzie was a shallow, pretentious bitch, but I had sense enough not to say so. Yesterday, she proved me right.

I'd come back from OPS over Iraq just in time to make chow, and was surprised not to see Jake wolfing it down as usual. The guy worked out so much in between flights—to keep himself good-to-go for Suzi—that he needed to take on fuel like a leaky B-1. When I got back to our stateroom, I discovered that not only was Jake not hungry, he was a world-class mess.

I found him sitting in his shorts on his rack, a *Dear Jake* letter crumpled on the deck at his feet and tears streaming down his face. I felt sorry for the poor bastard, but knew he'd be better off in the end. Meanwhile, I went over to sit beside him on his rack and try to buck him up as well as I could. I've never been especially glib when people have their lives ripped apart, so I just mumbled "Sorry, Dude" and reached out to give the back of his neck a comradely shake of sympathy.

If Jake had been feeling low to begin with, I opened the floodgates. He collapsed against my shoulder, blubbering like a child, his nose running, and tears washing down across his broad hairy chest. Jake didn't look much like a Marine Corps aviation hero and still less like his usual Chippendale-quality self. While I'd often admired what he had, I had enough sense not to put the moves on him. Somehow, though, sitting there with him looking like cat puke on the carpet and falling apart on my shoulder, I had never felt so turned on.

Call me a pervert! Maybe it was because he was so completely vulnerable. Maybe it was having his nearly naked body practically in my arms. Whatever the cause, my buddy Jake had my nine inches of Marine joystick inflating to do a vertical vector along the left leg of my flight suit faster than I'd have thought possible. Sanity demanded I get the hell off his rack, but he was such a fucking mess that I knew I had to sit there and let him wind down on his own.

Only he wasn't winding down. After I'd wrapped my arm around his broad shoulder and pulled him closer to commiserate, he stopped crying quite so much, but slipped into spasms of gut-wrenching sobs that made me wonder whether I should call somebody up from Medical to give him a shot. I knew how he'd hate to have his business spread around the ship, though, and held off for a few more minutes to give the poor sap a chance to find his bearing on his own.

What he found was a woodie of his own. I didn't notice it rising. I wasn't looking at his crotch, after all. By the time I saw the thing, it was impossible to miss—standing monster tall and threatening to rip through his briefs. I couldn't believe he was horny. Maybe it was my arm around his shoulder that made him remember his last run with slick Suzi. Maybe his body thought it wanted to be reamed out to make him forget his troubles. Maybe the gods do have a sense of humor. Whatever the reason, that big Marine dick throbbed away, counting down to trouble and I had a choice to make.

Only a real bastard would put the moves on a buddy who was falling to bits momentarily. Still, I had to do something. I couldn't have us sitting there forever with our dancing woodies while Jake sobbed my flight suit sodden. Ever the sage counselor, I reached out my free hand and gave his naked thigh a shake: "Dude, get a fucking grip."

He just sobbed the harder and bawled, "Look at my fucking dick. I haven't even beat off since we sailed, saving it all for Suzi—and now…"

I swear I wasn't trying to turn him on. I thought maybe the best thing I could do was play the situation for the ridiculous. I reached up and grabbed the cotton-clad knob pressing so hard to gain its freedom and started to say something about how even he was clever enough to bust a nut anytime he wanted to. I never got the chance. Jake moaned in abject torment as his dick throbbed upward against my palm and then shuddered slightly when it began oozing a sticky stream of pre-cum through the cotton and into my palm. The rest of his body, already wracked by sobs, gave a quiver that seemed to rattle his very soul and he blubbered, "Oh, God! I feel so… Rick, I know it's gross, but can I…"

He'd made my flight suit a mess and slimed my palm, but I wasn't so sure which was supposed to be gross—or what he wanted me to say. As it happened, he didn't need me to say much of anything. After a few seconds, he reached a trembling hand towards my zipper and had my flight suit open to my crotch before I could get anywhere near beginning to think.

His hand did the thinking for both of us, slipping inside my flight suit and up under my T-shirt to coast up across my tight, furry belly towards the stiff tits that had waited months for him without even bothering to hope. As he leaned forward slightly to get a fistful of chest hair and find my left tit, I snatched the shorts from his ass and gave his dick a hand.

The shock of acting to satisfy his need had stopped Jake's blubbering, but he was soon chanting "Oh, God! Oh, God! Oh, God!" as though only an incantation could work the magic his hard Marine body needed so much. Once he had a handful of hard tit, Jake redefined himself. The spurned lover in him died a sudden death, and a brutal, lecherous man-beast claimed its place. While one hand tore at the thick mat of rust-colored fur that lives across my pecs, the other snatched my T-shirt off and my flight suit down to leave me naked and at his deranged mercies. I let him have his way with me while I waxed his dolphin with one hand and cupped his huge tender nuts with the other.

When his mouth made a dive for my dick, I had to drop his nuts and clamp a paw around my knob to keep things kosher. If Jake had intended to gobble my crank for chow, he moved deeper into my crotch without a qualm—licking the thick, hairy base of my bone and lapping at my sweaty balls like a starving rottweiler with a fresh kill. Jake didn't seem much to care what he sucked as long as it smelled of sex so I decided I'd let him lap and suck and chew away for as long as I could stand the abuse. I even pushed his body backwards onto the bed and planted my nuts in his face so I could lean forward into his crotch and return the compliment. My mouth had no sooner wrapped around his left nut than the poor bastard started moaning again—only this time it wasn't the hapless moan of a dashed love, but the carnal, guttural moan of a feeding beast.

We rocked together, locked head to crotch, for nearly five minutes before I realized that his legs had spread, as though inviting me to see what he had been hiding up his ass all these months. My fingers slid down into his hairy crack, working his hard glutes wide as they went, prodding and prying towards the shithole the gods give Marines for fun. Jake's moans picked up both frequency and volume as I skidded a fuckfinger across his hole, playing chicken with his ass with all the heavy-handed action of a Fokker biplane in a MIG dogfight.

Jake's ass didn't want subtlety; it wanted action—and on its own terms. His lean hips arched powerfully upwards against my finger, scratching his ancient itch as my finger dodged and weaved, trying to escape the hungry pink maw that yearned for lean Marine meat. His teeth pulled at my nuts to distract me and, perhaps, to demand compliance, but I kept ahead of the game until his whole body bucked upwards against my hand. My fuckfinger sliced through my flyboy buddy's shithole in a swift, slick movement that left my nuts adrift in a gaping mouth and the tightest ass on the ship locked hard into heaven.

I finally decided to stop being a concerned friend worrying about what was going on inside Jake's jarhead brain. If he wanted something up his ass, I had just the thing. Almost before he could recover from the way my finger was twisting across the slick, hard curves of his prostate, I had my dick rubbered up and Jake's legs lifted towards the bottom of my upper rack. His feet locked there as his butt rolled forward, sliding his target hole into position and daring my ordnance to take it out.

I hesitated for a moment longer—not because I was confused. I had made up my mind what was going to happen whether Jake liked it or not, whatever it did to alter our relationship, whatever the Marine Corps thought about two of their Harrier jockeys fucking each other raw.

Now I hung above him, looking down as though for the first time at his incredible blue eyes and the glossy knot of black hair the Corps had left on his crown. His strong jaw and massive brow, his classic nose, and his eager kissable lips all called for a moment's admiration before I collected my prize and reamed his ass as raw as it deserved. A quick glance down across his furry chest and belly at the thick dick leaking love-lube into the mire spreading out from his belly button got me seriously in the mood to wrangle.

I looked down at his face one last time, halfway in love, and saw a tongue flick nervously across his wet lips but then he whispered, "Please, Rick—I have to know."

Just then, I wasn't sure what he meant. Just then, I didn't give a shit. I slammed my thick nine inches of mean-Marine joint through my buddy's shithole and sent him into a seizure that would have made Torquemada himself glow with the pride of accomplishment. Every nerve ending seemed immediately to explode as his body at once knotted tight around my dick and hurled helplessly up my shank to impale his virtue on the cruel altar of raw masculine need.

I slammed deep and quick and hard through Jake's guts, pounding a ricochet shot off his prostate and augering in somewhere up by his liver or pancreas. Whatever it was that bounced off the end of my dick shrieked silently out in terror and then flowed bravely back to caress my head in a semper fi tribute to the very essence of man.

Neither of us was much interested in specifics just then. Jake was trying to breathe—and not doing a good job of it. I was too busy fucking him hard up the ass to even think about mouth-to-mouth. That could come later, as I restocked my sperm-pods for another strafing run.

Meanwhile, I turned on the autopilot and let my dick direct the fire control. The relentless rhythmic in and out of our warrior breeding frenzy wasn't totally artless, of course. Now and again, I'd stay deep, stirring his organs with my muzzle even as my system locked and loaded to fire.

When I saw Jake's eyes open wide in delicious wonder, I pulled my dick all the way out of his ass to remind him what life would be like without me—and then slammed it deep and hard again to strain his shithole's ruins towards a breakdown of their own.

His feet soon slipped off the bottom of my rack and landed onto my butt, his heels stretching and prying at my crack—almost as though he dreamed he had a chance of getting at my ass. As my hips picked up their pace and rocked Jake's hole harder with every reaming thrust, I pinned his shoulders to the mattress and used my tongue on his face.

His lips tried to kiss mine, but I was in no romantic mood just then. I was fucking tail—hot, hard, tight Marine tail. Now that I had Jake just where he wanted him, I was determined to dick his ass until we both bled. The ancient crimson frenzy of the jungle fuck swept across my consciousness as I licked his salty cheeks and slammed my tongue into his ear, and soon I was amok and driving Jake towards any man's ultimate breakdown. His body bucked and twisted, hurling this way and that trying escape the agony and accentuate the ecstasy that every inch of my terrible shank was giving him.

Jake had long since surrendered, but surrender wasn't good enough. My body needed to consume his with absolute finality, to fuck it to jelly and then lick up the leavings. Tongue and dick locked into him, hole and hole, until there was no escape, no delay, no mercy—nothing but raw animal brutality.

One wave of relentless rapture after another washed across my consciousness, always rebounding with the next fuckthrust to crest to even more massive and miraculous heights.

As my hands and tongue and dick held Jake down and ripped his very being with a ferocity beyond mortal comprehension, my body finally exploded, thundering one laser-hot blast after another deep enough up into Jake's Marine guts to sear his soul forever.

Life and love and need and fear all spiraled together into the maelstrom, and I was swept away for a eternity that bred and bonded and fused us into the single being only warrior brothers can be. Like Achilles and Patroklos, we became twin shadows of the same perfection of spirit, two hard male animals who knew and answered a single call and were together consumed by its fierce, unutterable destiny.

Jake's eyes were tearing up again as I drifted back towards something approaching comprehension, but this time around he was driven more by awe at the possibilities that had opened up to him than he was worried about some transient and imagined grief. As I let my nine inches of hard breeder-barrel cool, he tightened his arms about my chest into a grateful hug and said, "Now I know."

Maybe sometime I'll ask him the full ins and outs of what he thinks he knows. Hearing him try to put the feeling into words might be interesting. Meanwhile, we have other ins and outs to worry about. *TARAWA* will be Stateside again in two months, but I don't think old Jake will be camped out at Suzi's door begging her to change her mind and take his ass back. Besides, in two month's time, who knows how much of his tight Marine ass he'll even have left?

BIG GUNS

Military deployments are funny things. On the one hand, each float is different in a lot of ways—the ports one visits; whether the bad guys are Iraqis, Iranians, Serbs, or whatever; and sometimes even the mission. On the other hand, the cold food and hot, cramped quarters, the uniforms and stupid rules all lend a sameness to time at sea until any deployment seems just like all the others. Time collapses into itself and a man can't tell last Tuesday morning from 1975.

Everywhere a man turns, he sees the ghosts of his youth, revitalized and restored by the ceaseless flood of hard young men who comprise the Corps. The haircuts and uniforms, the eager wide-eyed expressions and Marine-built bodies all conspire to blend one bulging bicep and goofy grin, one tight ass and massive set of pecs into the next until we really all do look alike and only a few really heroic figures stand out in memory above the meaty, muscled masses.

I realized all this yesterday afternoon as I stepped out onto the after gun deck and saw a Marine stretched out on his towel, lying like an especially satisfied lizard in the warm Mediterranean sun. That Marine, the living clone of PFC Tony Hammond, was naked but for his UDTs and the thick layer of sweat that speckled his powerful body. If you've never been in the service, you don't know how fine a Marine in UDTs can look.

They are officially diving trunks, but are worn as a "tropical uniform item" in lieu of trousers. Since no one wears underwear with the sublimely short UDTs, dicks and balls routinely dangle out of them and a Marine's huge bubble butt makes the khaki-colored cloth rise until nothing is secret but every glance becomes a sacred revelation. As I stood savoring the nameless Marine stretched out on the deck, my world warped back to my first deployment in 1978—and back to PFC Tony Hammond.

I had happened across him sunning on the deck, too—and lay down beside him to admire the view. I'd noticed him plenty in berthing and in the shower, of course, but he somehow looked even sexier covered by nothing but his UDTs and the sun-sparkled sweat oozing out of his pores. A Marine's ass is usually classic. We have flat guts and fine shoulders, but our asses sweep up off our narrow hips like suicidal balloons, determined to over-inflate until they explode in a paroxysm of meaty, martial muscle. A jarhead's butt swells high, but is rounded and firm, yet soft on the outside as a drifting cloud. Even when I was 18 and raw as an open wound, I knew what to do with a Marine's ass. Instinct, my dick, and boot camp had taught me well.

I took my time with Hammond, both to savor the ultimate conquest and because lying beside him in the Arabian sun was like drifting stingless on a golden sea of honey. I watched the rivulets of sweat ripple down his muscled back or drip from his flanks to splash into his towel. I admired his powerful biceps and strong thighs. Most of all, though, I watched his UDTs swell and darken as khaki cotton soaked up the sweat streaming out of his ass until his crotch was sodden glory that begged for my tongue without knowing it. Now and again I caught his eyes sweeping along my body and lingering on my ass, so I flipped over to give him a gander at my basket. Only about two inches of dick was hanging out of my shorts, but they kept him interested until I gave him a comradely jab to the shoulder and suggested we go work out.

Since we'd entered the Gulf, the gunners mates who maintained the Mount 51 gun turret had stood .50-cal watches. Mount 51 was always empty. We slipped inside and dogged down the door, tightening all 10 dogs so we'd have plenty of notice if anyone did try to disturb us. The heat had a palpable ferocity; the space was built to fit only one, but I didn't mind being shoved hard against Hammond's harder young body.

We slipped out of our UDTs and into each other's arms. For the longest time, we just stood there, our arms wrapped tight around the other, the sweat pouring from our bodies and dripping down between us as our dicks slipped together like eager eels. To this day, I can remember the sweet, salty taste of his sweat and the musk that wafted up from his armpits as my hands moved down his back to cup his perfect male ass with the reverence it deserved. As my palms slipped across those broad glutes on a pellicle of sweat, his young Marine body shivered with the delicious awakening of the beast within him, and he let slip a small squeak of such sublime sexuality that I wished the moment could be frozen in amber, as eternal as it was perfect.

Then Hammond sighed that long, drawn-out sigh a man makes when his deepest itch is about to be scratched, and I knew I was being selfish. It was time to move on. I slipped my face down to lick at his tits and chew at them lightly while Hammond wriggled and twisted and his hands tore at my head as though riddled with unthinking lust. I eventually worked my way to my knees to enjoy the long uncut dick I'd admired from afar. It wasn't the thickest dick I'd ever seen, but it was long and lean and in my face. It was heaven afloat. Even stiff and beating a frenzied tattoo against his bare, hard belly, that dick had enough floppy foreskin covering its head to crown him with soft, wrinkled glory.

His head peeked up through the russet wrinkles and oozed a slow, consistent trickle of pre-cum that overflowed the foreskin and drizzled down his dick in a sloppy disregard for Marine hygiene. Always eager to help a comrade, I began low—licking his hairy nuts clean and working upwards along his throbbing, bobbing bone. His crotch was thick with the aroma of man-musk and slick with sweat dripping down from above, but I didn't mind.

Today, I would make an eager meal of his nuts and lick him until he whimpered and begged to be fucked. In that distant, simpler time, though, even the heady scent of his musk and the texture of those low-slung nuts against my tongue wasn't enough to keep me from following Hammond's drizzling dick-dew to its source.

The crystal ooze stuck to the tip of my tongue when I drew it back into my mouth, coaxing out long, silken strands of dick-sugar that thinned as gravity tore the leavings from my mouth and finally broke, splattering the nectar back onto the root of its beginnings. I slurped at his sparkling stream, lapping it up like the dick-hound I had become until the outside of his bone was licked clean and I needed to go for the marrow.

When my tongue slipped between the soft thrum of his cocksock and the hot purple knob still nearly hidden from the world, Hammond's body gave another jolt and shiver and his hands slammed around my head, forcing my face down his dick. I locked my lips tight around the tender skin covering his head and let him push my suck-hole down his crank. Hammond needed it bad so I forgave his lack of finesse. I forgave the way he used my lips to rip his `skin back across his dickhead until it lay stretched inside-out along his shaft. I forgave the twist he gave my head to torque his tool against the back of my mouth. I even forgave the way his hips thrust forward, fucking his swollen knob down into the tight, tender tissues of my throat. My tongue needed to savor the taste of his tangy tool, to relish the feel and scent as my bumpy tongue ripped across his satin-slick shank and sucked up every rich atom of the refined masculine musk he had brewed there since his last shower. While I was doing all this forgiving, I sucked his dick until he popped the nut of his young life down into my jarhead gullet.

The process took a while, mind—but I don't remember it all now. Age has not dulled my memory of his long dick prodding down my throat or of the rich scent of his crotch or the way his hands tore frantically at my head, trying to ram his frantic, brutal rod through the back of my head. There was just so much going on, that my teenage brain couldn't handle everything and made do with small snatches of dick-sucking delight: his naked body rippling muscle and splashing sweat as his hips slammed back and forth, driving his dick deep; his swollen balls slamming into my chin as he reamed his Marine meat even farther yet down my throat; the feel of his ass in my hands as I held tight to keep from being fucked over onto my ass; and the glorious hardness and heat and taste of his surging uncut dick as it force-fed my face as though I were the very man-slut of creation.

Hammond was definitely in charge; all I had to do was bear down around his jarhead joint and suck up his creamy load. The heat and lack of oxygen made me even more light-headed than the scent of his crotch or the feel of his ass flexing away inside my hands. Years too soon, though, I heard his cautious murmurs grow to gungy Marine grunts as his dick exploded, pumping enough protein down my gullet to feed a Pakistani family of twelve for a month. If his body had been shuddering before, how he fell to pieces—his hips still twitching and heaving away, but his hands holding onto my head and shoulders to keep him from crashing into the kind of cosmic convulsions only a nut-busting blow job can deliver.

I played the good Marine and took care of my shipmate—*semper fi* to the end. Well, almost to the end, anyway. When I felt his cum-tube stop pulsing his load north, I pulled his dickhead out of my throat and let his hot spooge cascade across my tongue. An uncut dick that has just blown its wad is the touchiest creature known to modern science, so when my lips fluttered back up and over his still-swollen head, slurping and stroking across his exposed nerves on a layer of his own jism, I knew I would drop his ass flat. Hammond's body instinctively tried to do the foetal curl and slipped backwards against the gunner's chair before I was able to pin him solid enough to finish licking his bone clean. I even slipped my tongue into the tight smile of his piss-slit to dig up any shy stragglers; but once he was temporarily tapped out, I let his stiff dick slam back up against his belly while he stood to slide a snowball into his mouth.

He seemed to like his own jism—or maybe it was the taste of his balls or dick or the eager action of my tongue that made him purr. He was still sucking at air so much, it's a wonder he was able even to do that. I backed up and just admired for a minute or two. His gorgeously pumped Marine physique, the swollen tits I'd played with and the hard, hairless pecs that swept up from them, his natural meat and the randy chicken-delight look about his face were all such a rush that I was proud to have sucked his dick and chowed down his frothy load. Now that I had, there was only one more mission worth planning.

I wheeled his naked ass around and pushed his head down over the back of the gunner's seat so he wasn't wobbling about and his ass was sticking out where it belonged. My nose nuzzled deep between his proud Marine glutes, slipping as though on skates through the slick sweat and musk that lined the dark, secret crack of his ass. Hammond's body surged backwards, shoving his butt harder into my face as though he needed me to ram my whole head up his ass. First he had to find it—and keep his hole steady enough for me to take advantage of his warrior virtue.

When my nose skidded across his jarhead fuck-hole, his butt took hostages and demanded a ransom. My tongue paid it off, skipping around and darting acros his tight, pink pucker until we both needed for me to drill him deep. Once I had my tongue on his hole, he wriggled his ass, moaned once, and went straight into brain-lock. I kept my tongue busy, giving his shithole the same hard time I'd given his dick moments before, but I've had enough tongues up my ass to know that a Marine can never get enough. My lips locked solid around his hole to provide suction while my tongue flicked and fluttered and drilled up his ass. I was loyal until my jaw locked up tight, and I knew I had to use some other muscle. Then I pulled my face out of his ass and got down to business.

At the first feel of my hands on his shoulders, Hammond knew what he had coming to him. I heard him gasp and gurgle once and then his head reared back. I could see his jaw set, steadying him for the flash of pain he expected to portend yet another ecstasy. My thick PFC meat wasn't the kind of nine-inched dick a man could take without some trouble—especially not a tight-assed young PFC who, I discovered later, was virgin goods. If I'd known he had somehow slipped through boot camp without doing any more than choking down the occasional load, I might have been more gentle, but I doubt it. I was young and hard-charging and Hammond's tasty shithole was the dictionary illustration of good to go.

My knob was swollen so huge it took me about a dozen of my best butt-busting stabs just to get though the outside gates and another minute or two of twisting and shoving before I could ram my dick all the way home where it belonged. Hammond's body knotted up tight as a banker's fist, and that didn't make my passage to paradise any easier. In the end, though, Hammond got what he deserved—and I gave it to him as much and as long and as deep as he needed it.

I'd never felt an ass so tight. Even at the end of that first fuck, his tight shithole clawed at my dick, dragging at the skin of my shaft and pulling at my head like a Burmese rice picker with a run-away cam. His ass was hot and dry, but his guts were slick and clenched around my throbbing Marine tool with every soul-shattering thrust.

At first, all Hammond could do was gasp for air as though he were trying to shit out a baby rather than take it up the ass. Within ten or twelve minutes, though, his attitude changed for the better. His hard jarhead fanny started wriggling around my joint as it slammed deep. His hands reached back to cup my ass and pull my cheeks wide so he could dream of fingering my shithole. Maybe he thought I'd even let him do me deep as soon as I had nutted up his ass. Maybe he was right—but once I sank my shaft up his tight ass, I was in no hurry to let the worm turn.

By the time my hips really got going, we were both sweating so much our bodies kept slipping apart and splashing together with every sloppy, pounding fuckthrust. My hands left his shoulders and worked at twisting his tits for awhile before I had to hold his hips to really let him have it. His swollen glutes tore at my tool, clenching tighter as Hammond got with the program; and by the time my balls blew the first of many loads of my frothy jism up into Hammond's sperm-park, I'd managed to teach him the virtue of hard Marine workout sessions. I kept Hammond's ass full of my jism for most of the next four months—until he transferred to a new company at the end of the float.

I hated to see him go, of course. I've wondered from time to time in the years since, what happened to him. On the other hand, the nice thing about the Corps is that all those tight, muscle-bound asses are interchangeable. Hammond was fun, but easy to replace. Call me a slut to the Corps. As long as I have the Marines, I will be happy. Standing there on the after gun deck yesterday afternoon, watching that young PFC sweat, I realized he was probably only four or five years old when I lay down beside Hammond and got charming. We live now in a different world. I'd have to use a rubber to go up his ass. On the other hand, I am now a warrant officer—with my own stateroom. That means we didn't have to fuck inside the gun mount. As I took off my shirt to catch some rays and hunkered down beside the kid to learn his name was Anderson to get charming, though, I wondered whether our first fuck shouldn't be inside the gun mount. There is, after all, such a thing as Marine tradition.

FLIGHT TRAINING

I stopped working on my flight reports and looked up across the eighteen inches that separated Andy from me. The time had come to end the game of touchy-feelie we had been playing all afternoon. Life in the military is built around deciding whether a guy means what he says or is really hinting at deeper, more entertaining possibilities. There are more gay men in the military than you can shake a dick at, but until the Pentagon gets its act together, all a guy needs is one homophobic prick taken into his confidence to put a hell of a serious crimp into his future.

I was stationed aboard a certain LHA on its way to the Gulf when Captain Andy flew aboard with his Harrier squadron at Subic Bay. We were winding down our raj there and hauling the aircraft down to Singapore, so he would be aboard about a week for the transit and exercises scheduled along the way. I wasn't thrilled about getting a roommate. Roommates generally interfere with my after-hours R&R; but when Andy swaggered in, the usual bitches I'd been doing underway stopped being much of a concern.

Except for my dimples and his brown eyes to my green, we looked amazingly alike: over six feet tall, bright red hair, pug noses, strong brows and jaws, and power-packed muscles everywhere you care to look. Just then, I cared to look everywhere. A guy doesn't like to sound conceited, but you don't sail aboard Navy ships for years without knowing whether you have bait for the beast. I had it; Captain Andy had it, too. I had to wonder whether doing him hard wouldn't be the most fun I'd had since I'd stopped by my brother's dorm room the previous spring. In so many ways, Andy and I were brothers, too: both bound to the tight military family that breeds brothers by the dozens, both handsome and hard and ready.

When Andy slipped out of his flight suit and I discovered he was a freeballer, my internal queer alarm went off so loud Judge Crater probably heard it. For the next couple of hours, we sat at side-by-side desks while he blathered and I tried to filter through to the subtext—if there was one. He was a Marine captain. I was a Navy lieutenant (oddly enough, the same rank), so our positions in the pecking order didn't matter as far as who came and who went, if you know what I mean. Finally I gave up, looked into those amiable brown eyes, and asked, "Are you a top or a bottom?"

Marines are cute, but no one ever accused them of being quick. Subtexts aren't their usual bag. He looked at the racks in our room—mine on top and long since made, his on the bottom with the linen still stacked and waiting—and got lost between A and B: "The bottom is just fine."

This was going to be harder than I'd expected. Maybe he really was one of those straight Marines I keep reading about in Pentagon propaganda.

"No," I said with my version of a subtle, knowing smile, "Do you like to be on the top or the bottom? Most of you jarhead jet-jockeys seem to like taking better than giving." Frank talk finally got through the haze, but also made the guy blush red-pepper hot and stammer gibberish. Marines like being shown what to do—so I showed him.

I started slowly enough, reaching over to kiss his neck on the way to his right ear. My lips washed the blush from his face, but set shivers and gooseflesh in its place. He put his hand up, unsure whether to push me away or pull me closer; but when he brushed against my chest and felt my swollen tits through my T-shirt, I pulled my dog tags off and let my shirt follow them to the deck. Captain Andy was fascinated by my thick, red chest fur. I rose, rubbing my rough-textured pelt against his cheek, pulling his head against my breast until the racing cadence of my heart was unmistakable.

His broad hands slipped down from my shoulders to learn every inch of my strong flanks. When they instinctively drifted down, by easy degrees, to my khaki-clad ass, I knew he was a jarhead I could depend on for a thumping good time. The careless grating of his Corps-cropped head against my arms, the low puppy yelps of pleasure he was making as he nuzzled my pecs, and his scent of man-sweat all gave me the green light for stage two. Still, I couldn't help thinking that something about Captain Andy wasn't quite right. Most of my Marines would have had their legs spread toward the ceiling and their asses stretched wide for me by now. Andy fumbled about, seemingly uncertain, happy to let me have the con as he snuffled fecklessly around my tits.

I ordered all-head flank and pulled his ass out of the chair. His tags and shredded T-shirt joined mine on the deck so I could check out his set of hard Marine-built muscles. He wasn't as pumped as some of the enlisted grunts I'd done aboard, but they have dick to do all day but work out. Captain Andy was worlds more delectable than any other squid officer aboard.

Beads of sweat gleamed on his broad, tanned, hairless pecs. Hard, brown tits stood tall for the taking. His pointer-trim caught my fancy most of all, though. That's my pet name for the cute little fringe of fur clean-bodied men often have pointing dickward down from their belly-buttons. His was thick and tightly curled and leading just where I wanted to follow. When he'd changed out of his flight suit, I'd just gotten a glimpse of thigh; now I needed to fill my world with dick.

His did the trick just fine. Big men often have big dicks, but his was almost as fine as mine—and even more eager. Thick blue veins pulsed with expectation. Getting him naked had been a minor comedy; but once I plucked him bare, high drama began.

I tossed him backwards onto his unmade rack and slipped my face between his strong, unsure thighs. A unique mix of sweat and JP-5 fumes had cooked all day in his crotch until Escoffier would have turned from his tureen in envy. His hands held my head away for an instant, perhaps fearing what was to come; but the thrill of the moment and every macho Marine's hard-charging need to experience everything soon reminded him who was in charge. I started deep, slurping up one huge, low-hanging nut and then the other, sucking the savory sauce *du jour* from his wrinkled man-sack until I thought I'd never need dessert. I licked his thighs and the base of his glorious jet-jock joy-stick, working upward as it bounced hard against his pointer-trim and the lean warrior belly that lay beneath. I might be there still, snuffling along his shank like a harrier with a fresh, juicy bone, if a surge of crystal pre-cum hadn't splashed and sparkled against his belly, warning of the unlucky times in which we live.

If I couldn't suck his oversized dick until I gagged on his jarhead load, where should I go next? I could Trojan his tool and chow down—or shove my rubber-clad rod so far into his cute face that he'd have heartburn. His tits needed tweaking in the worst way. His full lips lay parted, begging in unconscious desperation for my tongue. The possibilities were endless—but, fortunately, he wasn't.

I didn't learn until later in the night that the asshole had been, until I came along, the rarest of marine meat: virgin. I might have enjoyed myself even more if I had known, but I just thought the bastard was shy. I don't blame myself for missing the signals. How could a jarhead get through OCS and flight school and then fly about with the fleet and *not* have his hole plumbed at least once? At least he had the good sense not to give me any trouble when I flipped his ass over and reached for the KY.

Captain Andy's jarhead butt was even better than most, firm and full and ready for all the fun I had to shove his way. Soft skin stretched taut over muscle that was hard and ready as coiled carbon steel; but, as my fingers slipped across the smooth curves of his Marine pleasure-mounds, his whole body writhed in schoolgirlish wriggles and that powerful warrior body melted in response to every delicious sensation of the moment. Those muscles stopped wriggling when my lubed finger snaked between them on the way to prying open his asshole. He locked up tight around me, desperate to have something thicker and longer finish the job.

One finger followed another, fighting against his frantic grip to make headway, until putting off the finale any longer would have been an act against nature. Fortunately for both of us, I'm a natural kind of guy. My dick was wrapped in rubber and greased for grunt in a hard-charging, light-speed flash. One hand lifted his ass into the air while the other forced his shoulders down against the mattress to provide maximum presentation. My thick nine inches found his pucker and dicked around with him for a while to be mean, sliding across his eager, quivering asshole, making him beg just a little more before he got what I had.

When I learned mercy and slammed into his hole, the reaction was well worth the wait. The magnificent bastard exploded forward like a shot—and would have made good his instinctive escape if my dickhead hadn't been swollen too big to get back out through his tight jarhead ass. Dick caught hard on the inside of his sphincters and they rebounded like a trampoline, pulling him back against my hips. I locked my hands over his shoulders to make sure his passing fear of the unknown wouldn't try again to overcome his deeper, more ancient need for dick.

By the time I was sliding outward again, Captain Andy had made peace with my presence. His cheeks were clenching tight along my crankshaft, his hands had reached back to cup my ass, and one masculine purr after another eased out into the night from between his lips to tell the world how he really felt about being fucked hard up the ass by the first Navy helo-jockey to come along.

As the sweaty smacks of my pelvis pounding into Andy's firm man-cheeks accelerated into a random noise akin to the patter of summer rainfall, his soft purrs and coos grew rapidly into the yelps of a young man having one very good time. My own grunts and growls were probably not far behind, but I was too fucking busy to take notes. His slick guts slipped insistently across the tender head of my dick, coaxing my crank to unheard-of thickness as it lured whole squadrons of whip-tailed kamikazes up from their hidden bases.

My lips tore into the back of his neck, slurping up his musk as they moved up across bare flesh and stubble to give his cute little ears a real licking. For a seeming eternity, I was content to suck and nip at his lobes, happy with the shivers that shook loose his muscular bedrock and sent him reeling. My tongue finished the job, twisting far into his ear as quickly and furiously as a vicious rumor, wreaking havoc in its path. I had his humpy body hooked fore and aft and was using it the way a cur dog would use a pedigree-bitch when I realized the one thing I was missing. I wanted an up-close-and-personal view of his face while I nailed him hard. Captain Andy needed to show me how much he liked being fucked by my thick naval dick.

Rolling his ass over didn't take a second. By now Andy was following orders like a Benedictine bootcamp. As though from long practice, his feet hooked onto the underside of my rack, rolling his hole upward into perfect position for me to finish using it the way any Marine hole deserved to be used. By now his eyes were worth watching—sparkling bright with that tell-tale glow bred of fuck-friction and the knowledge that he was having more fun than he could think about at one time.

The change of position also meant his lips could stretch upwards to mine, eager for the kind of reward his ass was earning with every nine-inch injection. Our tongues met and slipped apart again in the heaving give and take only two men locked together hook and tail can know. I felt his hands clawing at my back, pulling me down against him as he slipped towards the abyss that had lain hidden for an eternity within him, secret and sublime, like some black hole at the center of his being.

My crankshaft switched into overdrive, twisting new paths through his dick-demolished asshole with every savage stroke. My cadence quickened until the piston-fed flinches in his face subsumed into a prolonged seizure of satisfaction. Captain Andy's strong marine jaw slackened against his own selfish animal need to feed off more and more of my fuck-friction. His shithole was already bearing down so hard onto my rubbered root that spontaneous combustion lurked just ahead.

About the time my ballbag finally clenched up enough to stop slamming into his ass, his prostate must have popped like corn in a campfire. Those baby browns rolled back into his head, his legs and arms all flailed about in opposite directions, and that mean-Marine mouth twisted into blasphemies that would make even a congressman blush. By then, though, my own ream-rhythm was just as out of control.

My head remained stoically on station, hovering a foot above Andy's, recording his tortured face with some small fragment of consciousness; but my hips were long since amok, driving my dick deeper and better with every convulsive, grunt-loving grind.

I think Andy must have seized up first, because I felt every muscle in his ass clench solid at once. His arms clutched tight about me. Those delicious brown eyes slammed shut to discover the awful ecstasy that lay within. My time came a stroke later—and a stroke felt just like what I was having. This wasn't any ordinary buttfuck; what Captain Andy did to my dick was Nobel-quality physics. Whether because of the heat or the selfish grip his grunt guts had on my crank, my dick didn't just shoot sweet jism—it fucking exploded out through the top of my head until I knew for sure I'd fucked up a nut.

My hips bucked and heaved and pounded and ground until, when his good time was over, Andy reached up and clamped his hand over my mouth to shut me the hell up before we drew a fire party. By that time my balls were flushed dry; I'd pumped everything I had up his ass, but just didn't have the couth to call the end to a good thing.

I shut up all right, and managed to get my breath, but pulling out of Andy's ass was almost impossible. Not only were his hands and feet still wrapped tightly around me, but I'd developed the cramp of the century in my right leg. By the time I untangled our bodies, the cramp had made me lose my balance and splash down into the jarhead jism Andy had sprayed all over himself.

After taking my load, any normal man is happy to coast and cuddle for awhile to recharge his batteries before I slam more satisfaction out of his ass. Captain Andy was no normal man. His limitless need for dick was extravagant even by Marine standards. The slut just couldn't get enough, pestering me to do it again until I wondered how much more flesh I could rub from my bone.

When I finally begged off, he begged even louder, confessing that he'd been cherry until I came along. Shit, I had to do the decent thing and reconsider. Andy flew five missions in his aircraft during the next week; I lost track of the ones we flew together. After all, he was now my hard, lean warrior brother and we had a lifetime of love to cram into a few short days.

We did, too. Oh, sure—sometimes helping out a hunky shipmate can be a real pain in the ass, but then sometimes the hunky shipmates don't mind that at all. We all make allowances for family.

CAUGHT IN THE MIDDLE

That second day of my port visit to Abu Dhabi, I more or less talked myself into staying in my room and resting up. I needed it. The night before, I'd left the ship intending to find a young Marine to help share my hotel room and several well-packed loads of naval jism. Three Marine amphib ships lay tied up just aft of my carrier at the dock so finding a grunt to hump would be no problem. I suppose I figured deep down that since I had been flying missions against Iraq for the last six weeks and they'd done dick but float around in the Gulf jerking each other off, they owed me. On the other hand, I've never needed a reason to drill a tight Marine hole. Marine butts come with a reason to be fucked built in as factory equipment.

As it happened, though, I had gotten sidetracked by a cute little Arab sales clerk who wanted to do his part for the war effort. I didn't want to seem ungrateful so we'd gone through my entire rubber supply in eight frenzied hours; and by the time he limped out to greet the dawn, my dick was suggesting I try holy orders. At noon when I got up to drain it, my joint was well on the mend. I woke at five, healed, hungry, and horny. Time had taken care of the first; room service took care of the second. Yeah, I figured as I leaned back to let obscene amounts of hot hotel water stream down across my naked flesh for my first real shower in six months, now that I had rested and fed, the time had come for me to be really bad to the Corps.

The city was positively pullulating with Marine muscle by the time I ambled out to find adventure at sunset. Strolling the few blocks to the souk, I ignored the stock running in herds as too hard to cull. I sat for a time, slowly drinking a Pepsi and trying to decide whether to take home a lost-looking, well-shorn lamb I saw looking through pirate cassettes in a stall across the way. He was cute and fresh and hunky in a blue-eyed Marine way, but I watched him snatch up an MC Hammer tape as though it were the very Grail and decided I would keep looking. As so often happens, some passing god must have approved, because two young Apollos magically materialized at my side. They were alike enough to be brothers and gorgeous enough to melt marble. I had found my fun for the evening— warrior brothers far from home.

I don't generally go in for a *Marine a trois*. The Corps bonds men so close together that however much fucking fun they are, you always feel slightly a fifth wheel or visiting distant cousin afraid to ask why Uncle Jack is tied up in the basement. Ken and Luke were a pair of lance corporals good enough to make me break my rule. Kenny was an inch taller, at about five-eleven, and had green eyes to Luke's hazel, but both had worked their bodies into a classical perfection you seldom find even among Marines. Both blond and tanned, they looked so earnest as they cleared their throats and started to launch into their question, that I'd have done them on the spot. More to the point, something wholesome and uncomplicated in their natures proclaimed with a glance that they were really nice guys underneath their muscle and *Freshmen*-coverboy-quality good looks. They were, in short, the cream of the Marines—and if you've ever milked from that herd, you know how very thick and savory that cream can be.

Ken was clearly the dominant male. As Luke hung back, Kenny asked in a rambling sort of way whether I knew of another souk beyond a winding white overpass. He rambled on at tedious length describing the place, but I was having so much fun watching that I let him go. What they wanted was two blocks away. I could have given them directions in seconds and sent them on their way, but am I heel enough to send two American fighting men off to risk adventure on their own in an alien land? I tossed my Pepsi can into the trash, stood up, and told them with a grin that oozed charm about how I just happened to be on my way there now. Why didn't I show them the way? I chatted with Ken as I aimed them by easy degrees in roughly the right direction. A pharmacy appeared in our path, so I made the most of the chance, going in and buying two dozen rubbers. I like to think big.

As I expected, Ken tended to take point so I had no trouble hanging back to chat Luke up. After a few preliminaries, I used my best off-hand manner to observe in passing that since Ken was taller and had a killer basket, Luke must have found him hard to take. Shit, I went on as I waved my bag of party favors, I'd probably split his butt wide open. Still, if they felt like chancing it, I had a room at the Centre Hotel where they could spend the night if they wanted. Luke stopped stock still as I started and shot Ken a look. Were they that obvious? How should he react? Did *everyone* know? But Ken was just out of ear-shot, so it wasn't until I delivered them to their destination that my scheme could hatch.

I'm good stuff so I was fairly sure Luke and Ken would confer and Ken would decide spending a night of sin with his best buddy and a handsome stranger in a five-star hotel room wasn't a bad idea. I was right. I'll save you the details of the next hour. We shopped; we chatted; we went to my hotel for some $5 beers—and ended up naked in my room after one round.

Another reason I'm not big on threesomes is that one never knows where to start. I pushed the guys backwards onto my bed and told them to plow ahead as they always did; I'd join in when I was ready. Meanwhile, watching their hard Marine bodies at work would entertain me just fine.

Luke went for Ken's crank with an earnest relish bred of affection and continuing practice. I interrupted with the idea that since I was strange, maybe we should all use rubbers—whatever they did when they were working out aboard their `gaitor. Marines do take direction well. From the way they played with my cock-cowl, you'd have thought the kids had never seen one before.

Ken, lying back on my pillow with his arms folded behind his head, got off almost as much on my watching Luke at work between his legs as he did from the feel of his mate's mouth sliding up and down his hard Marine meat. Even from my chair, I could see I'd been right about Ken's cock: it was only an inch or so shorter than my own cruel nine inches, and nearly as thick. Luke took it like the trooper he was—to the hilt. When I saw Kenny's mouth start to gape open and those cat-green eyes of his slide blissfully shut, I knew I'd better get with the plan or all I'd have to show for the night would be a pile of grunt-filled rubbers. The question, though, was still where to start. I liked them both, but for some reason, even with his butt in the air as he sucked Ken's cock, I don't think Luke did quite as much for me as the leader of the band. Maybe I was partial to Kenny because he's more like me: green eyes, thick fur on the chest and belly, man-sized dick, and a what-the-fuck attitude that means I'll generally try anything once.

I slipped my fingers along Luke's tight fuck-trench as I walked by, and had to admit the soft skin atop his hard butt felt just fine. His ass did a little wriggle of appreciation as my fuckfinger found his shithole, almost begging me to do him right then. I continued up along his hard flanks and reached below to feel a bare, hard tit crowning a pec that would have done any body-builder proud. He was busy enough, though, I was sure he was having a good time. Poor Kenny was just lying there, neglected but for his dick. I made a show of stretching the rubber around my throbbing dickhead and working it down my joint before I hopped onto the bed, my knees straddling Ken's chest so I could shove my thick Navy dick down where it belonged.

I didn't bother with waiting for the usual tongue action. I'd done enough grunts to know they kept foreplay to a minimum. My rubbered rod slapped Kenny in the face a couple of times, as though to show I felt we were all fuckflick material. Then, as those slutty green eyes of his glowed bright, I slid my healthy joint of meat into his scrutable archaic smile and deep down his throat. For an instant I thought he was going to gag, but the trooper held his ground—and my root. I felt my hips give a little twist of contentment as my dick hollowed out a home in the soft tissues deep within Kenny's neck. His head was nearly buried in my crotch and, hence, lost to sight, but I reached back to play with the thick blond thatch on his chest. I alternately tweaked his tits and grabbed great handfuls of his soft fur to use as reins while my butt, clenching in a dick-driving reflex, drilled my dick harder and deeper into that beautiful Marine face with every fucking stroke.

I'd almost forgotten Luke, bobbing along behind me like a pump handle, but when my ass started bouncing off his head I made the most of the experience.

Soon my ass was rubbing the crown of his head, snatching shocks of his hair or grinding it against my butthole as I cinched up and drove dick deep down inside Ken's talented facehole. Fucking back and forth between the tingle on my ass and the tight heat that lived deep inside Ken's thick Marine throat, I think I could have gone on forever.

The gurgles beneath my loins told me my Marine fox wanted to breathe, so I eased out for a moment and improved my position. Now facing Luke, the curve of my dick fit Ken's throat better and I could feel my low-slung ballbag dragging across his face with every stroke. When my hands needed a change from the glorious feel of Ken's chest hair, I reached down to play with the tail wagging just beyond Luke's eager cocksucking head.

Luke was a born slut. My fingers had no sooner started sliding down his spine than he knew I was going for his butthole and tilted his ass as high as he could to give me more tail-room to play with. Both the boys had typical Marine butts—thick mounds of manmuscle that bounced and bobbed with a verve that shouted out raw animal sex. Their bulging arms and powerful chests and flat bellies are always fine, but I've always though Marine asses must be the gods' special gift to mankind.

When my right fuckfinger found Luke's asshole again, his butt climbed upward until it hit hand. Then, as he worked on Ken's crank, his ass torqued and twisted and tightened, using my finger to stretch his shithole, almost as though he were an Olympic buttfuck warming up for a championship match.

You see what I mean. There was just too much flesh and I had too much bone to keep still. The tight yearning of Luke's jism-locker needed satisfaction; anything short of doing him deep and quick would have been inhumane.

Ken was turning blue when I unrooted his face so he took a few minutes to gasp and pant, but that doesn't mean he didn't keep those green eyes glued on the action between his legs. I hopped off the bed and drizzled liquid lube down Luke's fuck-crack and along the length of my latexed lizard. I'm one considerate kind of guy. I even reached down for a fast feel of his naked, throbbing dick and to give his heavy nuts a quick squeeze of affection before I reamed him senseless. The vision of Luke's head lashing his buddy's log while his ass lay open for business, the sight of Ken watching and grinning like a loon as he lay staked out on my bed, the sound of heavy breathing and the soft, sweet slurp of cocksucking, the sodden smell of man and musk and sweat and sex in the air—a hundred sensations melded together as I parked my breech-bore against the pink buttpucker that pulsed with a fierce hunger between Luke's glorious glutes.

Ken almost drooled. He'd been in my place often enough to know what I was feeling: half lust, half excitement of the rut, half thrill of sexual conquest, half dominance over another man. That's too many halves, but then sex never does add up. I'd worried about Ken being possessive, but he was a bigger horn-dog than Luke. While his buddy was sucking his dick like a fiend, butt up and ready, I saw his Mona Lisa smile sneak back across his face just before he mouthed the words so Luke wouldn't hear: "Fuck the bitch hard."

Navy lieutenants follow orders pretty well too, even from Marine lance corporals. Luke's butthole had been nibbling my dick like a Chihuahua pup on the end of a mastodon steak. He wanted it bad. That's how he got it. I'm generally a considerate, laid-back kind of dude. All three of us knew, though, that consideration wasn't wanted. Luke needed to be used—and used hard, partly as a break from the same old dick, partly to prove he was attractive to other guys. Ken wanted to share, but needed to know I wasn't making love to his mate—I was just fucking him up the butt. Although I didn't belabor the point at the time, the glorious display of Marine muscle below me had pumped my `nads more than anything in years; the primal sexual savage that lurks just behind the tenuous veneer of civilization we're all so proud of wanted to ream those two beeves until they bleated.

I took Luke's waist firmly in hand so he wouldn't ricochet off the wall when I did him. I couldn't see his face, so I did the next best thing and kept my eyes locked on the greedy green windows to Ken's soul, watching every cruel flicker of satisfaction as I slammed the nine thick inches I know best in the world up his bitch's butt. Ready as it was, Luke's shithole couldn't handle what I had to offer. Nobody in the room was going to let a little discomfort get in the way, so I rammed full speed ahead. His paper-thin sphincters stretched impossibly tighter and then somehow scraped their way across the throbbing, swollen brutality of my knob until, cresting like a victorious Channel swimmer, they caught their breath on the far side of my trigger-ridge. Then came the long, bumpy slog down my log. I felt tight, hot flesh sliding around my joint and saw Luke's head leap off Ken's cock to bellow like a stuck bull. Ken reached up, laying a caring hand aside Luke's cheek, that belied the vicious look of triumph in his eyes. He kept his hand in place over the next several seconds. Long after I'd begun to gnash at the ruins of his buddy's asshole with my stiff red curlies and the need to show his love had passed, he asked in a self-satisfied, mocking tone, "Whatsamatter, Marine? Can't you take it?"

By then, of course, Luke proved what a tough little trooper he was. His guts were rippling along my crankshaft, driven more by the frenzied confusion of sensation than any conscious desire to do a good job. Almost at the moment I hit bottom, I saw gooseflesh sweep across his body like a breeze through a wheat field, gone almost as soon as it appeared, but marvelous and unmistakable in its passage. Luke's cocksucking slurps were replaced by moans of amazed contentment as his butt wriggled slightly on the base of my bone, as though scratching an itch buried nine inches up his guts.

When I began sliding my member up from his depths, the moan was replaced by an almost subsonic, grief-stricken groan that mourned the meat he was losing. My partner in pleasure sounded like a goatsucker with a sore craw, but I had no pity. My piston lifted faster with every inch until my corona caught, *slam*, against the innermost rim of his butt-muscle. Then I heaved back downwards, forcing a breath-robbing grunt from Luke's lungs. My hands had loosed his hips and were sliding along his flanks, exploring his massive chest, and, in a gesture perhaps dictated as much by amity as need, reaching down to grab and hold his shank while I did him harder and faster up the ass. Ken's throat had been so hot and tight and fine, I wasn't sure how long I could make my first load last.

Ken had ideas on that himself. Once I was slamming my hips hard into Luke's ass, I made the mistake of leaning across his back to nuzzle his neck and suck on his ear—partly because I wanted him at least to believe I didn't see him strictly as a piece of meat to be used and abused, and partly because I get off on sucking while I'm fucking. I guess maybe that makes me—*both* oral and anal-retentive, but I've never seen the point in hiring a shrink to find out. Ken used my diversion to his advantage, sneaking behind me like the back-stabbing bastard he was about to become and shoving his mammoth Marine prick where he thought it would do the most good.

I'm a top, not a bottom. When that thick dick broke the bounds of bias and made me the very man I love so much to make, I lunged forward and nearly fucked Luke's brain out through his nostrils. Prejudiced as I am against having my butt torn up, I have to admit Ken's cock felt fucking fine. Before I had recovered from the first, frenzied seizure that gripped my guts as they tried like hell to get out of his way, I felt his hands on my shoulder and his hot breath in my ear. He mirrored my vicious, butt-rending fuck-thrusts with his own, sliding up my ass whenever I slid out of his bitch's. His hands gripped my tits and twisted as I ground my chest-pelt into his buddy's back, rolling my hips up to drive my point home harder with every gut-wrenching Marine assault up my trench. When our cadence corresponded and we were locked together forever, a trinity of savage animals at rut, Ken started talking shit in my ear—growling, really: "You Navy flyboy shit. I'm gonna fucking blow you so full of Marine cream you're gonna need a fucking fire hose to come clean."

As he'd deliver an especially wicked thrust and send me into orbit, his voice would echo the special triumph man knows only when he's breeding. The harder he fucked me and the harder I fucked Luke, the bolder his bravado became and the more I knew I belonged to them both. Marines can be a very close group. Kenny was talking shit like a teamster with a blistered butt, but his invective was music to my ears. I was accepted as one of them. I could have slid back and forth between those two studly Marines, connected by meaty monorails of prime-quality U.S. government dick, forever. I could have. I didn't.

Between the tightness of Luke's butt and his heaving and grunting and moaning and the racket Ken was making in my ear—not to mention the thousand indescribable sensations bred by Ken's Marine cream-machine up my ass—I was a gone goose. Or goosee, I suppose; with limbs and bodies intertwined and slamming away, I didn't set gooser from goosed, master from slave, victor from vanquished. One minute I was stroking along in heaven, the next minute the joint exploded.

First it was my joint, then Ken's went off as soon as I spewed sperm and instinctively seized up my butt around his bone. Together, the two of us fell forward onto poor Luke, nailing his body to the bed. The meat up my ass made every sensation seem to last forever; I blasted and heaved and reamed cream until time itself seemed to lose its meaning and the universe was one intermeshed mess of muscle and mayhem. It was, in short, fucking awesome.

As we all ran out of steam (among other things), I looked up at the clock and saw it was only 2015. We were going to have a long, nasty, very busy night ahead. I tried to catch my breath, caught in that epic pile of bodies, and smelt our mingled sweat and felt our shared body heat and knew the meaning of contentment. We slid off Luke, only to discover the slut had left a puddle of spooge on my bedspread while we weren't looking. Naturally Kenny and I made him lick it up before we headed to the showers to hose down—again. Luke and I got our revenge on Ken, showing him what interservice cooperation can do to fuck somebody up hard. I expect we gave something of a thrill to the waiter who brought up our six-packs of beer and found us all hastily more or less wrapped in towels, standing in the ruins of the room.

I was too busy to notice at the time, but the things we got up to that night and over the next two days were the dictionary illustration of how fine sex can be.

IN A PERFECT WORLD...

Desert Storm was a blast—in a lot of different ways. I don't imagine the poor troopies camping out in the dunes for weeks on end had much fun but I know we pilots enjoyed the living fuck out of the war. Just launching off a carrier with two jet engines up your ass is a rush. The way that movie "Top Gun" described the thrill a pilot gets in his guts as he slams into a steep climb or inverted dive was dead on target. The truest line in the movie was where one jet-jock said he was having so much fun, his dick was hard. A lot of guys I know get hard every time they go up. Early on, I started freeballing under my flight-suit just so no shorts would cramp my nine inches of style. Half the time when I climb out of the cockpit, my dick is so uncontrollably pumped, my flight crew drools as I do my flyboy swagger across the flight-deck.

Last night, as I slammed off the *CARL VINSON* flightdeck on my way to bomb missile installations in Iraq and lose a load of my own while I was doing it, I couldn't help thinking back two years to the war and my last Gulf deployment.

When Desert Storm started, *everybody's* dicks stayed hard. Not only were we doing what we loved most—well, almost—but that was the first time we were actually getting to fire all those neat toys that each cost as much as a congressman. I suppose we shouldn't have been so gleeful; the guys on the other end of our lasers were dying in very nasty ways. But when you swoop down on a hardened hangar or let loose a Maverick at a column of tanks, you only feel good watching destruction zoom inevitably in on your target. Once the war started, I was in fighter-jock heaven.

The first thing I usually did after a mission was stroke into the head to pump out a load or two of thick, prime quality, US Grade-A flyboy spooge—unless I'd already done it inside my flightsuit. Sometimes a quick monkey-spank would help—for about twelve seconds. Then I'd head for the shower and see other guys in the squadron stripping off their sweat-soaked flight-suits and washing their dicks. The shower stalls have plastic curtains, but you know how much they hide.

Hitting my rack, one deck down from the flight-deck, was a waste of time. As if the jolt of the catapults and deafening roar engine thunder weren't enough reminders that other guys were getting to fly, the ship's 1-MC blasted out the Lone Ranger theme every time another sortie launched against Saddam and my unit launched against my belly.

Heading up across the Gulf from *CARL VINSON* the other night, I savored one night two years before when I learned what war was really all about. I landed aboard *RANGER* about 0430 after a long night in the air and headed for the usual workout in the showers. The ship was quiet. I stripped off my boots and flight-suit and realized I needed to tap a kidney before my slick-down.

I was standing, stiff dick in hand, using the pisser when my eyes wandered over to a mirror reflecting the showers behind me. Only one was occupied, but the frosted plastic curtain didn't hide the lizard-lashing that was going on inside—or that it was Chipmunk dick in action.

My roommate's name is Charles, but they've called him Chip since high school. When he started flying and needed a radio call-sign, "Chipmunk" just happened naturally. Like most men thrown together by the military for isolated months on end, we'd grown almost as close as brothers. The main difference was that my own brother had taken nearly nightly Jackson family jism infusions up the ass, while I had been hiding my hard-on from Chipmunk for the last four fucking months—and there he was slogging the log not six feet away. Any other time, I'd have headed for a stall and taken care of business on the sly. That morning, though, something snapped and I knew I had to fuck something better than my fist. If we were going to live like family, it was about fucking time young Chip got what I had to give.

Chipmunk's look of stark animal terror when I whipped back the curtain and reached out for his rod was classic, but he needed action too much to bitch. The bastard froze solid, but I didn't mind. His dick was enough sure to thaw us both out just fine. When my fingers wrapped around his stiff joy-stick, my thumb pressing downward on the top to keep it from flopping back up against his bare, hard belly, I felt his body tremble like a schoolgirl's.

Chip opened his luscious Ricky Nelson-like lips to form the word "What...." but no sound escaped from the swallow that seized him. His eyes fell to my thick nine inches of naval need and forgot all outrage or terror. If possible, he needed me even more than I needed him. As I held fast to his joint, one wave of Richter-class shocks after another shook his very foundations until, almost without thought, he reached across and lay his hand behind my neck, pulling me into the stall with him.

I shook my head. We were bound to be interrupted. I held fast to his bone with one hand and reached down for the shower hose with the other. I sprayed hot water across his strong, naked body, rinsing the soap from his flesh as though he were a stallion instead of a stud. Only when I needed to dry him did I drop his dick, letting it fly belly-up with a wet *smack*. I knew it would keep. I wrapped a towel around my waist and led him back to our stateroom, leaving my boots and flight-suit to fend for themselves. Something told me we'd be back in a couple of hours for some serious hosing down. I could pick them up then.

The slut barely waited until our door was closed before he attacked me. His hand slammed back behind my neck, pulling my mouth against his so his tongue could rape mine, sucking me into his mouth with a fierce passion bred of a hundred unfulfilled nights and the worse days between.

As he used my face as though I were some piece of meat, my hands found their way across his back and down his strong, muscled flanks. His damp skin was soft and smelled faintly of soap and sweat, but his hard muscles were every young boy's finest wet-dream come true. As our beard stubble raked and grated each other's face and my hands worked down to cup the grinding mounds of manmuscle that formed his beautiful flyboy butt, I felt his shivering return.

This time, I held him tighter—lifting his ass hard toward my hips, grinding our stiff dicks together in a dance too long delayed. His fresh, soapy scent blended with the stink of the day's sweat I still wore to put my pulse into overdrive.

I felt the stiff red carpet on my chest grinding into his soft skin, grating across the hard tits erupting like twin Vesuviuses from his strong, hairless pecs. My lips evaded his to maneuver south, tearing the taste from his neck as I moved towards his left ear lobe. I sucked like a starving calf when I got there, nibbling lightly with my teeth while Chipmunk helplessly shivered and groaned and then all but went limp in my arms as I shot my tongue into his ear.

I didn't need laser-guidance to drill deep enough to shut his brain down hard. I might still be there, standing just inside our door with Chipmunk in my arms and my tongue up his ear, if I hadn't felt the slick stain of our blended pre-cum oozing across my belly.

My dick instinctively started skidding up against Chipper's flat gut, pushing his joint along with it like twin toboggans sliding down an icy winter slope—only no pesky trees kept us from going as fast as we liked. Within seconds, our hips were heaving and grinding together, making up for the months we'd wasted with a frenzy unlike anything I'd ever experienced. I kept belly-fucking my buddy, harder and faster with every slippery stroke of my spooge-pistol, until I knew I was cocked and ready to go off.

The look of betrayal on his face when I pushed myself away from his man-hungry body was so classic I had to laugh, but when I locked my lips around his nuts and started nuzzling his aching `nads, tonguing and sucking his low-slung jism magazines like a cur dog in the street, his head fell backwards, his mouth slipped open. A low, almost subsonic moan crept up from the depths of his very soul to shudder through every fiber of my being. The sound of that glorious groan of satisfaction was more a turn-on than his deep brown eyes, his gloriously muscular body or thick naval weapon, or even the tight butt I knew I'd do before dawn broke.

For the first time in months, I was giving a man satisfaction. For some perverse reason I've never been able to put my dick on, giving has always been an even bigger pleasure to me than getting.

I kept giving—while my first load of the day drained back down out of my dick. When his balls were spit-shined and Bristol fashion, I eased my nose past his asshole, yearning for a simpler time when I could have given it the same sloppy treatment. I did manage to breathe in great lungfuls of air, thick with his man-musk and the scent of sweat melded with a faint memory of soap. Then I eased my face far enough away to enjoy the sight of my fingers slipping across the pulsing pink pucker that guarded the eager gates of my buddy's virtue.

They didn't guard it very well. My fingers slid upward, taunting his butthole with a possible poke or stretch—and the slut's butt-pucker would snatch out at my fuckfinger like Cujo after a month on a water diet. I kept up the action as my mouth moved upward, striking just above his fuck-furrow. There, at the base of his backbone, I started licking lightly, teasing the bumpy knobs of his spine with my tongue, grazing across Chip's naked, heaving flesh as light as butterfly's dream. By now he was leaning across the wash basin, writhing in a combination of agony and ecstasy from the delicious toll my fingers and tongue were taking. I eased carelessly upward, unhurried by any need but to enjoy myself, knowing my jet-jock buddy could take any tongue-lashing I could dish out.

I was the one close to the breaking point. Neither of us had touched my dick, but I was still so close to spewing sperm that I expected to taste it any moment. Some remote corner of my brain, the perfect warrior's backup guidance system, must have been thinking well ahead of the action. By the time I'd polished off the base of Chip's neck, one Houdini-like hand had rummaged through the drawer next to the basin and come up with the plastic bag that held my stash of rubbers.

As his ear called me back for a re-strike and I eased my chest against his back and felt my chest pelt prickle his hot back, I knew I couldn't keep out of the saddle much longer. Our first ride was going to be short, but we were going to have plenty of time to take the beasts out as often as we liked. While I used his ear and got an earful of moans and dirty talk from him in return, my military member had found itself hard-pressed. I only just managed to rubber him up before my buddy's cute little butt snatched hold of my best asset and started wriggling about, trying to get me right where he wanted me.

I wasn't up for an argument, so I yielded the point and pressed it home. My hands were under Chip's chest, gripping his shoulders from below—not to keep him from escaping, but to hold him close. As I pronged through into his aviator's ass, I raised my face and looked at his in the mirror. The parade of emotions that marched across my war buddy's face as I did him hard up the butt was at once so natural and remarkable that I know the next few moments will return in dreams until my final day.

One moment he was possessed by a hunger so sharp that it threatened to steal his soul. The next, as his slutty sea-pussy swallowed my dick whole, I saw the muscles of his face knot. I rammed everything I had hard up his ass: his eyes slammed shut, his jaw clenched tight, and clusters of muscles cobbled his temples. A second later, the lubed latex around my butt-pump had greased the skids of my pilgrim's progress and, as I felt the hot insides of his guts rippling their welcome along my crankshaft,

Chip's brown eyes opened to positively sparkle with satisfaction. As he gave me his finest shit-eating grin, his fanny did a little flourish, pressing backwards against my hips, stretching his hole around my joint, and scratching his insides like an itchy-backed bear who has finally found a stiff tree limb after an especially pesky winter. He was talking dirty at me again by now, so I was no gay blade.

I crashed headlong through his shit-chute, meating slick satisfaction with every tight new inch. When I felt my stiff red pubes slam home where they belonged, they ground into his asshole—as though polishing would make it any more perfect. Chip reached back, pulling my butt hard forward, greedy for every millimeter I might be holding back.

My lips eased around his ear as my stubbled cheek grated hard against his neck, eager for every sensation that would bind us together. I felt his soft, chestnut hair caught between my lips and tasted the sweat I'd already fucked out of him. Most perfect of all, though, was the look of sublime animal contentment reflected back as my hips began great rolling surges of dick thrusting up his tight slut-hole. My hands had worked their way down to his tits, tenderly twisting and tweaking in time with the pounding I was giving his guts. At the crest of every wave, I'd feel my swollen knob nudge some secret nook of his cranny to the breaking point and Chipper would give a little squirrely chirp of satisfaction to prove I'd fucked the last breath of air from his body.

I'd like to say we fucked on for hours. In a perfect world, that first glorious fuck would have lasted forever. I managed to pick up my ramming speed, locking us together in the savage cadence only two pilots far from home can know, banging myself harder and faster up my buddy's butt with every brutal, bestial bone-crunching, back-stabbing stroke. I found nature's snarls roaring past my lips. Breath came harder; the seconds slid together into an eternity. Then the universe exploded, blowing the tops of my heads off. My body convulsed in glory, my muscles seized solid—all except for my hips which kept ramming out of control until I was bone dry and holding on for dear life.

Sensations flooded one over the other as I spunked myself back to life: I felt my hands locked tight around Chip's waist to keep myself in the saddle, my nuts and thighs were swamped with overflow spooge spurting out the end of our rubber, my ass was fast in the grip of a selfish slut who wanted me to keep drilling him up the butt, and my chest was about to explode. I eased myself to a stop and collapsed, completely drained, onto Chipper's back. My hands trailed along his flanks to show I hadn't forgotten him, but I was (as they say in the Navy) broke dick down hard.

Fortunately, Chip was ready to take the con. You wouldn't think after all I'd done for the selfish bastard, the minute I'd pried his ass off my stiff dick he'd want to fuck me up the butt, would you? Believe it or not, though, that's all he had in his nasty little jet-jock mind.

As I was sucking at his balls, you can believe I admired his dick. It wasn't quite as long or thick as mine, of course—but a young warrior far from home can't have everything. He has me for a roommate; that should be enough. Not everyone would be willing to stretch out on his rack, feet to the overhead so he could be sodomized by some sex-crazed jet-jock just back from a bombing mission. Not everyone would donate one of his last six dozen rubbers for the enterprise or help the glorious goof get the fucker on right way up.

But, then, not everyone has the chance of digging his heels into Chipper's once-tight butt and looking up at those spaniel-brown eyes while the bastard fucks a world-class glow up your ass. I guess I'm just one great guy. In fact, over the next couple of weeks, in between missions over Iraq, my Chipmunk told me I'm fucking terrific. We were both sorry to see the war end—but you can believe we made the most of the few months we had together as *RANGER* made the long float home from victory.

Heading back down the slot from Iraq two nights ago, my dick hard and my missile racks empty, I couldn't keep my mind off my current roomie. I considered whether to risk opening myself up to him and spending the rest of the deployment in meaningless, hard-charging mansex of every description possible. I pondered whether he could take my nine inches up that tight little ass of his. I wondered what he'd sound like if I acquired his target and locked on.

By the time the wire caught my tailhook and my A-6 had slammed back home aboard *CARL VINSON*, I'd made up my mind that my shower could fucking wait. It was long since time for me to make another shipmate into a warrior brother and show him how good being a brother can be.

A MARINE INVASION

Since the Gulf war, the US military presence in the Kingdom of Saudi Arabia has been as low-key as both sides can possibly make it. In the Eastern Province, floating atop ARAMCO oil and neighboring on Kuwait, American military vehicles and personnel show up now and again. In the Najd, though, the situation is more sensitive. Closer to Makkah and in the center of the Saudi heartland, the winter capital Riyadh is a study in contrasts. One can still see the crumbling mud-brick fortress where Abdulaziz Al-Saud conquered a tribal rival and carved out the Kingdom—as well as the legend goes, the heads of the fortress's hapless defenders. Riyadh is the only capital on the planet where *mutawas,* religious police like something out of Monty Python, ensure all businesses are shut down during the day's five prayer calls. This stronghold of history and of Sunni Islam, though, is an architectural wonderland where modern skyscrapers built with petro-riches and the best creative minds money can buy show off the Kingdom's modern face.

I know all this, because I am stationed in Riyadh and love it. During my first months in the Kingdom, I wasn't able to see much. When regulations relaxed enough for us to get out and about—so long as we wore mufti—Morale and Welfare even arranged for guides to show us around the city. The Kingdom is not open for tourism, so the dragomans are unpracticed and often more trouble than they're worth. In my case, though, I got lucky—very lucky.

He was waiting for me outside the MWR office at noon on Thursday, just as scheduled. I'm not sure what I had expected, but Ali Muhammad Al-Khalid Al-Khalifa wasn't it. He is distantly related to the Bahraini amir, but had spent all his 19 years in Riyadh. Standing about 5'6" in his flowing white *thobe* and red-checkered *guttrah*, with the face of a cafe au lait cherub and huge black eyes soulful enough to break a tax collector's heart, the kid looked about 12. If ever a dragoman threw himself into his work, though, it was Ali.

His face split wide in a grin when he saw me. Even out of my uniform, my haircut gave me away. "I like Marines," he began and babbled on in awkward and simple but perfectly intelligible English about how we were the bulwark of Saudi democracy. Ever the diplomat, I let the oxymoron slide and asked where he was taking me. Sure enough, he had a full day planned: the gold souk, Justice Ministry Square, the shops on Wazir Street, Camel's Eye Park, a drive round the major palaces, and then, he said, "a surprise."

I felt a little silly having him hold my hand as he pulled me along through the souks and shops, but Saudis, like most Arabs, are a friendly folk and don't feel they're communicating unless they're within touching distance. They also like to ask what we could consider personal questions in getting acquainted. Ali spent almost as much time discovering that I was single and came from Colorado and liked to ride horses as he did telling me about Riyadh. By the time we were finished with our long list of palace drive-bys, we seemed like life-long friends. Ali liked Marines.

When he asked me to his villa for dinner, I was impressed. Purdah makes entertaining awkward, but when we got to his apartment, I saw there wouldn't be a problem. Not only were there no women in seclusion; no one else at all was around. As he sat down beside me on his couch, I wondered in passing how he was going to produce dinner and entertain at the same time. I shouldn't have doubted him.

He confessed again that he liked Marines—especially big, handsome US Marines with green eyes and red hair. Then he commiserated with me about the lack of female companionship in the Kingdom. It must be hard, he said, to make do without women. He looked so young and innocent, I couldn't believe he was headed where I thought he was headed; but when he rested a hand on my thigh and moved over to stroke The Monster, my name didn't need to be Burton or Lawrence to know my dinner would be protein rich and served up hot.

As his hand moved across my basket and coaxed my Marine advantages ever-more to life, he talked on in a soothing, sensual voice that could have mesmerized a mongoose. He liked Marines, he said. The knuckles of his other hand pressed against my Corps-built pecs and drifted down across my swollen tits. I like Marines myself, but our detachment was so small that I hadn't done any liking Marines in weeks. I needed to like hard and long in the worst way. Ali was fresh and eager. A glance at his lap told me he was naked as a haddock below his *thobe* and likeable as they come.

His fingers slipped inside my shirt, combing their way through my red fur. He must have liked hairy chests as well as Marines, too, but he didn't say so. He didn't say much of anything for a while because my shirt had come open and his mouth went down to lick me happy.

Getting to my tits can often be a problem. The thatch that thrives across my chest is stiff and thick so unless my nipples are really standing tall, a guy can get a mouthful of curlies before he has anything meatier to chew on. Young Ali was so cute and eager and close, though, that his getting my tits stiff was the last worry on my mind. As his lips yielded to frantic flicks of his bumpy tongue and thence to the sharp, insistent edge of his teeth, my major duty was deciding which hole I was going to blow my load into. Fortunately, although his slick lips knew their business, Ali's hips were so narrow and his butt filled out the back of his *thobe* so fine, I didn't have to ponder the problem very long.

Before I tapped my gusher of American crude, though, I intended to set an All-Arabian record for foreplay. My hands caught fistfuls of his hair and used it to smear his face across my chest, grinding his nose against my pecs as his teeth tore away at my tits. The little slut was already moaning away like a *houri*—only no phantom of paradise could possibly be as good at processing fresh tit as Ali.

Even as he chewed away at my chest, his hands were unbuttoning my jeans and freeing my dick to stand taller and prouder than the minarets of Makkah itself. The minute he heard my shank slap up against my belly with a *thwack*, his head pulled away from my grasp and scoped out the view. One hand cupped my low-slung nuts while the other took the measure of my Marine weapon. Since both hands were full, he managed to kick a bowl overflowing with rubbers from beneath the couch. Multi-colored packets of plastic joy-pouches spilled across the rug like the guts of a ruptured pinata, but I was feeling too festive to much notice.

Ali's voice was prayerful as he amended his credo: "I like Marines—I like Christians." I lacked the heart—and time—to explain that religion had little to do with my being natural meat. He slowly worked my foreskin up and down as though it were some freshly discovered holy relic, sniffing my knob and rubbing my raw, tender virtue across his smooth face until my slick streaks of crystal pre-cum darkened his cheeks with massive potential for Gulf-quality pleasure. I only half noticed when the slut's practiced paw slipped a thin rubber down my shank, but I noticed plenty when Ali's full, hot lips locked tight around the tip of my foreskin and as his stud-sucker went into overdrive. Normally my foreskin is long enough to hide most of my head until I am ready to use the fucker, but Ali had my knob so hard and swollen and grungy that a cresting cum-slit caught the full brunt of his first attack.

The kid's miraculous talent for sucking uncut dick was as sweet and subtle as it was surprising to find in a Muslim. He didn't jerk the head bare like some rapine barbarian. The rubber did keep him from diving hasty and headlong beneath my straining cocksock with his tongue. Ali was perfectly ready to tear into my cum-slit and urge upward the streams of pre-cum oozing up in thick, crystal abundance while he waited with lip-smackiing patience for nature to take its inevitable course.

My thick jarhead lizard was as lust-struck as Ali was dedicated to dick. His lips were soon gliding with slick ferocity around the top inch of my knob and coaxing more cock out into the open with every sadistic slurp. His faced twisted around to give his hands better access to my nuts so he could crack them open and spill out their creamy pleasure. I knew he wouldn't be happy until I sprayed my massive Marine load up into his tight little man-hungry Arabian maw.

I shoved his face hard down across my knob, stripping my latexed lizard foreskin away until my jism-jet was pointing smack down his gullet. His throat wasn't nearly big enough to take my head whole, but that didn't matter. The back of his mouth and first inch or so of his throat were hot and tight and itching to do their bit for international relations. By twisting his head around my shank, I was able to make him gurgle and grunt like a recruit in a boot camp shower, but his military service was *too* good.

I'd tried to be patient and considerate and a '90s kind of lover. I hadn't rolled my hips up against his cute young face. I hadn't flexed my ass to drive my load up into my dick and lock it in firing position. I hadn't even slammed my heathen hose deep enough down his throat to make him smurf. I was almost able to stand his suction and tonguing and the twisting his gullet was giving my head. Despite all my good intentions, though, he was too much, too soon for this Marine. Before I knew what the sand-surfing sneak was up to, he had my balls in his fists and was squeezing away like a Shi'ite zealot with a new pair of thumbscrews.

My feet instinctively flew into the air and landed low around his back, forcing his face harder up against my belly. Since my hands were on his head, he had nowhere to go but down—and my load had nowhere to gush but up. From the way my mean Marine cream seemed to fly up through my dick and blast out the top of my head, I should have blown his foxy little face halfway to Damascus. Instead, he hunkered down hard and took it all the harder—slurping and sucking up more when I threatened to run dry until he had chugged my load and the industrial-strength membrane that kept it from him halfway down his gullet.

That bone-shattering load didn't just blow up and out, though. It was sucked up by Ali's demanding, almost demonic spooge vacuum. Each ripple of jism coursed up through my throbbing tool, feeling for all the world like an elephant being sucked through a pinhole from the safety of a spacecraft into the hungry, limitless void beyond. The glorious, unfamiliar tenacity of that sublime suction and the cruel rapture that ripped upwards from my dick, shredding my soul and showing me a glimpse of Xanadu itself, suddenly fused solid every circuit breaker in my over-loaded brain. As reality collapsed into a singularity of ecstasy, the pain in my nuts somehow offset the pleasure in my heads and kept me spewing sperm like a six-day virgin with a world-class suction slut dangling off the end of my dick.

My heels bucked him harder against my flat, firm belly with every gut-wrenching, ball-blasting, mind-numbing stroke of my shank through his face. Despite all the heaving and howling I was doing, young Ali was worlds too busy to make a fuss. I somehow managed to regain some vague awareness of the universe and my place in it and was even eventually able to pry the cocksucker's frantic face off the ruins of my throbbing knob—just as the last big glob of my jarhead jism blasted up from my exploding spooge arsenal. He took the round full in the face, looking up at me for all the world like Bambi as my glob of creamy jism dripped slowly down his tawny cheek. I shoved my dick into the mess and let the last tortured leavings of my load ooze out to join their comrades as I smeared my way across his cheek and jaw and up into his glistening black curls.

I rolled him over onto his back and pinned him to the couch and so I could lick my load from his cute young face. I've licked enough of my jism off my fingers over the years to relish the taste, but blended with the salty taste of his sweat and some scent of the mysterious East, my frothy cream was a whole new adventure in exotic cuisine. His hands pulled at my head, smearing my face across his. When he was licked clean enough to lunch with the village vicar, our spooge-lubed lips met and settled in to get acquainted. His body bucked upwards against mine as we did the tongue tango, and I couldn't miss the hard force of his lust-struck bone grinding upwards against my belly.

My dick was still stiff and good-to-go, but the burning in my nuts warned me I should take a break before doing him hard up that tight Arabian ass of his or I was sure to fuck myself into a rupture. Besides, the way he was squirming under my tongue-lashing begged for some quiet, quality time before I rode his ass into the ground.

My lips left his to skid across his cheek to give him a real Marine earful. The gorgeous bastard had been frantic enough with my dick and then tongue probing away at his tonsils, but when my tongue tore up into his ear-hole, digging relentlessly down towards his brainstem, I thought the kid was going to shit from pure satisfaction. He screamed and bucked and clawed away at my back even as he was trying to gulp in enough air to live through the best time of his young life. My tongue showed him no mercy, darting deep and wet into his ear and slurping at his lobe until his body was racked by gooseflesh-fed seizures and, for a long, convulsive moment, he stopped bothering to breathe altogether.

Since dead dragomans can be inconvenient to explain—and aren't nearly as much fun as the live variety—I reclaimed my tongue from his head and slipped it down across his chest to tease his tits. They were already hard and standing tall, meaty purple towers of need that begged for all the American military assistance I could command. The aid came crashing in, with my bumpy tongue slurping and twisting around his tit-stalks to establish the beachhead. Then my wet lips pulsed up and down along his tender tits to secure the field. I used just enough pressure to make him beg for more and just enough spit to lube our slick love. When I let the cruel edge of my teeth tease his tits with the delicious prospect of danger, his body erupted in spastic shivers of delight and his surrender was complete. Once more, gooseflesh consumed his firm, hairless torso and low moans of raw animal pleasure jolted upwards from the very depths of his soul.

I molested those meaty tits until they were rubbed insensible and then ducked deep into his pits to lap away the man-musk our day together in the desert heat had bred there for me. While my nose and tongue and lips raked his pits for their tangy treasure, my hands wandered across his soft skin and the tight knots of lust-struck muscle that writhed below it. When one hand drifted across his lean belly and felt the hot, slick sea of pre-cum that had oozed out of his throbbing dick, I knew the time had come for me to show him how macho Marines suck dick.

I was in no rush, mind. First there was the pool of dick-honey to massage up across his hard, lean belly. Then his small, boyish balls needed to be licked and sucked and tongued into shape. By the time his lizard was latexed and my lips coasted down over his teak-colored knob on layers of packaged passion floating on a sea of Ali Muhammad's own natural dick-lube, my young guide was quivering helplessly away just this side of Paradise. I was between his thighs, their soft skin and musky smell wrapped tight around my head in case I should try to escape. My tongue flickered down across his tender head, slip-sliding spit and pre-cum around his knob and down into his cum-slit. My lips followed, slipping around his corona and sliding down his thick shank, while his narrow hips went wild with dick-fed delight.

I kept one hand on his belly to hold him down and snaked the other beneath his nuts, first to pay them back for the nut-cracking he'd given me, then to pry open his eager little ass. As my head bobbed in counterpoint to his cock and his adolescent hips force-fed me Saudi shank at seven inches a pop, I dribbled spit down his dick until his balls were awash and his ass-crack was slicker than a sergeant's wetdream.

He naturally rolled his ass upwards as he fucked my face, so spreading his tight, muscular brown buttocks wide was no problem. I let my thumb slip along the narrow defile of his ass-crack as he humped his way up into my face. Every thrust of those narrow hips dragged my slick thumb across his tight pucker and made him bark with pleasure. I was so busy with his tool slamming into the back of my throat, I didn't worry too much about showing his hole a good time. That would come later.

As it happened, though, young Ali didn't want to wait. Every sortie of my thumb strafing his shithole made him wriggle that tight ass harder until he was half impaled on my hand.

Whether I'd pushed just the right button with my anal intruder or sucked him too happy for my own good, the little slut chose that moment to blow his wad up into my *semper fi* face. Even though I couldn't taste it through the wrapping, it hit this Marine's spot dead on. I kicked up the suction into overdrive and paid him back in part for the way he'd nearly sucked up one of my nuts just minutes before. I think Ali must have missed the point, though. He was too busy thrashing around and screaming in Arabic and trying to rip the back of my head off to see the overall picture.

Looking back, I have no clue where he got the load he blew into my face. Either he was some freak of nature or hadn't blown his load in months. His nuts were small and tender, but the rest of his glands must have been on steroids. All I know is that he humped my face and spewed sperm until his creamy good time was back-flushing like a Turkish crapper, gushing out the end of his rubber and washing down over his balls. By the time the kid finally humped and shuddered to a stop, my own balls were stoked and loaded for butt.

As I lifted my face off his joint and looked up at the sweaty stud gasping for breath, I don't think I'd ever been so turned on. The decent thing to would have been to hold him close and murmur sweet nothings in his ear while he recovered and then, maybe, work up to getting mine back.

Fortunately, though, in situations where foxy teenage boys are lying naked and prostrate a dick-length away, Marines don't tend to do the decent thing.

I had his log latexed and his legs spread and lifted before Ali Baba could say "Open, Sesame." A quick dollop of his own jism wiped up off his nuts and rubbed against that gorgeous brown pucker was all the lube he got before my thick knob broke his tight ass to the saddle. He'd liked the feel of my thumb, but when my egg-sized knob ripped upwards through his guts and tore satisfaction from every slick, hot inch of his shit-chute, he fucking loved life.

He greeted my infidel insertion with a howl like a siren. His body clenched tight around my Marine meat while my hips slammed hard against his tight, brown ass. I'd no sooner given my cum-slit a quick jab against his gizzard that I pulled back and almost out, just for the selfish pleasure of slamming my way back down where I belonged. His eyes opened wide with unspeakable pleasure as I picked up my ramming speed and slammed harder and harder down into his tight ass with every delicious stroke. The howl finally devolved to feral grunts that welcomed every brutal thrust of my Marine invasion, but his body knew better than to run up the white flag too soon.

Instead, the slut turned Quisling against himself, wriggling his ass along my slashing column of Marine man-meat, spurring my butt with his heels to force me into the deepest, most secret depths of his love-tunnel. Above the rasp of my own breath, I heard nothing but the sweaty *smack* of flesh against flesh and *slurp* of my thick dick drilling snicker-snack through the ruins of his shit-hole and his little grunts of contented pleasure. My dick so swelled and throbbed inside the dry heat of his teenage ass that I wasn't sure which of them would split open first.

As it happened, I looked down into those incredible brown eyes with their youthful wonder and innocence and felt my second load of the afternoon blow. In the last brief second of full awareness, I hunkered down against Ali's torso and let my hips do their worst. Hours or seconds later, when I again regained charge of my body and destiny, I discovered I'd fucked us both onto the floor and halfway over to the window. My nuts were burning again, but the fuck-friction along the length of my shank had been salved with nature's own best balm, trapped tight against my gut-wrenching tool in one slight blessing of safe-sex techniques.

Now, though, it was Ali's turn to take advantage of my distraction. I'd no sooner dumped the last of my load down his spooge-filled shit-hole than he was behind me, slamming his dick up my ass. He wasn't half bad, either. I didn't give him the kind of ride he deserved, but Ali didn't much mind. We both knew that before the long Arabian night was over, Ali Muhammad would be a dozen rubbers poorer and we would both have plenty of perfection to remember.

IN LOVE AND LUST

I re-read the letter for about the thousandth time. Just looking at Dave's handwriting gave me a rush—knowing that the hand that held the pen also beat him off. Every time I got to the part about him coming to town, I got hard. The letter was couched in the careless, profane, abusive language we sailors use with one another, but the tone was unmistakably affectionate.

We hadn't seen each other since I left the *NEW JERSEY* months before to transfer to shore duty at FTG Pearl Harbor, but we'd spent almost two years together in the ship's Combat Information Center. Since we were both STG2s [second class petty officer sonar techs], we worked side by side, slept in the same berthing, and grew ever-closer together as the CIC duty roster slowly changed over the months. By the time I'd asked for my transfer, I'd become Davy's best friend; he had become the center of my universe and the cause of my greatest torment.

I was in my rack reading a Charlie Chan novel when Dave reported aboard. Combat Systems berthing aboard the NEW JERSEY was always hotter than a Marine's butthole, so we usually kept our rack curtains open when we weren't sleeping.

Every little breeze the ancient fans could crank out helped some. Because we'd just come back from a week's sea trials, I hadn't been on the town for a while, and my ballbag was swollen tight. When I looked across at that ass, I lost all interest in helping Mr. Chan solve his pesky tropical murder. Dave's middle rack was right across from mine so when I looked up from novel and found him stowing shit into his rack-pan, all I could really see was that beautiful bubble-butt. He was wearing his cracker jacks and, bent over as he was, that ass was an outrage against modern morality. Two tight clumps of muscle, each a man-sized handful, stuck out at the world.

When he straightened up and said his name was Dave Dalton, I saw that the eyes would be a problem, too. They were as green as a cat's and surrounded by long, doe-like lashes the chestnut color of his thick, wavy hair. His face was OK—a strong jaw, high cheekbones, perfect nose, blinding Hollywood teeth, and all the rest that goes with the All-American face—but it was set on that awesome body besides. The gorgeous bastard was the avatar of my dream-hunk. I was fucked.

After four years in the Navy, I'd gotten really good at pretending studs didn't inflate my crank. For the first several months Dave was aboard, I had no problems. I kept my lurid little mind busy with jerk-off fantasies involving that tight ass and those green eyes. The more I got to know Dave, though, the more I liked him. I think our real problems must have started when I noticed him after his shower. I made it a rule to save my pecker checking for the baths because I figure there's no percentage in tormenting myself with USN meat. When I woke up from a nooner to find his freshly showered dick practically in my face as he was toweling his hair, I nearly reached for the gusto. It was only in front of me for seconds, but all I've had to do ever since is close my eyes to see it—beautiful, uncut, thick, about eight inches long, and complete with a generous flourish of skin at the tip. That perfect peter stretched out over his egg-sized balls like a snake over a log. From that day on, life grew progressively harder. The next few weeks were tolerable because we were about to go on WESTPAC, and the CO was working the living shit out of everybody. Aboard, I didn't have time to think of dick. On my few days off, I'd go to the Castro and find some fine young face to fuck until the image of that snake faded back a bit into the jungle undergrowth. Once we got underway, though, my cool turned to shit.

For one thing, Dave and I were in the same duty section—working side by side at the sonar console. We were off at the same time so when he wanted to hang out, play UNO or Trivial Pursuit, or just shoot the shit, I was generally around. The nights were obviously the worst. Like most guys aboard, he slept naked in the heat. He often kept his curtains pulled shut for privacy's sake and so he could ready himself to sleep without bothering others; but when berthing was unusually hot, I'd look over in the middle of the night to see the red battlelight reflected off his hard, lean body. Dave is usually a belly sleeper. He liked to curve his right leg beneath him and face the bulkhead—which meant that those two handfuls of ass were pointed directly at me, begging for it. Four feet away, I'd try to sleep and fail. The muscular back running from his wide shoulders down to his narrow waist would have been bad enough, but that ass was just too much. I'd shut my curtains and swelter until I'd spanked a couple of monkey loads into a handy sock. Those were the good nights. After an unusually rough day, he'd be restless. He'd pitch and turn and usually end up on his side, arms wrapped around his pillow with his dick sprawling out across the mattress from under his chestnut curls and his nutsack draped down across his solid thigh. Then I didn't have to deal with the ass, but his massive, hairless chest crowned by gorgeous tits was even worse. His stomach was so flat that even when he was asleep, it seemed rock-solid.

One night around midnight, three weeks or so out of Alameda, my crank was rubbed raw so I was trying to sleep without shooting off again while I watched him toss and turn. Sure enough, he clutched his pillow and began to smile as his dick started swelling. The head was first, creeping out like a reclusive cyclops as the skin ruffle slowly stretched back over the head I'd never seen. In no time, he was up off the mattress and had grown to about ten inches. By the time the skin had completely exposed his plum-sized head, that cock was stiff as iron, and standing tall way past his navel. With every beat of his heart, the dick would throb, and pound itself against the center of his belly. The larger he grew, the more he throbbed and the wider the bastard grinned. I was nearly cumming from watching the show when I saw him jerk awake. His eyes darted around the compartment to see whether anyone else was awake and, once reassured, pulled his curtains shut. I heard him spit into his hand a couple times and then all was quiet save for the glorious sound of flesh against bone. After about five minutes he started to hiss something like a steam locomotive running dry. I heard his limbs jerk, his breathing stop, and, after a few minutes, the rustle of cloth. Soon afterwards, Dave opened his curtains, rolled over onto his belly, and drifted off into the sleep of the just with his pucker peeking out at me from the smile of those tight cheeks, leaving me to put another blister on my dick trying to squeeze out enough spunk to get to sleep.

The next week, we pulled into Pearl for four days and Dave and I did the tourist bit. That was my first time in Hawaii and I loved it. During the day, we drank, hiked up Diamond Head, swam, lay in the tropic sun, drank, and cruised Waikiki. Nights, we spent drinking. Our last night in town, Dave said I was on my own. I suspected he was headed for Hotel Street and some cheap, meaningless sex—just what I needed myself. I'd looked up the number of the local gay information service our first day in port, so I knew about the Kuhio District and its bath, bar, and other family businesses down in Waikiki—just a sixty-cent bus ride from Pearl.

That afternoon, evening, and until six the next morning, I fucked everything that would move—asses, faces, hands. I went through more Trojans than the Mycenean armies, but when I got back to the ship, I knew I could handle the pressure—for a while. The following months strengthened our bonds. When we stopped in Chinhae, a pack of us hired a taxi for the trip to Pusan.

Dave and I ended up in the Florida Club. The "hostesses" were insistent and I'd had enough to drink that when Dave suggested we take them upstairs for the evening, the idea seemed to have merit. We ended up in bedrooms separated only by a curtain so I was able to enjoy the sounds he made as he humped. I'd gotten excited enough to hop into the saddle myself and was riding away, dreaming that the slack hole beneath me was really Dave's tight virgin ass, when who should burst in with his monster cock waving about but dangerous Dave himself. He was yelling some shit about a rat roughly the size of a pony, which was supposed to have run through our rooms. I hadn't seen anything, but then I'd had my eyes closed in fantasy. I could easily have missed a circus troupe of three unicorns and a mastodon. All four of us spent the next ten minutes looking for the phantom rat.

Dave finally tired of the safari and dragged his still-rigid dick back to bed. Fortunately, he neglected to close the curtains—so for the rest of the night I was able to watch his ass in action as it rammed that monster man-meat home.

He pronged the wench four times before we left; I was more or less constantly in the saddle. She certainly wasn't much—loose and gushing the whole time and interesting as a theology seminar, but Dave's example was inspiration itself. I hoped against hope that I could pump enough socially acceptable spunk to dry up my pump. Besides, there's something about two guys going wenching together that strengthens the ties of male bonding.

We went on to Yokusuka, Hong Kong, and the PI, but I was able to avoid wenching until we hit Subic. The Philippines was a kind of Disneyland for sailors, so I knew there was no way to avoid doing it there.

The night we got in, I streaked out the gate and down to a famous gay bar on Rizal Boulevard. I found a meaningless, transient relationship, which was consummated in a flea-trap hotel down by the Olongapo Casino. The guy was nearly as bad as the Korean bitch, but at least I got off enough to be sure I could trust myself the next night. I'd already promised to go up to Bo Barrito with Dave. A three-peso, thirty minute jeepney ride from the base, "the barrio" comprised a quarter-mile stretch of highway with cheap, well-stocked whorehouses on either side of the dusty road. For about seven bucks, a sailor could get wasted, hire a girl and room for the night, and still have money left over to get drunk the next morning.

What the Ka'aba is to Muslims, Bo Barrito was to squids. Dave and I started off with other guys from the ship but ended up in a joint called The Buzzard Inn. The rooms were better than usual, but Dave apparently had trouble with his wench. We parted about midnight and by 0030, he was at my door, fuming about the static he was getting from "his bitch." I thought fast and invited him in, suggesting that the two of us spend the night pronging mine.

I'd started off already, dreaming away of Dave's tight, hot little hole as I got the girl (who had the sweet, if inaccurate name of Baby Ruth) warmed up. As Dave shucked his clothes, I suggested he take up where I had left off. When the girl saw Dave's tool, she shied away, but I gently reminded her that I had paid her "bar fine" and had the documents to prove it. She let Dave have his way—with me watching every fucking move. With my running commentary, constant suggestions, and encouragement, Dave set to. I sat at the end of the bed, watching his dick sliding in and out of her and dreaming that it was me. Once he was underway, I moved even closer and played with them as they fucked. By this time, I was impressed and moved around so that the wench could suck me off as Dave was ramming his swollen rod into her. It wasn't the kind of blowjob I would have liked, but certainly was better than nothing. He lasted about ten minutes the first time, then I hopped aboard while he did the color commentary. I insisted that he move up to let her blow him, just inches away from my face. The vision filled me with a passion unlike anything I'd ever known, but was frustrating as hell because I knew that was as close as I would ever get to his dick.

For our second go-round, we used the ever-popular sandwich ploy: Dave on the bottom impaling Baby Ruth, me atop her fucking her ass as though all I needed to do was ram hard enough and I'd be through to him. Looking past her at his face as his lips parted and eyes clinched shut while he shot off inside her, I delivered the best load of my life. We bucked and thrashed like animals. It was great! One or the other of us was at her for the rest of the night. By the time we caught a jeepney for the base the next day, we were almost as intimate as I'd have wished.

As I re-read the letter yet again, that night in Bo Barrito, the high point of the *WESTPAC*, lived in my mind over and over, like some loop-projector gone wrong. We'd had other fun times, but for weeks afterwards, that night haunted my sleeping and waking hours until I knew I had to get away from the *NEW JERSEY* before either My Secret spewed out or my sanity unraveled. I'd liked Hawaii and, since I was about due for a shore billet, I decided to ask for a transfer to Pearl. We had one last blow-out at the Terror Club in Sembawang, Singapore before I left—and promised to keep in touch. Since then, I'd gotten a few cards, and now The Letter.

When I picked Dave up at the airport the next Saturday, I had fears on several counts. First, of course, I didn't want to let My Secret slip out after keeping it hidden for so long. Not only would I lose his respect, but if anyone else found out who I was, my career could end in mid-stroke. Then, too, one always feels awkward when meeting old friends after you've grown apart. By the time we'd downed our first brews, though, I knew that nothing had changed. We were still so close that I could often tell what he was thinking from a glance. We spent the rest of the night drinking and, by the time we finished off the last of the case at my apartment, we were the dictionary illustration of "shit-faced."

I'd taken digs in Salt Lake, but hadn't gotten around to finding a roommate yet, so there was plenty of room—but only one bed. Dave insisted that I use it. After all the beer I'd drunk, I more or less passed out as soon as my head hit horizontal. Dave was still up, finishing his shower and turning off the lights. I hadn't been out long, though, when I felt Dave shaking my shoulder. I looked up and saw him starkers, with his hair still deranged from the shower. He mumbled something about the air conditioner being too cold on the floor and did I mind if he climbed in with me.

If I'd been sober, I'd have come up with some reason why it wasn't a good idea. Fortunately, I was drunk enough that I thought I'd be able to sleep through the night without raping anybody. I rolled over and he slipped into the bed in his belly-down position. I winked out.

I think I woke up once to feel his arm lying across my chest, but otherwise slept like a drunken sailor. The next morning, I drifted up to the twilight state between sleep and life with a piss hard-on. My subconscious was debating whether I could put off waking up to pee until later when I felt a fly on my forehead. I brushed it away and discovered that the guy with me was brushing my hair out of my face. I automatically snuggled closer, put my arm around his waist, and asked how he'd slept. The nickel only dropped when I heard Davy's voice. I opened my eyes and remembered who the guy was. I must have turned about nine different shades of purple trying to straighten things out. He just looked at me with a crooked little smile as I was blathering about thinking he was some lady I'd brought home to pleasure. When I ran out of spiel, he reached over and put my hand onto his mammoth, blood-gorged crank.

As those green eyes bore into my soul, David said he'd been trying since his second week aboard to penetrate the veil that separated our souls. Often he was sure he could feel my lust burning, but he'd never had the guts to put his ass on the line. He asked if I'd noticed that he slept naked, with his curtains open. He asked if I didn't think it strange that he'd chase around a Pusan whorehouse while I was trying to screw. Didn't I think his coming to my room at the Buzzard Inn mean *something*? Why hadn't I had a fucking clue? Surely I must have known when he climbed into bed the night before what he had in mind? As he reviewed our past, propped up on one elbow, looking into my depths, he explained how he'd gone slowly ape-shit while we were aboard. Now, however, he'd decided he had nothing to lose.

As quickly as I realized how lucky I was, I began to mourn the time we'd wasted. I asked the bastard when he had to report to his new command and when he said he only had until Thursday, I was desolate. Then he smiled and suggested that I get a roommate. His new command was NAVCAMEASTPAC in Wahiawa—about twenty minutes away from my joint—from both of them. When I was trying to adjust to this new set of affairs, he began a gentle rocking of his hips, pushing his huge hump-horn into my hand. As I figured out he was using my paw to beat off, I also discovered that the candy store was open and unguarded—and I should let rational thought wait until much, much later. I ducked down under the sheet, which had trapped the warmth of our bodies in against the morning coolness, and gave him a licking. I used my tongue on his nuts, his stem, his head, his butt and tits—and everything else I could reach. Starting slowly, I grew wilder by easy stages until I was gagging myself on his impossible peter and he was working me over better than any fist-fucking fantasy.

He lifted his mouth from my meat and pulled me above him. His legs grasped my ass as he practically forced me into his ass. My hands on his shoulders, looking down into those eyes of joy and need, I felt myself lose control before I was completely inside him. My hips went wild; I slammed against his beautiful butt, driven forward by nearly three years of unproven passion finally released. When I had filled his ass with my load, he grinned and taunted me that I was a one-stroke artist. He seemed to recall it had taken me 45 minutes with a certain wench in The Buzzard. I ground my hips into his ass some more and tweaked his tits while I reminded him that while he was a world-class bitch, he was no fucking wench.

I think Davy must have liked that, because he nodded, laying his hands on my ass with a smile. I managed to wriggle from his embrace and insisted it was his turn to show his stuff. I reached under the mattress and dug out my KY. Perhaps someday he would stretch me out enough to just hop on, but until then, we were going to take things slowly: I was going to do the work. I slathered his pole with enough KY to lube a small Harrier before I climbed up. As I began to play with my stiff meat, I lowered myself onto his as gently as a lovestruck guy could. At first I had no luck, but quite suddenly he gave a little shove with his hips and rammed himself through the gates. I yelled like a stuck motherfucker on speed and reached round to squeeze his nuts, reminding him that I was in charge of this fucking evolution. He lightened his grip on my dick and told me not to get cute; but he kept still and let me take what he had at my own pace. I didn't want anything to rip that would take too long to heal. If he was going to be around, I wanted tomorrow to be as good as today. Straining to the max, my guts on fire, I finally worked him inside me and began the slow rocking motion that forced my prostate against him.

I let him begin a slow rotation as I applied myself to playing with his tits and, leaning far enough forward, kissing him as I'd never kissed anyone before. This time he was the dickhead that shot off years too soon. I'd just put my tongue into his mouth as his hips seized control of his stock. It flew in and out like a piston, drawing my guts on the down-stroke, making me want to explode on the up. The pressure on my prostate was so great that, for the first time in my life, I came from anal agonecstasy alone. As he forced his juices into me, mine surged from my meat and flew against his chest, into his face and hair, and onto the wall behind. As his dick grew still, I squeezed his ballbag again—this time to force out every drop. I forced what was left of my ass as tight as I could when I pulled myself upwards, squeezing him dry. I lay atop him, wriggling about on his hard body, separated only by a thin layer of my own spunk.

We kissed and cuddled until, still wrapped together, we fell into a deep, profound sleep for a few more hours. I was first to wake when the sun hit our bed and woke him with my dick. Since that day, I have thought of no other person. Except for duty days—which we have arranged to have in common—we have made love at least once every day. After work, we have a couple of beers, jog or work out, take a long shower, and spend the rest of the evening in bed, making slow love as we chat, watch TV, or just watch each other and admire nature. We have become more than lovers, more than friends. We have become one spirit in two vessels, whole only when linked together and, once linked, needful of nothing else. We both have two years before our next rotation, and it looks as though we'll both leave the Navy then unless there is some way they could guarantee us the same duty station. Although I can't believe it could be true, Davy seems in love and in lust with me as much as I am with him.

One night last week, as we lay in each other's arms to let our bodies recover and our spunk dry, we finally finished the Charlie Chan mystery together. I'd lost interest that day in my rack when Davy's ass burst into my universe, but he ran across the book in the closet and thought we should make it ours. Tomorrow we're going to have little black camels tattooed on our butts. We've talked it over and think every sailor should have a tattoo where it counts most. Charlie Chan might even agree.

TWO BLOND SIGNALMEN

Even in port, Fetshak and Fetterling were a pair. They reported aboard about the same time and were both boot camp signalmen, so it was natural for them to buddy up. They were together so much, though, that before long the crew stopped making jokes about how they were "very special friends"—just in case they really were. Something about them convinced you that they belonged together even though you couldn't put your finger on exactly what it was. Their division officer juggled the duty roster so they could share a watch. By the time we had left San Diego for our six-month deployment to the Gulf, everyone had gotten used to seeing them move about the ship, nun-like, in a pair, sharing unspoken thoughts and wordless smiles at the rest of the world.

I worked in another division, so I didn't have much to do with them on a day-to-day basis—but like everyone else aboard, I knew who they were. They stood out. One of them alone would have made my crank inflate. Seeing them both stroke about the ship like young, studly bookends gave me dreams.

They were always talked about together—in the beginning as "Fetshak and Fetterling." That made them sound like a Czech law-firm so they soon became "Fetch and Fett." Both were blond with gleaming blue eyes and a raw sexuality that could coax pre-cum from a mummy. Fetch was about two inches taller and had more of a chin, but Fett had freckles and a boyish surfer quality that was hard to resist. Since they were both SMSN's (signalman seamen) by the time the deployment rolled around, they had to be about twenty. Their pug noses and great floppy shocks of blond hair made them seem younger, but the muscles they found in the ship's weightroom showed they were men. I soon discovered that neither really needed muscles to prove they were legal tender.

On a frigate, you get used to seeing guys walking through passageways on the way to a shower dressed in a towel or less. Younger seamen fresh out of bootcamp are used to being naked—and like to show what they have. They almost never bother with towels. The deployment was still young when I met them headed towards a shower just after taps one night. I stopped to shoot the shit for a minute so I could scope them out; I have no clue now what I said. I do remember every freckle and hair on their hard, young bodies. I'll never be able to forget the meaty, wrinkled foreskins that dangled below their dorks. Uncut dick isn't impossible to find, but finding two out of two hanging off bodies like theirs is about as likely as being hit by lightning while you're in a vat of pudding backstage at the opera. Since I was standing there staring at what was bobbing between their hairless thighs, it was obviously possible—but I knew I'd have to review the scene again and again with my hand sliding along my slick crank before I'd really believe my eyes. Fetch's dick was slightly longer. Its eye poked through the bobbing, wrinkled mass hanging low between his thighs to wink at me. But Fett's dick was thicker and completely covered by an extra-large cocksock that dangled a tassel of flesh all the way off the end of his joint. I probably only held them up for twenty seconds or so, but it was enough.

Junior officers in the Navy don't get a lot of sleep underway. What little time I did get off was spent getting off—lying in my rack with my hand stroking the nine thick inches I know best in the world, dreaming of sucking those two slabs of choice government property at once until their seamen semen gushed hot, creamy streams into my face. The images of their bodies remained so fresh in my mind that I could savor the tangy taste of their jism as it dripped in juicy fantasy down into my mouth. Sometimes I'd put those classic uncut dicks out of my mind—and dream of reaming the twin hairless bubblebutts I had seen as they walked away from me. Both sets of cheeks were full and firm and seemed to grind and squirm together like a bag of cats on the way to the river.

One night about three weeks later, I was relieved from my bridge watch at 11:45 and decided to take a few minute to unwind before I went down to my rack. Since Navy ships travel without outside lights, the bridge and lookout watches get used to seeing in next to no light. That night, though, there was a crescent moon that sparkled off the water and made me want to be alone to pull my shit together. Well, let's face it. My roommate was in my stateroom and I needed to find someplace quiet to jerk off for the third time that day. I left the bridge and headed up one level to the signal bridge to be alone. It's just a bare deck except for the signal shack—a little metal room where the SM's store their signal flags and hang out when they don't want to be found.

That's how I found Fetch and Fett: hanging out. I stood by the railing, looking out towards the water and the moon and thinking of hard young muscle as I lashed my lizard. The noise of a sump pump with a loose seal tore through the noise of the ship's engines behind me and made me turn around to investigate. There, through the open door of the signal shack, I saw two moon-struck, naked bodies folded together in the 69 position, heaving and humping away. Somehow, even a dozen feet away, I knew the perfect butt I saw bobbing up and down above a mass of blond hair belonged to Fetch. How many nights had they come up here? Even though it was wide open, they probably had found the best place to fuck on the ship—- easy to get to and, best of all, abandoned after dark. I leaned against the rail and took my time enjoying the show, sliding my palm where I'd dreamed of feeling their lips. I watched as each young man's hands slid over the other's hard, lean body -- spreading butts, feeling up flanks, and generally having one fine fucking time. I'd spent so much time fantasizing about those bodies that I didn't want to get too close for fear they would dissolve into the moonlight before I'd shot off. My fear eased as they grew louder. Soon their moans and dick-stifled grunts were loud enough to bore through the drone of the engines and the whooosh of the bow churning through the water. My brain told me not to spoil the picture, but my dick took charge. I ambled over for a closer look.

Fett was lying on a signal flag locker and Fetch on top. Both of them were too far gone to notice me standing in the doorway—until I slid my fingers between the cheeks of Fetch's gorgeous butt. At first, he didn't bother to count hands and discover he had a third one gliding across his flesh. When my fuckfinger found his shithole, though, his brain finally took a muster and reacted. That hard ass jumped half-way up my hand. When his dick flew out of Fett's throat, the kid knew something was up and opened his eyes. Those bright blue eyes of his widened and I heard him gag, "It's Mr. Jackson!" as much as he could with a mouthful of meat headed back down into his gullet.

They had seen my stiff dick outlined by the moonlight and knew what I wanted—what I was about to take. I let them suck on. I knew that later my tongue would slide up inside those skin-clad cocks until I'd stretched them raw, but I was in no hurry. We had five months before us. Just now I was more interested in the fuck-finger I'd buried up Fetch's tight, quivering butt. As his lizard lifted from the depths of Fett's throat, his butthole gobbled ever-farther up my finger. My hand felt fine sliding in and out of his tight, hairless ass—but I hadn't spent the last three weeks dreaming about a fingerfuck. I unhanded Fetch's hole, reached out to grab his narrow hips, kicked off my trou, and put my nine thick inches between his hard mounds of manmuscle. At first, I leaned over to feel my hard, swollen tits dig through the pelt of stiff red hair that covers my chest to rub against Fetch's muscled back. I stroked my hands along his flanks and up to his shoulders as though he were a holy relic. One hand eased down to molest Fett's butt even as I started to prick harder against Fetch's fuckhole. Feeling my flesh rub against theirs and their animal heat warm me in the midnight breeze that gushed through the open door, I would have almost been content to stay there forever. Almost.

My hips drove my dick harder against Fetch's quivering pucker until I had eased inside almost without knowing it. Fetch knew it plenty. When I broke into his shitchute, his body let out a squeal like a bat caught in a blender. He arched upward as the painful pleasure of my fucking dick ricocheted through his body. His back slammed me upright as he heaved himself off Fett's body to get comfortable on my dick. I heard Fett's incredibly thick manhood slam against his belly with a sloppy wet *smack*. So much prime enlisted manmeat lay below me that I wasn't sure what to do with my hands, but my lizard lashed deeper into Fetch's guts with every fierce, soul-shattering stroke. It knew what it wanted and took it by right of discovery. I'd found it; now I was going to fuck it. My hands were wrapped around Fetch's body, letting his tits dig into my forearms as I humped his ass. I heard Fett gag as I fucked Fetch's butt harder and faster, driving his dick deeper with every stroke into the foxy cocksucker that lay trapped below him. The thought of that meat slamming down into Fett's face just got me even more excited. I picked Fetch up and nailed him against the bulkhead, my hands on his pecs, so I could get at his butt without worrying about smurfing poor Fett.

Fetch twisted and moaned on the end of my dick like a Subic Bay whore on a payday weekend. Every *smack* of my hips against his hard butt forced a low animal grunt up from his guts and made him gasp harder for breath. His face was turned toward the door, though, and the moonlit grin on his face told me he was doing almost as well as I was. Fett was the odd man out. I started to suggest he hop in front of Fetch so he'd have something to ream, too; but I got selfish. Since I wanted to nail Fett as soon as I was finished with his buddy, I wanted his ass dry and tight. Besides, these enlisted sluts had probably been doing each other since the deployment started. This was my night to get some. I ordered the seaman up my ass with his tongue.

One thing you have to give sailors, they know how to follow orders. I got busy slamming everything I had down Fetch's fuckhole and lost track of Fett for awhile. When I did notice him again, he was lapping at my shithole the way a cocker spaniel licks his dick. That tongue slid along the hairy crack of my ass, zipped around my twitching pink pucker, and slid deep into my hole. His nose ground along my ass as his hands gripped my thighs to hold on. It couldn't have been easy. My ass was pounding away like a pile-driver stuck in overdrive, jamming my joint up into Fetch's writhing body. He twisted and torqued and grunted and moaned until I regretted not having closed the signal shack door. Modesty didn't slow me up any, though, so I guess deep down I was too horny to give a shit. The feel of his slick prostate bouncing off my dickhead, the slick ripples of his satin shitchute stroking along my crankshaft, the firm pressure of the blind end of his guts as my cum-slit scratched away at the most secret, tender itch he kept buried deep inside his sea-pussy, the way he wriggled his butt along my length—all these and a hundred other sensations kept my brain just short of overload. There was the tight grip of his sphincter around the base of my shaft. My stiff red pubes ground into his tortured fuckhole like fresh Brillo. His sweaty back slid along my chest and belly as his hands joined Fett's on my butt, trying to cram my whole body up into his foxy tight ass. All the time, Fett's tongue was dancing around and into my hole as his face smeared itself up my ass. I fucked myself into a frenzy between the best ass I'd had in years and a tongue hot enough to melt molybdenum. Those incredible sensations blended together with my own snuffled grunts and the slurping up my ass and the moans echoing off the bulkhead in front of me to lull me into a warm fog that dulled my consciousness enough to keep me reaming away long after I should have creamed butt. For the first time in my life, I felt like a fucking machine. I could screw butt forever.

Eventually, of course, I blew it straight up Fetch's tight squid butt. It was his fault, too. I'd been doing fine with his moans and grunts, but when he started in with long, drawn-out prayers of "Yeeeessss" and "Oh, god!" I couldn't hold back.

My guts turned to plasma and blasted out through my dick. I felt so good that, for a minute, I thought I was having a stroke. Every nerve in my body seemed to flame out at once until I came to, eventually, to find my hands clawing at Fetch's pecs, my teeth dug into his neck like a tomcat's, and my balls slick with premium-quality Annapolis spooge that had overflowed his enlisted ass to gush back out at me with every stroke. Fett was beneath me now, lapping at my balls and his buddy's butt as my naval shaft reamed away on autopilot. I fucked on even after my nuts were dry. That slick spooge-filled butt was just too good to give up. I could tell from the way Fetch was wriggling his ass on my joint like a bear against a pine that he didn't want it to end, either.

When I finally did pull my stiff dick out into the night air, it wasn't there long. I reached down, grabbed Fett by his surfer-blond hair, lifted him towards the flag locker, bent him double, and rammed my seaman-slicked joint up his ass. He let out a howl, too, but we all knew what was good for him. His shithole was even tighter than Fetch's had been when I started.

Belatedly it occurred to me that these two cocksuckers must not have been doing much buttwork, but that was going to change from now on out. Having just pumped the load of my life up Fetch, I was in no hurry to bust another nut up Fett's guts. The night was young, and I was going to enjoy myself. I sent Fetch forward so Fett could suck his asshole. I'd found my rhythm again and watching Fett slurp my spooge out of his buddy's butt made me even harder. I noticed again that Fetch was a twister who loved to wriggle his ass around anything you poked up inside it.

By the time I'd started to feel my next load rising, I called Fetch to sit on his buddy's shoulders so I could suck him off. Since I'd let him feel my thick commissioned dick, it only seemed fair I get to know his enlisted joint. The `skin was pulled back slightly, but there was still enough soft, wrinkled meat to make anyone happy. My tongue slithered between his `skin and the hard, throbbing dickhead that lay buried below. I felt his need almost at once. Even before I could strip away the taste of man from below his cocksock, the slut's hips began fucking himself into my face.

I picked up my own speed, ramming away into Fett's tight ass while I sucked sweet sailor dick. Fett's butt seemed to have a shorter stroke and smaller bore than Fetch's, but it was slick and full of craving. That hungry butthole gripped hold of my Annapolis-trainednine inches like a lottery check.

The perfect feel of Fetch's meat fucking my face was as much a rush. Locked around Fetch's swollen dickhead, my lips sucked up a steady flow of pre-cum oozing like magical syrup across my flicking tongue and sliding up and back along his hot, throb as the motion of his body swayed his dork down my throat.

Soon I was slamming back and forth like a see-saw. Fetch would fuck my head back, driving me forward up into his buddy's ass. Then I'd jerk several inches out of that tight sailor butt and start the process over again. Several times, I pulled completely out of Fett's ass and let my slick dick slide awhile along the tight, bare crack between his classic cheeks. Then I'd have the fun of breaking back into his butt. My crankshaft was stretching his ass, but it was nothing compared to what my swollen dickhead could do. I knew I was going to use these two assholes often during the months again so it was time they learned what to expect.

Fetch came before I was really ready. I loved the feel of his soft foreskin sliding up and over his head, the tight feel of his man-sized meat in my mouth, the soft brush of his blond bush against my nose. When I heard his breath change from a gasp to a growl and felt his hands clutching at my head, though, I knew fighting nature wouldn't do any good. Fetch was a young animal in heat and wasn't about to do anything except pump his nut down my gullet.

That's where he started, too. I'd had his dickhead in my mouth, but he shoved it straight back, raping my throat in his ecstasy. I felt his cum-tube pulse jism, but he was too far back for me to savor the sauce. The kid "fuck"-ed and "Oh, shit"-ted and screamed until I half expected the whole ship to hear us. When his spasms had begun to ease off, I worked my face off his dick enough to feel his creamy enlisted spooge shooting off the back of my mouth, slathering down across my tongue, and making every tastebud in my head sing harmony. I sucked the rest of his load up from his ballsack until he squirmed and pried my face off his dick. I'd long since discovered how sensitive uncut meat was once it had done its job, so I didn't take his rejection personally. Besides, I had another squid-shoot of my own cumming up.

I lifted Fett into the air and motioned for Fetch to take his place on the flag locker. Once his ass was spread, I porked Fett back down—right up his buddy's butt. Fetch had been opened up fine when I pulled out, but the excitement of shooting off had made him a tight-assed sailor again. When Fett's dick slammed through to dig for my jism, Fetch reared upward again—slamming me into Fett and Fett even deeper into Fetch. The noise and confusion of getting us all stroking along in common cadence was too much for me. I reached around to grab them both, catching Fetch around the neck and Fett at his hard belly. Then I juiced sailor ass for the second time that hour. This time around I was able to keep track of every sensation—of the way my dickhead pulsed as it launched a load of cream up Fett's ass, of the way his butthole felt grinding along my pubes, of the sounds the two boys made as I fucked one into the other. We were all drenched in sweat by now, so holding on was hard—but letting go was impossible. I shot and ground and reamed for what seemed like forever. My prostate work must have been up to the usual Jackson standards, because Fett started to lose it next. His butthole tightened harder and harder around my crank as he juiced the butt below him. He was such a tight-ass I half expected my joint to break off at the nub.

I was finishing up business when I heard Fetch say something about shitting white for a week.

Later on, after we'd unplugged ourselves and disentangled our legs and arms, I explained that he was going to be shitting cream for more than any week. If these two wanted to do the nasty on aboard my ship, then they were going to do it the right way—with me at the helm. I was going to be on their asses until they knew all there was to know about being a seaman—and all three of us knew their introduction into the naval service would take the whole fucking deployment.

JARHEAD SURRENDER

The first time I saw Spence padding towards the shower, I knew that sooner or later he was going to be mine. I had zero clue how I was going to manage giving him the hard Marine dicking a perfect male body like his deserved, but I knew the naked truth of Destiny when I saw it swinging between his legs.

Coming from different companies, we didn't know each other back then, but Marines embarked to the Arabian Gulf for six months at a stretch on a ship like *Tarawa* are used to making new acquaintances. Enlisted Marines are really much better at catching the right eye and luring a tight asshole into a gun mount or fan room for anything from a quick knob job to a six-alarm jarhead orgy; but we officers aren't exactly monks, even if we do have to be more careful. We have more to lose if some Navy homophobe should catch us working out with one of our men—or with each other.

I had several regular bitches aboard, and we got together several times a week when our various roommates were ashore or flying; but, sweet as they were, one look at Spence made me realize how much I had been missing out of life. I stood in the shower room and practically gawked, rather the way one would stare at a Michelangelo marble found amongst the detritus of a suburban yard sale. Everything about him was exciting and arresting and pumped full of a Byronic, bone-busting electricity that jolted me stiff and kept me that way, waking and sleeping, for weeks.

Glossy black hair and cat-green eyes set the theme of his powerfully magnetic *GQ* appeal. A broad brow and strong jaw with high cheekbones between were curiously at odds with an almost feminine nose and lips. His smooth skin was tanned and soft and stretched over such a wonderland of rippled muscle that at first glance he seemed hardly human—and upon more careful study was proved to be truly divine. His back and flanks were hairless as a virgin's hope, yet glossy black curls flourished thick and rich and soft across his chest and down over his flat belly to lose themselves into the glories of his crotch. Much later, I discovered his ass-crack was as innocent of hair as his broad chest was guilty—yet his other cheeks were framed by an omnipresent five-o'clock shadow that would have made any spaghetti Western casting director drool buckets.

I've always considered myself a top. Unlike most Marines, I've never liked being fucked and almost never have been. Spence was so mind-numbingly, soul-shatteringly gorgeous, though, that one look at his long, thick, uncut dick and the low-slung nuts he had packed full of good times started my ass twitching like a spastic mongoose hyped up on speed.

Like the good Marine I was, I spent days and weeks on mission planning—especially in the nightly dreams that left my balls aching with yearning and my sheets sodden with wasted wads of jism. I did some recon, talking to Spence a coupleof times in the wardroom, but couldn't decide whether he was completely without guile or just half-witted. It wasn't until our port visit in Jebal Ali that destiny and persistence threw us together off the ship and gave me the chance I craved so much.

Jebal Ali is nothing but a port facility and a whole lot of sand, so most of us Marines went into Dubai for liberty. Pancho Villa's in the Astoria Hotel is *the* best Mexican restaurant and bar in the Gulf and, consequently, the obvious place to find fellow Marines far from home. Don't ask where the bar or hotel got their names or why they wound up in a place like Dubai; I don't explain life, I just live it.

When I finally made my way up the line of squids and jarheads wanting inside Pancho's, I had no trouble at all finding Spence. He was sitting at the main bar in front of enough empty margarita glasses to stock a TJ whorehouse. I doubt he was as waxed as he pretended, but I didn't care. In the way military men on liberty are inclined to do, we recognized each other as coming from *Tarawa* and started buying each other drinks. I lost little time in working the conversation around to how long it had been since I had been laid. OK. So I lied. I'd really spent most of the night before pumping one load after another into a couple of second lieutenants; but, fine as they were and horny as I was, I didn't much enjoy the spectacle. They weren't Spence so, in a very real sense, they hadn't counted.

The few straight Marines on the ship—and those who pretended to be— had no trouble finding Russian hookers in the hotels down by the Gold Souk so getting laid in Dubai is no problem if a man is willing to settle for anything. Personally, I'd have rather screwed my hand than bothered to pay for some slack-twatted Slavic slut, but I didn't bother mentioning that to Spence. Both he and I intuitively pretended we were marooned in a wilderness of forced celibacy and wanton deprivation as we bemoaned our common fate.

After four or five more drinks, Spence stopped dicking the dog and gave me the opening we needed. When he said he was horny enough to fuck anything alive or dead, I made my move and countered that I was so fucking horny, I'd even fuck *him* up the ass. We bantered back and forth about who was the horniest and which of us would doubtless be the tightest fuck and scream louder until I decided we'd gone far enough that I could ease into stage two without fear of feigned outrage.

I offered him something like a tail-tontine: we'd get a room and several bottles of booze and drink shots until one of us passed out. The guy who was left conscious could then ream out his unconscious buddy for as long as he wanted and no one would ever know. Even the poor blister-butted bitch would never be sure how much fun had been had at his expense. I saw the greedy bastard's green eyes glow bright behind his doe-length lashes and realized for the first time that he probably needed me as much as I wanted him. Had I lurked in his dreams the way he had haunted mine? I'm damned good looking and built Marine-tight. I'd never had any trouble finding men who craved my dick up their asses, but Spence had such an ethereal, otherworldly beauty that it never occurred to me he would be one of them. Somehow that realization just made my ass itch all the more.

We were checked into room 1017 before you could say "Jose Cuervo." I pulled off my shirt, partly to give Spence a look at the thick, rust-colored thatch that covers my broad pecs and flat belly and partly just because the combination of booze and Arabian Gulf and pumping testosterone had made me hot as fried fuck. He returned the favor, proving that he was even more savory up close than he had been at a safe distance in the *Tarawa* shower. I dragged the cheap plastic glasses out of the john and cracked open the first bottle of tequila.

We talked shit as we sat side by side on the bed and drank like Marines on liberty. I don't remember anything we said. The booze I had swilled downstairs had already given me a serious buzz and the sight of Spence's hard, sweat-speckled young body just inches away distracted me plenty. Everything about the guy excited me: the serious bulge in his basket, the way his tits swelled hard and firm, his cock-suckable lips and smoldering green eyes. Before long, I wasn't sure whether the rush I had going was true love or merely the after effects of good tequila—but I was damned well going to find out.

In case you haven't spent much time in hotel rooms with Marines, I should confess that when we can't find any bullets to stop, we show our manhood two ways: by drinking and by fucking. Marines drink to show how much they can hold— and love getting shit-faced, puddle-puking, piss-pants drunk, with a couple of fist fights thrown in on the side if at all possible. The only thing we love more, of course, is what happens when we are off by ourselves and show how much jism we can pump or how much dick we can take deep. Since I'd already decided I needed to feel Spence's gorgeous jarhead joint slammed up my ass, neither of us had anything to gain by waiting. As soon as I indecently could, I pretended to be drunker than I was and keeled over backwards onto the bed, seemingly unconscious and defenseless as a goat at an Iraqi barbecue.

Spence didn't waste any time getting my sneakers and Levis stripped off and tossed across the room. Then, for the longest time, I didn't know what was going on. When I finally risked cracking open an eye to peek out at him, I saw the poor sappy bastard standing next to the bed and looking down at my naked Marine body, doing everything but slaver. I couldn't see his stiff dick just then, but I felt it not long afterwards—pressing against my right shin as Spence licked his way up my thigh.

I'd expected to be fucked hard up the ass the minute I passed out. I wasn't sure whether I could take the pain or not, but Spence was so fucking gorgeous, I knew I had to try. What I wasn't prepared for this foreplay shit. It felt fine—it felt fucking fantastic. I just wasn't sure how long I could last without spraying loose my load. If you've ever lusted after a man for weeks and then had to just lie still and let him lick and suck and slurp at your body for seemingly hours on end, you could appreciate what hell heaven can be.

He started low, behind my knee, and licked his way towards my nuts. Summer in the Gulf is a sweaty business, so I'm sure my crotch must have been ranker than five-day roadkill; but Spence tore into me. First he lapped my poor balls raw and then took turns sucking one nut after the other into his mouth, pulling his head backwards, straining my sperm-cords against his teeth as he threatened to swallow me whole. I couldn't help moaning and twisting about in pleasure, but Spence either didn't notice or thought I was dreaming—or didn't give a fuck by that point whether I was playing possum or not.

My tortured dick had never felt so forgotten and alone. It throbbed, neglected and pouting, against my belly, oozing pre-cum and threatening to split down the seam if I didn't get relief on the fucking double. The more I moaned and the bigger my bone swelled, the more Spence humped my leg and tore at my nuts like a pit bull with a problem.

His hands were everywhere at once—grabbing great fistfuls of my chest fur, tweaking my tits, sliding down along my legs and up along my flanks. The only place they weren't was on my dick. I'd have given a month's pay just then to have him take me in hand and pump out a load, but the crazy bastard seemed determined to chew my balls off instead. I could feel the wet slickness of his dick-honey oozing out onto my leg as he humped away. My hips couldn't resist arching instinctively upwards to grind against his face. Spence was too busy to notice, gobbling down more and more of my nutsack, chewing greedily, relentlessly on for what seemed like a Brahma lifetime of eternities.

His gorgeous jarhead face slurped sensations out of my crotch that I'd never dreamed possible, but not even the mind-numbing raptures he was ripping from my soul could keep my dick down. It danced and throbbed and bobbed and oozed until I was sure my big head would explode if my little one didn't in one quick Marine hurry. Just seconds before I would have given up pretending and reached down to spank my shank, Spence spit out what was left of my nuts and eased his face upwards. With the instincts of a Torquemada, he started at the base of my bone and lapped his way slowly upwards.

By the time he had reached the top, I could feel my ample foreskin stretched halfway down my knob. Even after he was on station, though, Spence took things slowly enough it's a wonder I didn't rupture. Being another of those rarest of beasts—an uncut Marine—he knew how to do maximum damage. He kissed the tender frenum that holds my foreskin down tight and then flicked his tongue into its folds. Then, after he had licked up all the man-musk I had there, he eased his lips around the underside of my unit and kept on easing until my whole swollen knob was inside his mouth and celebrating life.

The first hints of his suction pumped up a double dick-tickle of sap, which blended with his spit and seemed to turn his bumpy tongue into relentless waves of satin, which slipped and flicked and fluttered around the exposed upper half of my dickhead. For the briefest and most sublime of moments, his tongue tip prodded at the very font of my dick-honey and I just had to sneak another look down at him. Fortunately, he was too busy to notice whether my eyes were open so I made the most of the opportunity, burning into my brain every bob and twist of his face around my knob. One day when I am old and sere, I will look back on that magical night of liberty in Dubai and remember how hot a young Marine can burn in the desert.

When his tongue pried its way between my tight `skin and the hard, purple country still hiding deep inside it, I couldn't help moaning again. Michelangelo's *David* would have groaned in rapture if it had felt Spence's mouth wrapped around his dick and his tongue digging deep. Just about the time my foreskin gave up and popped behind my trigger-ridge, I saw Spence's throat start to pulse. His suction went from gentle to vicious to downright criminal as his tongue ripped rapine across the hyper-tender tissues of my tool, digging deep for the secret treasures of musk my foreskin had hidden away just for him. The top and back of his mouth went after me next, polishing my knob as though it were a bowling ball in need of intensive rehabilitation.

I might have held out a minute or two longer if he hadn't grabbed my ballbag with his hand. God knows I tried to draw the moment out forever. Except for not being able to put my hand onto the back of his head and grind his gorgeous jarhead face down even harder onto my dick, that knob-job was the very definition of a good time on liberty, perfect in every way —and it didn't cost me a dime. At least, it didn't cost me right then. Later, of course, I would have to pay out the ass.

For some reason, my dick didn't give me the usual warning of impending pleasure. One second I was basking in the warm fuzzy glow of contentment bred by a quart of tequila and my shipmate's face wrapped tight around my bone. In the next heartbeat, my guts turned inside out and lashed upwards through my dick with the power and ferocity of a Johnstown Flood gushing through a gnat's nostril. I half-way panicked as, for the first time in my life, I had zero conscious control over what my load was doing. Spence pounded his face down on my dick and sucked even harder. All I could do was hang on to my bearing and let the gorgeous bastard suck my guts dry as he pulled at my spit-slicked balls as though they were his personal Grail. I must have wriggled and groaned, but fortunately Spence was too busy chugging down my creamy commissioned load to notice.

He snatched up one bone-busting wave of jism after another until my balls ached from the combined pressure of rupturing wide and being crunched and fisted from the outside. Just as I was sure the top of my other head was going to pop off, too, Spence finally let up on the suction and set his tongue more seriously to work, scraping across the tender tissues of my knob to tease the last whip-tailed little holdouts up to join the festival in his mouth. It was only when he unclenched his fist from my ballbag that I noticed he'd also had an aggressive finger prodding towards my asshole. I had never before felt so used, so much like the cheapest of sluts—or so blissfully alive. After blasting out a week's worth of jism, my dick by rights should have checked into rehab. Instead, it stayed at attention, roughly caressing Spence's tongue, sliding slowly between his succulent lips, and begging for more rough, Marine-quality liberty.

Spence apparently had other ideas. Once he'd milked my dick for a selfish good time, he decided to flip me over and score some serious ass. I thought the moment I had been craving—and fearing—for so long was finally at hand. Once again, though, the bastard surprised me. Spence went straight for my ass all right, but not with the hard Marine dick I'd expected. He didn't even slip me the finger to test the temperature of my lust. Instead, he spread my glutes wide and slammed his face hard between them, first sliding his nose across my shithole like a hog after truffles and then locking his lips around my butt-pucker to administer just the kiss of life every shit-faced young Marine needs on liberty.

Most of the Marines in my experience love sucking ass only slightly less than choking on dick and having the dog-shit fucked out of them. Spence was far from being the first jarhead ass-lick I've had lapping at my hole over the years, but I'd never felt anything remotely like him. There was none of the tentative tasting stabs or slow swipes of his tongue across my ass to test how well I'd wiped away my last shit. Whether because he thought I was unconscious or just because he was a whore, Spence didn't worry about what anyone would think of him. He was indifferent to moral or ethical or aesthetic issues. He wanted to suck my ass and that was what he was going to do—long and hard and as raw as he could manage.

Once his lips were sealed around my shithole, he spent the next many minutes teasing my ass as his beard stubble grated the skin from my glutes. Spence cranked up his suction, lifting my pink lips up even higher than they could leap on their own, but he didn't drill deep at first. Instead, he fluttered and flounced about my helplessly quivering pucker, dancing lightly around the rim like a whole tribe of woodland sprites about a mid-summer fairy ring.

Only rarely would he make a lightning-quick guerrilla raid directly across my hole. My ass knew well enough what he was doing, but that knowledge bred only increasingly frantic desperation. If his lips and dancing tongue made my heads spin and my shithole beg for mercy, those bolts of lingual lightning sent jolts of raw masculine energy ripping up every nerve until my brain and reflex centers were short-circuited with more heart-stopping pleasure than anything mortal should have to endure. I would no sooner start to recover from one assault against my eager virtue, than Spence would slip me the tongue again and hurl my poor pulsing ass back towards the abyss.

After what may have been ten or twenty minutes but felt at once like ten seconds or ten centuries, Spence stopped slurping around my ass and dug right in, ripping my shithole wide with his bumpy tongue. I heard myself bellow aloud and felt my glutes clench impossibly tighter around his face, but the ass-lick was either too busy or insouciant to care. My legs splayed wide, my fingers clawed at the bedspread, and my breath came in great rasping gasps; but Spence's face was buried so deep up my butt that he would have missed the second coming

Just as I was sure he had licked and sucked away all the rapture I had, the creature would move to new tender turf and start afresh. Not content with sucking and rasping away like a love-struck leech, Spence prodded his tongue up my ass and stroked it across my inner sphincters like a cat licking its chops. Thinking of cats and cream, I suddenly realized what other cream had so recently been washing across his talented tongue. The image of faint vestiges of my own spunk being lapped across the inside of my shithole by his hunky jarhead tongue was so deliciously wicked that my ass cinched up hard around that bumpy anal invader and hung on tight out of sheer, unregenerate cussedness.

In my experience, nothing addles a man's brain faster than having his tail licked. I tried to hold on, to enjoy every lap and flutter and slurp; but years before I was ready, my mind skidded off the highway to happiness and started seriously spinning its wheels. Time slowed to a shuddering stop as space folded in upon itself; the cosmos lost its form and devolved to chaos. All that was left was a warm glow of absolute contentment that spread upwards from my ass and radiated forever outwards like the previous Big Bang of creation.

When the stars started spinning again, I realized three things right off. First came the tragic news that Spence had pulled his tongue out of my ass. Next I learned that my leg had been twisted into the same uncomfortable position for so long it had cramped up something fierce. Then I realized my ass wouldn't be empty for long—not if I knew anything about Marine psychology.

As though still asleep, I eased my leg straight and waited valiantly to be raped. Sure enough, I felt Spence's breath in my ear and his arms take up their station on either side of my shoulders. Yet again, though, I was disappointed with a gratuitous reprieve. His lips leaned low against my neck and kissed and licked their way across to my right ear and cheek. My heart raced into overdrive and goose bumps raced each other headlong across my flesh as I smelled the musk of my own ass on those lips.

I yearned more than anything to lick those sweet, nasty lips clean and kiss my shipmate until he smurfed. Some inner voice, though, wiser and less selfish than I, told me Spence needed the fantasy more than I needed yet another thrill. He needed to take me unawares, to rape me completely insensible, to blast his wide load up my helpless ass and, like any other spraying tomcat, to mark me as his own for all time.

He eased his naked body down onto mine and lay almost worshipfully atop his plundered spoils, his strong hands sliding along my flanks as his tongue tore deep enough down to tickle my brainstem. The hot rasp of his panting breath in my ear and the fierce, determined prodding of his musky tongue were good enough to melt Frosty himself. Then I felt the hard pressure of his swollen crank lying between my glutes, oozing seeming buckets of slick pre-cum into the small of my back. The hard presence of his dick launched more shivers up my spine to tangle hopelessly together with those his brutal tongue-fuck was tearing out of my brain.

That monster dick had looked big and beautiful and enticing swinging safely between his legs in the shower; but, as my butt clenched along that throbbing shaft, it felt more like a redwood with a bad attitude. There was no fucking way Spence would be able to get that swollen freak of nature up my ass. In a way, I was almost as relieved as I was disappointed. I had to let Spence try, of course, but then I'd pretend to wake up and I'd make my tight-assed limitations up to him in many, many other ways. Then, just as I breathed a slow, disappointed sigh of relief, an odd thing happened.

While I was enjoying having my ear reamed, Spence's hands reached down to cup and caress my furry pecs and drill my tits hard into his palms. I suddenly realized how nice it would be just to lie in his arms forever, not fucking but just being his. I let a couple more groggy moans slip loose and then wriggled my sweaty body against his in absolute contentment. Spence pretended to wriggle back, rolling his hips upwards, covertly easing his dick down into my ass-crack. Then the selfish fuck slammed that sequoia-sized shank against my poor shithole and changed all the rules of physics.

Was it all the spit he'd drooled up my ass that slipped him in? Maybe it was the lifetime supply of dick-honey he was gushing loose. Maybe uncut meat slides in easier than the few trimmed jobs I'd had in the past. Maybe the brutal, selfish, cocksucking bastard just didn't give a shit how much he hurt me. I wouldn't have cared in his place. The cruel truth was that although getting that dick up my ass was physically impossible, neither Spence nor his dick knew that.

There is no way to describe what having that monster Marine dick slammed up my ass did to my body, but there is no way to forget it, either. For an instant, I wasn't sure what had happened. Then, about the time Spence's hips crashed hard against my glutes, my guts exploded with white-hot shards of shrapnel that ripped and seared their way through my very soul. Looking back, I am surprised my asshole didn't hurt. I know it was broken wide open because it hurt like hell later. I suppose shock numbed the nerves that should have warned my brain how much doom was rolling my way. In any event, instead of my butthole, it was my guts that flashed into flames as Spence's ten or so thick inches of Marine unit stabbed me in the back and pushed my innards first loose and then completely aside.

I didn't bother pretending to wake up—with that monster dick up my ass at last, I was worlds beyond pretense, and it would have been a waste of time anyway. Spence had scored his fantasy rape, only it was no fantasy. I screamed and bucked and twisted, trying to tame the savagery of his dick if not to escape it completely. Try as I might, however, that dick was just too damned big to shit out and too fucking mean to accommodate. The more I struggled, the more firmly his shaft stabbed me deep until he threatened to fuck loose an organ and immolate me, willing and eager, on the altar of his lust.

Most Marines love nothing better than a rough fuck—a trait I've always used to advantage myself. I didn't realize what a very good time old Spence was having until, as he fucked my face down into the pillow, he pulled his tongue out to bite my ear and growled, "That's it, bitch! Take it fucking all!" His words may have been less than romantic, but the tone and temper of his voice echoed directly down from our jungle origins, the savage grunts of the cave man as he fucked those he had conquered, the triumphant howl of the *Homo erectus* breaching the infinite and making it his own.

The next many minutes are a fragmented kaleidoscope of mangled images that rattled about my numbed consciousness like a grenade with a pulled pin, threatening at any moment to shatter my sanity to bits yet proving beyond question that I was alive as never before to the true nature of man. I remember the rough feel of his pubes grinding into the ruined remnants of my virtue as his glossy chest fur scraped along my back and his hands tore at my pecs and the stiff tits that crowned them.

His lips were everywhere—on my ears and neck and straddling backwards from the bared teeth he locked into the knotted muscles of my shoulder so he could hold my impaled body down for his pleasure. The slick textures of his sweaty skin sliding along mine and the rabid thrusts of his hips pounding against my ass and the musky sex-pumped scent of man all washed over me in blissful waves of incipient rapture. My hands raped his flanks and back, and, most of all, his ass, pulling his huge dick ever deeper into me to do its worst. Most of all, though, I felt his powerful Marine dick stirring the flames in my belly, crudely at first and then, as my guts ripped loose and joined the whirlwind of his fuck-frenzy, with all the brutal rhythm and inevitable certainty of any other tribal sacrifice. His vicious grunts and profane swearing, his howls of triumph and my muted moans of submission all soon blended into a sublime symphony of savage man at rut that counted our cadence and at once dragged our hard warrior bodies back to the very dawn of time and carried our soaring souls forward towards the ultimate transcendent experience.

Spence fucked me in and out of semi-consciousness for so long my guts forgot what life before him had been. As waves of sensation crested high and washed across my being, I heard him calling me all the names he knew so well: Slut. Whore. Bitch. Cunt. I relished each more than the last and tried to clench my shattered man-gash tight enough to be worthy of them. My prostate was soon slammed to the same shreds as the rest of my ass, but it was only when Spence reached down to drag my knee up towards my shoulder and force my ass higher into the air that my buttnut caught the full fury of his dick. Every slashing stroke rubbed my prostate the right way until I knew my bladder was about to explode. I clamped down harder to keep from pissing the bed, but I wasn't strong enough to hold back the wildcat-quality gusher that jetted far and wide and long. Fortunately for the hotel's housekeeping staff, what blew wasn't piss, but great globs of ivory-colored cream—the sweet fruits of this Marine's first anal orgasm.

Neither of us had touched my dick since before Spence slammed up my ass, but we forgot to bother telling my dick that. The smells and textures and feel of being taken so absolutely by the Marine I'd craved so long, the pressure on my prostate, and the verbal abuse Spence was spewing my way had all conspired to blow off the top of my head and sent my second huge load of the evening spraying in all directions. As I surrendered absolutely and my nuts exploded, the ruins of my fuckhole clamped involuntarily down and pressed my prostate all the harder against the cruel inevitability of Spence's surging shank, in turn setting off even more spectacular salvos of spumy spooge.

The harder I nutted, the harder and faster and deeper Spence fucked my ass—and the wilder and wider my dick showered sperm in every direction. My body shielded Spence from the worst of the blasts, but his legs soon dripped cream, as I did from one throbbing head to the other. I couldn't breathe or scream or think—all I could do was bounce back and forth along Spence's express monorail to nirvana and let the jism fly. Finally, ages after I had slipped into the Void, I reached up and pulled Spence in after me.

I was too busy trying to survive to read the signs, but I'm sure they were there: the staggered fuck-thrusts, the balls rising high, the clawing fingers and agonized breath. The first I knew of Spence's pleasure was the bellow that ripped past my ear and ricocheted around the room like shrapnel in a tank.

You'd have thought Spence was the bull being gored by the way he carried on as his hips humped my ass faster than a buck rabbit with a live wire up his ass. When the flaming shank that had so long been stretching at my innards ruptured wide with hot, soothing cream, I felt a dozen sensations at once, including a selfish relief that his jism would quench the fire up my ass and a satisfaction at having achieved my mission goals —and lived to enjoy the experience.

Maybe most of all, though, was the simple age-old pleasure of having another man's essence up my ass—of knowing that I could carry part of him with me forever. Long after he pulled out his dick, long after Nature forced me to shit out his seed, the warmth they left up my ass would glow bright and comforting.

What had started as mere lust for another cute young jarhead had matured into the ancient bond of warrior brotherhood few non-Marines can understand. As Spence collapsed onto my back, a sweaty hulking shadow of his former glory, I knew from his moan and kiss and the gentle stroke of his hand along my flanks that he felt the same ineffable but unbreakable connection. I also knew that my dick was still hard as a DI's heart and that Spence's ass was mine.

Having nutted twice already in as many hours, it took me halfway to forever to blow load number three up where it belonged; but, then, I was in no rush. If my thick nine inches of hard Marine meat were rough on Spence's ass, oh, well. Life is hard, but so was my dick. I gave my buddy a few short breaks so he could lick the drying medley of jism and musk and salty sweat from my chest and so I could suck his nasty balls and dick— among other things. I even held him in my arms for a time and cuddled the way they do in books, our mouths locked together as our hands and bodies and souls learned each other's secrets.

For most of the next few hours, though, I fucked Spence hard enough to make a rhinoceros bleed—and Spence took everything I had like the Marine he was.

By the time I was finished, so was Spence, for awhile anyway.

We fell asleep, one sublimely sticky tangle of arms and legs. Spence awoke me some hours later, back lapping at my asshole like a starving pussy with a fresh batch of cream.

Whether he hoped to start something or just wanted some of his own back, I have no idea. I thought about rolling over and teaching him not to awaken a Marine on liberty, but, instead, I smiled and drifted off to sleep again for a few more hours— and let him to lick on to our hearts' content.

I knew I would need every ounce of strength I could summon before we left our hotel room. Hard as service in the Corps can be, liberty can be a vastly more draining experience. We had both surrendered to the inevitable, but still had three days of liberty ahead of us before we had to drag our asses back to the boat—and the rest of our lives together.

BAD CONDUCT DISCHARGE

Maybe I subconsciously went out looking for trouble. Otherwise I wouldn't have been standing at one of the few stores in town savvy enough to sell what they call gay erotica. When my eyes drifted from all the lovely naked coverboys to the ass writhing about inside Greg's shorts, though, I couldn't help myself. I know fate when I see it. I also know a big, bouncing, jarhead butt when I see it—one with every bit as much raw sex appeal as any of the glossy, airbrushed studs on the covers.

Marines don't have much trouble identifying one another. In Greg's case especially, no one needed to call Sherlock Holmes in to solve any mystery about what he did for a living. For one thing, we were standing not five miles from the second largest Marine base on the planet. He had the savory haircut we call a "high and tight"—nearly shaved on the back and sides and long enough on top that a guy can just get a fistful of hair if he needs a good grip to hold his man's hole in place. Marines are always built, but Greg's body was pumped way past perfection. His gorgeous blue eyes and bulging basket betrayed the wary excitement anyone would expect of a savory young Marine in public caught sorting through salacious pictures of very naked, very succulent young men.

After eight years of seeing thousands of United States Marines' butts in shipboard showers, moving over obstacle courses, lying hard and ready in barracks bays, or bouncing off the end of my bone, I didn't need any subtle clues to know Greg was a fellow jarhead. The physical conditioning the Corps puts us through guarantees any Marine is going to have a firm, full butt—and one that can take any abuse I slam its way. Sometimes older officers back in the rear can sag a bit, but I have yet to see a Marine ass that wasn't better than anything else you could find in a magazine. One look at Greg's butt told me two things at once: he was young Marine meat in its prime and I was going to nail his ass before the evening was out.

If a guy pays careful attention near Marine bases, perhaps once a year he will see the living image of Corps-pumped perfection: ripe mounds of the hardest Marine man-muscle that clench and grind and wriggle about on their own, begging to be dicked deep and trained to like it. Such perfect glutes live beneath the soft, hairless skin of late adolescence and revel in the realization that full manhood is finally upon them. They keep themselves in the fighting trim boot camp has endowed them with and are eager to wrangle at the slightest sniff of a fellow Marine's thick, hard dick.

Asses like Greg's don't just look pretty or give their owners something pleasant to sit on. Like the most insidious and obsessive of science fiction creatures, they subvert the minds and destinies of the lean, lithesome studs who carry them about, demanding to be taken out into the world where dick swings free and throbs ready and eager to please

Like any of his breed, Greg's butt sniffed out the instinctive spoor of sex before either of us was consciously aware what was going on. I doubt Greg even saw me standing behind him, but his butt knew I was there and knew what we both needed. When I slid my hand across the hard, full country of his right cheek, his ass did everything except leap out of his shorts and rape my arm. By the time Greg's nasty little military mind finally registered my presence and about-faced, the only question in those sky-blue eyes was how soon I could slam him happy.

He used the short trip back to my lair to introduce himself just as Greg. Marines usually use titles or last names, but not when we meet as strangers to do our wild thing. At least, we had been strangers moments before. I couldn't help thinking, as I looked past his ass to relish his strong, poster-boy face and the way muscle rippled with his every movement, that I had known him half past forever.

The Corps molds men's psyches as firmly as it does their bodies; so, in a larger sense, I really did know Greg. I was ignorant of his last name and completely clueless about his blood type, but I knew well the searing lust that pulsed through his veins because it flamed high and hot and ready within my own. Sharing the deepest and most profound secrets of our souls, in a very real sense we were blood brothers to the Corps.

He was obviously so young that he had to be a private or PFC and spoke with a border-state accent that hinted seductively of a farmboy background rife with adventures hidden away in hay lofts and behind barns. Almost by the time my door clicked shut behind us, we were naked and in each other's arms. Seductive hints about his true nature were the last thing I was worrying about. In fact, to reassure the kid later how little I cared about his identity, I pulled off his tags and tossed them onto the clothes that littered my deck.

Greg didn't appear to notice. He was too busy slamming his swollen dick into my belly, desperately prying my glutes wide with his hands, and probing away to discover what my tonsils tasted like. To be fair, my hands were busy, as well. Call me a slut, but there's something agreeable about running my hands across the broad, rippling back of a perfectly built 19-year-old Marine with a boy's enthusiasm to complement his man's muscles. The feel of all that pent-up beef just waiting to explode with sperm naturally makes a man let his hands wander slowly down to cup overflowing palms around the finest kind of ass ever bred for mortal pleasure.

Once I had Greg firmly in hand, one thing led inevitably to another. Before I was ready to take notes, I had my tongue drilling into his right ear and both fuckfingers ripping raw rapture from his tight little asshole. Normally I like to step back and admire the lean young bodies I bring home for hard Marine workouts, but Greg was so foxy and so fucking desperate to be dicked, I decided I could wait until afterwards for anything approaching aesthetic appreciation.

The way his butthole reacted to my skidding, probing fuckfingers told me I was on the right track. His glutes were so full and powerful that just reaching the bottom of his asscrack was worth of a NAM—if not a Good fucking Conduct Medal. Once I was on station, the young slut's shithole targeted my fingers and moved in for the kill. I was so busy tongue-fucking his head and getting off on the way his pucker pulsed beneath my probing touch that I wasn't prepared when it suddenly became the Hole from Hell and charged halfway up my hand.

The way Greg's shithole stretched wide and chowed down on my fingers made me feel fine, but that was nothing compared with his reaction: he screamed, shivered, slammed forward into me, and nearly knocked me over onto my ass—all while his slick sphincters tried to rip my fingers off at the knuckle. Under the circumstances, there was only one thing for me to do.

I dragged his ass into my bedroom so I could have my bucket of party tools within easy reach. Since neither of us could bear to unhand the other, travelling was awkward enough to remind me of one of those three-legged races that supposedly thrilled Middle America in the good old days. Whatever the inconvenience, my sense of mission was not to be denied. I eventually managed to maneuver Greg's desperate jarhead ass close enough to throw it onto my rack without either of us breaking a vital bone.

As he lay there before me, naked and panting hard with a lust so lupine it did everything but howl at the moon, I rubbered up as quickly as I knew how—and used even that time to memorize every hard, cobbled muscle he had. When I am old and sere, I shall look back on that panting boy with his hard, swollen tits and broad hairless pecs, his flat belly and big, stiff dick; I shall look back and remember that day and know that whatever else I had achieved or failed in my life, I had done young Greg — hard and deep and until my nuts ruptured wide with raw Marine rapture.

His blue eyes focused onto the thick dick standing tall and fierce against my belly the same way any sensible mongoose stares at a cobra. I saw his tongue flick nervously out across his full lower lip and thought I heard a soft sigh echo the fears of his conscious mind, even as his legs lifted high to liberate the lusts of his loins. I had seen his kind before—desperately needing a world-class reaming to prove he was a man, yet wondering whether I might not have *too* much to do the job. Could he take everything I had to give without losing his bearing? Would I be as rough as he craved without ripping loose anything he might need later in life?

There was only one way to find out. I moved between his uplifted thighs and spent a moment caressing his chest and flanks and even stroking my hand along the hard-charging shaft of his loaded Marine weapon. Suddenly I knew how Michelangelo must have felt when he first saw the model of *David*. I could have knelt there forever, worshipping his lean, masculine perfection. Greg, however, had the impatience of youth and absolutely no present appreciation of the glories of Renaissance sculpture. He wanted to be fucked. He wanted my stiff nine inches of Marine meat slammed far enough up his ass to dislodge his molars. Then he wanted me to stir his pot until he boiled and had to be fucked some more.

As luck would have it, I had something of the kind in mind myself. I locked my elbows behind his knees and leaned low so I wouldn't miss a single flinch or grimace or scream of infernal agony. My first three or four thrusts disappointed us both. Greg had gulped my fuckfingers like a starving shark, but his shithole was way too tight to take my swollen sergeant's shank the way we wanted. Like a mountie, though, a Marine always gets his man. If he couldn't stretch wide enough for me to slam his ass to satisfaction, then I would just have to storm that beach myself.

My pelvis reared back, arching my butt towards the overhead and flaring it so wide in anticipation that I could almost feel my own hole asking for trouble. Then I clenched my butt tight and swung it forward. I held his knees and shoulders in place long enough for my pile to drive deep, shunting his shithole aside like a thoughtless promise and burying my swollen knob nine deep inches up the hottest, tightest, most gloriously fuckable young Marine ass I'd done all day.

Most men don't run screaming into the night when I first ream them out, but that's only because they're incapable of any movement beyond the familiar gut-wrenching scream and the odd paralytic shudder or two. Once I had him well and truly staked out on my mattress, young Greg proved that Marines really do have what it takes. His eyes widened like a carp's and his mouth gaped wide to match, but for the longest time he didn't make a noise. After ten or fifteen seconds, I stopped waiting for the usual shriek and ground my pubes as far down into Greg's tight asscrack as I could manage.

Only when my dick stirred up trouble with his prostate and liver did my young little lust-struck Lazarus coast back to life and let loose a sigh of such sublime contentment that I wondered in passing whether I might be losing my touch. Was I over the hill, or was young Greg just such a chronic jarhead slut that he could take like a man anything I could slam his way?

I hadn't had a challenge like Greg since a very busy weekend with a satyr of a major and his captain bitch the year before. As I eased half my dick upward and got ready to poke him again, only harder; the bastard smiled at me. It wasn't the sappy romantic smile a shit-faced sailor gives you if you scratch his itch for him, but the cocky, self-possessed grin of a stoic standing up to the village bully. Maybe, given the otherworldly look in his eyes, it was more the smile of a saint heading for the stake, yet sure of present salvation. Whatever the source of that loopy grin, my mission was clear: I had to wipe it off Greg's puerile jarhead face and teach the boot some respect.

The next crash of our roughly rutting bodies together didn't crack wide the earth, but I saw some of that cockiness fade from Greg's eyes. The next stroke was harder and faster and deeper; and, as my hips found their cock-driving cadence, I switched mission control over to my little head. For a time, I was happy just to slam the living shit out of Greg's ass, changing position and rhythm and angle and even the depth of my stroke to keep him off guard and maximize my meaty good time.

Within a couple of minutes, my rubber-clad dick was ripping that smile off my young acolyte's face and leaving awe in its place. Our bodies heaved together like colliding planets as I fucked his body up my bed. Soon his cute little jar-head was slamming into the wall, and we were both too fucking busy to care. When I finally got around to taking pity on him and lifted his heaving hardbody off the bed, fucking him from my lap up against the wall like some barroom brawl run amok, I had long since proved my point and taught the kid to respect his elders.

By then, I was just using his ass for some mongo R&R—to bust the biggest, slowest, most semper fi nut of my life. That doesn't mean I was in any hurry. His ass was so hot and tight and deep that I had all the time in the world. Now and again I felt my balls start to rise and eased off. Greg's hands clawing at my back and the stiff thrill of his syrupy dick boning my belly didn't help keep me stoic. The feral grunts I fucked from him and the way his teeth stayed locked into my shoulder forced my load to percolate north. The sweat streaming from our bodies kept our outsides slick; the juices of Greg's ass somehow greased our skids as well and sent us soaring into orbit.

As you might expect, the kid was first to lose control. Whether my dick's ripping the shit out of his prostate was to blame, or his own peter's prodding into my belly did the trick, I neither know nor care. I am sure the selfish bastard brought me back to earth when he seized up tight and slipped into convulsions that made a congressional budget hearing look organized. Even with me slamming his ass into the wall, he howled and twitched and bit at my neck, spraying so much sperm so far and so wide there was only one thing for me to do: blast the biggest, baddest good time since Caligua up into his hot, heaving roller-coaster ride of a shithole.

I might have held off even longer, except that I got the mental image of his full, firm butt wrapped around my dick and milking it dry. When I saw I couldn't hold off another second, I picked up my ramming speed, held him tighter, and reamed away like a bastard. The last thing I remember was savoring the combined scents of our two sweaty bodies melded with the tangy smell of the jarhead jism that seemed suddenly to be everywhere at once. The sweetness of the smell and the slickness of our hard bodies and the tormented animal sounds we were both bellowing out into the void sent me over the edge and into the most perfect of mortal oblivions.

When my heart started up again, I discovered myself flat on my back with Greg's wet tongue lapping a good portion of his load off my chest and belly. I would like to say that I rolled the dogface right over and slammed him again—sideways. Maybe in my old age, that's the way I'll remember it. To be absolutely candid, though, I had fucked myself halfway into a coma and didn't do dick for the next five or ten minutes but suck at air and admire the show.

Greg had a lot to admire so I took my time recovering. We both knew that before we headed back to base the next morning, we would need all the Marine strength we had going. I can report, though, that when he eased his ass out of my car and limped towards his morning formation, young Greg knew for sure that he had met his match—for the following weekend, at least.

LIFE IS GOOD

All things considered, I like the way my life has turned out. I have an obscenely well-paying job for a certain software maker in Washington state. Living in the great Northwest is satisfying, if sometimes a bit damp. I have love and friends and no troubles beyond the occasional pesky bug in my code. Life is good.

Driving back up to Redmond the other week, I realized that somewhere along the way, I had grown staid and middle-aged. For the first time, I regretted my loss of youth and innocence —not that I would be the callow 18-year-old virgin I was for anything in the world anymore.

I pulled over to top off my tank at the same station in the small mountain hamlet of Fort Klamath where I had pumped gas and diesel during my youth, back in the halcyon days of the 1970s. So many aging generations look back on a halcyon youth that the term has become almost a cliche, but ours really was. Stonewall and Vietnam were in the recent past; HIV lurked safely unknown in the future. For the first time in history, young American men could be who they were and enjoy the hell out of life. For men of the mid-1970s, life was one long fucking party.

Unless, of course, they lived in Fort Klamath, Oregon. Growing up, I knew I was marooned at the very end of the earth and that no adventure would ever come my way. To make matters worse, I was a cute kid—the sort who looks 13 when he's really 18 and is carded well into his 30s. Every time a man would look me over and consider, the term "jail bait" would pop into his mind and he would drive off down the road, leaving us both disappointed. I didn't mind at first, but as my eighteenth summer wound down and college loomed on the horizon, I began to wonder whether I would ever get laid.

Back then, not four persons on the planet had heard of the spotted owl, and most of our business came from huge, lumbering logging trucks, pulling in for diesel and to give their drivers a break. Sometimes the drivers would go next door to the Cozy Kitchen for something to eat; sometimes they would just stretch their muscles while I filled them up.

Pete, if that really was his name, stretched his muscle plenty, but he was the first of those logging drivers to fill me up instead. He was the first to ask. I saw the look, of course, and watched him savor my ass and broad shoulders and cherry-boy face, but by then I had lost hope. When he got around to asking how old I was, I was so surprised and happy that I nearly shat. He didn't believe me right off, but I'd long since taken to carrying my driver's license with me, just in case. Once he was sure, he didn't waste a whole lot of time: "How'd you like to show me where y'all keep your crapper?"

Pete didn't figure in any of the nightly dreams I'd had of that day. He was old, for starters—in his 30s! He had beard stubble and smelled of dust and diesel and dead pines, but he had another, more ancient, smell, too. His body was still mostly hard, but spreading through the middle and, once he got naked, I was astounded at how much hair a primate could have and not be a gorilla. Still, Big Peter was my chance and I took it—or we took each other.

The door had no sooner clicked behind us than Pete was pulling off his flannel and jeans, ready to knock off a piece and get back on the road. I was nervous and afraid and eager and a thousand other things, but I was naked and ready for him before his jeans hit the floor. It was just as well I didn't dally.

Without a word, a huge hand reached out and grabbed me behind the neck, pulling my face against his in a crushing kiss that took my breath away and left my heart racing for days. The rough beard stubble ground against my cheeks, but it was his big, stiff dick slashing upwards against my belly that really convinced me deep down that my boyhood was fated to end at last.

His other hand skidded hard down until it found my virgin ass and locked on for the kill. As his tongue and lips taught me what to do, his palm roughly massaged my glutes, first grinding one against the other and then parting the two. When he shoved his hand down into my ass crack, I thought my heads would pop off from sheer excitement. The gloriously wicked feel of another man's hand where mine had been so often, grating across my hungry asshole and pinching it wild sent bolts of electric rapture ricocheting up my spine.

Old Pete didn't waste a lot of time feeling me up, though. I had just realized for sure that he was rubbing me the right way when he pulled away, put his hand on my head, pushed down, and proved what a romantic he was: "Suck my dick, kid."

I'd never even touched another man's crank before, let alone licked one. Starting with Pete's was a major-league shock. For one thing, it was nearly ten inches long and almost as thick as my wrist. Like my unit, his was uncut—and deliciously nasty. I don't just mean it had huge blue veins pulsing along its length, though it did that, too. The really nasty part was the smell.

I don't know how long he'd been driving through the summer heat, but that crotch smelled like a dead llama that's been left out in the rain too long. Sweat and musk had cooked together in his jeans to make a smell I'd never imagined possible. Then, when his hands shoved my face onto his dick, I got another jolt.

I didn't realize at the time that uncut dick doesn't have to be rank, but Pete's must have set a record. When I slid a tentative tongue into the wrinkled crown of his foreskin to scoop up the clear, sweet pre-cum he seemed to have so much of, my tongue erupted with the taste of sweat and stale piss and some stuff I later discovered was called *dickcheese*. The weird thing about the stench of his crotch and the awful taste of his dick was how I couldn't get enough of them. Everything I knew told me I should be revolted. I should be gagging my guts out at the stench. Instead, everything I was made me reach up and pull his `skin back, stripping his huge louring knob of its protection and leaving every nasty speck that lived there for my tongue to gobble down like a starving sailor on a goat farm.

Maybe instinct drove me on; maybe I just didn't know what I liked. I couldn't help myself. I tore at his tender meat, slurping away with my tongue and lips and would have done more if I'd been able to cram his dick into my mouth. God knows I tried, but Pete's monster log was just too big. I was so clueless that I didn't wonder how I was going to take up my virgin ass what I couldn't even get in my mouth; I was too busy licking everything from my chops to his pubes to care. I just knew I was finally in heaven.

Pete must have thought so, too. His head slipped back in pleasure, his mouth gaped wide, and he talked an endless stream dirty enough that I'd have taken notes if I hadn't been so busy sucking his big, nasty logger dick. His hands didn't take any chances and held my head tight, grinding my mouth and tongue to whatever part of his dick he thought needed the most polishing. Between the fumes and the gloriously unfamiliar tastes and the way my heart was racing and pounding in my ears, I almost passed out— and might have done if the sex-crazed bastard hadn't kept me just where he wanted me: on my knees, between his legs, vacuuming his big, ugly dick.

At one point, maybe I got too rough because Pete's hands aimed my face lower to lap at his hairy nuts. The taste of that revisited crotch was a kinder, gentler flavor than the raunch of his unwashed crank, but I had plenty to work with to keep me busy. When I sucked one nut at a time into my mouth and tugged gently on his sperm-cords, Pete didn't know whether to scream or moan so he did both at once—swearing all the while.

Just when I thought I was going to get to take it up the ass, he showed me that I was a long way from finished learning about foreplay. Leaning over the washbasin and spreading his cheeks, he showed me a tangle of thick, matted black hairs and a pulsing pink pucker and said, "OK, Kid. Now suck my asshole until I tell you to stop—but don't get any ideas."

If his crotch had stunk, his asscrack was a whole new definition of vile; but, once again, when my tongue finally worked up the nerve to give it a taste-test, something deep in my brain kicked in and made me go for the gusto. I didn't like the way his hairs prickled at my face, but my lips and tongue loved the taste and smell and throbbing texture of his shithole. Once I had locked my cock-sucking lips around his hole and started digging my tongue into his ass, Pete unhanded his glutes and leaned forward onto the basin. Now and again, he would help keep me up his ass by wriggling his butt against my face to work my tongue deeper.

The whole time I was sucking his shithole and keeping his nasty dick well in hand, the bastard moaned and talked dirty and groaned and cussed me out—and I couldn't get enough of his abuse. I felt at once like the lowest, wickedest slut of creation and better than I'd ever imagine I could feel. If the feel of his tangy shithole quivering against my tongue and his dick slowly fucking my hand was what sex was all about, I was for it.

When I stopped to take a breath and let my jaw uncramp, Pete pretended to take offense and growled, "The work too hard for you, Kid? OK. You just let me take care of things."

In no time at all, he had me bent over the basin, my feet kicked wide and his big leaky dick pushed against my asshole. Remember, this was in the days before rubbers and lube. Back in the raw, anything-goes seventies, when a guy wanted to fuck, that's all there was to it. If the asshole he was reaming wide was virgin meat or wasn't ready or broke open, the fucker didn't care.

In Pete's case, the fucker didn't care. He wasn't in that service station john to find true love. He wanted to bust a nut and I had the hole he was going to use—one way or another. I knew of course that his dick would hurt. It stood to reason. I braced myself against the basin and the wall and hung on. I thought I was ready for the pain. I was wrong.

At first, nothing much happened. I guess I was tighter even than Pete expected because he had a hell of a time getting up my ass. The more he reared back and pounded that thick dick against my hole, only to have it bounce off, the madder he got. Finally he said something about "Okay, bitch" and reached low to grab my shoulders from below. He eased his ass low and then pulled me backwards, pressing his monster logger dick against my virgin hole. First I felt pressure, then discomfort. Then the whole fucking world exploded as he reamed his way hard enough against my shithole to pop it loose.

To this day I have no idea of the details. I just know one minute he held me helpless in his arms and the next every nerve I had was exploding in agony. Oddly enough, my ass didn't hurt more than anywhere else. I felt his dick up inside me, of course, but the first waves of pain were too fierce to put a name to—even if my body had known what name to choose.

Pete's dick didn't bother lying fallow for me to get comfortable. The instant his hips slammed against my butt, he was on the rise again, surging upwards and taking my guts with them. Then he would change his angle slightly and stab in again. Instead of getting better, the pain mounted from unbearable to indescribable and then beyond. I wanted to scream out, but nothing in my body worked. With his dick filling my body, I couldn't breathe or talk or even pass out. I hung on, hoping that the endless surging waves of pain or lack of air would finally knock me out so that he could have my ass without killing me.

After the first two or three slashing strokes, I had to piss but nothing would come out. I've since learned all about prostates, but Pete knew how to dick mine like a master. He picked up speed and ferocity as his hands tightened on my shoulders and his breath roared into my right ear. The harder he sliced his way through my guts, the more certain I was I'd never let another man use me. Then, slowly, an odd thing happened.

The waves of pain were as fierce and brutal and unforgiving as ever, but my body gradually learned what to do with them. The sharp edges of agony blurred into contentment and then into pleasure. The matted fur from his chest and belly grated against the naked skin of my back as his dick humped my wounded hole like a buck rabbit on Benzedrine. He had long since stopped talking and was now just growling and snorting and grunting as he used my shithole harder and deeper with every brutal, selfish, glorious thrust.

Those blurred edges of pain soon glowed with unexpected glory as the blood and juices of my ass lubed his dick and greased the skids of lust. His teeth tore at the back of my neck and I felt my dick explode, spraying my legs and the washbasin with the biggest, baddest load of jism in my young life. I couldn't believe my dick had gone off by itself, but that disbelief was very low on a very long list.

I couldn't believe how right Pete felt up my ass. I couldn't believe the surging waves of rapture his every jab sent rampaging through my soul. I couldn't believe that I actually had a man's dick up my ass, finally. Most of all, I couldn't believe how time and space folded in around us, trapping us together in a shifting warp of raw, timeless, animal power. That slow-motion eternity caressed me from the inside, stealing a divine spark of energy from Pete's huge dick and radiating it outward to hold us together, one being with a single purpose. I felt myself slip away to join the consciousness up my ass and fuse with it forever as time skidded to a stop.

Something jolted me back to life. I think it was the feel of Pete's gushers of creamy jism splashing up inside my ass. It may have been his screaming or his biting my neck like a deranged tomcat. Maybe it was even the rabid way he was grinding the shattered ruins of my ass with his pubes. Whatever got me back with the program, even an ex-virgin like me knew that Pete was pumping enough jism up my ass to last a Siberian winter. Some instinct made me reach low between my legs and grab his nuts to squeeze the last drops up through his rampaging dick and into my ass. Pete just kept on yelling and spurting and bucking against me until I was sure the old bastard was having some kind of an attack.

When he finally did run dry, the rest was anticlimactic. He collapsed onto me for a few seconds while he caught his breath and then pulled his dick out of what little was left of my ass. I looked around, expecting to see several organs dangling from the thing, and saw only a splotch or two of blood and cum. He tousled my hair, saying something like "You're a good fuck, kid. You're okay." Then he pulled on his clothes and walked out the door.

I took longer, first making sure I wasn't bleeding too much and then cleaning up the mess I'd made when I nutted. By the time I was dressed and had limped outside, Pete and his truck were gone. I left the station a couple weeks later to go off to school and never saw him again. I like to think he stopped by again later and was sorry to see me gone. I know I went off my feed for three days after he left—not from grief. I just didn't want to have to shit out the load he'd pumped up my ass until I absolutely had to.

In a metaphysical, Zen sort of way, I guess that load is still there where he left it. I know I was never the same after that glorious summer day of my youth. Pete wasn't anything remotely like my ideal man, but he was my first—and that makes him as special as they come.

"One of my Navy bitches once asked me a riddle: What's the difference between a gay jarhead and a straight one?
His answer was: 'a six-pack.'
That may not be totally accurate, however.
I once needed almost half a case to get
a lance corporal's legs in the air."
- The immortal words of the esteemed
military sex chronicle, Rick Jackson

He's ready, willing, and able... he's a

SAILOR BOY
by
Ken Smith

An Erotic Novella

STARbooks Press
Sarasota, FL

One
HANGING AROUND

Brad hung from the ceiling like a succulent portion of prime meat, his acorn-brown body clothed in a small leather jock and black leather harness which held him there. His pink-palmed hands glistened with sweat, handcuffed behind his back. The contraption wasn't uncomfortable, and the room was pleasantly warm. But he couldn't believe he had allowed himself to get into this position! He wasn't afraid—slightly apprehensive, maybe.

The young guy who had welcomed him into this mansion was pleasant and attractive, but Brad soon realized he wasn't the punter. He had talked little and had ushered Brad into one of the many rooms, where he had offered Brad a spliff, explaining that the gentleman was delayed and he may have to wait a short while. He also informed Brad he would be required to be placed in a harness. Brad agreed.

Uncharacteristically, Brad puffed on the drugged cigarette and settled into a four-seat leather settee, allowing some classical music from an ultra expensive stereo system to seduce him. The reward for his services was to be a good deal more than usual—one hundred pounds—which he'd eagerly accepted.

The seductive soft music was the last thing he could remember.

Gently he rotated his harnessed body, in a room that was blacker than black—not a chink of light finding a way into his searching eyes. An aroma of expensive cologne was apparent and had an arousing effect on him. Classical music floated around the room, but he was unaware of its direction. Brad found it comforting as it wrapped around his nakedness.

Who the punter was, he had no idea. The voice at the end of the phone had only given the address and said he had a client for him. Brad guessed that that voice belonged to the young guy who had invited him in.

Brad was unsure how long he'd been suspended there—maybe hours, maybe less? The spliff and alcohol had made him lose his ability to reason. Possibly the punter had already had sex with him? He really didn't know. Brad reassured himself that he was safe, albeit in a strange way. The client was obviously wealthy, and wealthy punters were seldom the cruel type. It was, he guessed, the client's way of getting his kicks—all punters had their own way of getting off.

"If my mum could see me now," he mused, "dangling like a smoked kipper. What would she make of her adorable son, who she thought was still a virgin?" Brad laughed inwardly as that thought entered his mind, and hummed to the music. There was little else he could do; not even reach an itch on his bottom that had begun to annoy him. "The things people do for sex or money," he smiled, and scratched as close to the annoying itch as possible.

He was becoming slightly irritable, hanging there, and wished the punter would soon appear, but the claustrophobic feeling of being boxed in wasn't worrying, and in some ways was similar to the confines of a mess-deck when darkened. For a moment he wondered if he was in the same room where he had smoked the spliff, it having a similar distinct smell of leather; and when he had called out, his voice echoed, indicating that the room was of a similar size.

A match suddenly struck in the far corner of the room and for a brief moment that area was illuminated. Spinning in the direction of the fiery glow, Brad absorbed as much of his surrounding as possible, but by the time his eyes had settled on the area of brightness, the glow had subsided.

A waft of tobacco smoke sailed toward him, its sweet aroma, comforting. In the direction of the bright glow, he could barely make out the silhouette of a man's head, as he puffed on the pipe, firing it up to its full potential. He appeared to be sitting in a winged armchair with his back toward Brad.

"I'm Brad," Brad whispered in a soft voice, with just a hint of nervousness. "What can I do to please you, Sir?"

"Are you comfortable and warm enough, Brad?" The man was well spoken, his voice warm. Brad confirmed that he was fine. He would have said so, anyway, regardless of his discomfort. He was, after all, on uncharted waters.

"If you wish to leave, please say so."

Those words reassured Brad he was in no danger and, feeling safe, he began to become sexually aroused by this unexplored situation. "I'm ready to please you, Sir," he seduced, enticing the man with his 'come to bed' tone.

The man, who Brad guessed was quite mature, inquired if he had any other clients to visit. Lying, but he didn't know why, Brad confirmed that he did.

"I shall pay you two hundred pounds to cover your other clients," the man suggested, his voice very authoritative. It felt more like a command than an offer, but Brad accepted. It was the intrigue of his position, the sexual excitement of the unknown that made him agree; but such a large sum of money must have been an influence.

An agreement reached, the man raised himself from the chair and began to walk toward Brad. Brad was mesmerized by the glowing pipe in the Mystery Man's hand as he came closer, and his heart began beating fast with each silent step toward his vulnerable body....

Two
INITIATION

Brad's days as a rent boy had started early. It wasn't planned and it wasn't for the money, although that was a bonus, providing him with many pleasures other boys of his age couldn't afford.

He had always suspected that he was gay and had not the slightest hang-up about it. He reckoned he knew at the age of ten that girls were not all they were cracked up to be, and guys' bodies were just wonderful. He even thought, if men were supposed to have sex with women, why weren't there places in men's chests for women's breasts to slot into? He was sure that they would always get in the way, and found them repulsive things. Yes, women served a purpose, they could produce more men, but apart from that, he wasn't in the least bit interested. Brad didn't hate women; after all, his mum was one and he loved her dearly. Also, he wasn't sexist, although some may have found his reasoning so. No, men were what he adored. Men were what he wanted. And men were what he would get!

Brad knew that he was a most beautiful young boy, and to observe men go wild over him made him feel even more so. Although he knew the power of his beauty, he was not narcissistic. Almost all of his punters fell in love with him, treating him like an Adonis, but he loved them equally and gave every ounce of himself to each, yet was always open and honest, making it clear that he wasn't theirs forever. They respected his truthfulness and found it refreshing to be with a youth who clearly loved himself and what he was doing. It was almost a divine gift to be able to share such beauty in an uninhibited way, and Brad was proud of it. In fact, the punter's money meant little to him. It was the love of men he adored, and he couldn't get enough of their attention.

The first time Brad was paid for sex was during a lunch break whilst still at school. A toilet in a nearby park was always popular with young men, and Brad would sit in the sunshine beside it, watching their comings and goings. It was something he really enjoyed. At bedtime, those delicious men provided him with fantasies whilst wanking, or became visitors in his regular wet dreams. It was also in this park that his awareness of his own beauty became apparent.

A variety of men would cruise him whilst he ate his snack or did his homework. Few ever spoke, but many offered him a smile. His admirers came from all walks of life. He'd felt the sexual desire of telephone engineers, bank managers, milk men and construction workers; observing their eyes seducing him. It gave him great joy and his young body would tingle with sexual pleasure. Often he became aroused.

With so much passion paraded before him, it was surprising he rarely entered the toilet himself, and only then to have a pee. On the occasions he did go for a pee, he noticed the men peeing but not peeing, and observed their eyes searching his for the slightest interest. He seldom gave them full eye contact, but often looked lower down, admiring their sex and long for something as big and beautiful to grow from his small frame.

But one lunch break, on a glorious day in June, with the temperature in the eighties, Brad was sitting in the park in his shortest of shorts, having just finished a P.E. lesson. As usual, he was close by the toilet, watching the guys come and go.

Along the path and between the flower beds, he saw a young guy, about twenty, moving toward him. At first he didn't recognize him, but then realized he had seen him before, but dressed in a suit. He looked decidedly different in his jeans. Brad was stunned by his bare-chested sexiness and excitedly focussed on the guy's bulging crotch. When he had seen the guy in his suit there was no indication of the shape of his body. But now, with the guy wearing only tight denim jeans, Brad could see everything which made him a man.

Passing closer than he needed, as he walked toward the toilet, the guy offered Brad a pleasant smile. Brad gave him one in return. He had never followed anyone into the toilet before, but this guy was so manly, so sexually stunning, that an overwhelming urge to discover what was hidden inside his pants urged Brad to do so. Excited and aroused, Brad followed him in.

Inside the rather smelly toilet, he discovered that the guy had entered a cubicle. Brad stood at the urinal, pretending to pee, hoping he would soon come out. After a couple of men had genuinely used the convenience, he began to feel self-conscious standing there doing nothing. He decided to leave but just as quickly changed his mind. He'd never been inside a cubicle before, except at school, and was curious. Tiptoeing, although he didn't know why, he entered the cubicle alongside the occupied one; gently closing the door.

Brad's body shivered slightly. He felt guilty knowing he was doing something he shouldn't but it was also his excitement that was making him shake. He didn't need to go to the toilet but pulled his shorts and pants down anyway; sitting on the wet and cold seat.

Whilst waiting for the guy to emerge, he began to amuse himself by reading the scribble on the door and walls. The school toilets also had writing on them but nothing as explicit and exciting as this. With his interest so fixed, he had completely forgotten about the guy in the adjoining cubicle. Some of the stories were so erotic he began to gently toss. Unnoticed to him, however, there was a large circular hole in the dividing wall. On becoming aware of this, he was shocked to discover an eye peering through. Brad stopped tossing.

Moving forward, he bent and peered through the hole and watched with amazement, disbelief and desire, as his manly neighbor carefully caressed himself. Brad thought it so sexy, so beautiful, and desperately wished he could reach through and grasp the solid sex. Aroused by that stimulating sight, he began rubbing his cock vigorously.

He had no idea why he did what he next did. Perhaps the desire for this man to touch him was too great to resist, or some subconscious urge rushed through him, because he pushed his youthful erection through the opening. The sudden warmth was unexpected. The firmness of the mouth and softness of lips and tongue made him come instantly. The heat of the young man's mouth that worked over his sex was just sensational!

Stunned, Brad sat back on the bowl, his body quivering, the sensation sending shivers throughout his slender frame. Peering back through the hole, he discovered that the guy was now rubbing himself very fast. Filled with an overwhelming urge for that huge sex inside of his own mouth, he parted his lips over the opening. Instantly, it was filled by the thick, firm flesh; its sweet and sour liquid gushing down his throat the moment his mouth moved to the base. Brad drained the huge cock, desperate to savour more. He was even reluctant to release it back to its owner after he'd swallowed the milky mouthful. Brad could not describe the excitement that surged through his body. He was ecstatic! He was liberated. He was gay for sure!

The episode was so enjoyable, Brad wanted to repeat it again and began to relive the moment, wanking furiously whilst recalling every detail but stopping briefly when five-pound note was pushed through the hole. Written on it was, "Thanks, boy."

It was for Brad the beginning of a very fruitful, rent-boy life, both sexuality and financially.

Brad appeared a good deal younger than his age, his tanned skin silk-smooth. His small frame, which weighed under eight stone, had well-defined muscles for his size, including both his arms and legs. His backside was a treat to behold, with full rounded buttocks, the likes of which you only find on black boys. His face was a dream: lips full; nose slender but slightly fuller at the nostrils; cheeks unblemished and thin; ears, small and dainty. But his "come to bed" eyes were the icing on the cake. Large and blue, they were adorned with long, rich-brown eyelashes and topped with light-brown eyebrows. A matching crop of curly blond hair fell sexily over one eye.

Some would say that he was as pretty as a girl. Brad would say that that was an insult.

Other features only men and boys had the privilege of seeing —making them almost pee their pants—were the tiniest of nipples on his chest, his micro-dot navel, and his long, thin sex with its tuft of cock hair.

Great Masters dreamed of boys like Brad and would have been honoured to place his beauty upon canvass or mould a statue in his likeness. But who would have known beauty could be born of beauty!

It was on Brad's fifteenth birthday that a butterfly was born of a butterfly. On this day he was adorned with a sailor's uniform, having joined the Royal Navy. Every sailor on every ship must have gasped in awe as he slipped into his bum-hugging bell-bottoms, white front, sailor's collar and cap. For Brad it wasn't a working uniform, it was his second skin. And whilst other baby sailors complained that their clothes itched, or were too tight, or their caps were too large or small, and even cried with homesickness, Brad carefully adorned himself with the pleasure and joy of decorating a Christmas tree.

The ritual complete, he admired himself in a mirror and although he didn't wish to comment, he knew he looked wonderful beyond words. Instinctively, he knew he had been given the key to his success. The Navy would be his shelter, his home, his daily job, but his career would be giving sexual pleasure to men. The Navy was the perfect place to be: respectable, revered, reputable but, above all, rife with men!

Thus, Brad's life as a sailor began, but his initial training was no simple task and he needed every ounce of courage to get through it.

There were those in the Navy for whom beauty held very little meaning who even found it a weakness, something to be despised in or beaten from a boy. The harsh and cruel physical training instructors were the worst, but even they were careful with their cruelty toward Brad because, thankfully, he was good at most sports. Thus protected by his sports skills, they could only resort to verbal abuse. It soon became apparent to Brad that they were threatened by his sexuality, discovering their own suppressed sexual desires.

In order to make his training easier, Brad made a point of seducing those in authority, using his looks, charm, and skills. Intuitively, he knew those who would bed him, given the chance, rewarding them with seductive smiles or allowing them as close as possible to his body, within the bounds of their duties.

The swimming instructor was one such tutor Brad knew had fallen in love with him, and whilst he taught Brad to swim, would touch those parts he shouldn't. Brad found this pleasurable and did not dissuade him but, more importantly, he could use the instructor's friendship and authority as a protective measure against those who would make his life hell, deciding that he was a useful authority figure to have on his side. But Brad never allowed the instructor inside his trunks, however, he could do very little about providing the Instructor with oodles of delicious nakedness when he showered, even the occasional friendly smack on his bare bum. Even so, Brad would be the first to confess that he did find the instructor good-looking and tossed himself silly over him on many a night.

Although sexually desired by many, Brad decided he would keep his own sexual needs distanced from those who were training him. There would be plenty of time after he'd established himself and secured a good position to begin his sexual career. He would only allow his tutors the simplest of sexual stimulation in order to achieve his goals. Touching the erection beneath his swimming trunks was enough reward for the swimming instructor; who appeared amply satisfied, fully aware of the boundaries he should not cross.

When it came to choosing a trade, although he was capable of various excellent positions within the Navy, Brad chose to become a seaman. He would be working in the open air, on the upper-deck. This would keep his body fit and trim. He knew the majority of the work would be mundane—scrubbing decks, repairing ropes, painting, or general duties—but he would be with the real men of the Navy, and there would be plenty of beefy bodies to admire, even envy.

One would have thought that there would be little to learn if you were to spend your days scrubbing, tying knots and the like. How untrue! The Seamanship Manual was a daunting book to master and Brad was instructed on many different subjects—navigation, lifeboat drill, gunnery (his specialist subject), and a host of other subjects people took for granted.

The instructions on tying various knots, however, were very interesting. Brad could see a potential use for that information in his sexual career!

His months of training sailed swiftly by but without any sexual encounters with other ratings. There was rumor that they placed a substance in the drink to subdue sexual libido. Brad could not believe this because he was always wanking, which made him wonder if the other rumor "wanking makes you blind" might come true.

But the opportunity to touch other boy sailors often came about on the sports field, and Brad took every advantage, regularly grabbing the glorious parts of his shipmates. The greedy hands and occasionally mouths that gripped his cock were too numerous to mention. Brad made a mental note of those doing it more often than most.

Also, when they showered, he would observe the eyes of those who admired his nakedness. Brad considered this to be part of his training for his career as a rent boy. Understanding body language and eye contact would be an essential requirement. But bedding his mess mates was not among his priorities; he thought it might be too easy.

The important sexual encounters would be with the brass. These would be a challenge and the most rewarding. Of course, being gay in the Royal Navy was illegal and to be caught would mean curtains for himself and the officer, but fear of being caught, or seducing those who would risk their careers, would be added excitement.

Of the instructors who trained him, Brad guessed he could have bedded at least three, definitely, and maybe two who would have done it but would have lived a life of guilt until he'd left training. The swimming instructor was a cert, and during his last lesson attempted to slip his hand beneath Brad's trunks. Brad responded with a "treading on thin ice" look and the instructor brushed the incident aside with a nervous smile.

Come the end of training Brad's head had been filled with an encyclopaedia of information, most useful, some not. He knew many ways to tie a person up, although that wasn't the purpose of the knot training. He'd also seen every kind of naked body and cock, and was amazed at the different types. There was the scrumptiously small, horrendously huge, laughably little, tortured and twisted, bent upward or down. In fact he could describe them forever. The only thing they all had in common: they all longed for a hole to put them in!

But if he could chose his favorite cock, it would be longish but not over long; not too thick, uncut, have a small tuft of hair, and, hopefully, belong to a Greek god. But Brad was only too aware that if he was to pursue his chosen career, he would be unable to choose his favourite dick because the majority of the packets would come wrapped. And until the moment he unwrapped them, he would have no idea of what his present contained. Brad was truly looking forward to that because every day would be like Christmas, but he wouldn't be unwrapping presents, he would be unwrapping men!

His training complete, Brad waited in eager anticipation for his first draft, not to mention that first present!

Three
SHIP AHOY!

Brad's first draft was to be a small frigate based at Portsmouth. The train journey from Ipswich was very pleasant. Brad enjoyed travelling but, being a country lad, it did make him feel homesick as he was whisked through fields and tree-lined cuttings.

About halfway through the journey it unexpectedly took on a new dimension and became extremely interesting. A youngish suited gentleman, travelling to the city, was giving him those unmistakable looks that said, "I wish I could dive in your knickers." Brad played with the guy's emotions, giving him regular eye-contact and spreading his bell-bottomed legs, revealing their shape and the bulge in his crotch.

Their compartment was comparatively empty. Several times Brad seductively ran his hand up his leg and teasingly over his crotch. The guy desperately focused his eyes into a book but the magnetism of Brad's suggestiveness forced him increasingly to look in the young sailor's direction; mostly at the expanding crotch. Unable to contain the sexual urges rushing through his wanting body, the guy rose from his seat and began to head down the carriage. Brad was quick to observe that the man was extremely aroused, proof positive of the pulling power of his uniform.

Sensuously, Brad offered his prey a smouldering smile as he headed toward the exit, parting his lips and sliding his tongue erotically between them.

Hastily, the man moved down the corridor, falling from side to side as the train rushed them toward London. With some difficulty he opened the sliding door between carriages, nervously glancing back in Brad's direction. The message was quite clear and Brad rose from his seat as the subconscious signal 'to follow' flashed between them.

The fifteen minutes in the toilet was bliss for both, more so for Brad. Greedily the man mouthed the serge material and then the cotton underwear beneath, eventually releasing Brad's long sex and sucking upon it furiously, feasting frantically on the young sailor-boy.

Brad came twice, the first being so quick, he thought the guy deserved more for his money. Also, once was not sufficient to satisfy his own lust. Little conversation passed between them but ample money for his services did.

His devilish deed done, Brad didn't return to his seat; the buffet beckoned him to toast his successes, passing his seamanship exams and passing his pulling a punter practical. Both passed with flying colors, he thought.

A double rum roasted his throat and belly as he lay back in the buffet car. After it had taken effect, he began wondering if there were more clients on the train and how many he could service before he reached London.

The echoes of the Tannoy, repeating the station's name, woke Brad from a much-needed sleep. The rum, far from increasing his sexual activity, had sent him into slumber. His early morning departure, combined with the passionate sexual servitude, had obviously exhausted him, but he did have another train to catch, and as he brought himself to full awareness, fancied there might be an opportunity to find other clients before reaching Portsmouth.

Inside the station's cottage, more an act of curiosity, Brad watched rent boys and potential clients going through the motions of washing hands, having invisible pees, and changing cubicles in search of the body that met their requirements. Brad didn't stay and had a pretend pee between two guys with erections, but being sure to send signals of disinterest, then disappeared into the underground railway system where a sausage-shaped tube shot him through the bowels of the earth and across London to the next mainline station, where he boarded the Pompey train.

During the Portsmouth journey, Brad began to plan his life. He decided sailors, officers, or any other servicemen would not be clients, after all. He would stick to civilians and would not reveal to anyone on board that he was gay. If his plans were to be successful he felt that his two identities needed to be separate. There was no way he could rent a flat in which to service clients, so he would have to work the streets, cottages and bars, going back to a punter's home or doing it in public places. He would advertise but it would have to be worded carefully. There could be other problems. The ship would be at sea for weeks or even months, and cruising in his uniform could also prove difficult, what with the Military Police. He would need to find his own, less conspicuous corner.

Gay clubs and pubs were definitely out because the undercover guys—

the navy had their own—would have them under surveillance for sure. Still, the idea of popping into a gay pub dressed in a sailor's suit would be absolutely divine, for it would turn a few heads and pull the punters. Therefore he would need to seek out a quiet park with a cottage, or perhaps the sea-front and funfair would be good places. Gay trippers or guys on longer holidays were bound to provide a variety of voluptuous adventures.

Brad could visualize it all as he watched the blurred fields race by his window. The carriage became a sports car, whisking him along country lanes. At his side was a man's man— muscular, slim, tanned, and tormentingly titillating. With each gear change, Brad's body was shot with a surge of submissive sexual desire as the masculine hand manipulated the gear stick's thick, round head.

"Portsmouth! This is Portsmouth!" A feminine voice welcomed him to this seaside town.

Brad hadn't noticed the train slow, or the approach of the station, having fallen asleep. Passengers hustled and bustled, desperate to alight, swinging open doors whilst the train was still in motion. Why was everyone always in such a hurry?

He waited until most had left the carriage before adjusting his crotch, which had become proud in his pants, then carefully placed his cap upon his head and stepped from the train into this unromantic station.

After a brief walk, the thick-bricked, reddish-brown dockyard wall loomed high above him. The words PORTSMOUTH DOCKYARD, in wrought iron, stared down at his insignificant presence. Two green gates stood open wide, a large, toothless, hungry mouth, eager to devour him. Brad, completely unaffected by its daunting presence, strutted confidently into its awaiting mouth, canvas kit bag slung upon his shoulder.

An over-friendly dockyard policeman directed him to his ship, after checking his paperwork. Brad thanked him politely.

Passing Nelson's infamous H.M.S. Victory, Brad paid it little attention and was more interested in the various sailors and dockyard workers going about their duties. Casually he made his way toward his ship, dodging trains, which used the roads as well as other traffic. He was also keeping a wary eye on the huge cranes, lest they drop something upon him.

After a sweaty, fifteen minute walk, he was in sight of the main harbor with a parade of ships moored along its length, each with its own special characteristics. There were an enormous, flat-topped aircraft-carrier, a couple of minute minesweepers, some frigates, with a good deal of fire-power, and a dreary depot ship. A black submarine was also docked, only its conning tower visible. It looked dwarfed against the mighty carrier. At the far end of the mooring bays, lying in dry dock, he found his frigate.

Brad was thankful he'd not been drafted to a carrier or a submarine, but this rust-bucket did little to fill him with joyful abandon. Between the patches of red lead paint and the blotches of yellow lead paint, there were splashes of ship's grey and a good deal of brown rust. Brad's new home resembled a patchwork quilt of the most morbid colors. His head dropped in dismay.

Over the ship a small army of worker-ant sailors chipped, hammered, scraped and painted. Some used yellow, some red, and a few grey. There appeared to be little organization, and Brad wondered if they were painting over each other sections, or chipping away freshly laid paint.

A selection of sailors hung from yardarms or swung over the ship's side in cat cradles, paint brushes slopping, hammers hammering. All the while bodies rushed up and down the gangway, arms filled with an assortment of odd items. Brad's home was in the process of a refit.

Among the descenders of the gangway came a Noble Knight, naked to the waist, his red-yellow-blue-grey overalls folded over his backside, the sleeves tied about his waist. Giving Brad a warm smile, he asked his name, checking if Brad was his new recruit. Brad acknowledged with a half salute but hesitated before completing the action. Dressed as he was, the Noble Knight was very unlikely to be an officer.

Greg, which was the Knight's name, grabbed Brad's kit bag with his muscular, tattooed arm and hand, hoisting it effortlessly onto his shoulder, then springing up the gangway like a young gazelle, checked briefly to see if Brad was following.

"Oh, my Greek god!" whispered Brad, as he watched the hunk of hormones ascend before him, and his boyhood bulged in his bell-bottoms!

With a hint of self consciousness creeping into his mind, for he looked so new in this muddled mess of mucky men, he gingerly followed Greg over the gangway and onto the quarterdeck.

Beneath the ensign flapping in the breeze, like a long-lost lover, Greg awaited his boy prince. And, Brad, overcome by the hustle and bustle and Greg's naked chest, almost forgot to salute this hallowed section of the ship.

Together they moved below decks, into the mess deck, where Greg introduced himself. He would be Brad's boss. There were many bosses above Greg but he would be his number-one boss, the one who would give him his orders or who Brad should see if he had problems. The next thing Greg did was give Brad a large brown parcel tied with string. The only thing Brad wanted to give Greg, was a kiss!

"How sweet," thought Brad, "he's only known me a few minutes, and he's already giving me presents." Almost believing it was a present, Brad unwrapped it with childlike wonderment. It's contents totally baffled him, causing Greg to laugh, a beautiful laugh. Brad's present was a canvas hammock.

While Greg demonstrated how to assemble all the pieces and how to sling it, Brad could only wonder how both would fit into it!

The hammock slinging mastered, Brad took in his new home. The contents of this mess deck, this metal marvel, were minimal. A thousand pipes and wires with ambiguous markings zigzagged across the deck-head, then vanished through the bulkheads. Six four-seater tables stood in the centre, bolted to the deck. A bank of silver lockers, also bolted in place, covered one bulkhead. Above, on the deck-head, were iron roller bars and hooks. This was where the hammocks were slung at night. Over the hatch, leading to the deck above, a Tannoy mouthed the occasional order or request for someone to do something or contact someone else, then switched to an unidentifiable radio station. Luxury of luxuries, in one corner stood a solitary fridge. Not a TV in sight, nor an armchair, nor any other furniture that would make it more homey. Only a few formica chairs, with tubular metal frames, stood under each table.

Brad's first thought, "How could thirty boys and men live together in this small space without killing each other?"

Along the port side of the mess ran a long deep well, filled with thick, black, gooey oil. Running along its length, one of the propeller shafts. The stench was sickening.

"Shouldn't that be on the outside of the ship?" wondered Brad. "Is this an old ship?" he shyly asked his Noble Knight.

"Old? The Germans sunk it in the First World War and it was raised from the deep," laughed Greg, and rubbed his big hand over Brad's locks.

"He loves me!" delighted Brad, and laughed along with him.

It was time for a tour, and both began a trek around the rust bucket, which did look better on the inside. Greg pointing out places of importance—canteen, NAAFI, heads and showers. Also, places out-of-bounds, such as the communications office, officers' mess deck, and the like.

During the tour, Brad registered with various departments— pay office, sick bay, galley and stores—each stamping his draft card. As they walked about, he noticed several sailors giving him the eye. However, the Master-at-Arms, the ship's policeman, was stone-faced and so cold, you could have frozen ice cubes in his butt. Brad listened nervously as he laid down the law. Bradhated him instantly. Mercifully, most of the rest of the crew seemed jolly and Brad thought he would be happy.

Along the Burma Road, the main passage running through the ship, a bulkhead of sailors chucked chirpy comments at Greg as he escorted Brad below decks.

"Cradle snatching, Greg!" one beer-bellied sailor barracked.

"Who's the bit of s-k-i-n?" slithered another. Skin was the sailor term for a pretty boy.

But when one rating, almost as handsome as Greg, gave a loud wolf-whistle and began singing, "Love is a Many Splendored Thing," Brad began to wonder if Greg fancied boys. And although he'd ruled out having sex with sailors, since meeting Greg he knew he would love to dive into his pants. Already he was in love! Greg was charming, big and strong, yet soft and cuddly. In fact, Brad couldn't wait to see him naked, which prompted him to ask whether they were to live in the same mess. When Greg confirmed that that was so, Brad's face erupted red, and the bulge in his bell-bottoms just exploded!

During their tour, although Brad had been taught all the naval terms: heads for toilets, bulkhead, deck-head and deck, for wall, ceiling and floor, and so on. But he still found himself saying things like stairs instead of ladders, which caused Greg to tease him. Brad soon realized that being on a ship was like being in another world, with its own language, humor, rules and punishments. No longer was he a baby-sailor in a Training Establishment. This was the "big boys" navy, in more than one sense of the word!

Back in the mess, Brad began to stow his kit, but he was no longer alone. The working day had finished, although sailors would always be working somewhere, and the mess deck had filled with the bodies that lived there. The place was buzzing with chatter, laughter, and bodies in various states of undress. That delighted Brad!

As far as those naked bodies' looks went, they ranged from the unbearably ugly, to the sheer gorgeousness of Greg. But Brad had already decided that only his Noble Knight stood the remotest chance of ripping the pants from his eager body, and if that were possible, now would be the perfect time. He was unbelievably horny!

In the mess deck, sailors laughed and swore, and swore, and swore. They also groped cocks and butts, kissed—cheeky kisses —and talked filthy, dirty talk. But it all meant nothing sexual. It was only their way of surviving this often difficult life. The sexual banter and constant touching were purely acts of comradeship. Brad reckoned it would be extremely difficult to discover for sure who among these kissing, cuddling, groping men would be those who really did fancy boys.

Greg was constantly being teased about his new skin, but it affected him not in the least, and he gave as good as he took. Brad was captivated by his fellow messmates and found their wit, and the speed with which remarks were parried and countered, brilliant.

Later that evening, Greg was preparing to go ashore. Wrapped in a towel, he headed to the deck above and the showers. Brad, overcome with the desire to see him naked, quickly stripped and dashed after him.

As expected, the showers were spotlessly clean but completely outdated. Brad abandoned his attempt to get the water to the temperature of his liking and plunged into the cold, lumpy spray. Greg was in the shower opposite, his shower curtain drawn. Brad left his open. He didn't mind who saw his body. In fact, he wanted them to.

After five minutes Greg's curtain swished open. He looked surprised to see Brad but commented that he liked his boys to keep themselves clean. Brad gave him a grin, pleased that he had pleased him, then, as soon as the opportunity presented itself, dropped his gaze between Greg's muscular thighs.

Brad gasped! Greg's cock was gigantic! It hung, semi-hard from being soaped, almost to his knee, and must have been as thick as Brad's own arm, and was a good three inches longer than his sex. Swamped by a sudden surge of shyness, he drew his curtain closed as blood burst into his cheeks and cock.

Did he imagine it, or did Greg give him that knowing smile? Brad wondered. One thing for sure, he knew what he'd be tossing over tonight!

Ten-thirty and the Tannoy sounded "Pipe Down" and the lights went out. Only the red night-light remained lit, but after a while that became as bright as any ordinary bulb, illuminating the mess in a seductive, warm glow.

A kindly old Sea Salt had helped Brad sling his hammock and even provided him with a hammock stretcher to place between the nettles, to stop the contraption wrapping around him like a cocoon. After several failed attempts, to much laughter from fellow sailors, Brad finally managed to manipulate his body into the monster.

The canvas contraption was decidedly uncomfortable, and Brad was sure he would not sleep. Also, the noise of the ship was unbearable. Fans hummed, pipes clinked and clanked, and duty sailors constantly came and went. It seemed as if the ship were alive, everything with a voice of its own.

His wank over Greg's juicy giant took a while to materialize. Most of the hammocks touched, the slightest movement making the others move. At sea this would not be a problem as all would be swinging and swaying, but here in port, Brad thought twice about each movement he made. However, when the hammock next to his, containing a delightfully young stoker, began to take on a steady rhythm, Brad became aroused by the thought of the lad tossing and commenced his own steady caress. Then, filling his thoughts with his face foraging in Greg's furry forest, he began a more forceful rub of his cock.

"Wanking again, Spider?" a voice next to the stoker teased.

Brad stopped instantly!

"Just rocking myself to sleep," came the unconcerned reply.

Hammocks began to swing, accompanied by grunts, groans, oohs and aahs. Feeling instantly relaxed, realizing wanking was an acceptable occurrence, Brad resumed rubbing his cock whilst Greg did all manner of naughty things to him during his fantasy.

Four
THE FIRST CRUISE

Brad made good use of the period in dry dock whilst the ship underwent its refit. He ventured into every crevice of the ship that was permissible, until he knew the ship's contents and superstructure, finding secret and secluded places, should he need them for sexual favors.

It was impossible to know everyone on the frigate but he became acquainted with as many as possible, especially those it was useful to know, logging in his memory a whole range of faces. Definitely he noted those who were good-looking or gave him lingering lustful looks. His feelings for Greg, though, came as an unexpected emotional experience, and over the months they became closely bonded. And although Greg had never given him the slightest indication that he would like to have sex, Brad was sure he was falling in love. That was something he hoped he could avoid as it would most certainly put paid to his rent boy plans. Unfortunately, Greg was such a wonderful guy, and dare he admit it, fitted his vision of a boyfriend perfectly.

Continuing with his plans, on the days when he was allowed ashore, Brad found a park in which to cruise. Its cottage, which had a good few users, was hidden from view by a clump of tall bushes, set in a far corner. He decided he would use this place to begin with, but his plan was to advertise his services in a local paper. That advert would read, "Young lad seeks local work. Anything considered." Added to this would be the phone number of one of a pair of call boxes situated close by the cottage. Brad was pleased to have found a pair of call boxes, as his further plan was to use one number for the advert and the other for regular clients when he had found them. He was sure he would soon discover whether a caller was looking for sex. In any event, if there was some confusion, he need only replace the receiver. Should someone else answer, he expected they would inform the caller they had the wrong number. Anyway, he was fairly confident the system would work.

Whenever the opportunity presented itself, and if the weather was fine, Brad would venture to the park. In his sailor's uniform, he reckoned he received double the interest from guys, unlike his schoolboy days. Men no longer seemed so shy or too scared to chat. And although his age was not a lot greater, he suspected his uniform's maturing qualities must have given them more confidence. Of course, a good few who made contact were not guys. Curiously, many were old ladies or young mums with kids in tow. But he chatted to them all and felt it important that he should appear as normal as possible, without putting off potential clients. As yet, he had not placed the advert. He decided to wait until he was absolutely confident and comfortable with his plans.

During a Friday afternoon, when he was off watch, Brad once again found himself in the park, cruising the cottage. Without warning, the sky opened and threw its contents of acid rain down upon him. Brad had no choice but to dive for cover into the cottage.

Inside the sparkling, red-tiled loo, with its pungent smell of bleachy substances, he discovered a blond boy, with a fair amount of teenage spots dotted his flushed cheeks. Brad observed him as he stood at the urinal, checking if he had an erection and wondering if he was competition, another rent boy. Brad hadn't seen him enter and guessed he must have been there for some time. After the lad had looked across a couple of times and offered shy smiles, Brad guessed he most likely wasn't a rent boy but was bunking school.

Walking to the door, Brad lingered by the entrance, checking the rain situation and if anyone was about. Rain continued to tip down and was getting heavier by the second.

While occupied with the contents of the sky, he was unexpectedly grabbed from behind, the greedy hands clutching his crotch with a greater force than the lad realized. It was a desperate grasp and Brad yelped in surprise on contact. The boy released his grasp instantly.

Brad spun around and looked directly into the lad's eyes. He appeared frightened and concerned that he'd made a big mistake. Brad released a cunning grin, but could not believe his own ears when he told the boy he charged for sex.

The lad nervously fumbled in his trouser pocket, producing a trembling hand filled with loose change. Pitifully he held it toward Brad, who scooped the two pound of coins from the shaking fingers. Grasping the boy's shoulder, Brad led him into a cubicle.

Inside their secure, solid cell, Brad became excited by what was about to happen. He hadn't had sex since the train journey. His thoughts suddenly flashed back to his first sex in the park toilet by his school, suspecting this boy was in a similar state of sexual awareness. If anything, he should be paying the boy. Feeling guilty, Brad decided he would put matters right and give the lad the time of his life.

Even before he had touched the youth, the boy's hands had begun to grope, and his mouth pressed hungrily on Brad's. Taking control, Brad calmed him with gentler kisses and caresses. But it was quite a task, the youth was so sexually charged, Brad thought his nectarous little neophyte would come in his pants before he'd even got them off.

The excitement of the lad was so electrifying it unleashed in Brad his own spark of sexual desire, exploding his passion to please. If something turned him on more than anything, it was knowing a person desperately desired him.

Ravenously he removed the lad's jumper and T-shirt, eager to get to his nakedness. Willing to assist with his disrobing, the boy unfastened his trousers, dropping them to his ankles. The old-fashioned, all-in-one underwear was simply stunning and looked so sexy against the youth's skin.

Sailing on a seductive sea of passion, Brad searched for the soft skin beneath the flannel material, his fingers working desperately on the buttons. Rapidly they popped open, down as far as the boy's navel. With each button a little more of the prize was revealed. Urged on by that erotic sight, Brad kissed, licked and gently bit at the boyish body. Excitedly, the boy began running his fingers through the blondish hair on the head that was ravishing him.

Popping the penultimate button open, the boy's pubic hair was revealed. Meanwhile, Brad's tongue was searching the indented navel.

The cold, hard, tiled floor was not comfortable for his knees but Brad barely noticed as he ran his hands beneath each short leg of the snugly fitting underwear, caressing the boy's buttocks. Simultaneously, his mouth kissed at the tuft of cock hair and at the erection beneath the soft flannel. All the while, the lad releasing whimpers of pleasure, eager for Brad to commence the caress that would make him come.

Brad unzipped his own fly, releasing himself from his bell-bottoms and commenced his own caressing, ready for the climax of his luscious lad. As Brad sprung the final button open, the boy's mouthwatering morsel met his mouth and he delightfully devoured it.

The exhilarated emissions of a deep, breaking voice, whispering, "I'm coming! I'm coming!" were all Brad needed to come himself; and as one stream of liquid left his body, another entered as the boy gave a final thrust and shot his load.

Leaving the cubicle, a jubilant Brad returned the money to the lad, saying, "That one's on me." And the boy bounced from the cottage, beaming a smile from ear to ear, but not before giving Brad a kiss-of-life kiss.

Having had a wondrous sex session, Brad decided he would cruise around the Pompey bars, have a few beers, and savor the episode whilst it was fresh in his mind. But cruising can be a funny game. Some days nothing happened, and then there were days like this when, out of the blue, sex fell in your lap.

No sooner had the boy left when a guy, fairly scruffily dressed, about twenty, entered. He obviously hadn't found shelter and was drowned with the deluge of water that had drenched him. Brad lingered, his built-in sexometer signalling that this was a punter. Sure enough, in a matter of minutes he was propositioned and found himself accompanying the guy, whose name was Tommy, through a labyrinth of back streets.

A price had been agreed, also what could and could not take place. Sucking each other was in. Screwing him was in, but being screwed was out. Brad thought that being screwed was a special act to be done by a man who he cherished and would be cherished by him. Greg for instance. Yes, Greg could screw him anytime, any day, any night and anywhere!

They reached Tommy's flat in a short while. It was strange but they chatted during their journey as if they were old buddies who had known each other all their young lives. Tommy was really pleasant and had good looks. He was also married with a pregnant wife. That came as a real shock.

Brad was totally disinterested in women and wasn't sure he could handle both Tommy and his wife, but he remembered that being a rent boy meant one needed to be flexible and forthcoming.

Inside Tommy's bedroom, Brad was stunned by this living, sexual fantasy as he lay on top of Tommy screwing, whilst his pregnant wife thumbed through erotic magazines of naked guys. She was clearly excited by her husband's passiveness and at one point, when Tommy said it was painful, told him not to be such a baby.

The bizarre bisexual romp reached its climax with Tommy screwing his plump pregnant wife whilst she gave Brad his first female blowjob. All in all, if was fun, all three thoroughly enjoying themselves. Tommy and his wife certainly did, becoming regular clients. But when it came to screwing Tommy's wife, Brad declined.

He finally found his way to the NAAFI. As usual it buzzed with servicemen in various states of soberiety. Women and men from all three services chatted, danced, and sucked on each other's face. Only the more agreeable act of guys kissing guys was missing.

Brad chose a secluded spot where he could admire the good-lookers and ignore all advances from females. He did spot a couple of sailors he recognized from his ship, but didn't know their names, and remained on his own. But sex was the last thing he needed at present. Even so, being highly sexed, he doubted he'd be able to resist the temptation should it be on offer.

Although he was on his own, he wasn't a loner. The rent boy life he'd chosen would not lend itself to going ashore with mates. On those occasions he did venture out with them, he found their heterosexual aggressiveness and full-of-themselves attitude really pissed him off. And the way they treated service women like cheap tarts made his blood boil. Brad reckoned he could call himself a tart. But he certainly wasn't cheap!

His peaceful solitude was degradingly disturbed by an onslaught of tipsy WRENS who began rubbing his locks and mothering him with "pretty boy" comments. Reluctantly, he submitted to their whims and was wrestled onto the dance floor.

A lipsticked mouth began to devour his face as the elephantine owner engulfed his small frame. With the alcohol he'd consumed and the heady odour of her perfume, he began to feel very giddy himself. He was sure he would throw up.

A group of sailors from his ship caught sight of him and were amused by the spectacle as Brad resigned himself to his female fate. If nothing else, it would do his image no harm and he would definitely have the piss taken from him back on board as those sailors had begun to holler "Go for it, Bambi!" encouragement.

"Bambi" was the nickname he'd been christened with by fellow shipmates. All sailors eventually got one and they nearly always stuck, remaining with them for the rest of their naval lives. Brad was quite happy with his name; others had less desirable names like Tosser, Balloon, Scruff and Winkle.

Winkle was a sad soul, but a real sweetie. His surname was Perry. Sailors gave him so much stick. Winkle was accused of everything from wearing women's clothes to wanking in public. And there was no doubt in Brad's mind that he was gay. In fact there was no doubt in anyone's mind. He was campier than an Indian reservation.

No matter how often sailors told Winkle to act more manly, he just couldn't. One guy even claimed that he'd seen Winkle giving the Master-at-Arms a blowjob, but that was beyond belief. It was doubtful that even the Master-at-Arms's wife would dare do such a thing!

Winkle was also accused of wearing make-up, and all manner of things that would make other sailors feel more manly about themselves. Brad seldom became involved in the sarcasm, but he had to admit, when Winkle was getting his verbal battering, it could be hilarious. Some sailors were just too good at inventing stories, and there was always a new one to be heard at least once a week.

Brad had reached the point of suffocation by the buxom bird who wrestled him around the dance floor, when a welcomed hand reached out and rescued him, just as he was about to be sucked inside-out by her spongy lips. The girl hardly noticed him slip away and was already in search of another vulnerable soul to seduce.

He could have kissed Greg for his timely intervention. He could have kissed him, anyway! Greg's smile simply dissolved him, and the warmth of his huge hand on his shoulder, as he led him away, sent a salvo of sexual shells exploding throughout Brad's body.

The NAAFI had many forms of entertainment, apart from drinking yourself stupid, but the most popular was the five lane bowling alley. And that is where Greg and Brad found themselves, balls in hand.

Everything Greg did, Brad found sexy. The big black ball, as large as Greg's biceps, effortlessly raised and rolled along the runway by his muscular arms, drew admiring glances from Brad, and he commented how Greg made it look so simple. Greg had already scored three strikes, whilst Brad had only managed to hit ten pins. He could play better but pretended he couldn't. It was a cunning attempt to lure Greg into a bit of close-up coaching. He would do anything to get his favourite body close to him.

Greg's solid chest pressed hard against Brad's back, his masculine mitt cupping both Brad's and the ball. Together they moved forward, simultaneously crouching on the forward swing, sailing the ball toward the ten phallic symbols. Side by side they watched the spinning sphere target the pins, Greg's arm slung over Brad's shoulder.

Egg met sperms with an almighty crash!

STRIKE! flashed onto the electronic scoreboard.

Brad swung to face Greg, jumped into the air, released a yelp of delight, gave Greg a hug, then almost kissed him as their faces rubbed together. Greg returned the affection, as always, with a rough rub of Brad's locks.

The game was eventually won by Greg by a clear one hundred points, but Brad was sure he was winning the game of love. Even more certain than before, he was sure that Greg would be the first sailor to screw him.

They continued to chat and drink after the game, occasionally interrupted by Greg's mates or women who fancied him. Greg politely turned down the female offers. Brad hoped this was because Greg would rather be with him.

Come eleven, Brad left his would-be-lover and returned to the ship. He would only have four hours kip before going on watch.

Five
STORMY WEATHER

Full steam ahead! Brad had placed the advertisement, confident he would soon reap its rewards.

The frigate resembled a ship, at last, the patchwork quilt now a bright ship's grey. Brass sparkled, woodwork looked fresh, either scrubbed with salt water to make it white, or coated in varnish. An embargo of stores and ammunition had been brought on board, and every spare hole—apart from Brad's!—had been filled with something. She had also taken on her full complement of crew, and now began to resemble a fighting machine, if that was possible for such an old ship, especially one supposedly raised from the ocean bed.

Brad's watch, keeping timetable was less erratic now, which allowed him to plan his visits to the park and cottage, plus allocate time for trade.

For the past week things had been manic, and every piece of machinery had been checked and re-checked for gremlins. The ship's company had also been paraded in their best uniforms in the presence of the officers and captain, plus a Rear Admiral weighted down with scrambled egg and medals. Greg even had medal and Brad thought that impressive. Maybe he too would get one, one day, for sexual services rendered to sailors, or get an extra special gong for services rendered to Greg!

Brad had specialized in gunnery during his seamanship training and his post on board was with the million-pound missile system fitted during the refit. Missiles that could knock a fly from a cow's backside from a hundred miles or so. Being a pacifist, he hoped he would never see the evil things fired at anything other than a practice target, but he had to admit, they were rather erotic objects. And polishing a huge, pointed hunk of horror often got his hormones humming, and he sometimes wondered whether they had been designed by gays. Even the word, weapon, had its double entendre, and comments such as "How's your big weapon today, Bambi-baby?" were not uncommon during a day's teasing.

As well as the missiles, Brad also used other means of destruction: four inch guns, hand grenades, and small and automatic firearms. He'd become familiar with them all and had even won an award for the most accurate shot with firearms. But hand grenades filled him with some trepidation, often wondering if they would explode as soon as he released the pin.

Hand grenades were used to signal submarines during exercises, and on one occasion during an exercise, he'd pulled the pin and walked onto the bridge asking when he was required to toss it into the ocean. His presence was greeted by a bridge of officers hitting the deck and an avalanche of abuse from the Captain. Needless to say, his feet never touched the ground as he was whisked away to feel the wrath of the Gunnery Officer. So long as he only killed cardboard cut-outs, he didn't mind using weapons, but he did have reservations about some of the crazy crew and prayed that those in possession of such powerful means of destruction had had the contents of their heads checked. Personally, he wouldn't let half of them loose with anything more powerful than a cucumber!

Brad tried not to worry himself unduly on the morals of mass destruction. And if a missile did hit his ship, he would know little about it. A can opener could have sunk it!

Sod's Law prevails. Especially so in the Royal Navy.

Brad might have guessed that all the gathering of stores and double checking of everything with a movable part, or half a brain - which included a good percentage of the crew— indicated that something was in the air.

Pulling in a hawser thicker than Greg's manhood, Brad and the rest of the seaman reluctantly released the ship's hold on the quay side, and with a deafening series of blasts from the siren, she slipped solemnly seaward.

While Brad and his mates sweated in the sunshine from their strenuous task, he could think only of the telephone ringing in the park, and all those disappointed lusty landlubbers going to waste, not to mention that extra cash.

For Brad this was his first real time at sea, a feeling of excitement and nervousness rocking his emotions, the slight swell of the sea doing the same to his body and, regrettably, his stomach. The last time he'd been on water he was ten, and that was only a rowing boat on a boating lake on the Isle of Wight. On that occasion he and his friend were caught in a tremendous thunderstorm, and the boat sank. Luckily, help was at hand but the water only came up to his bottom. Nevertheless, it was still an unnerving experience. At least he could now swim, and the way the old ship moaned and groaned, he wondered if he might yet have to!

Within an hour of clearing Portsmouth's Outer Spit Buoy, Brad's stomach had settled the gentle movement of the ship no longer bothering him. He was more than thankful for that because the last thing he wanted was to be one of those seasick sailors who spent the majority of a trip throwing up. Also, when it came to getting sympathy from shipmates, should you become seasick, forget it! Sailors were wicked beyond belief and did all manner of things to make a person feel worse. Dangling fatty bacon rinds from noses, or sucking runny egg yolks were only a couple of treats to torment and turn a sickened stomach.

The majority of the crew was unaware as to where they were headed, but Brad had a mate in the communications office and had managed to squeeze some information from him. He was pleased to discover the trip was only for a short period and was in fact an exercise in the Atlantic, accompanied by several ships from different nations.

Everything in the navy had a name and the oncoming exercise was called Shake Up.

Shake Up was the understatement of the year. On the second day of this grueling, watch on, watch off, exercise, the glorious summer weather turned into a mini-hurricane!

Being at sea in a storm force twelve is bad enough. Being at sea in a bucket, with no stabilisers, in a force twelve, is beyond a joke! On the third day, every small ship with a captain who had half a brain, headed for the shelter of shore. Captain Kamikaze, the nickname was one of many to spring from the lower deck, decided his ship and sailors would brave the elements, come hell or high water. And as sure as there was a hole in his arse, both came!

Hundred-foot waves look lovely when you watch them from ashore, crashing onto rocks or riding up a beach. If, however, you are in a bucket set at the top of one one moment, at the bottom of one the next, going through one the next, it's a different kettle of fish, or rather, bucket of sailors!

The old frigate shrieked as her riveted, metal plates worked against each other when she thudded into wave after wave of the green-grey liquid. Such was their force, the ship would shudder to a halt as they struck the bows as she ploughed through the onslaught of water. Several attempts to turn the vessel away from the storm were abandoned when she lurched forty-five degrees and the port guardrails buckled under the weight of water.

Bodies, bowls, cups, plates and food—anything that wasn't lashed down—scattered across the mess decks as she rolled over, and within seconds the ship resembled a floating garbage can, not a dry patch below decks. In fact, Brad thought that there might be more water inside than out. Thankfully, the watertight doors did their job and the savage sea failed to sink her.

But life went on regardless, and amidst the water, spew and food, broken plates, cups and bones, Brad and his fellow sailors worked, ate, slept, wanked, and wondered why the hell they were there!

Finally, in their wisdom, the powers-to-be cancelled the exercise, but Captain Kamikaze decided to have his own private exercise and pushed his men to the brink, determined that his crew would not crack, even though the ship possibly might, right down the middle!

Eventually, it had become so dangerous to move about the ship, Brad, like many of his mates, had ceased returning to their mess to crash at the end of a watch. Instead, they dropped wherever they stood, or crammed themselves in corners for safety. But sleep had become a rarity, and life had almost become one continuous watch as the workload of cleaning and keeping the ship in a watertight condition overwhelmed them. In fact, a good fifty of the crew were either seasick or damaged in some way. Even the galley had closed, as such, because only one chef remained in full working order, and another had sliced the top of his finger off. As always, humor gave the sailors strength. Rumor that the captain had eaten the finger, raising their spirits. A further rumor that the chef had been fingering his bottom beforehand gave the sailors extra joy.

The galley chefless, for the final two day of the abandoned exercise the crew lived on Irish stew and dumplings, cooked by a couple of Stokers and by poor, commandeered Winkle. Jokes as to whether Winkle was any good with turnovers and tarts, came from every quarter.

Greg remained Brad's protector throughout the storm and kept him safely by his side. He even gave him regular gulps of his rum. Brad thought he could do the work of twenty men after sinking those, but that fantasy soon fizzled out.

For Brad's first time at sea, it was an experience he would never forget, and one he hoped would not be repeated too soon. Perhaps the most pleasing episode for him was when Greg and had braved the weather to lash down a cutter. After their task had been accomplished, shivering and soaked to their skins, both climbed into a small locker space and cuddled close together.

On the final day of the exercise the storm had blown itself out. It was the strangest feeling for Brad, because his body continually felt as though it were rocking and swaying, even though the sea was now flat calm. But the cost of Captain Kamikaze's cozy cruise was high: two broken arms, one broken leg, broken cups, plates, bumps and bruises too numerous to mention. And, of course, there was the famous finger that, hopefully, had been eaten by him!

It was impossible to believe the ship had weathered a hurricane as it sailed back into Pompey on this sun-drenched afternoon. Once again it sparkled as new, the crew not on duty having been promised shore leave if they could rebuild it to its former glory. Thankfully, Brad wasn't, he would be heading for the park as soon as they docked, if he could muster the energy. Like never before in his life, he was absolutely shagged!

Six
PARK AND RIDE

Brad was happy and as horny as hell as he made his way through the dockyard and toward the park. En route, he checked out various dockyard cottages for any available punters. Most were empty, apart from genuine users. He did receive a minimal mental undressing from a boiler-suited dockyard worker, but reckoned there was no money to be had.

Reaching the park, first he checked out the cottage. Again, it was punterless. Sexily he strolled to the far side of the park, past a kiddies' play area with its noisy youngsters and distraught mothers, and plonked himself beside the call boxes. After a good hour's wait, which he spent watching feathered birds and cuddly clouds flit across the sky, the phone rang. A sudden rush of uncertainty swept through him and he was of two minds whether to answer it. But the phone wasn't aware of his indecision and persisted with its ringing. After a quick scan of his surroundings, Brad entered the red booth and took up the phone. He was surprised anyone had called at all, it being a week since the advert was placed.

The man on the other end sounded more nervous than himself, and it took him several minutes to get around to sex. For one moment, Brad actually thought he was seeking a person to undertake some gardening. In which case he would be definitely out of luck.

They discussed the usual things: prices, what could and could not take place. Brad gave the client a description of himself and his age, but tried not to sound desperate for sex himself. The guy said he would call back in five minutes. Brad's concern increased.

For the first minute or so, he tried to relax while he awaited the return call, but then began to wonder if he was being set up. He wondered if the caller was the police, military or otherwise. At this very moment was an unmarked police car racing to the scene of the crime? Brad scanned the bushes and flower beds, and all entry points for anyone who might resemble plain clothes policemen, but the only humans were pregnant, buggy-pushing mothers.

He checked his watch for the umpteenth time. Eight of the five minutes had already passed. His concern increased. Should he leave? he wondered. But he couldn't see the point in that. This situation was bound to happen, and the caller would have been just as wary.

Brad jumped, the ringing phone startling him. He let it ring twice again before answering. Relieved, he listened to the same guy give directions to where they should meet. It would take some minutes to get there. Brad asked how they would recognize each other. The punter would give absolutely no details of himself. This caused Brad even more concern, but he guessed the guy would probably check him out from a distance. If he didn't like what was on offer, he wouldn't make contact.

Brad walked briskly along the street, carving a path through shoppers, paying little attention to anyone. He'd switched to automatic pilot, oblivious to everything and everyone, apart from the job at hand, homing in on his punter like a cruise missile. Like an athlete, he was determined to keep his thoughts focused so any doubts which developed would be quickly quashed. It was, after all, a new experience, and although it filled him with a good deal of fear, it also thrilled and excited him.

Nearing the meeting point, a not-so-busy back street, he checked his uniform, ensuring he looked appetising. Tilting his cap sexily on his head and springing a few locks from beneath, he turned into Admirals Road. Taking two deep breaths, he walked the final hundred yards in a brisk, confident stride.

The sports car, red and gleaming, seductively slid to a halt beside him. Where it had come from, he hadn't noticed. He also hadn't noticed the driver and was transfixed by this sexy, cigar shape with its throbbing cylinders purring in his ears. His only thought. He wanted one!

Brad heard his name mentioned as he was offered a ride, releasing him from his hypnotic trance. Looking directly into the man's eyes, he offered up a scrumptious smile. The guy looked pleasant enough. About forty. And by the expression on his face, was delighted with what he'd purchased, but not paid for. Accepting the invite, Brad hopped over the door into the passenger seat, the phallic feast roaring away before he'd even settled himself. In a matter of minutes they were free from the city streets and heading toward the very expensive seafront dwellings, at an average speed of 100 mph.

"This man is rich. Very rich!" was Brad's only thought as he sank into the leather upholstery.

Reaching toward the dash, his punter flicked the cassette player on, releasing some pop music that sounded too young for him, using the opportunity to stroke his sailor boy's thigh. Brad gave his punter a warm smile, confirming his actions were welcome. The palm remained over his cock throughout the journey, only the occasional gear change removing it. Brad was excited, thrilled by the race toward the punter's home.

Arriving in front of a palace, Brad's jaw fell open in amazement. His punter was a Saudi prince or some oil baron. His frigate would fit three times into this mansion. Brad didn't speak as they entered lest his voice break something, but the punter appeared less inhibited by his own wealth and ushered him immediately into a bathroom with inch-thick golden carpet and gold-plated taps, and requested him to bathe.

"Perhaps he thinks I'm a dirty boy?" mused Brad. "Well, I am. But a clean, dirty boy!"

Whatever the punter's reason for wanting him to bathe, Brad wasn't bothered. This was a luxury he was going to relish. He couldn't remember the last time he lay in a scented bath. And after the gentleman had left, he selected what appeared to be the most expensive ingredients from the marble shelf and tipped more than required into the steaming water.

A good half hour later, after towelling himself dry with a luxurious towel almost as large as himself, and slipping into a skimpy pair of white shorts at the guy's request, Brad emerged from the steam filled room wondering if he'd occupied the bath longer than acceptable. Looking as delectable as a Danish on a doily, he walked bare foot into the en-suite bedroom. Scented and seductively warm, it was furnished with only the best money could buy, only it was *pink*! Everything was pink or a shade of pink. But Brad had to admit, it looked beautiful. Feminine maybe, but beautiful.

Resembling one of the many boy statues guarding the doorways, Brad moved toward his client, his dazzling white shorts flashing bright against his sun-tanned skin. He looked exquisite, exciting and so edible!

John, his punter, beckoned him onto the king-size bed, where he lay upon silk sheets dressed in a Karate-type outfit as white as Brad's shorts. Brad obeyed.

Gently placing his willing body beside John's, Brad made the first move and began kissing and caressing. Using all of his seductive skills, he moved his fingers into John's hairy chest, tweaking his tits. John responded by running his palms over Brad's delicate chest, then beneath his shorts and over his cock, rubbing it softly.

Moving down to the thick, stiffening shaft, Brad was totally bewildered when his caresses to that gorgeous giant were rebuffed and, with a swift movement, he was quickly spun over John's lap, the huge cock pressing against his own. Brad whimpered, sending his punter wild, and began to wriggle into a sucking position. Again his advances were rebuffed, John pulling him away.

Brad was confused, wondering if he was blowing the trick, but John continued to tormentingly caress his sailor's youthful sex beneath the tight white shorts, at one point almost making Brad shoot his stuff.

Pulling his massive dick from his Karate-type outfit, John slipped it beneath one leg of the skin-tight shorts, bringing it into contact with Brad's pre-cum-oozing cock. There was barely room for both pricks as John's cock swelled, pressing hard against his sailor boy's tender thigh, squeezing even more pre-cum beneath the taut material.

Enthusiastically, he worked their cocks together, thrusting hard and fast against Brad's thigh, cock and balls, almost to the point of filling his shorts with cum. Then, just at that critical moment, John stopped.

Brad had no idea what was coming next!

Thwack! Thwack!

For a brief moment, at the start of this "naughty boy" punishment, Brad was sure he would burst out laughing but managed to contain himself. If anything would turn John off, then that surely would. It was another first for him and he hadn't the faintest idea of what to do. Should he pretend to cry, or tell him to stop, or ask to be hit harder? He certainly didn't fancy that. Already his cute little arse was turning a shade of red.

"Have I been a naughty boy?" Brad whimpered.

It was all John needed to spur him into action, and his hand commenced a steady striking of the shorts-clad cheeks.

Sex rubbed frantically against sex as the Master's hand struck the naughty boy, Brad offering words of encouragement and muffled cries. With a flurry of stiff spanks and rapid cock thrusting, Brad's tight shorts were filled with an ocean of orgasmic juices.

Shorts filled with subsiding cocks and cum, Brad smiled. He had serviced his first big-time punter. John said he would love to give him a good spanking again, very soon. Brad gave him the number of the "regular's" call box and explained that he was often at sea, sometime for long periods, and if he wanted to know when he was back to port, he should watch for his advertisement.

As promised, John kindly returned him to town where Brad headed for the NAAFI.

He hoped he would bump into Greg.

Seven
FROM LITTLE ACORNS...

Six months had passed since Brad joined the rust bucket. Calling the old ship the "rust bucket" was a bit unfair, really, because he loved the little ship and was truly at home and happy on her. He'd made friends with many sailors and the harassment he had early on in his life hardly existed.

He was also madly in love with Greg. He had finally admitted this to himself when he realized he was constantly searching Greg out, just to be by his side. Also, his regular nightly wanks were always fantasies of Greg doing what his punters did to him, and more. But the main reason he knew he was in love was that he wanted to be fucked by him. And how desperately he wanted that. But how he could bring this about, he had no idea.

Did Greg fancy boys or not? This was the question to which he had no answer. Greg wasn't married and had never had a wife. In fact he'd not even seen him with a girl, and definitely not a boy. And because they had become almost as close as lovers, Brad wondered if Greg might have similar feelings.

Despite Brad's sexual awareness and experience with guys, he still couldn't find the courage to take their friendship that one step further. If he did and he was wrong, and it destroyed their obvious love for one another, he would not be able to live on the same ship anymore.

Love, being what it is, can be a hard lion to tame and Brad wrestled with the animal many times. Sexually, he had more than enough punters for his over-passionate prick, his punters numbering ten. But the need for that one special person to embrace and make love to him ate away at his insides, and he knew that the day was approaching fast when the urge to proposition Greg would be too great to resist. He could only live in hope that Greg would be the one to make that dramatic move. He was, after all, the man, and wasn't it the man's place to make the first move? But perhaps Greg was unaware of how deep his feelings were and needed an unmistakable signal. Maybe he would need to be more risky when they larked—a more affectionate cuddle, a good grope, maybe a full-blown kiss. They would be bold moves but he expected Greg would take them in his stride. But would they succeed in sowing a sexual seedling? Brad decided that he must sow that seed soon.

The weeks passed by, Greg and Brad doing what they always did, iring their weapons, working on the upper deck, and other seaman's duties. They also went ashore as often as they could. Brad to his punters, Greg with his mates. As yet, Brad still hadn't found an opportunity to make his love for Greg known. It was so difficult because they were always in the company of fellow sailors, and this was something that needed to be done in private. Then, one afternoon after they had been working hard greasing the mechanical parts of the missile bay in order to beat the bathroom rush Greg said that they could nip into the showers before the others. Brad's mind raced when "seed sowing opportunity" sprang to mind. And, before leaving the missile bay, he rubbed his bare back against some greasy cogs.

As expected, the showers were empty. Taking cubicles opposite one another, both chatted whilst soaping their fine bodies. Brad could no longer hold back as he lovingly feasted on Greg's muscular torso. "Greg, can you wash my back please? I can't reach the grease," he bravely asked.

Naturally, Greg obliged. Brad knew he would and climbed into the cubicle beside him, the fine, warm spray cascading over their naked bodies. Greg began pressing firmly into the grease, occasionally re-soaping his hands and whilst his thick but gentle fingers worked, Brad gently edged his soapy bottom into Greg's semi-proud sex. Seductively, he rotated his delicious buttocks into his stud-man's crotch, his own cock rising to a full erection.

Yes, they had touched each other many times, seen each other naked, and even seen their stiff sexes, but never all three at the same time.

Brad knew the power of his own beauty and the power of touch, and whilst Greg's fingers worked over his silken skin, he used the combination of these sexually stimulating actions just long enough to sow that magic seed.

Body cleansed, Brad returned to his own cubicle then turned and thanked Greg, allowing his youthful cock to point proudly toward his man. He was positive his ploy had worked. How could it not? Greg's hands had been over his tender skin and he had felt Brad's soft, willing, bare buttocks pressing against his cock. And now having seen how aroused he had made Brad become, Greg could be in no doubt Brad was his for the taking. If Greg fancied him, the seed must surely have been sown. All Brad need do now was wait for that seed to grow into a giant oak.

The first sign of the sprouting sapling came sooner than Brad expected. On the upper deck, attempting to make a Turk's Head in a length of rope, he was unexpectedly lassoed by Greg's arms.

A Turk's Head was a difficult monster to master. It was a kind of clenched fist moulded on the end of a rope. When held upright, it resembled the head of a prick. Hence the sailor's expression, "He needs a good Turking."

Greg's sweaty chest pressed against Brad's bare back. He could feel the nipples, as firm as .22 bullets, pushing against him. And whilst both their hands worked on the phallic symbol, Greg's rum-smelling breath caressed Brad's neck, his lips occasionally brushing the nape. Brad went stiff in his shorts as he felt the solid sex pressing into the small of his back. Greg was his!

The instruction over, Greg moved on, lending assistance to another sailor, but Brad didn't mind, he was sure their relationship was developing fast, and to remind himself of that special embrace, he lovingly placed the Turk's Head inside his locker, positive he would hold the real thing very soon.

Returning to sea once again, Greg and Brad and the rest of the gun's crew tested their weapons. But when would Greg test his weapon on him was foremost in Brad's mind?

The missiles hit their targets with monotonous accuracy but the guns missed regularly. Unlike his last voyage, the sea paid more respect to its occupants. This time it wasn't an exercise and they were on their way to Amsterdam, a courtesy visit.

Proudly showing the British flag, sailors and ships were a regular pastime of the Royal Navy. The regular pastime of the crew, however, was to get paralytically pissed once ashore, defeating the object. Brad seldom got drunk but Greg often got merry.

Amsterdam was adorable with its tulips and pretty, young men. Sex was seldom far from Brad's thoughts, and the fields of tulips reminded him of the obvious, with their bulbous heads and thinner stems. But sex did not appear on his agenda during the visit. He did, however, find himself in the red-light district, greeted by breasts of various shapes and sizes pressed against window panes, a most unwelcome sight. Sadly, he never found young guys with gorgeous cocks and butts pressed against any. Yes, he'd heard that there were gay haunts, but it was too risky, and the guys he'd gone ashore with were certainly not interested in those. Confirming his thoughts, the number of his mates slowly diminished, every couple of houses another sailor slipping into the sea of seedy sexual sublimity. In fact, he even found himself under pressure to perform and an image exercise was necessary. Succumbing to his mates' wishes, he sulkily slipped into the pot noodle of promiscuity himself but only until they had disappeared themselves, then slipped out again.

Amsterdam was fun but sexless and he was pleased to get back to port and his regular punters.

Eight
HOME AND AWAY

Days, weeks and months flashed by. Brad's punters were ticking over as regular as clockwork. The advertising system worked well, only the regulars' phone box now required, most new punters coming by word of mouth. But Brad's life was not all ships and punters. Whenever possible, usually on a long weekend break, he would visit his mum, pleased to be back in the countryside.

One person his beloved countryside didn't posses anymore was his best pal, Malc. He'd been sent away to a special school to help him recover after the accident. But one person who was still around was Liam, his favorite farmhand, his big, *real* man.

It may or may not have been intentional, but on this first day of his weekend break, Brad found himself heading toward the hay barn, dressed in his bum-hugging shorts and sporting a baggy yellow T-shirt. But he was not alone. With him was Paul, a junior seaman. Paul was a very shy lad, and as much as Brad was crazily in love with Greg, he had an irresistible urge to discover whether Paul had similar sexual interests as himself.

Together they laughed and joked, wrestled and played, Paul obviously loving the freedom of the countryside. Also, there could be little doubt in Brad's mind he was loving the close contact as they entwined their bodies, the tell-tale tenting in Paul's oversized shorts all too apparent.

Yes, Brad had seen this pretty, black-haired boy's fine offering of sex when sturdy and stiff, a boy whose skin was as white as snow, defining the boyish bush of black pubics, the only hair apparent on that delicate torso apart from a wisp under each armpit. Yes, he had observed the rounded white buttocks, also sporting only a wisp of hair between that beckoning, virgin crevice. But not once had he been as close as they were today, heads buried in bulging crotches, young hearts pounding in anticipation.

It was always difficult to know at what point to move things along, but this time Brad decided to wait. There was always tonight when they bunked down, if things had begun to look more promising. Not that they didn't look promising already! If there was any guilt in his mind that he was being unfaithful to Greg, Brad soon let those thoughts alone. He would simply think of Paul as another punter. And anyway, a boy needs his sex!

With the mixture of gropes, grapples and the steep climb, the boys were soon puffing by the time the reached the hay barn. It was Brad's eyes which were the first to sparkle with delight when they caught sight of the half-naked Liam, muscles rippling, effortlessly lifting bales from the trailer hooked to the back of his tractor. Brad glimpsed Paul's cheerful face. An unmistakable sparkle shone in those deep brown eyes as he watched in awe. A surge of naughtiness suddenly swept throughout Brad's body, mostly his crotch, when he immediately decided to move things along.

Paul was in for one hell of a wonderful surprise!

"Brad!" greeted Liam, heaving a bale about the same weight as Paul into the barn.

"Liam!" Brad returned, moving over to his man and wrapping friendly, wanting arms around his favorite farm hand. "This is Paul. He wanted to see your big.... bundle!" Brad winked. Paul stood shyly by, unconsciously adjusting his crotch.

"Behave, Brad!" grinned Liam, "or I'll have to spank you again!"

Paul released a shy smile as Brad bent over and his shorts tightened over his buttocks. Whether that image held some excitement for him, Brad had no idea. But he was damn sure he was going to find out!

With the assistance of Paul and Brad, Liam soon had all of the bales stacked in the barn.

"Reckon we could wrestle Liam to the ground?" urged Brad, grasping Paul by the wrist, urging him into action.

"I told you, Brad. Behave! I know you're a bigger boy now, but not so big I can't put you over my knee."

"Are you a bigger boy?" teased Brad, almost dragging Paul toward Liam's sweaty, smooth body, knowing only too well what treat lay beneath those denim cutoffs .

There was no doubt that Paul had grasped the situation, an increasing awareness now tenting his baggy shorts. And unexpectedly, it was his small frame that sprang forward in giggles and excitement and threw itself upon the laughing Liam.

Without effort, Liam lifted Paul above his head, like a weight-lifter pushing 200 pounds, and tossed him into a stack of soft hay. Brad, having joined them at that precise moment, had inadvertently grabbed at Paul's shorts. And as Paul sailed through the air, off they came!

Liam and Brad stared down at the red-faced, half-naked youth, his cock pointing excitedly skyward. "I think Paul's pleased to see you!" giggled Brad.

Liam plucked the playful Brad from the hay-strewn earth, fell beside Paul, spun Brad over his knee and began to spank his shorts-clad bum. Sensing that that wasn't humiliating enough, with a smart downward movement, he whisked away Brad's shorts and resumed his spanking on the bare backside. Brad's cock sprang outward, jamming itself between Liam's strong thighs. With each slap of his arse, Brad thrust his cock hard between them, dribbling pre-cum over the cut-down denim.

Paul could not believe what was happening, his face redder than before. But this time it was not red with embarrassment but with the desire to be involved. Desperately, he began to rub on his ever-swelling sex.

"Harder, Liam. Harder!" enthused Brad, placing his palm between Liam's thighs and levering the giant cock from within the denim prison. Liam continued his playful striking, but only enough to redden his favorite boy's bum.

Reaching out and grasping Paul's ankles, with a smart tug Brad pulled the youth downward until the boy's cock was before him. Parting his lips,

Brad sent his mouth deep into the fluffy bush of black hair. Paul squealed!

"You naughty, naughty boy!" scolded Liam, striking Brad's bottom with the hardest smack yet, then rolled him from his lap.

Brad continued to savor Paul's stiff cock. Already he'd come, Brad gulping down the teenage juices. But sensing the lad could come again and probably again, he continued to work along the six-inch length, teasing more cum toward the bulging bud.

Liam was now eager for his own prick to be gorged upon. Moving down on Brad's sex, firing up his own passion, he began to lick and slurp on that bulging thickness that he'd savoured many times before. Shuffling himself toward Paul, he offered his own mammoth cock to the pretty face, first spreading his pre-cum over the lad's kissable lips. Paul instinctively licked the silver strands away but was unsure whether to swallow the enormous shaft before his cute, boyish face. Never before had he done such a thing!

Brad sensed the lad's indecision and stopped sucking, then moved himself into a sixty-nine position with Liam taking the opposite side to Paul. Whilst kissing his young sailor passionately, Brad pushing his tongue deep into the hot, moist throat, Liam moved over the young lad's sex and began sucking upon it ravenously. In order to show Paul how to suck a big cock, Brad opened his mouth wide, pushing deeper and deeper until all of Liam's shaft had disappeared into the depths of his tight throat.

Paul watched in amazement as the shaft reappeared like some magical, sword-swallowing trick. Brad kissed him again, placed his palm on the back of his cropped hair and gently pulled him over Liam's swollen shaft. Excitedly, Brad watched as the bulbous, throbbing head vanished, followed by the first four inches, then with some effort, the remaining four.

Briefly, Liam stopped sucking the lad, eager to see who he was being sucked by. On discovering the pretty boy's face buried into his cock hair and the whole of his cock-shaft swallowed, gasped, "That's it my lovely lad. Suck it good and hard! Suck it all the way down!"

All three cocks were ramming home like pistons, Liam moving from Brad's to Paul's and back, Brad and Paul doing five deep thrusts apiece down upon Liam's.

It was Paul who came first, his small buttocks hammering his young cock frantically into Liam's large mouth, sending spunk swirling over Liam's tongue as he lapped away at the swollen head of the boy's sex. Liam's own torrent of cum came seconds later, causing Paul to cough and pull his mouth away. Quickly it was replaced by Brad's, who gratefully swallowed the remaining wealth of cum, that being more than half.

Meanwhile, Paul had moved swiftly down on Brad's sex, discovering he loved the taste of fresh cum, and was now sucking furiously. Liam, loving the sight of that, continued to thrust his own cock deep into the depths of Brad's throat, sensing more spunk rising inside his thick shaft, all the while gripping tightly onto Paul's head, watching his pretty face bobbing up and down, making him take all of Brad's sex he was blissfully sucking upon.

A second deluge of cum escaped from Liam's sex, causing Brad to shoot a multitude of juices from his own cock. Large amounts dribbled from Paul's mouth as he desperately tried to swallow the surge. Not wishing any to be wasted, Liam raised the boy's head and began lapping around the lush, spunk- covered lips, darting his tongue deep into the youth's throat in order to get the last remaining droplets. With a final flurry of sucks, slurps, kisses and cuddles, all three were spent.

It was Sunday morning, the final hours before Paul and Brad would return to ship. Silently, Brad moved into the bathroom for a pee. Before returning, he slipped his mum's ever-useful Nivea cream into his palm. Barely breathing, he slid beneath Paul's duvet and snuggled up.

"Brad. Your mum!" warned Paul.

"Church," whispered Brad, kissing gently on the white nape of his neck, then biting tenderly into the black spikes of Paul's cropped hair. Paul just loved that.

"Thought we might have another bit of fun before we go back," Brad coaxed, bringing his palm upon Paul's sex.

Paul was stiff but wasn't sure. "I don't know. It's not right!"

"It was all right yesterday. Right inside your mouth!" Brad teased.

Paul released a nervous giggle. "But what if someone finds out?"

"Who?"

Brad felt Paul's body relax and succumb to his advances. Rolling over, he brought their faces together. Mouths locked upon mouths, and tongues explored.

"You won't tell, will you? Back on board," Paul pleaded.

"Tell? Why should I?"

Cautiously, a hand moved down on Brad's cock and began to stroke. "That's nice," Brad seduced, reciprocating.

For some while both boys explored, kissing chests, nipples, tummies, mouths and cocks.

"Want me to suck you off?" suggested Brad.

"Please!"

Brad slipped deeper beneath the duvet and began to savour the fine, six-inch, slim cock. Unknown to Paul, the Nivea had been opened and Brad's fingers had scooped a fair-sized dollop onto them.

With a deep gasp, Paul called out, "What you doing!" but the pleasure of being sucked so deeply caused him to gasp again, this time with great delight.

Gently Brad massaged the virgin passage, each new thrust adding another finger. Paul writhed excitedly upon the probing digits, even though some pain was apparent.

Professionally, Brad moved between the slim white legs, parting them with his strong body. All the while he continued to suck his boy sailor, careful not to bring him off.

Paul hardly noticed the three fingers being replaced by a solid, thick cock, such was Brad's expertise. And with a smooth swift stab, Brad's cock had sunk to the depths of the tight virgin hole.

Paul was in another blissful world. All he was aware of was the amazing sensation of a tongue deep in his throat, a greased palm moving rapidly over his sex, and an indescribable sensation of something sending fire deep within his body.

Crying out and pleading for Brad not to stop, his cum sprayed between both naked bodies as he shuddered with the amazing sensation.

Brad breathed rapid and deep, thrusting hard and fast into the soft, round buttocks. Paul screeched loudly and his arse tightened around the penetrating shaft when Brad's cock thickened and exploded streams of spunk into its dark depths.

The boys fell apart, both exhausted and spent, sweat streaming over their silken bodies.

"Like that?" asked Brad.

"Oh, yes! You done that to anyone before?"

"Nope. You're my first."

"Honest?" Paul gushed.

"Honest."

As Brad and Paul's weekend break came to an end, one thing was certain: Brad had brought a virgin sailor home with him, but he wasn't taking one back!

* * *

Christmas had come and gone and the January snows had melted. The little rust bucket was now bobbing in Far East waters and Brad's punters were far from his thoughts. He wouldn't see them for the next five months. Greg still hadn't made love to him but they were closer than ever. Brad had also been promoted to Able Seaman.

Hong Kong was beyond his wildest dreams. One day, when he had made enough money, he would bring his mum here. She would absolutely adore it. The clothes and the materials they were made from were magnificent. The young Chinese boys were delectable and mouth-watering. Brad adored their slanting eyes and their jet-black hair, not to mention their slim, dark-skinned bodies.

Hong Kong was a capitalistic beehive that buzzed continuously, night and day. There was always something to see or do or have. Brad was disappointed that he'd missed the Chinese New Year as that would have been a treat, but he did purchase a Bonanza box of fire-crackers for the next bonfire night or any celebrations that might spring up—his seventeenth birthday, for instance.

Brad visited loads of places during his visit, including Kowloon and

Aberdeen. Aberdeen was an eye-opener. It was a shantytown of fishing boats.

Photography had become his hobby and he'd purchased a Nikon camera, which was very cheap over there. Brad took roll after roll of pictures of this special visit. At least one roll contained only pictures of Greg in various moods and states of undress. One actually showed his semi-erect cock, and Brad was surprised that the film was developed without problem.

One of his favorite snaps was taken in Aberdeen, a picture of a young, naked Chinese boy standing on the deck of a fishing boat, fish laid about him drying in the sunshine, the lad casually pissing over them. After seeing that, he wondered should he remove fish from his diet. Disgusting or not, it was a gem of a picture, and he even entered it in an amateur photography competition, but he didn't win.

On the outward and return journeys to the Far East, the ship also popped into Gibraltar, Malta, Singapore and Aden, passing through the Suez Canal on the last leg. They also crossed the Equator, which was a really camp affair. The Navy had a "Crossing the Line" tradition. Watching butch strapping sailors dress in drag and camping it up as they chased the Skins around the upper-deck was amusing and erotic, especially when they wrestled with the naked, soapy Skins in an attempt to give them a decent dunking in King Neptune's pool. Naturally, Brad got caught several times, going through the dunking and shaving ceremony.

Brad enjoyed all the ports he visited apart from Aden, which was far too hot, also there was a bit of a war going on at the time. Singapore was brilliant, but the Tiger beer was a little stronger than he'd anticipated and Brad got legless on his first run ashore. But without doubt, Hong Kong was unsurpassed. Malta was his favourite of the others. The inhabitants were extremely friendly, a special friendship built with the British during the war. But the water was foul and whatever you mixed with it, you couldn't alter the taste. Brad became a cola addict.

Brad loved his trip abroad, and with the absence of sex with his punters, was falling in love with Greg even more. But no matter how much he enjoyed himself, he continually dreamt of good old England and its crummy weather, and longed to get back home.

As he worked on the upper-deck in the drizzling rain, Brad knew he was back home for sure. Foremost in his mind as they entered port was his punters—he hadn't had sex in five months!

The advert had been placed, but would it work after such a long absence?

Within an hour of docking, Brad was in the park sitting beside the telephone kiosks. Almost as soon as he sat on the bench, the phone rang. Brad couldn't believe his luck as he chatted to Spanking John, with the supersonic sports car. They arranged to meet at the usual place.

Brad was doubly pleased. Not only did the system work after such a long time, but Spanking John was easy cash, a gentleman, and jolly good fun. But no sooner had he replaced the receiver, when it rang again! It was Sam the Skinhead. He sounded desperate! Brad guessed, he too hadn't had sex for some time and arranged to meet after his bottom had had a jolly good spanking.

Bottom rosy red, Brad was chauffeured by taxi across town to Sam's. Sam was one client who took some getting used to. Water sports was his game. On their first meeting, Brad actually thought Sam was going to take him swimming or surf-boarding, or some other harmless wet fun.

At Sam's abode, on that first meeting, both boys sat on the floor in their underpants, talking dirty talk whilst filling their bellies with large amounts of liquid, mostly beer.

Brad was totally stunned when, asking if he could use the loo, Sam wouldn't allow him!

"Pee your pants!" Sam excitedly pleaded, pressing his cute, boyish face and shaven head into his boy sailor's bulging belly.

Brad's tummy was so full it was impossible not to, and the steaming golden liquid soaked through his tight underpants, over Sam's head and face, then down his own thigh muscles and brown legs. It was at that point that he realized why the floor was covered in plastic. Not, as he had thought, because Sam was in the process of re-decorating.

But the more he met Sam, the more he understood about water sport and what was required of him. It was immense fun and they often broke down in fits of giggles as they splashed and sprayed. Screwing never took place. It was blowjobs and bubbles. Easy money and wonderful fun.

Discounting Spanking John, Splashing Sam came out top of his Punter of the Year award—Brad receiving a regular soaking. Nicknaming his punters was a habit caught from the Royal Navy. It also added humor to the business of selling his sex. If he wasn't able to enjoy it, wasn't able to laugh at it, wasn't able to sleep at night because of it, he would no longer do it. Since the start of his rent boy life, he promised himself he would rigidly adhere to those rules.

Of the other punters Brad met on a regular basis, one was a guy who dressed him as a schoolboy, and another put him in a mini-skirt. But most didn't want any special effects. They wanted sex, pure and simple. And although he wouldn't allow anyone to screw him, saving it for that special person, he was not short of punters.

Generally, Brad was happy. And should someday Greg and he make love, unhappiness would be an impossibility.

Nine
SHATTERED DREAMS

Although unhappiness was a word seldom used by Brad, it could not be kept from his life forever. It was after he had been on the frigate for nearly two years that it entered his life with great force. Yes, in that time there had been tears and arguments, even with Greg, but nothing had prepared him for the oncoming event.

News reached Brad that Greg had received a draft and was to be posted to another establishment. That shattering information reached him, not from Greg but from another rating, hitting him with such an unexpected force, how he didn't burst into tears there and then, as the enormity of his love for Greg engulfed him, he would never know.

Brad's legs sped him from the ship and over the gangway into the darkness of the evening, he found himself sitting in a cubicle of a dockyard toilet, confused and crying for all his worth. Try as he did to convince himself that he was being silly, and Greg and he were just friends, he could not stop the flood of tears. Such was his unhappiness, he doubted if he could even return to the mess-deck and face the one person he loved more than any other without totally breaking down and bringing undue attention on himself, and more seriously, upon Greg.

God, how cruel! Hadn't he saved himself for Greg? His virginity was still intact. A valuable and precious jewel, for Greg and Greg alone! Was he being punished for his promiscuity, and was this the price he'd never expected to pay? Would he not have stopped being a rent boy, instantly, if Greg had asked him to be his boyfriend, to be his lover, even his dog?

He would kill himself because there could be no life without Greg.

The dry dock beside the toilet was empty. He would do it there. It wouldn't take long for his soiled body to drop the one hundred feet, a foot for every punter he'd slept with.

"Bastards! Fucking bastards!" he shouted, accompanied by more tears as he slammed his fist against the cubicle door.

"Okay, in there, mate?" a concerned dockyard worker inquired.

Brad composed himself. "Well, okay. Caught me damn finger in the lock," he quickly offered.

The dockyard worker grunted and laughed and continued to wash the day's grease and grime from his grubby face. Brad sucked in a deep breath and walked briskly from the cubicle, avoiding eye-contact with the docky, who turned and gave a concerned smile. Brad reassured him with a nod of his head.

The urge to kill himself was causing Brad to tremble, fear of contemplating such drastic action rushing through him. Sucking in more gulps of sea air, tears rushing down his cheeks, he began a solemn walk toward the dry dock. His mind raced in confusion, wondering if he should go to Greg and tell him straight that he wanted to be his boyfriend, that he wanted Greg to be the only person in the universe to make love to him, that he was his and his alone.

Dejected, head bowed and shoulders slouched, he moved closer to the edge of the dry dock. His tears had stopped flowing, now drying white on his baby-brown face. Eyes opening wide, they were suddenly filled with serious intent.

He took a step forward, peering into the dark depths of the dry dock. Like a hungry, toothless mouth it awaited the minute morsel of a body to provide it with a simple snack.

Brad began breathing rapidly as he took another pensive step toward the edge. His right toe slipped over and his mind blanked. A loud clash, metal against metal, unexpectedly resonated throughout his body, bolting his head upright. His white cap flew away, releasing the hair from beneath, and began sailing down, down, deep into the darkness below, vanishing like a dot on a TV screen. Terrified, Brad stepped backwards, releasing a yelp as his body collided with another, sending him forward again, perilously close to the edge.

Greg's firm hand fell upon his shoulder, holding him as rigid as Moses' staff, gently easing him to safety. "You okay, Brad? Been searching for you, all over. Got something to tell you."

"I'm fine. Got caught short. Had to pop into the dockies loo." Brad nodded toward the cottage, but was aware he would be unable to hide his true feelings from Greg, knowing with one inquisitive glance from him, his soul would be stripped bare like a carcass in the Kalahari Desert.

Greg folded a friendly arm about his boy sailor and his hand, as always, moved into the locks and ruffled the hair. Nothing was said about what Brad was doing beside the dry dock, or about his tearful appearance. But Brad knew that Greg would have been concerned. Perhaps Greg did love him more than mere friendship. He really hoped so.

On their stroll back to the ship, Brad almost blurted out the whole "I love you madly" bit, but a single soothing smile from Greg dropped the words back into his throat.

"When are you leaving?" Brad bravely asked, losing part of "leaving" in a nervous cough. It was the weekend. Sooner than expected. So little time to be with Greg.

There could be no more rent boy romps, he thought, as he walked sadly behind Greg and up over the gangway, just as he had done all that time ago when his Noble Knight carried his kit-bag and gave him his very first present in the mess-deck below, even if it was a hammock!

Unfortunately, these memories set the tears flowing once more, and he rushed past Greg into the heads below, sobbing for all he was worth.

His unhappiness was unbearable and he didn't think he could cope. Desperately, he wanted to be as close to his man as possible, and yet to be so close would only cause him more pain, constantly reminded that come the weekend they would be together no more.

Those final days were filled with unbearable emotions as they worked together, Greg determined to keep him busy and his mind free from the oncoming departure. But there was a more serious reason for the extra work.

Brad would soon be sitting a Leading Seaman's exam. Greg had said that he was so bright, he would be the youngest Leading Hand ever. Greg was up for promotion to petty officer, hence his draft. Brad had no doubt that he would make a brilliant petty officer, and the uniform could only enhance his already beautiful body. So, they worked harder than ever, Greg imparting every ounce of knowledge into Brad's brain.

As Brad promised, not once during their final days did he venture ashore to his punters. Instead, he became Greg's second skin, seldom leaving his side.

All too soon it was Friday night. Greg's mates decided to hold a draft party for him and all got pretty pissed. Bubbly and booze flowed freely, with Greg getting a gulp of everyone's rum, a good deal of which he passed to Brad.

It was well known in the mess-deck that Greg and Brad were inseparable buddies, but when their mates began teasing them, asking when were they going to kiss each other goodbye, Brad was totally unprepared when Greg's rum-smelling mouth dropped a smacker right onto his lips. After which, Brad daringly pulled their faces back together, grabbing an extra few moments of that marvellous mouth.

Roars of approving laughter and table thumping echoed around the drunken sailors. No doubt a good few would have loved to be kissing Greg, and more than a good few kissing Brad.

Pipe Down sounded. Greg bent toward Brad. "Tomorrow I'll take you ashore and we'll say our final goodbye," he whispered.

With those loving words simmering in his soul, Brad slung his hammock and jumped in, and with a final smile from Greg, he drifted into slumber. As always, Greg was never far from his thoughts and he dreamt that they were in a cathedral getting married, Greg in his Petty Officer's uniform, Brad in white, naturally. United as one for the rest of their lives, madly in love, till death parted them.

Ten
THE LAST GOODBYE

Greg and Brad strolled over the gangway wearing their best uniforms with their gold badges, Greg's with its medal ribbon. Normally, Greg wouldn't wear his uniform whilst ashore but as he was going on draft, he was obliged to.

Away from the dockyard and close by the railway station, Greg popped his kit-bag into the digs he was to stay at overnight, he wouldn't be returning to the ship.

"Was it possible to enjoy this day," Brad wondered. Already he was feeling overwhelmed with emotion. But he would be brave, he decided, as there could be no doubt in his mind that Greg was also hurting inside.

Where to begin their final day's fun together was quickly resolved, the first pub, of course! Together they sat in unbearable silence, Brad thinking about what Greg was thinking and, no doubt, Greg pondering Brad's thoughts. Eventually, the double rum they both ordered softened their sorrow and sparked them into an adventurous mood.

Fairgrounds were a good place to release suppressed, emotional sorrow, and as they rolled up over the world on the big wheel, Brad released a sizable scream, tucking his arm through Greg's, who instinctively pulled him close.

Fortunately, it was a wonderful day and the sun blessed them with each rotation of the giant cog. Happily, they rode on almost all of the rides, Brad clutching Greg's torso tightly on most. After several rides together on the bumper cars, they parted, taking separate cars in order to give each other a good bumping.

Strangely, sexual thoughts seldom entered Brad's mind during this friendly frolic, which was unusual, as almost every day the urge for Greg to make love to him reared its beautiful head. But on this very special day, they were inseparable friends, bonded as strong as book and cover, one protecting the other.

Greg couldn't decide which ride to try next and Brad suggested the ghost train, mainly so they could be closer together. It wasn't at all frightening in the darkness but Brad screamed several times, holding onto his man, and for a brief instant their lips touched, Greg giving Brad a hug and squeeze.

Upon bursting into daylight, Greg noticed a tear had slipped from Brad's eye, the tell-tale white streak still visible. Greg suggested it was time for another rum and they whisked away to the NAAFI.

Brad didn't fancy being around other sailors during this precious moment in his life, but both had always enjoyed their ten-pin bowling. No doubt, Greg had this in mind.

Several times Brad tangled with his tears as different activities reminded him of the wonderful days they had shared together. How could he not feel like a defenseless child? Greg was his teacher, his mentor, his friend and, unbeknown to Greg, his love.

During their game of bowls, Greg folded his arms about Brad and cupped both Brad's hand and the ball, just as he had done on their very fist game, claiming Brad still hadn't grasped the technique. Brad recalled their first dance-like duet and the strike that followed. Overcome with a surge of emotion, he was unable to contain the crescendo of tears cascading over his face, and ran from the bowling alley. Greg didn't follow. One of them needed to be strong, but even his hand brushed his eye and caught a tear.

The game wasn't continued. With each hour being eaten away, emotions were becoming heightened, more so for Brad, and Greg guessed fellow sailors were not the best of brethren to be with at present.

They took a cab to Portsdown Hill to watch the sun sink into the sea. Old sailors would say that you could hear it hiss when it hit the water.

Sitting in their solitude, Greg melted Brad like Demerara sugar in hot tea when he innocently told him that he was the most beautiful person that he had ever known. And although those words were magical for Brad, they brought another flurry of tears and Greg needed to cuddle him with all of his might in order to console him. Not all of the tears were Brad's.

The final hours until closing time were spent in a lively disco, devoid of sailors. Brad and Greg concentrated on the fun times they had had over the past years. Both got fairly drunk, Brad more so than Greg. Both danced with girls but Brad was really dancing with and for Greg, most of his gyrating gestures aimed at him. Brad's girl grasped the situation fairly quickly but didn't appear to mind. Perhaps she too had had to say goodbye to a sailor sometime in a past life.

Finally, when the bar had closed and with a good deal of coaxing from the doorman, they left the disco and climbed into a cab. Soon Brad became glued to Greg's body. But, all too soon, the taxi pulled alongside the digs and both got out. This was it. The dreaded moment. The final goodbye!

Brad knew it would be impossible to stay composed. Already he could feel the emotion exploding inside of him.

"If you love me...."

"What?"

"Oh, please say you love me! If you don't, just let me go." Awash with tears, the words exploded from Brad's sodden face over a saddened Greg.

"You'd better stay with me tonight. I'll make it all right with the ship," consoled Greg, wrapping a comforting arm around his young sailor boy and gently eased Brad up the solid stone steps of the Regency style building. Brad's legs folded beneath him, either through drink or the emotional state he found himself in, or both.

Inside the digs, Greg removed his kit-bag from the double bed whilst Brad stood in silence. What on earth had he done? He'd just destroyed their friendship. He'd stepped out-of-bounds and there was no taking back of words, especially those spoken with such passion.

Oh, that he could step from the cab and relive that part of his life. But would he have done it any differently? Could he have done it differently? He loved Greg so badly, he just had to let him know. No way could he have said goodbye and watched Greg disappear into another world, forever, without first telling him that he loved him, almost beyond the bounds of reason.

Brad's body began to sway. Greg quickly moved to his side and steadied him. Holding his boy sailor square on, he carefully kissed his forehead and, cupping his reddened cheeks in both hands, pushed away the tears with each thumb. "Bedtime for you, my boy," he whispered, in his kindly but authoritative manner.

Lovingly, Greg unzipped Brad's top and removed his sailor collar and white front, revealing the delicate brown chest. Brad's legs buckled beneath him but he was skilfully scooped up and laid, childlike, onto the bed.

Brad giggled, cried and said sorry, all at the same time whilst Greg removed Brad's shoes. Leaning over the vulnerable voluptuous vision, Greg unfastened the bell-bottoms waistband and unzipped the fly. Then, grabbing both trouser legs, he whisked them down.

In his brilliant white briefs, Brad lay naked, beautiful, beckoning and bewildered, his smooth, scrumptiously seductive body submissively sedated. Without effort, Greg lifted the weightless torso and pulled the duvet from beneath and covered his baby sailor, then stripped naked and slipped in beside him. With a couple of moans and groans, Brad turned on his side and snuggled his buttocks into Greg's lap.

The presence of his man's hot, naked body pressing against his brought Brad into a new awareness. Excitedly he ripped off his briefs and pushed his submissive buttocks harder into Greg. Instantly his cock stood proud. So hard was his sex, he thought the head would burst. Greg was hard; Brad could feel the stiff sex as he nestled his boy buttocks into the fluffy cock hair. He had waited so long for this moment, but as desperate as he was for Greg to make love to him, he couldn't bring himself to make the first move. If it was to be special, then Greg would have to be the one.

Side by side they lay. Greg sighed, a deep, manly sigh and his hot breath wafted over the nape of Brad's neck and between his shoulder blades, his arm moving around Brad's slender waist. Greg whimpered as his hand wrapped around Brad's cock and his heart raced excitedly in anticipation.

But Brad had fallen fast asleep!

Eleven
LOVE AT LAST

Brad dreamed. Erratically, scenes of his young life flashed through his mind, finally being marooned in a not so pleasant one. Sweat trickled over his brow and from beneath his armpits. Restlessly, he tossed and turned as he wrestled with the unwelcome invaders of his mind. With a start, his whole body shook and suddenly he was awake, and Greg's face was before his blurry eyes.

Through the curtains, the first light of dawn broke, a single shaft of sunlight slicing Greg in two. Brad smiled. He was safe. Greg returned his smile and moved closer, their hot bodies touching chest against chest. Lovingly, Greg cupped both palms beneath Brad's face, giving him a long loving kiss. Brad wanted to wrap his arms tightly around his man but his body froze, Greg's unexpected passionate embrace paralyzing him like some virile venom.

"Good morning," whispered Greg as their lips parted.

Greedily, Brad grasped Greg's head with both hands, fingers feeding into his hair, kissing him frantically over every inch of his unshaven face. Crazily, he kissed Greg's mouth, ears, eyes and nose, then lips again and yet more lips, devouring every centimetre of Greg's face, his nostrils sucking the scent of early morning sweat. There would be no turning back this time. Greg was his!

Greg freed himself from the fierce embrace, separating their faces, fearing he might be eaten alive, Brad's cute face red-raw from early morning stubble rubbing against it.

Meanwhile, Brad had dived his hand between Greg's thighs. Pleasantly pleased, he found the giant sex standing proud and powerful, his own penetrating power reaching its full potential, pre-cum seeping from it. Taking Greg's hand, Brad placed it onto his own cock, whilst drawing Greg's foreskin gently over the bulging head. Their lips met again. Brad wrapped himself around his prince, panting in pleasure as they worked themselves to the point of coming.

Soon they were licking wildly over each other's body and suddenly they found themselves head to tail. Brad lavishly licked on the massive cock, then accepted all of it into his small, tender mouth. Greg gasped as Brad went deeper than he thought possible, watching in amazement as his sailor boy's face sank to the base.

Furiously Brad worked Greg's cock, eager for a similar response, but Greg had never done this to a guy before and was reluctant to swallow the young sex before his face. Brad, however, was a skilled and irresistible lover, and he teased his youthful erection into Greg's mouth. Surprising himself, Greg accepted it all.

Charged by the sensation of that long-awaited mouth sucking his sex, a sliver of cum slid from his cock into Greg's working mouth. Greg went wild, eager to savor the whole sackful, his own sex solid and ready to burst a jet of cum into his young sailor's mouth. Sensing this, Brad pulled away. The only thing he wanted was for Greg to make tender love to him. He wanted his man to fuck him and come inside of him. To surrender to the one person he truly loved, for whom it would be so special.

Desperate not to kill the lovemaking stone dead, but knowing that he needed lubrication, Brad said he needed to pee. Unromantically he peed in the sink, taking the opportunity to collect a sachet of lube from his bell-bottoms. Before snuggling back between Greg's beefy biceps, he tore open the sachet.

Shivering with nervousness and excitement, inflamed by a cock the size of Greg's, he lubed into his bottom. Greg asked if he was OK. Brad said he was fine, cuddling closely into his man, kissing him passionately, darting his tongue tormentingly into Greg's mouth, bringing him to the point of being ready to please and be pleased. Greg was more than ready, his bursting cock well greased by Brad's nimble fingers.

Slipping his right leg beneath Greg's waist and wrapping the other around him, Brad moved his brown buttocks over the waiting cock. Cupping Brad's covetous cheeks, Greg began a slow penetration whilst Brad continued to kiss and bite on earlobes.

A sudden yelp issued from Brad's mouth as Greg's cock broke through the incredibly tight channel. Greg stopped instantly.

"Don't stop!" begged Brad.

Breathing deeply now, Brad relaxed his buttocks. Greg was halfway in. Already Brad's bottom felt numb and he wasn't sure if he had legs anymore.

Though not fully in, Greg began a steady rhythm, and with each forward thrust, more and more of his cock disappeared, his massive meat massaged his sailor boy's willing buttocks.

With a satisfied sigh, as the final fraction of Greg's solid shaft slipped from sight, Brad got his man at last.

Robustly they rode each other, Brad digging his nails into Greg's back and biting hard into his biceps. He was beyond pain now and lovingly accepted all of Greg as the cock was thrust deep and hard into his buttocks. At long last his man was making love to him. And as they drove their bodies together, Brad cried for more, more and even more!

In a final fusion of flesh, Greg released a manly gasp as his hot cum gushed into the hole of his sensuous sailor. Simultaneously, Brad released a shuddering sigh, sending streams of semen sailing over their sticky bodies.

Satisfied and spent, they remained locked in each other's arms, whispering words of love until Greg's sex softened and slipped out. Brad was ecstatic, crazy in love. Blissfully unaware of the rest of the world and forgetting that Greg would be leaving this day, he lay beside his prince, unable to believe that his deepest dream had become reality. Happy and content, wrapped around his man like a baby Koala, he drifted back into early morning slumber.

Twelve
CLASH OF CYMBALS

The soft click of a closing door clashed in Brad's brain with the resonance of a pair of cymbals meeting each other. Waking with a start, his muddled brain began absorbing information, assisting in the recognition of his whereabouts. The time this took was minuscule but for Brad it felt like an eternity.

An onslaught of information provided him with the answers, and turning to the empty space beside him, tears were quickly teased from his tired eyes when he realized Greg had gone.

Naked, Brad leapt from the bed and, tripping over the quilt, rushed to the door, flinging it open. A hotel guest jumped back in surprise when he was greeted by Brad's full nudity but in Brad's state, the guest didn't exist. Crazily, he screamed Greg's name along the length of the corridor, the echo bouncing from wall to wall. There was no reply. Tears flooded his eyes, descending both cheeks and dripping onto his naked chest.

Returning to the room and dashing to the window, he stared into the sunlit street. Greg was two floors below, walking upright and proud, kit-bag slung upon his shoulder. Gallantly, he strode in his manly manner along the pavement. Frantically, Brad struggled with the window but couldn't release the catch. In desperation and almost hysterical, he smashed his fist against the pane, screaming Greg's name. If Greg heard him or not, he could not know. Defeated, he stood in silence as Greg boldly disappeared from view.

Brad wrestled with his uniform. He might be able to catch Greg. But all was in vain. Being in such an emotional state, the task appeared beyond possibility, and eventually he fell onto the bed, crying into the pillow. An hour later the landlady was thumping upon his door, requesting him to vacate the room. Brad had cried himself to sleep.

This time he dressed without difficulty. Sorrowfully and silently, he went through the motion, almost on automatic pilot. He peered from the window for a second time just in case Greg should be returning, but he knew he wouldn't be. His teacher, friend, and now lover, had finally left him. He was on his own. Never in his young life had he felt so alone. Greg hadn't even kissed him goodbye!

A second call from the landlady and Brad decided to leave. Woefully, he reached into the wardrobe, and something fell to the wooden floor, hitting it with a clunk. Eagerly, he dived down and scooped it up. Tightly he grasped the treasure lest it escape him, giving it a delighted squeeze, and managed a smile. Lovingly, he removed the slip of paper inserted in Greg's gold ring. He knew it wasn't a letter but a weekend pass, but checked anyway. The only writing belonging to Greg was his signature. For Brad that was enough. He would treasure it always. A few tears began to form as he slipped the ring onto each of his small fingers, searching for one it would fit. It didn't fit any properly, so he left it on his wedding finger which, pleasingly, was the closest.

Brad levitated along the corridor, gently caressing the precious gold band. There could be no doubt in his mind that Greg did love him so much he was unable to say goodbye.

Thirteen
ALL ALONE

A clock somewhere in the distance struck twelve. Brad had wandered around for the past few hours in a trance-like state, still unable to come to terms with feeling like half a person, Greg's absence left a gaping hole in his persona.

God had once again been kind and the sun rolled in and out of gigantic, fluffy clouds. Brad rubbed at the ring on his finger. Hopefully, a genie would appear and grant him three wishes. He only needed one!

Brad wondered how far Greg was into his journey and how much he would be thinking about him. And like himself, was he feeling that his soul had been torn from his body and scattered for life's scavengers to feed upon? He doubted if there was life after death, but was there life after love?

The same clock, or was it another, struck half-past the hour. Brad felt he needed some spiritual support. Although it was Sunday, he was thinking of the double rum kind.

He bumped into a bar along a back street, well away from any of the sailor haunts. The place was such a dump! And although the dump appeared as though a customer only came in at each parting of the waves, the owner still had the nerve to ask him for identification. Brad sucked sarcastically through his teeth but produced his ID. It was a regular happening for him, looking as boyish as he did.

A rum-on-the-rocks, topped with a Coke for a change, was duly produced and paid for, but not by him. Sitting at the corner of the bar was a prostitute who, with a flash of her false eyelashes, indicated to the bar man that the honors were hers. Brad nodded a surprised thank you in her direction and then reluctantly strode toward her beckoning nail-varnished finger.

"This is camp!" he mused. "A pro cruising a pro!" and wondered should he play a game with her and see who could pick up whom.

Brad hadn't the slightest interest in females so there was no point in doing so, but he was bored and it could prove fun and raise his spirits. But he had to admit, she was a scrumptious- looking girl, about nineteen, he guessed, and plonked himself on an adjacent stool.

"You're a good looker," he teased, playing the straight game.

"You're Brad, aren't you?" came her sledgehammer reply.

Brad almost fell from his stool and could return with little more than, "Yep!"

"You're well known, you know?" she smiled, thoroughly enjoying herself, knowing she held a handful of trumps.

Brad looked decidedly embarrassed. "Well know for what?" he wondered. She didn't mean well known for what he thought she meant? Well know for that ! Well known for sex! "Oh god! I've been sussed. How? By whom?" he tortured himself. "No, she's winding me up. She's playing me at my own game, and winning!" he concluded.

Brad submissively twisted a lock of hair around his finger, pulling the curl out and letting it bounce back into place. Was there a reply in his brain, or should he jump from the stool and tell her that he must be off?

He took a deep breath and a hefty gulp of rum then requested her name: Rosemary. Hardly a Fillipino name, he thought, but guessed it was her "working" name. He never used one himself, he was happy with the one he'd been christened with, and thought it wouldn't matter if punters knew his real name—until now, that was!

"What did you mean, I am well known?" Brad inquired with a rum-assisted, nervous laugh.

Rose, as he decided to call her, ran through a list of his punters. She knew them all. "You're good at your job, sweetie," she winked, massaging his ego.

Brad knew that he was good at his job, both of them in fact. But he wanted to know more about this "pay as you play" grapevine that he was part of but not privy to. Because he always returned to his ship or went to the NAAFI after servicing a punter, he never had the privilege of meeting other rent boys or girls. Apparently, they all knew one another and watched over each other, swapping good punter advice or passing on clients they could not cater to, for one reason or the other.

Rose informed him that the majority of his clients were the cream, and a few local rent boys were more than jealous. He was somewhat concerned by this. He was an easy going guy and for the life of him, didn't want to upset any applecarts, especially those full of pretty boys. Rose said he wasn't to worry, there were no boys who wished him any harm.

"Do you swing, sweetie?" she casually tossed into the conversation.

She was either chatting him up or teasing, Brad figured. He knew it wasn't uncommon for girls to want to get off with gay guys. Often, he had had calls from women wanting his services and put them off by saying that he was gay. Usually, they knew exactly what he was, and that was precisely what they wanted. But maybe Rose was thinking of providing him with a new variety of client—married couple threesomes and the like. Brad said he was sorry but he didn't. Rose gave him a bunny rabbit look and said that that was a pity as she had nothing to do for an hour.

So, thought Brad, it was an offer. He gave Rose's hand an intimate squeeze, saying, "Thanks, anyway."

They became instant friends and Brad gave Rose his ship's address, which he'd never done to anyone before.

More than sufficient rum rolled down Brad's throat as they talked about anything and everything, eventually venturing into his love affair with Greg. He wished he hadn't done that as it brought an inevitable flood of tears.

Brad showed Rose Greg's gold ring and said he was fearful of losing it because it was too large for his fingers. Rose was clearly in sympathy for this pretty rent boy sailor, and, taking one of the thin gold necklaces from her neck, offered it to Brad. He wasn't sure what he was supposed to do with it, so Rose slipped Greg's ring from his finger and threaded it onto the golden strand. Brad leant forward, as requested, and Rose placed it around his neck and fastened the clasp, giving him a huge smacker on the cheek.

Brad smiled and thanked her whilst she removed her rouge-red lip print with a tissue, then ruffled his hair. It reminded him of Greg, but Brad didn't mind. She began to chastise him, explaining that he'd broken one of the golden rent boy rules, explaining that it was impossible to do his work if he fell in love.

"You don't fall in love with punters. You don't fall in love with anybody!" she scolded, giving him a friendly poke in the tummy. There could be only two solutions, either he stopped being a rent boy right now, or he went straight back on the streets and got himself a punter. She knew only too well how lovers often never returned.

Brad thought hard on her words. Could he really carry on with this renting game knowing his heart and soul were pining for Greg, or would that pass over the months once he got back into it?

"I can get you a punter, now!" suggested Rose, urging him into action, or maybe she thought he needed to free himself from thoughts of Greg, even free himself permanently from his lover.

"I've heard from a rent boy friend of a nice guy who's been after you for a long time," she informed. "I can fix it for you."

Brad, not totally legless but quite merry and unable to make a serious decision, agreed. What harm could there be in it? And he could do with some extra cash.

Rose slid sexily across the empty bar and made a phone call. Brad went to her side when she beckoned him, and, taking up the phone, chatted with the guy on the other end. The conversation was short and Brad's face beamed a little during it. The receiver was replaced and lifted once more, and, selecting a taxi cab number, he phoned a cab.

Climbing into the taxi, Brad gave Rose a hug and kiss, avoiding her lips, and said, "Goodbye." Rose asked him to keep in touch.

The taxi trolled around the town stopping at almost every traffic light. Still the sun shone and appeared to get brighter as they headed into the countryside, eventually stopping at a huge house. Brad paid the driver and gave him a tip. A handsome youth opened the door to the house and invited Brad in.

In a massive room, Brad sat on a leather settee and listened as the youth explained that he would be required to be placed into a harness. Brad agreed.

A spliff was handed to him, which he had never tried before. Cautiously, he puffed of the drugged cigarette. Within minutes it began to take effect. Drowsy from the booze and puff, and not too sure of his whereabouts, he was ushered into another room and prepared for his punter.

Fourteen
HANGING AROUND

Brad watched with great anticipation as the glowing pipe was placed onto a piece of furniture. It appeared as if it were floating in space.

Closer and closer came the unknown man with unknown intentions. Brad's heart raced as the fearsome black figure continued toward him. Brad's initial excitement instantly drained from his body and his heart gave a huge thud, and then another. He was sure it hit the inside of his ribcage.

He began to breathe deeply, his heart thumping hard and fast, sweat seeping from his forehead and armpits. He wasn't afraid; he was terrified. In fact, he was petrified! This black figure was about to fetch some sadistic implement and beat the crap out of him and there was nothing he could do about it. Scream perhaps!

"Sir! Sir!" Brad pitifully called after the brutal black beast.

Stopping short of the doorway, the dreaded dark demon reached beside it. With a swift flick of his fingers the dimmer switch was spun, raising the lighting, and Brad was welcomed into a world of furniture, ornaments and double bed.

Standing tall and slim, dressed from head to ankles in a tightly fitting, black leather outfit, including fearsome face mask, was his punter. Brad released a burst of relieved laughter, realizing he wasn't going to be beaten stupid, but also because he was still stoned and found the spectacle ludicrous and laughable.

He couldn't apologize enough for his hysterical outburst as the punter came toward him, but still giggled during each apology. Mark (the client had finally offered up his name) laughed along with him, suggesting that maybe Brad had had too much puff. Brad agreed and apologized again.

The mood soon changed as Mark moved closer toward Brad's bound body and began to slowly circumnavigate the suspended torso, occasionally stroking a finger over the silken skin. Brad remained silent, allowing Mark to formulate his own fantasies.

Behind him now, Mark kissed at the powerful young shoulders and biceps, then over the nape of Brad's neck and behind his ears. Brad's breathing relaxed, in fact, he was almost asleep, the puff taking a second swipe at his over-indulgent body. Mark, unaware his purchase was almost in slumber, worked his way to the tight, firm buttocks and was biting into them. Gently he rotated his kinky kebab and began a tongue search of Brad's navel, avoiding the boyish bulge beneath the leather jock, saving it until last.

Brad's eyes opened and closed in baby-like fashion as he came ever closer to a slumbering state. His head tilted to one side sending his unruly hair flopping peek-a-boo over his forehead.

Biting, but not too hard, Mark nibbled on Brad's nipples, each firming slightly with the attention they had been given. Kissing now, ever more passionately, Mark's mouth moved around Brad's chest, brushing against

Greg's gold ring and Rose's chain.

A moan rose from Brad's mouth, but it was not one of passionate response. He was fast asleep!

Undeterred or unaware, Mark continue his tantalizing tour of the fine-featured figure. Tenderly, he teased and tweaked from tip to toe every centimeter of his covetous creature. Brad began to bulge in his leather jock as the masked head mouthed and manipulated its contents. It was a subconscious act as Brad had drifted into a sexual dream of Greg and himself making love on some exotic island. Mark was aware of only his own sexual arousal and that of Brad's unfolding before his wanting eyes. His sailor stimulated sufficiently, Mark moved for the prize!

Popping open the press-studs on either side of the leather jock, Brad's proud prick pushed the shiny sheath clear. Mark moved upon the mouthwatering meat and it vanished into the blackness of his menacing mask.

With a start, Brad awoke form the loving embraces of Greg, to the sight of a black leather face lusting upon his sex. Without hesitation, he screamed, "Stop! I can't do this." Then, more subdued, "I'm sorry, Mark. I can't do this."

Mark stopped sucking instantly, and, raising himself level with the sad, boyish face, looked quizzingly into the wet eyes and saw that Brad was distressed. Swiftly, he released Brad from the harness lest he had done anything to harm him, but was sure he hadn't. Brad began to sob.

An invisible bell was sounded, summoning the youth who had welcomed Brad into the house, who was then dispatched, returning with Brad's uniform and two large rums. Between sobs and sips, Brad slipped into his clothing.

Mark and Brad lay side by side on the double bed, sipping their drinks, whilst Brad unloaded the sorry tale of Greg for the second time this day. Mark listened with compassion, stroking at Brad's body and comforting him, but also because he still desired it for himself, even though he knew that that was no longer possible. It was clear to Mark that Brad was crazily in love with Greg. Likewise, it was now unmistakably clear to Brad.

They chatted for a long while, Mark still dressed in his outfit, Brad still having no idea what he looked like or who he was. The only possible clue was a ring on Mark's finger with the letters MTC entwined around each other. M obviously for Mark.

Having unloaded his life onto Mark and not given him the sex he'd desired, Brad didn't take any money, but Mark insisted he take the cab fare back to his ship. Brad accepted the money with a loving kiss, which Mark took as an act of gratitude and friendship, sadly for him, not one of sexual promise.

The cab sped Brad to his ship, all lights green this time.

"Rose is such a clever girl," he thought. She had guessed that he was truly in love and his rent boy days were done, and proved it to him the best

Fifteen
NEW BEGINNINGS

Over the next six months, Brad became his own slave-master as the ship went to sea and back many times, preparing itself for a war. A war with whom, no one really knew. Any war would do! They never went anywhere special or exotic, mainly patrolling around the British coast and the occasional trip to France. Brad hardly ventured ashore; he hardly did anything anymore, not even wank. His life was now one of celibacy and self-imposed slavery.

No more punters had entered his life, his rent boy days definitely done. He regretted not informing his favorite clients that he had ceased his servicing, and felt that he should have explained. Often he thought of the phone ringing, unanswered, in the park.

Try as he desperately did, he could not help pining after Greg, and now that he had passed his exams and been promoted, he thought of Greg even more—now that he was doing Greg's job.

Like Greg, he too was fair when dishing out orders and punishments, but a good few of his mates had said that he'd changed. Perhaps a good few knew the reason why, and Greg's rings which hung around his neck on Rose's chain, was a dead give-away. He hadn't even looked Rose up to thank her, such was his sadness. He hadn't completely gone down the pan in a depressed kind of way, his life had certainly changed.

On a couple of occasions, he'd tried to trace Greg but without luck. And it was difficult to ask anyone in authority of his whereabouts without raising a few eyebrows. Mainly, he asked sailors from other ships who were friends of Greg whether they knew of his draft, but even that could give some the wrong idea, and it wasn't advisable to show too much interest in any one person.

At night he would caress Greg's ring and think of their days together, and hope that some day they would meet up again. Occasionally, he would slip the ring from the chain and wear it whilst sleeping, but he never wore it whilst working for fear of losing it.

Luckily, he loved the navy and was mostly occupied. He was also aware of the dangers of being preoccupied with other matters, when the sea was rough and the waves were crashing over himself and his mates, other than falling over the ship's side.

A new baby sailor had joined the ship and Brad had taken him under his wing, teaching him everything that Greg had taught him. But he kept the lad well-distanced, in a loving kind of way. No way would he want this youngster to become too attached and go what he was going through, should they part.

It was approaching three years since Brad had joined the frigate, which was a long time for a sailor to remain on one ship, so when a draft order was issued for him, it came as no surprise. What was a shock was that his new draft was to a minesweeper.

Being a small ship, everyone on board had a good deal of responsibility, and as he'd only recently been promoted to Leading Seaman, Brad felt obliged to have his draft confirmed. Sure enough, it was correct and he was congratulated on his posting. After all, he was the youngest Leading Hand in the fleet, just as Greg said he would be.

There was no party before he left but he cracked some cans with mates and had a few tots of rum. The baby sailor was unconcerned at his leaving, and Brad was relieved for that.

Scotland was where his minesweeper was based, a good way to travel, but Brad didn't mind. The train journey to London was uneventful but he had the pleasure of travelling on the Flying Scotsman from London to Scotland.

During his journey, he recalled his first train journey after training, and the punter he pulled. No such thing was going to happen this time, but he recognized the looks he was getting from interested parties.

"If you only knew!" he inwardly laughed as a young soldier cruised him.

The Flying Scotsman was welcomed with bagpipes, pomp and ceremony. Not for him, but for the tourists. Brad adored the kilts and knew of a few punters who would have loved to have seen him dressed in one of those.

An old crock of a Navy bus bumped and shook him to Rosyth dockyard, where he met his minesweeper. It was so small, compared to his frigate, and Brad was pretty sure it would be a bouncy bugger in a storm.

Saluting the quarterdeck, Brad offered his papers to the Officer-of-the-Day, who in turn directed him to the Captain's cabin. Outside, Brad made himself smart for the meeting, and, giving a sharp tap on the door was bade enter.

He felt relaxed and at ease as he chatted to Commander Tamworth-Cotrill, and he thought that they would get along well. They talked about his last ship and his good reports, and the Captain congratulated Brad on his promotion. Half and hour and the chat was over and he was welcomed on board. The Captain called for the duty Petty Officer.

Brad shook the Captain's hand firmly, then quite suddenly thought, "I know this man!"

"Sir," a soft but authoritative voice called from the cabin door in reply to the Captain's command. Brad turned in its direction.

Standing in the doorway stood a Noble Knight adorned in a Petty Officer's uniform. Brad gasped—Greg looked more gorgeous than ever.

Brad was speechless, his mouth agape and turned toward the Captain, catching sight of the ring upon his let hand. The entwined letters MTC were unmistakable. Mark Tamworth-Cotrill released a smile and simply said, "Please show Leading Seaman Trent to his quarters, Petty Officer."

"Yes, Sir!" a stunned Greg almost stammered.

Leaving the Captain's cabin, Brad caressed Greg's ring, which he had worn for luck. "Thank you. Oh, thank you!" he whispered.

Closing the cabin behind them, Greg and Brad moved toward each other, and without thought of who might be watching, threw themselves together. Fiercely embracing and passionately kissing, both whispered, "I love you."

THE STAR RECRUIT
by William Cozad

"...I whacked my big dick raw while fantasizing about him."

After high school graduation, I joined the Navy. I'd seen their television commercial about "Go Navy" and was persuaded. Besides, I thought that Navy Crackerjack uniform was the sexiest clothing item ever designed.

The idea of running away to sea appealed to me. I wanted to get away from my small, boring Midwestern town. I wanted to see the world. I wanted to be around the horny guys on a ship. I figured something homo was bound to happen.

At the recruiting office in the capital city, I signed up, took the test and was given a group physical exam with other 18-year-old guys, and was sworn in.

My folks were glad to see me go away because that was one less mouth to feed. I never got along with my stepfather who tried to boss me around.

The Navy put us recruits on a plane and flew us away to San Diego, California.

The reality of boot camp at the Naval Training Center was nothing like I expected. They sheared off our hair, issued us uniforms, and the training started.

The chief got us up before daylight and marched us to the chow hall. There were calisthenics and marching on the grinder, with the chief in our face bitching and calling his names. There was endless instruction and stuff to memorize like general orders, Navy traditions, rifles and knots to tie.

It was hot in the summer and the training was hard. Chowing down, I gained some weight. The only guy in the company who had an easy time was Andrews. He'd been a Sea Scout and could assemble a rifle and tie the knots faster than the chief, who was a bosun's mate. The chief made Andrews the example for the rest of us to be like.

I'd checked Andrews out in the showers. He was my age, tall, smooth and muscular, swimmer's build with buzz-cut brown hair and bright hazel eyes. He had a fat, uncut dick and big balls.

One night I was dreaming about Andrews. I had the hots for him just like I had for that football jock back in high school who barely knew I existed. I never saw the jock naked or got a whiff of his crotch. But I whacked my big dick raw while fantasizing about him. The saltpeter in the chow cut my libido, but I still had wet dreams about Andrews. He knew I admired him and wasn't jealous of him like some of the other guys were because the chief treated him special and the rest of us like animals to be whipped into shape and made into sailors.

Suddenly, I was shaken from sleep, with a flashlight shining in my eyes. It was Andrews in the flesh.

"Time for your watch," he said.

"Uh yeah, okay."

I rubbed the sleep out of my eyes.

"Hurry up."

I jumped out of my rack and put on my dungarees, blue chambray shirt, boots and white hat. My dick was still semihard from the horny dream of Andrews in the showers that had threatened to be wet in more ways than one.

Andrews left and I went to the head and managed to pee even with my boner. I took my sweet time.

Andrews barged into the head.

'Whatcha doing, jacking off? Oh man, I gotta piss or bust a gut."

He stood at the urinal beside me and whipped out his big dick. I watched him skin it back and let go with a spray of piss. He shook the golden drops off his dick and it stiffened.

"I get so fucking horny. Used to getting pussy...."

Fascinated by his macho talk and big meat, I reached over and grabbed his hot, throbbing cock that was nine thick inches, the biggest one I'd ever seen. I stroked the loose skin over the bulbous crimson crown that glistened and clear goo.

"What the fuck you doing?" he growled.

"Just giving you a helping hand, buddy."

"If some chief or officer finds that post deserted, we're in deep shit. If they catch us messing around, we'll get tossed in the brig and given an undesirable discharge."

Still, he didn't stop me from playing with his big dick. I leaned over and took a few slides on his meat.

"Oh, shit yeah," he sighed.

Kneeling on the concrete floor, I bobbed my head up and down on Andrews's hard dick. I'd never sucked a dick before in my life. His meat was rubbery and the crown tasted, well, "tangy."

He rubbed my head. He clasped it and shoved his dick down my throat. I had trouble breathing. I figured he'd choke me with his humongous dick.

"Fucking you in your face, cocksucker. Like it, don'tcha? Yeah, keep sucking on it. Get me off, queer recruit punk."

His dick got hard as a rock. I stroked my boner while he plugged my throat.

"Oh, shit. Oh, Jesus. fucking Christ, I'm coming!"

His massive prick exploded. Gobs and gobs of hot, creamy cum filled my throat and mouth. I kept my lips fastened around his dick, but the overflow of jizz ran out of the corners of my mouth and trickled down my chin.

He yanked his dick out of my mouth. I licked my lips, tasting his sweet cum. His dick stayed stiff. I wasn't sure what to expect when he maneuvered me over into a stall. There were no doors on them. I was worried because he was so macho he might stomp my ass or try to drown me 'in the toilet bowl.

He sat down on the toilet. The next thing I knew he wrapped his luscious lips around my dick, which had softened slightly out of fear but got hard as a rock. The feeling of his warm, wet mouth on my big dick was the best sensation I ever felt. I couldn't believe that the star seaman recruit in our boot-camp company was sucking my dick. He man aged to tug down my dungarees and boxers. His hands clamped my bare butt while he gobbled up my boner.

He rubbed my steamy asscrack. He punched his finger into my butthole and finger-fucked me. All the while he slurped and slobbered on my dick.

Watching him suck my cock was the homiest sight I'd ever seen, with his pouty lips wrapped around my meat. He sucked up a storm and diddled my butthole with his finger.

I'd never been so hot before in my life. The feeling was too good to last. He grabbed my dangling balls and wrenched them. That took me over the edge. With his finger all the way up my chute, I let go with the biggest orgasm of my life.

To my surprise and delight, the sailor drank every drop of my load. He kept his mouth on my meat until my dick softened.

He leaped up off the toilet. I started to pull up my pants. But he spun me around and positioned me over the commode, I braced my hands on the bulkhead.

Looking over my shoulder, I watched the sailor get down on his knees. He spread my buttcheeks. I was shocked when he dove into my asscrack and lapped at it. He darted his tongue up my asshole and tongue-fucked it.

My dick sprang to life again. He reached up between my legs and stroked my dick while he tongued my asshole. He finally came up for air.

I fooled around in the Sea Scouts, but it was mostly circle jerks for money. When I saw your cute butt in the showers and the way you gawked at me, I knew that you wanted the same thing I did."

The sailor stood up behind me. His mega-dick was at full mast and oozing clear pre-cum. Holding his dick, he smeared the goo into my crack. His dick felt like a hot poker.

"Oh, Andrews, your dick's too big," I whimpered.

That didn't stop him. He punched his bloated prick into my asshole.

"Whoa, shit!" I yelped.

"Stay still. Get used to it I've busted cherry holes before."

"But I'm a guy."

He was right. I felt my ass-ring expand around his dick. I wanted it. I wanted the sailor to fuck me. I backed up on his big dick and let him know.

"Hot, tight shithole. it's tighter than pussy," he said.

He clutched my waist and slid his big dick in and out.

"Fuck me, Andrews. Fuck my virgin butt," I whispered

"You got it, punk recruit. You're mine now."

He reached up under my T-shirt and tweaked my nipples. I'd never before realized how sensitive they were.

"Keep fucking me with your big dick, you horny stud."

He throttled my butthole. His dungarees chafed against my bare skin while he humped away.

"Fuck me harder. Deeper. Faster," he pleaded.

He pulled out all the stops. He rammed my ass hard.

and fast, creating sensations that put me into orbit. My head spun. My asshole was on fire.

"More. Don't stop," I gasped. "More!"

And so he literally tore up my ass with his big dick.

"Oh my god, it's so big and hard. Shoot it, Andrews! Shoot it!"

He thudded my guts with his exposed dangling balls slapping against my asscheeks.

"Here it comes!" he rasped.

He crammed his exploding dick all the way inside me and creamed my guts with his cum.

My asshole spasmed and I was aware of my own hard dick raining cum-drops all over the commode and floor.

The sailor was breathing heavy and kept his cock buried. up my butthole until it softened and plopped out.

I was about to turn around, but the sailor kept a tight hold on me. Kneeling down, he buried his face between my ass mounds and slurped some of his cum out of my asshole. Then he stood up.

I turned around, bent down and cleaned off his cock.

Both of us quickly got our uniforms squared away.

"Better go stand your watch," he said.

I left the head and went out to the patio behind the barracks. I walked my post in a military manner, the best I could with my sore ass. But I wasn't looking for intruders. All I could think about was Andrews the star recruit and the basic training with him that made a real Navy man out of me.

Three tales of Raw Recruits on their way to deeper understandings of life in the military

BUSFUCKINGRIDES
by
Mark Wildyr

A New Erotic Novella

TWINS

Pvt. Johnny Wallen's first permanent assignment for the Air Force after completing advanced training two weeks earlier whisked him straight from a cornfield to a weapons lab computer in the far-off southwest. Shy, naïve Johnny had coped reasonably well so far. It was almost like having a regular job: once his shift was through, he was free. No details, no harassment, no nothing. Most of the guys he worked with were okay, too. Their biggest complaint about him? He was a loner.

One Saturday morning, he was in the downtown library indulging a passion for history, most recently, western and southwestern history. It was only a short drive to fascinating places where incredible events had occurred a hundred years ago, but his pay wouldn't cover the expense of a car. Maybe someday he'd be able to afford one.

As Johnny manipulated the library's catalog computer, he noticed a young woman about his age across the rotunda. Man, he'd like to get next to somebody like her! Oh yeah, she was just dying to cozy up to a corn fed, shit-shoveler like him. He put her age at twenty, twenty-one even, older than him by a couple of years. Short brown hair with red highlights. Tall for a woman, but what a shape! Dressed classy. So far out of his league he was surprised he was allowed to look—which he did on the sly when she took the machine beside him and began skipping through menus. She looked over briefly and bestowed a smile. Beautiful green eyes with long lashes. He wondered if they were fake? Broad mouth with full lips. What was it the magazines called them? Pouty? Yeah, that was it. Smooth, clear complexion. Small ears. Man, was she pretty. Beautiful even. She caught him staring again.

Embarrassed, he headed for the stacks to find a volume on western range wars in the 1800's. He took the fire stairs, climbed to the third floor and spent five minutes at the shelves before settling at a study cubicle with his book. Almost immediately the same girl showed up and began prowling the shelves. Johnny caught glimpses of her now and then through gaps in the stacks. Intimidated by her presence, he concentrated on concentrating. Her low, throaty voice sent shivers down his spine when she asked to share his reading table. Unable to manage his voice, he nodded, and then blushed when that bad thing in his pants started acting up. He always tripped on his tongue or his cock when a girl was around. Must be why he was still a virgin. Was that right? Could guys be virgins? Well, anyway, he'd never gotten any.

Across the table from him, she daintily opened her book. A moment later, she startled him again. "Do you have a pen I could borrow? I seem to have left mine in the car."

S… sure," he stammered, rushing to hold out a ninety-cent BIC and inadvertently brushing her hand. His neck flamed furiously.

"How cute," she cooed. "You're blushing. Am I making you uncomfortable? I can move if you want."

"N… no! It's all right. I'm just sorta shy."

"How quaint. Most boys… men your age are throwing themselves all over a girl. It's nice to meet one with manners for a change. My name's Darla. What's yours?"

"Johnny. Johnny Wallen. Private," he added unnecessarily, glancing down at the uniform blouse bare of any stripes.

"I haven't seen you here before, Johnny."

"I'm new. Just got here last week. Took me this long to find the place," he blurted.

She took out a pad and wrote something in it, then returned his pen, clasping his hand as he accepted it. "Thank you, Johnny," she said, licking her ruby lips. "And it was a pleasure to meet you."

The way she held his hand in both of hers, the wet lips, the direct gaze into his eyes all got to him. His cock shot to attention, pressing painfully against his trousers. "Welcome," he managed.

She gripped his hand tightly with a little smile curling her lips. "Can I buy you a cup of coffee?"

"Yes, ma'am. Uh, no, ma'am. I'd like to, but I can't," he almost moaned.

"Ma'am? My name's Darla, remember?" She stood and tugged on his hand. She was stronger than she looked, and he came halfway out of his chair. He was mortified. She saw his condition. She was probably disgusted with him.

"Stand up, Johnny."

"I can't," he said, dropping his eyes.

"How sweet. You're embarrassed. Well, I'm not. Please stand up for me, Johnny." So he did, his hands cupped in front of him. She grasped a wrist in each hand and pulled them apart. His trousers stuck out obscenely. "That looks interesting," she cooed, as she covered him with a hand. A tremor jolted him. Nobody… but *nobody* had ever touched him there. "Feels interesting, too," she added, running her hand down to his balls.

Johnny backed into the table and almost fell on his ass. She pushed him deeper into the cubicle, out of sight of the door. "You listen for someone coming, okay?" With that, she knelt and placed her perfect cheek against his erection. He would've run away in panic if he'd been able to get anything to work except his cock, which was working just fine when she opened his trousers. The head peeked out eagerly.

"Johnny!" she exclaimed. "You are one well-hung stud." Her words embarrassed him, but he forgot all about that when she took him in her mouth. Although he had no experience to judge by, he figured she was very good. Within minutes, he crouched over and moaned his way to an orgasm. He tried to warn her, but it was a feeble effort, because instead of getting out of the way, she took all of his stuff without losing a drop. Then she stood and surprised him again by kissing him on the mouth. He wasn't sure he liked that, considering where that mouth had been. Her tongue tasted strange. Was it because of his stuff? In a moment he forgot all of that and reached for her, but she eluded his grasp.

"There, now, did you like it?"

"Yes," he panted, hurriedly stuffing himself back in his pants. "Can... we have that cup of coffee now? I'll buy."

"I don't see why not," she cooed, but when they left the building she suddenly recalled that she had something else to do and left him in the parking lot staring at the rear end of a LeBaron. At the very moment the coupe turned onto the main thoroughfare, Johnny Wallen emerged from his shell and resolved to find her. If she'd do that for him, heck, she'd probably do the other, too. And he desperately wanted to do that... well, not at that moment exactly, because his thing was pretty well played out, but when the guys bragged about fucking a slit, he wanted to know what they were talking about. She had a name, a car, and most important, he'd spotted a small triangular parking decal that read Riverside View Apartments, so he'd play detective and find her. He wondered if she would mind him tracking her down like a deer back home during hunting season. Naw, he reasoned, not after she went down on him like that. She must like him. Girl wouldn't do that if she didn't.

The telephone book and bus schedule told him where to find the apartments and how to get to them. Unfortunately, that didn't bolster his courage sufficiently to do anything about it. He returned to base and dreamed that night about his new girlfriend. Well, she *would* be when he found her again.

By Thursday night, Johnny had become obsessed with Darla. Darla...what a beautiful name. And it fit her. She was a Darla right down to her toes! To hell with it! He'd do it! When his shift ended, Johnny took a long shower, shaved for the second time that day, and slapped on so much after-shave he almost couldn't stand himself. He hoped it would wear off on the ride over. Two bus transfers later, he stood before a huge apartment complex and wondered how in the hell he'd locate Darla. Somehow, he didn't think asking at the office would be very smart. First he had to get in the place, because there was a sentry box in the middle of the entry, damned near like the ones at the base. It was unmanned, and he walked through the gate unchallenged. He made two rounds of the big place but didn't spot her car. He went back to the base that night and jacked off before his roommates came back from town.

Saturday, he tried to do some reading at the library, but eventually gave in to a strong urge and boarded a bus. There was still no LeBaron in the parking lot, but he found a little stone half-wall out of sight of the gates where he could sit and watch. If they didn't get him for loitering, maybe he'd spot her when she came in.

An hour and a half later, he questioned whether this was a good idea. Johnny was as patient as Job at squirrel hunting, but not at playing detective. He decided to catch the next bus. A red blur caught his eye as he looked up from the bus schedule. It was the LeBaron!

Johnny trotted after the car as it pulled into a parking spot halfway down the long complex. He was still too far away when she strode confidently across the walk toward a stairwell and disappeared from sight. He was afraid he had lost her, but she reappeared on the second story walkway and entered a corner apartment.

Now he knew where she lived, but had no idea what to do about it. Privacy was sacred to him, and he was uncomfortable violating someone else's. He circled the entire building trying to get up the nerve to knock on that door, finally hesitating outside the apartment. He could hear nothing. Well, maybe some faint music of some kind. A door opened down the way, and a gray-haired man emerged. Panicked at being caught listening at the door, Johnny rapped softly on a panel. Maybe she wouldn't hear, and he could sneak away when the old man disappeared.

The door suddenly opened on a handsome young man. His fine brows creased somewhat at the sight of an airman on his threshold. "May I help you?" he asked in a deep baritone.

"Uh… is Darla home?"

The young man's face cleared immediately. "Oh, are you a friend of Darla's? I'm Darin, her brother. Come on in."

"Johnny Wallen," he responded, accepting the firm handshake. "Uh, I met your sister at the library a few days ago."

"Oh," he said. "Well, have a seat. She just got in so she's removing her face or something in the bathroom. I'll let her know you're here."

Johnny looked around the place while Darin rapped on the bathroom door and mumbled something. Nice place. Expensive. His eyes fell on a framed picture on the table. Brother and sister stood side by side. Not just brother and sister, twins!

"So you figured it out," Darin said, handing a cola of some kind in a glass to Johnny. "We're twins. Fraternal twins, of course, though we look identical." The two men made small talk for a few minutes, and Johnny learned that Darin was a law student and that Darla worked downtown somewhere. Darin rose. "Look, I've got to go get ready. I was about to go out. Make yourself comfortable. She just got her face off, so now she'll have to put it on again. Might take some time." With a broad smile, he disappeared into a bedroom, closing the door behind him. Nice fellow, Johnny thought. He wished he could be confident and gracious like that guy.

Darla appeared ten minutes later. She hadn't spent the time putting on her face. She wore no makeup except a faint lip color, and the absence didn't detract from her appearance one whit. She looked like a million dollars in loose, beige slacks and tie-around shirt. He stood, already poking out a little.

She laughed throatily. "Johnny. You tracked me down. You didn't tell me you were a detective. What was it, car license?"

"Parking permit," he admitted sheepishly. "I hope you're not mad at me."

"It's hard to be mad at you, Johnny." She approached and patted his cheek. Suddenly, she leaned forward and kissed him. He glanced guiltily toward her brother's closed door. "Don't worry about Darin. We'll go to my room if you'll be more comfortable." She walked up behind him when he stopped in the middle of the bedroom. "I've thought about that day in the library a lot."

"M... me, too," he stuttered. Her hands closed on his thighs and caressed his package.

"This time, I want you to strip naked," she said, caressing his cock.

"You, too!" he said as he unbuttoned his shirt.

"No, no, no. There's something you've got to understand, Johnny. I'm a virgin, and the best way to stay that way is keep my clothes in place. There are other ways to have fun. Is that a problem?"

"No," he hastened to agree, slipping his trousers and shorts off all at one time. Then suddenly, he felt strange standing naked before this beauty while she was still clothed. Especially, when she walked around him, viewing him from every angle. All four of his cheeks blushed.

"You are one hunky man," she breathed, moving against him from behind. Her hands circled his chest, playing with the light sprinkling of hair. "I like a man with hair on his chest," she cooed.

For the next few minutes, he felt like an automaton, moving when and how she dictated. But he forgave her everything when she leaned over him on the bed and ran her tongue down his belly and over his hard cock. She murmured softly while she licked and sucked at his balls. When she took him in her mouth, he about lost it. He pulled her up on his chest before he ruined it all by coming too early. He wasn't used to having a beautiful woman look at him naked. Hell, he wasn't used to a beautiful woman, period!

Accommodatingly, she kissed him long and deep, and this time he didn't even think about where her mouth had been. He just enjoyed it! As she pulled away, he slipped his hand between he legs. He froze!

"What the hell!" he gasped, his hand closing on something that should not have been there.

"Busted!" a baritone voice said. Darin sat back on his heels and pulled off a wig. Instantly, he was the handsome young law student. Johnny couldn't believe he'd been so stupid when the man shrugged out of his blouse and unfastened the bra to reveal a well-shaped, masculine trunk. "That's better." Very matter-of-factly, the young man lowered himself to Johnny's groin again.

"Get away from me!" Johnny cried, his voice rising alarmingly. Darin ignored him. His mouth closed on Johnny's still rampant cock. Damned if it didn't still feel good. He lay there, allowing the young man his way, closing his eyes and conjuring the image of Darla taking him in the library, but it morphed into the handsome brother. Darin worked at him slowly, carefully, thoroughly. Hands reached up to stroke his nipples, hands that were obviously masculine. Why hadn't he seen it before?

The pressure of Darin's naked chest, the talented mouth, the hands roving his torso pulled him to the edge. When Darin raised his head once, then slid slowly down the entire length of Johnny's cock, the young airman flew into the abyss. He spasmed. His legs trembled. His hands flew to Darin's head, holding it tight against his crotch. Cum pumped out of him into the youth's mouth as Johnny's hips ground into him. It seemed to go on forever.

Drained of semen, drained of energy, drained of horror and revulsion, Johnny lay motionlessly on the bed as Darin crawled up his torso and looked him deep in the eyes. "That... that was you in the library, too, wasn't it?" Johnny asked. Darin nodded. "Why? Why'd you dress up like that?"

Darin rolled off him and propped his head on an elbow. "It started when we were little. We were so alike nobody could tell us apart. We used to change places a lot. Clear up until we were young teenagers. Darla lives in California now, but she keeps some of her things here for when she visits. Last year one of the clubs had a freak party... you know, where you dress up crazy. I went as Darla. One of the hunks who'd never had a homoerotic thought in his life came on to me even though he knew it was me, not my sister. I sucked his cock and left him begging for more. Later on, I tried it on my own, you know like I met you at the library. Guys who would've punched my lights out couldn't wait to offer their cocks to Darla. You're the only one who tracked me down."

"You're qu... uh, gay."

Darin's broke into a broad smile. "I'd say so, wouldn't you?"

"But you act so..."

"Macho? Yeah, not many people know the true me. Keep up a pretty good front."

"I feel like an ass," Johnny said a little bitterly. Belatedly, he reached for his shorts to cover his groin.

"Why? You liked it, didn't you?"

"I've never done anything queer in my life!"

Darin smiled again. "Yeah, you've limited your experience to women. How many have there been?"

"A few," Johnny lied. "Why did you pick on me?"

"Because you're one good-looking son-of-a-bitch. I noticed you right away at the catalog, but when you walked back to the stacks, I was lost. You've got a stride that makes me want to come in my pants."

"Don't talk shit," Johnny said, not totally displeased.

"No, really. It's long and graceful, and says get out of my way, here comes a man." Johnny blushed. Darin laughed softly. "I like the way you do that. Nobody's ever told you how attractive you are before, have they?"

"No, because I'm not."

"What do your women say when you fuck them?" Johnny flushed again. "Be damned," Darin said. "You've never fucked anyone, have you?" He stood and shrugged out of his sister's slacks. Once again, Johnny wondered how he could have been fooled. Darin was well formed. Hell, he had a cock as big as his own. Darin saw him looking and lifted his cock. "Usually I tuck it between my legs and wear this tight pair of underpants. It doesn't feel all that good, and I decided not to wear them today. Guess I should've."

As he started to lie down beside him again, Johnny scrambled to the side of the bed. "What are you going to do?"

"Take it easy. Just lie back. Close your eyes. Think of Darla, if you want to. I'll take it nice and slow."

Johnny thought his skin would crawl when Darin touched him, but it only trembled at the light touch. He closed his eyes, but Darla would not come. Gradually he relaxed as Darin caressed his body from head to toe. Eyes still closed, he felt Darin's tongue replace the fingers. He feebly protested when the other boy's lips touched his, turning his head slightly. Darin moved on, kissing his eyes, his nose, and then started downward again. When Darin reached his groin, Johnny responded. Slowly, his cock grew under the insistent prodding of Darin's lips. When he was hard, Darin threw his legs over Johnny's. Johnny's eyes flew open. Mesmerized, Johnny watched helplessly as Darin leaned forward, placing his penis against his own. He grasped both organs in his hand and began to stroke them slowly. The feelings it evoked astounded him. He could come that way, Johnny realized.

Suddenly, Darin took him in his mouth again, briefly, and then simply sat down on him. A sheath of warm, damp flesh shrouded his cock as Darin's sphincter slowly slid down his entire length. He gasped. Darin grinned at him, a handsome, crooked smile. Shit! Darin was as pretty... no... as beautiful as his sister, just without the softness, the femininity. His mind went blank as Darin began to rotate his hips.

"Look at me, Johnny," Darin said quietly. "Look at me. See that it's me doing this for you. Look at me and understand that you're not turned off. It's a man sitting on your cock, and it's stayed strong and hard. I can feel it inside me, and it's as hard for Darin as it ever was for Darla."

"Shut up!" Johnny said, but there was no sting in his voice.

"You won't ever be able to say you're a virgin again, Johnny. You're fucking somebody."

"No... you're fucking me."

"Same thing. Touch me, Johnny," Darin demanded, lifting himself almost all the way off the cock impaling him and then sitting down again, causing Johnny to gasp. "Touch me!"

Johnny's hand reached out and made contact with a leg. Darin placed it on his cock. Johnny left his hand where it was, loosely clasping the erect column.

"Jack me off, Johnny. Make me come." Johnny's hand disobeyed his will, slowly pumped the other boy's big cock while Darin rotated his hips. "This is what I wanted the first time I saw you. Handsome, hunky Johnny. I saw a man, and I wanted him. Do it, Johnny," Darin panted, moving his hips up and down more rapidly. Johnny pumped harder. "Oh, yeah! Here I come, flyboy! You did it good!" Darin's cock jumped in his hand, delivering a steady stream of thick, milky semen.

Johnny didn't even notice it covered his hand. He was only aware of what was happening to his cock. Darin's ass grabbed it and caressed it, loved it, massaged it. Lost now, Johnny turned on his side, dumping the other boy onto the bed. Desperately seeking to maintain contact, Johnny lunged against Darin's butt, entering the boy again. He held Darin's hips while he battered his insides with his hungry cock. He fucked, turning once again so that he awkwardly lay atop Darin, still battering him with his hips, his balls slapping Darin's round buttocks, his cock penetrating deeper and deeper. Although he felt the approaching storm, it still took him by surprise. He gushed, he spewed, he fed his cum into the law student. He fucked even after he was drained, finally shuddering to a halt. He rested, still inside Darin, seeking to control his breathing. He remained that way until Darin's voice broke the spell.

"That was wonderful, Johnny!"

Suddenly mortified, he jerked himself out and lunged through a doorway into the bathroom. Now he knew how Darin got into the room from his own bedroom. The bath had pass-through doors. He washed himself, almost whimpering in loathing at what he was cleaning from his flesh. He dressed in a panic while his groin was still wet. It soaked through his trousers but he didn't care. He had to get out of there.

Johnny fled the apartment without speaking to Darin again. He was almost running by the time he reached the bus stop. Something seemed to be chasing him. He glanced around. Nothing. The worst of his panic attack was over by the time the bus came. He sat alone at the back, trying to come to grips with what had happened to him. Darla wasn't Darla. Darla was Darin. And even after he'd found out, he let himself be seduced in the vilest, dirtiest, most horrible way imaginable. His manhood tried to crawl up inside him.

The entire next week he made mistakes at his job that brought censure down on his head. Lt. Morrison, his boss, gave him a tongue-lashing more than once. By the end of the week, he'd managed to get a handle on himself. He was afraid to leave the base, but forced himself to go to a nightclub Saturday night with some other guys.

His buddies knew some of the regulars and tossed a girl his way. She was blonde, big-busted, and brassy. She was also older than he was, but he didn't give a shit. He just needed to know. It was agony sitting at the table and trying to take part in the inane conversation swirling around him. He tried talking to the woman, but found it difficult, so out of desperation he dragged her to the dance floor. Dancing was not one of his social skills, but with a little instruction from her, he managed not to tromp all over her feet. During one of the slow numbers, he looked down at her and blurted: "I want to feel your tits."

"What?" she asked in amazement. "What kinda girl do you think I am, bozo?"

"Please!" he begged. "I *need* to feel them."

"They're right up against you, honey."

"No, I need to feel them with my hands. I wouldn't ask if I didn't need to."

Suddenly, she laughed, and led him from the floor. They claimed their drinks from the table of airmen and their girls and made the rounds of the big, crowded room until they found a deserted booth in the back.

"Okay, big boy," she said as she scooted into the vinyl seat, "but if you're gonna cop a feel, so am I."

Only when he slid his hand up her brassiere and touched soft mounds of flesh with large aureoles and exaggerated nipples did his mind accept what his other senses told him. She was a real woman. This was the first time he'd ever felt a woman's tits like this.

"Oh, my," she cooed as her hand found his cock. "You're a big one."

"Let's go somewhere."

"Now? The evening's young. What's your rush?"

"I need it. Now. Please. Can't you feel?"

She took him home to her small, messy apartment, not at all like Darla's... Darin's large, neat place. He tore off his clothes, and his cock sprang free, bobbing in the air eagerly. She laughed, and lay back on the bed. He wasted no time on foreplay, merely fell atop her and made an easy, warm entry.

Johnny assaulted her for fifteen minutes, drawing moans and cries from her. He figured she got it at least three times, especially after he found her clit and rubbed it while he fed her his cock. Finally, his balls began to draw up. The feeling came over him. He was near. It was going... to... be... *good*...! He came, gushing a geyser. He clutched her to him as if seeking comfort. When he was through it, he didn't know what to do next.

"Well, that was quite a ride, flyboy. You fuck good, even if your technique could use some work. You learn that watching the bulls on the farm?"

That struck him as funny, and he started giggling. "Yeah, I guess. You wanta go back to the club? I got a little money left."

She kissed the top of his head. "No, it's too late. How you gonna get home, honey? You can stay here, if you want."

"No, I got duty tomorrow," he lied, not knowing why. "Bus or walk or hitch, I guess."

"I'll give you a ride if you'll put that big cock away and let me get dressed."

Neither of them spoke much on the ride to the base. He sneaked covert glances at the first girl he'd ever fucked. Girl. Woman. She had to be in her late twenties. Had ten years on him probably, but she was kind of all right looking. Good body, pleasingly plump. Be fat in another few years.

She let him out at the gate. "I'll be at the club next Saturday, Johnny. I'd like to see you again. Teach you how to treat a woman. But," she added meaningfully, "can't teach *you* much about getting down and dirty. Like I said, you fuck good, kid."

Johnny strutted through the gate and walked the half-mile to his barracks deep in thought. He'd fucked his first girl. And his first guy, too. The thought shook him. He turned his mind back to the woman. What was her name? Helen? He relived the incident. It was great. Yeah, it was, but... the Earth didn't move. It was good, but like the Lieutenant was always saying, it wasn't *cataclysmic*. Well, next Saturday, he'd damn well make it cataclysmic! She'd practically committed to fuck him again. And he'd do it, too! Like the bull she accused him of imitating.

Johnny performed his work quite satisfactorily, even apologizing to his boss for being so lousy the week before and promising it wouldn't happen again. He went into town early Saturday afternoon to stop by the library. He'd neglected his reading these past two weeks. He found the book he wanted and hid out in one of the alcoves up in the stacks, devouring half of the book on range wars. When he finally closed it, he realized he hadn't absorbed a damned thing. Too wound up about tonight, he guessed.

He ate at a McDonald's and spruced himself up in the men's room afterward. When he stepped outside it wasn't even dark yet. What the hell was he going to do now? What time should he show up at the nightclub?

Johnny walked across to a small park and sat down on an iron bench. What was wrong with him? He felt on edge, itchy. Was he that fucking anxious? Half an hour later, he got up and walked to the bus stop. When the bus brought him to his destination, he got out and walked through the unmanned sentry gate. The stairs to the second floor seemed steeper than he remembered. When the door opened, the handsome law student stared at him for a moment and then asked in a deep baritone, "Which twin did you come to see?"

"Darin," Johnny answered, stepping through the doorway.

When the beautiful young man took him in his arms, it was the most natural feeling in the world. Yes, it was gonna be *cataclysmic*! He could just tell.

RAD

Corporal Josef T. Radinsky, US Infantry, stretched his long legs and leaned back against the bench seat of the last municipal bus to the base that night. Although he preferred to nap on the six-mile ride, the bus driver wanted to talk, so he made an effort to be sociable.

"Joe Radinsky," he responded when the driver introduced himself as Adam Hall. "Joe's okay, but mostly they call me Rad."

Then came the bios. Rad was twenty and hailed from the east. Enlisted after high school to escape his domineering father and a very unstable sweetheart, spending the last two years in an infantry unit. Probably quit and go to school somewhere in another year. Ran a squad in a basic training unit, so he had stripes, not chevrons and was proud of it. Preferred Budweiser, but was getting to like the local Coors. No hobbies, but he did all right with a cue stick.

Adam, of a similar age, was native born, single, no current girlfriend, lived alone, went to college by day and drove a city bus by night. Collected stamps, pussy, and swizzle sticks. Coors Light was his drink, hands down. By the time the bus pulled up at the base HQ, the blond civilian and the brown-haired GI had agreed to a night on the town Friday, after Adam's last run at midnight.

Rad wasn't sure if the recruits this session were dumber, duller, and lazier than usual, or if it was too much beer with an uninteresting bitch last night. At any rate, the week brought problems with his squad that put him in a bad light with the platoon sergeant, a twice-busted SFC named Muleson but inevitably called Mule… Sgt. Mule, to the boots. Half of Mule's problems had been initiated with a private named Dill, christened 'Pickle' by the squad who suspected he was queer and picked on him unmercifully. Although the smartest, Pickle was also the weakest, the slowest, and the most timid, constantly earning the squad's shit details, what did not make Mule happy.

Rad tried individual instruction, personal physical training, and everything else he could think of, but Pickle neither improved nor gave up. Since he had no intention of re-upping, Rad had little chance of a third stripe, but Pickle was making that an absolutely certainty. A leader of men should be able to make a soldier out of the guy.

By Friday, he was ready for a night off. He boarded the bus and received a thumbs-up from Adam. Good! He needed some booze and gash tonight. The booze he had aplenty in the two hours before the bars closed and at Adam's place afterward, but the only unclaimed females by the time they got to the Mint were a couple of two-o'clock-doxies. Nonetheless, he hooked one and fucked her on the floor of Adam's living room while his new buddy snored solo through an alcoholic dream in the bedroom. Rad was so drunk he through the gal was pretty good.

The following Friday, he wore civvies, which helped sometimes and hurt others. Some gals dug a uniform, others dialed 911 at the sight of one. He hit the Mint early; Adam was to join him after his shift. Rad connected with a good-looking blond, but she was as nasty a drunk as his girlfriend back home, so he and Adam went back to the apartment stag. Pissed off and frustrated, Rad sat up to drink the rest of the beer they'd brought, although Adam crashed earlier.

Rad tried out Adam's shower before sacking out on the couch in his shorts. On the brink of passing out anyway, he fell asleep quickly. The blond appeared in his dream, much nicer than in real life. The first thing he knew, they were both naked, and she went down on him with that pretty mouth. Shit! If he didn't wake up soon, he'd have a wet dream.

Rad came awake slowly. "Hey, babe," he mumbled groggily and caressed the head at his groin. The mouth was doing wonderful things to his cock. His eyes flew open! A naked Adam knelt beside the sofa, his head moving in slow circles as he bobbed up and down on Rad's erection. Stunned, Rad lay there, doing nothing. Just as he decided to knock the guy's block off, his balls tingled, and he let loose with one hell of an ejaculation. He'd changed his mind and decided to play possum until Adam's mouth fixed on a nipple.

"What the fuck!" Rad yelled, shoving the naked youth away from him. Adam had a big cock at about half-staff when he fell back on his ass. "You fucking queer! What'd you do to me?"

Adam wiped his mouth calmly and leaned back on his elbows. His cock was rampant now, but he didn't seem to mind. In fact, he acted proud of it. "Come on, man. Don't tell me you didn't like it. You sure came a lot."

"You cocksucker, I was asleep."

"Hey, you wanted to bust your balls, and you did. What's the big deal? You want to do me now?" Adam might have been dumb enough to make a remark like that, but he was smart enough to stay down when Rad slugged him. The outraged soldier dressed and reeled uncertainly out the door into the half-light of dawn. He threw up three times before completing the eight-mile hike to the barracks, where he fell into bed and snarled at anyone looking to snare him for some Saturday detail.

Rad caught a ride into town with the company clerk, Nicholas Hahn, the next Friday night. Hahn was a friend, but not particularly a buddy. He was too straight-laced for most of the guys. A straight arrow with a brain on top, the cadre joked. Dark-headed, olive-skinned Nick was all right, was just a loner, Rad decided. Hell, he wasn't even going into town to hit the bars; he was headed for some museum or the other. But Rad wasn't ready to face Adam Hall on the bus, so he hitched the ride. It didn't do him much good since Adam showed up at the Mint later that night.

Rad took a chance and snagged the same blond because she was the sexiest broad in the place, but the problem was that she knew it. She was all over him early in the evening, even chasing off a couple of other decent looking skirts. Then she switched over to drinking Long Island Iced Tea, and things went straight down the tubes. She acted so snotty when they started to go to her place that he refused to get into the car. She roared off leaving him standing in the rapidly emptying parking lot at closing time.

"Oughta know better," Adam said with a smile as he pulled up in his convertible. Damn his hide, it wasn't even a smug smile, just friendly. "She's bad news. Thought you'd found that out last week."

"Slow learner," Rad muttered and turned away.

"You need a ride, buddy. I'll take you to the base. No strings."

Rad hesitated. He didn't want to get in the cocksucker's car, but he didn't relish the idea of walking back to the barracks, and his money was pretty well spent. "No funny stuff," he grumbled, reaching for the door handle. They drove in silence for a short distance before Adam asked if Rad really wanted to go back to the base. "What the hell else is there to do?" the GI responded.

"Couple of six-packs in my frig."

"No thanks."

"Your precious cock's safe... unless you want it sucked again."

"Fuck you, Hall. I'm no faggot."

"If I thought you were, I wouldn't be interested. I like straight guys. Hell, Rad, I don't find somebody I'm interested in very often... guys, I mean, but you're sure as hell one. Come on, I'll behave."

Rad didn't agree, but neither did he put up a fuss when Adam turned down his own street. He took his time getting out of the car and climbing to the second-story apartment. Adam already had the caps off two tall bottles. Rad accepted one and flopped down on the sofa to watch a little TV. They stared at a couple of talking heads until things became a little more comfortable. Adam acted like a regular guy, extolling the virtues of the Steelers over the Cowboys.

He tensed up when Adam said goodnight and headed for the bedroom. The GI tossed restlessly on the narrow divan for a while, alert for any false moves. Gradually, he acknowledged Adam was going to honor his word, then began wondering how he felt about that. Shit, he'd almost been looking forward to slugging the guy again. Fuck it!

He wasn't surprised when he got an erection in the shower. The little blond bitch was responsible for that. Rad did not actually intend to go into the bedroom when he had dried off, but that's what happened. Adam turned

- 274 -

and looked at him. The bathroom light revealed Rad's naked, rampant condition. Adam threw back the covers.

Adam took his time and did things right. He licked Rad's balls, sucked his tits, pulled the chest hair with his teeth, and made admiring noise over how big Rad was. At length, he got down to business and sucked Rad's cock into his mouth. Rad just laid back and let it happen. He was a little surprised that Adam could take his entire seven inches, but the guy didn't have any trouble at all. When he got it, Rad had to admit that the orgasm was pretty good. He fell asleep while Adam was still licking his cock and groin.

Rad stayed on base all week. He wouldn't consciously admit he was avoiding Adam, but that was the reality. That cocksucker was better than any of his girlfriends, and that worried Rad. He got hard in the shower more than once, thinking about it. Not only that, he became absolutely certain that Pickle would go down on him in a heartbeat. Even worse, he exchanged a couple of friendly words with Spec4 "Rosie" Rosenthal, who was the battalion's only known-for-sure queer. The Old Man only tolerated him because he was the best motor pool boss in the division.

Friday night, Rad missed a ride with Nick so he took the bus, sitting in the back and trying to avoid the meaningful looks Adam shot him in the big rear view mirror. Rad chose another nightclub for safety's sake, but the brunette he'd latched onto ditched him—reluctantly, he thought—for some paunch with a wad of cash. Well, fuck her, he thought. Hope she likes the old fart's flabby belly flopping all over her while she's getting fucked tonight. She sure as hell ain't going to get her hands on *my* flat, six-pack…

Of course, he wouldn't get in her tight little pussy, either. The thought made him irritable, and it wasn't long before he caused enough trouble to get barred out. He walked across the street to the Mint, but didn't make it through the door. He crawled into Adam's convertible to rest a few minutes and didn't remember a thing until he heard a female voice exclaim that there was someone in Adam's car. Adam took one look and sent the babe packing. That night, Rad stood naked in the middle of the apartment while Adam knelt before him and swallowed his cock again. Hell, he didn't even put up a fuss when the kid played with his ass while he sucked him.

Mortified, Rad hid out on the base for two solid weeks. His boot squad pulled KP on the first weekend, so he had an excuse. When the second weekend rolled around, he had to face the fact that he was hiding. He talked a lot to Nick, the company clerk, and discovered he was a pretty good all-round guy, and not just a brain. They watched a couple of ball games together and shot some pool. Nick could just about hold his own with the cue.

Nick was a talker, but not about himself. He came from the Midwest somewhere, but Rad had no clue why he'd enlisted. Running from something, probably. A woman? Nick had the dark, saturnine good looks a lot of women liked. He was on the light side, but kept in shape at the gym. He wasn't a teetotaler either Rad soon discovered when they went to the EM Club. Nick had two Tom Collins while Rad got blasted on beer.

Rad had reluctantly agreed to go with Nick to a show of some kind the following weekend, but the platoon's CO, Second Lieutenant John Fallon, invaded the dayroom on Thursday night, eyed the five or six men standing at attention, and zeroed in on Rad for some bullshit TDY. The Lieutenant's ass was chapped because he'd been ordered to deliver something to another unit about three hundred miles distant, but the old man wouldn't lend him his helicopter.

Friday morning, Rad drove out the front gates in a Humvee with a pissed-off officer beside him and some dumb-shit package in the back. To make matters worse, the damned weather was sulking, too. They finished the last hundred miles in a driving rainstorm that turned into sleet and then snow as they climbed up from the desert into the mountains. The Lieutenant, who was newly married, refused overnight accommodations, so they started back for the base shortly before sundown. They did not get far. State troopers had closed the main road because of flash flooding, stranding them in a town that sat on the desert at the edge of the mountains.

Lt. Fallon sniffed out a decent restaurant, and Rad had steak and lobster for the first time since his Uncle Ivan bought him a meal the day before he enlisted. Rad was aware that the officer, who turned his attention to him, had stopped being pissed.

"Not such a bad deal after all," Fallon said as he pushed his plate away. "Good meal, good room at a decent motel. Sorry we couldn't get separate rooms, but at least we got a king-sized bed," he said, referring to the fact that other stranded motorists were snapping up rooms all over town.

"We'll make do, sir," Rad felt obligated to comment. The Lieutenant was an enigma to Rad. Most officers held themselves apart from their men, but not to the extent that Fallon did. He was due to receive his silver bar and a reassignment soon. It really didn't matter, because Mule would run the platoon like he always did.

The Lieutenant adroitly drew him out so that before they retired, Fallon knew more about him than anyone else in the unit. Rad wasn't sure he liked that. Fortunately, his CO unbent a little and they shared a bottle before turning in. Bourbon wasn't Rad's drink, but it was alcohol.

Something woke Rad in the middle of the night. Fallon's hip was against his. Rad edged away, but the officer shifted again. Pretty soon, Rad was at the edge of the big bed, and the Lieutenant relentlessly followed. Rad flopped on his side heavily, hoping that would rouse the man enough to move over. It didn't. Rad's groin was tight against Fallon's butt. Disconcerted, the GI didn't know what to do. Maybe he should just sack out on the floor.

The movement was almost undetectable, but it was real. Fallon's butt pressed against him a bit harder. Shit! What was going on? Rad thought of Adam, and his cock stirred. The movement came again, this time unmistakable. Fallon was grinding his butt against Rad's cock. He hardened.

Suddenly, the Lieutenant's hand snaked back and grasped Rad's semi-erect cock. "I knew you'd have a big one," the officer said. "I always like to see you at attention because your pants bulge more than anyone else's." The hand skinned him back and forth a couple of times. Rad said nothing, couldn't have if he'd tried. "At first," Fallon went on, "I thought you went around with a hard-on, but decided it was just plain big. I was right."

Fallon pulled down his shorts. My God! The man wanted to be fucked! He couldn't! He'd shrivel up like a prune. But his cock, throbbing rampant and eager, made a liar out of him. Fallon moved against him again, parting his cheeks, and grasping Rad's cock, positioning it. "Now!" he whispered urgently.

So help him, Rad lunged. Flesh enfolded him, accepted him, drew him in. He plunged deeper, drawing a gasp from the Lieutenant.

"But... you're married!" Rad managed to squeeze out of his voice box.

"For six months," the officer said, reaching around to pull Rad atop him. "But my college roommate did this for two years. I was beginning to miss it. Had my eye on you from the first. Wondered what it'd be like." with you."

So Rad showed him. If a thing was worth doing, do it the best you can, was his philosophy. He threw it to Fallon partly out of lust and partly on behalf of enlisted men everywhere, screwing the commissioned officers. Well, if that was the case, the officers would get a fucking they'd well remember!

Rad came to the brink three times, but eased off to keep himself from shooting. The fourth time, he kept right on going and emptied his balls violently inside the Lieutenant. Halfway through his orgasm, he realized that the Lieutenant was having one of his own. The man's muscles grabbed him and worked him back to excitement, so Rad fucked him again, Fallon's cries of 'harder' and 'deeper' fading to helpless moans. Damned if the guy didn't come again, just before Rad. They'd both done some moaning and groaning by then.

When Rad came out of the bathroom after cleaning up, the Lieutenant spoke to him. "I didn't pick you because I saw any weakness in you, Radinsky. To the contrary, I picked you because you were the best-looking, manliest guy in the outfit who still had a little sensitivity. Needless to say, we'll both be in trouble if this gets out. So we'll never mention it again. Oh, and by the way: You were everything I thought you would be. More, actually. Thanks."

"Yes, sir. Thank you, sir," was all Rad could think to say. Strangely, he slept like a log for the rest of the night.

They were back to being officer and enlisted man the next morning. Rad could tell no difference in the Lieutenant as they started the long drive back. Rad went into his barracks that evening a frustrated man. He had the damndest story and couldn't tell it to a soul. Sunday, he looked up Adam and fucked him so hard in the mouth the guy almost strangled to death. Adam ate it up!

Rad chased women like crazy for a month after that, but when he tired of the party scene and being broke all the time he took to buddying with Nick. Nick was safe; he didn't make demands on anyone. Nick took him by surprise when he suggested they take a three-day pass and drive a hundred miles to the state fair at San Pablo. "It's not only the fair," Nick explained. "The state's art museum and natural history museum are there, too."

It took some doing but Nick convinced him, in part because San Pablo also claimed the largest nightclub in the southwest. As soon as the eight-week training session ended, the two non-coms started wrangling for their passes.

Nick was the same on base or off, in uniform or out, solemn, serious, and about the time Rad would think Nick was dull, the latter would pull some fact out of the air and relate it in a way that piqued the young corporal's interest. Before they were halfway to San Pablo, Rad was looking forward to some of those museums, just as long as they didn't get in the way of partying at the Grotto, San Pablo's fabled nightclub.

Rad found the museums more interesting that he'd expected because Nick explained things in a way that made him think. They drove outside of town to where old Indians had drawn pictures on black lava rocks. They were just hen scratches until Nick made him practically feel the ancient artisans' presence. Rad took another look at his traveling companion. He was an interesting guy.

Rad returned the favor that night at the Grotto. This was his element, and he led Nick around by the nose, coaxing him into relaxing and halfway enjoying himself. They hooked up with two *chicas*, as they called them around there, and fucked them back in the motel room.

"Hey, man, you done good!" Rad said as soon as the door closed on the two girls. "Fucked her so she squealed."

"Yeah," Nick seemed a little embarrassed. Rad guessed that to him that was something to be done in private, not shared with others.

The next day was spent at the State Fair. Rad made a half-assed date with some gal who rode the rides with him most of the afternoon. Nick rode a couple of times, but spent most of his time at the exhibits and free shows. The milk cows probably touched his midwestern soul.

He was a little pissed that Nick wouldn't go to the Grotto that night, but came off it when his friend tossed over his car keys. Rad spent a couple of hours at the joint, but conscious that he was driving someone else's car, took it easy on the beer. The girl never showed up, and he allowed several others to slip through his fingers while waiting for her. It was only midnight when he tossed in the towel and went back to the motel with a couple of six-packs. If Nick didn't want to go partying with him, at least they could share a few brews in the room.

Nick seemed surprised he was backing so early... and alone, but he readily accepted a beer and popped the top. Nick was watching some documentary on Nazi Germany, and Rad got a kick out of the old Sherman's and M-1's and especially the Jeeps. Even the helmets were different. Hell, their current headgear looked more likes the Nazis' than the old steel pots the GIs wore back then.

Rad cleaned up a little before turning into the sack. Nick was already in his bed. The room grew quiet, but Rad wasn't sleepy, just tired. "Sorry, man," Rad said to the darkness after awhile. "I'm not a very good buddy for you."

"Hell, you're not. I've had fun so far."

"Sure. That's why you didn't go with me tonight."

"Man, that wasn't it." A pause. "I didn't want to cramp your style."

"Cramp my style! We did all right last night."

"No, *you* did all right. You found your girl, and you found one for me. Whether I wanted her or not," Nick added in a lower voice.

"You didn't want her? What the hell you talking about. You fucked her eyes out, buddy."

"Yeah." The word was completely lacking in enthusiasm. Rad lay with his hands behind his head trying to figure out what that meant until Nick spoke again. "Thank you for coming with me, Joe. I've... well, I've admired you for a long time."

"You admired me?" Rad asked incredulously. "What the hell for? You're the guy with the brain."

"Yeah, but you're the guy with the cool. Everybody likes you, Joe.

Wants to be like you. Hell, even I do sometimes. And you showed me some of it last night, but… I don't have what it takes. I guess I enjoyed myself okay, but I didn't want to try it again tonight."

A little irritated, Rad snapped. "What *did* you want to do?"

"Hang out with you."

That stumped him. "Hell, we hung out all day. Well, except when I was with that broad. And when you went off to look at the exhibits. And tonight," he finished lamely. "Why the hell you want to hang out with me?" he asked in an exasperated voice.

"Tonight, when we watched that documentary, I had a good time. It was fun watching you analyze that old equipment and talk about how things are different today. You've got a good brain, too, Joe. I like it when you use it."

"Be damned. So let's hang. What do you want to talk about?"

"You. Tell me about Josef T. Radinsky."

Rad amazed himself, opening up to his friend as completely as he had to Lt. Fallon. At that thought, he discovered he had an erection. "Look, if we're going to jaw all night, come on over here where we don't have to talk so loud."

"I… can't."

"Can't? Why the hell not?"

"I just can't, Joe. Please don't ask me why."

Rad lay staring at the dark ceiling. He knew why. Nick had a hard-on, too. "Why did you join the army, Nick?" he asked suddenly.

"Seemed like the thing to do."

"I did it to get away from my father and a crazy girlfriend. Who were you getting away from?" Silence met his question. "I answered all your questions; you answer mine. Who?"

"A friend. Please, Joe. If I answer any more questions, you won't want to have anything to do with me."

"Did you fuck him or suck him? Or did he do it to you? Answer me, dammit!"

"Neither," came the subdued reply. "But he would've if I hadn't got away."

"Come here, Nick," Rad's voice was sharper than he'd intended. "Please."

It took a long time before Nick moved. He crawled into the bed shivering although it wasn't cold in the room.

"Why are you shaking?" Rad demanded.

"I'm afraid of you, Joe. Have been ever since I laid eyes on you. Wanted to be your friend, but knew you were dangerous."

- 280 -

"Have you ever been with a man… done it, I mean?" Nick did not answer. "All right, I'll go first," Rad said. "One guy's sucked my cock a few times, and I fucked another… once."

Nick gave a little gasp. "You? Man, I never thought…"

"Neither did I, but I did. And right now I want you."

Nick laid a palsied hand on his chest. "Is that the truth? You want me?"

"Feel for yourself," Rad invited. An eager hand grasped his hard cock.

Nick let out a gasp. "I knew it was big, but I didn't know it was that big."

Rad quickly slipped off Nick's shorts. "Damn, you're no slouch in the cock department either."

"I never dreamed you'd ever feel me. Tell me what to do, Joe."

"Come here," Rad said, pulling Nick's head to him. They were both shocked when their lips touched. Overcoming surprise at his own actions, Rad forced his tongue into Nick's mouth.

"Man," Nick panted when they parted. "Sure didn't feel like that with that girl!" Following instructions at first, and his instincts later, Nick sucked Rad's nipples until they hurt, rubbed his chest until the hair got sore, eagerly felt his flat belly with his hands, his face, his tongue. A little more tentatively, he sucked Rad's big balls and finally took the tip of his hard cock into his mouth. Nick stayed high up on the head, not going down much beyond the glans, but it got the job done. Rad shouted a warning, but not in time. The first gob of cum went right in Nick's mouth. The second hit him on his cheek as he kept pumping the big cock. The third got him in the eye. Nick held still and accepted the remainder of Rad's seed right in his face, after which he rested his head on Rad's hairless belly. Reaching for a handy bath towel, Rad carefully wiped his cum off Nick's face. His hand on the other man's naked shoulder felt good.

"Sorry," Nick apologized. "I shoulda tried to take it, but I panicked. Next time, I will, I promise… if you'll let me try it again"

"Yeah, okay. But right now, I want you to do something for me," he said, snapping on the bedside lamp. "C'mon, Jack off."

Slowly, self-consciously, flushing from embarrassment, Nick grasped himself and started skinning his bone. As he watched his friend, Rad felt himself stir again. He placed Nick's other hand on his cock, and it grew harder. Nick's lips parted, his eyes glazed. Suddenly, Rad reached out and stopped his friend. Startled, Nick looked over at him, a question in his eyes.

Deliberately, Rad rose and moved between Nick's knees. He leaned forward. "Wet it for me," he ordered.

Obediently, Nick sucked the revived cock into is mouth, taking more of it this time, prepared to keep his promise. When it was wet with saliva and fully rampant, Rad withdrew. He saw the sudden fear in Nick's eyes when he lifted the two, bronzed legs over his shoulder.

"Oh," Nick's voice quailed slightly. "I don't know…"

"Hush. Relax. Enjoy."

Relax, Nick did not. Nor did he hush. He howled, first from fear, then from pain, and finally from ecstasy. "Oh, *fuck* me, Joe! Oh, *man*… That feels so good! Why does it feel so fucking *good*? Fuck it; I don't care," he babbled. "Harder. Fuck me *harder*, Joe. *Give* it to me. Give me your big cock! I didn't think… I could take it all, but… I *did*, man. All of it! Oh, *man*…" On and on, he talked and moaned.

When Rad got close, he grabbed Nick's cock and stroked him steadily while humping his ass. Suddenly, Nick shouted aloud and, wrapping his slender legs around Rad, shot endless rounds of warm, milky cum between them. While shooting, his ass grabbed Rad's cock and squeezed, causing Rad to explode with a force that stunned them both. As he pumped his seed into his Nick's spasming butt, Rad recognized that he had finally found what he was looking for.

BUSFUCKINGRIDE

The cross-country bus ride turned boring within the first fifty miles. Pvt Jimmy B. Mackey would have gone home by train if not for the poker game a couple of nights ago. On the other hand, he'd be boarding an airliner if he'd won the last hand. Now, as a penance for gambling he'd spend four days and nights on a frigging bus to get back to Tennessee. He smiled wryly as he recalled one of his platoon buddies describing the journey.

"Shit, Mackey! That ain't no bus ride. That's a busfuckingride!" The expletive, probably the most common in US Army vernacular, vividly conveyed that it was something more than an ordinary bus ride.

Jimmy had looked forward to that day every minute of the eight miserable weeks of basic infantry training at Fort Ord, California with its freezing dawn beach ranges where it was too fucking cold to even pull a trigger on a damned rifle, much less hit the target—Maggie's Drawers being the norm until the sun came up. The field jackets, gloves, scarves and other crap worn in a vain attempt to keep the piercing ocean winds from slicing out your liver became just so much awkward, added weight to lug around.

Now he was out! Free! After a two-week leave, he would report to Ft. Dix, New Jersey on his way to fucking Germany! Life would be different there! There'd be booze and frauleins all over the place. In the meantime, there'd be moonshine and down-home girls!

At least the frigging bus was big, with plush, partially reclining seats, and an inboard head. Jimmy chose a window seat in the rear on the driver's side a couple of rows ahead of the toilet, calculating that his position was far enough removed so as not to catch the smell, yet close enough so everyone wouldn't know he was going to lop out his cock and piss… or whatever.

He threw his military-style carry all in the overhead compartment and sat watching the other passengers board. Great! The seat backs were tall enough to give him a little privacy, good for stacking Z's when the time came. Typical of GI thinking, Jimmy B. Mackey figured that every minute asleep was a minute closer to home.

There was nobody of interest boarding until a pert gal in a short skirt and tight sweater slid her trim ass in a seat two rows up on the right side of the bus. Shit! A college kid flopped down beside her. Oh, well, he'd been without for better than eight weeks, so he could wait a little longer. Besides, what the hell could you do on a public bus? Still, some feminine conversation would have been welcome.

When the bus ended up only about two-thirds full he rested a little easier. He wouldn't have to share his seat with some two-ton fatso. He couldn't abide sweaty blimps who smelled like they never bathed whether they did or not!

The last person aboard was a young kid who looked to be high school aged. Jimmy saw him eye the uniform as he took the seat across the aisle. It was funny how many people reacted to his Class-A khakis. There were uniforms all over California, but people still took notice. Made him feel sort of proud. At the same time it annoyed the shit out of him because he liked his privacy. The kid smiled and nodded; Jimmy gave him a curt one back.

When the driver closed the door and pulled out of the LA terminal, all the passengers were at least two rows in front of him except for the kid right across the way. Good! It ought to be a quiet ride, Jimmy thought as he opened the sports magazine he'd bought in the gift shop. The excited chatter of a new adventure died away to a steady drone. The filtered air was fresh enough to be halfway pleasant.

Somewhere in the first five pages, he dropped off, and by the time he opened his eyes again the light was beginning to go. The kid across from him had scooted over to the aisle to avoid the setting sun's glare. Shoulda planned better, sonny boy.

The kid noticed he was awake. "Army, huh?" he opened. "Infantry?"

Jimmy nodded, not really wanting to strike up a conversation. He heard the subdued chatter of the college man and the pretty girl a couple of rows up. "Yeah, how'd you know?"

"Blue braid," the boy answered proudly. "My big brother's in the infantry. He's over in Germany."

"That's where I'm headed after a leave. Some place called Ulm."

"That's near Munich. My brother was there for a while."

"How'd he like it?"

"A lot. He's in Berlin now, but I think he liked the countryside more. Said things were better a year ago. People are getting tired of the GI's now."

"Yeah, they rub a little raw sometimes."

"You mind if I come over and talk some."

There it was, exactly what Jimmy had feared, but what the hell. "Sure, come on over," he said graciously. "My name's Jimmy Mackey," he held out a hand. The kid took it and said, "Will" back at him.

Jimmy guessed that answering a host of questions about Ft. Ord and the last eight weeks and Tennessee and the last twenty-years was preferable to staring out into the gathering night. He excused himself and slid by the kid to empty his bladder in the closet-sized head behind him. When he returned to his seat the bus was streaking by streetlights.

"Guess we're supposed to stop here for a rest," the kid volunteered when Jimmy was seated again. "You wanta get something to eat."

"Sure. Why not?"

It was while they were munching on surprisingly good hamburgers at a little Formica table in the restaurant that Jimmy caught on that the kid was passing him glances from under lowered lashes. Jimmy was proud of the way he looked in his uniform, but after half a day on a bus, he must be pretty wilted. Ah, the power of the uniform.

With a little bit of envy, he noticed the laughter and the banter swirling around the chick and frat boy's table. He envied guys who could do that. Jimmy tended to sports and hunting and fishing talk, and so far he'd found damned few girls who responded to that for very long except for a few who *looked* like athletes, hunters, and fisher... persons. After he ran out of patter, Jimmy always wanted to get physical, and after eight weeks of nothing, not even pulling his own pud, he *needed* to get physical!

Will must have been reading his mind. "Is it true that they give you that stuff?"

Startled back to the present, Jimmy blinked. "What stuff?"

"That soft-peter stuff to keep you from getting horny?"

"Beats me. Might be in the food, although the entire cadre ate the stuff, too. But there's no fucking privacy, so you couldn't do anything even if you wanted."

"Didn't you go on passes?"

"Sure. But the girls I met wanted cold hard cash, and I've never paid for it in my life. Went off on my own once and met a nice girl, but that's what she was, a nice girl. Every time I wanted to neck, she told me how much Jesus loved me."

"Those others, the ones who wanted money, they were prostitutes?"

"No, they were whores. Prostitutes had more class."

The kid snickered. "Did you do it to any of them?"

"Nope. They all looked like what they were?"

At the driver's first call for boarding, Jimmy headed for the men's room to drain the last drop of coffee before getting back on the bus. As he finished and was about to tuck it back into his pants, Will showed up and took his own leak.

The kid didn't even ask this time, just sat down beside Jimmy like that was his own seat. Neither of them said a word as the bus maneuvered the town's avenues, running through alternating patches of light and dark. Finally they hit the open stretch of highway and Will leaned over to him.

"Guess it's not working on you."

"What's not working?"

"That soft peter stuff. Looked like you were getting big back there at the urinal."

"Nope, that's about normal," Jimmy said, trying to get off the subject.

"Wow! You must be big!"

Jimmy couldn't help sending the kid a quick glance. Jeez, was this how the kids talked today? That woulda got you a knuckle sandwich back home, unless, of course, you were kidding around with your buddies.

"I'm pretty big, too," Will went on, ignoring being ignored. "At least that's what they say at school."

"How old are you, kid?"

"Eighteen."

"Eighteen, and you're still talking about cock size? Grow up."

Will shut up, but he didn't seem chastened. After another mile or so, he started back in. "Can I feel it?"

"What the fuck! You retarded or something?"

"Fixated," the kid said easily. "Fixated on big cocks. Looking for the biggest one I can find."

"Why, you gonna suck it or something?"

"Naw, but I can make it feel real good."

"How's that?" The boy made a pumping motion with his fist. "Shit, kid," Jimmy snorted. "I quit jacking off years ago."

"A man can't go eight weeks without wanting *somebody* to do something for him. You don't like how it feels, just tell me to quit."

"Fuck, Will, there's other people on the bus."

"Yeah, but it's pitch black, and everybody's in front of us. We can see anybody coming." The kid didn't wait for approval; he slid his hand over Jimmy's leg. "Oh, man, it is big. Can I feel it?"

"Shit, thought you was!" Jimmy groused, spreading his legs.

The kid was on him in a second. One hand sheathed the rapidly hardening cock running down his pant leg, the other rubbed the GI's flat belly. Keeping a sharp eye on the front of the bus, Jimmy let the kid play. By the time Will pulled his cock and balls out of the top of his khakis, Jimmy had hit his zenith, as big and hard as he got.

"Geez!" Will breathed. "How big is it?"

"Shit, I never measured it," Jimmy answered. "Big enough to do the job."

"Were you the biggest one in school? I am, or that's what they say, anyway."

"That's what I used to hear," Jimmy said modestly.

"How about in your squad?"

"I guess. Never saw them hard, but I'd say it ranked right up there."

"How about your platoon?"

"Shit, where we going with this? The company? The battalion? King Kong of the Army? How the hell do I know? What's with you and big cocks, anyway?"

I just like big ones. What's the biggest you've ever seen?"

"For the last time, kid, I don't go around looking at cocks. Now shut up about it and do what you gotta do.

Will had already lost interest in the subject. He was now engrossed in making Jimmy's dick perform tricks. He pressed the long, thick organ flat against the GI's lean belly and watched it spring back up into the air. He made it dance by tickling the private's balls. Then he suddenly freed his own cock.

"Not bad, huh?" the kid bragged.

Despite himself, Jimmy looked. "Not bad."

"But you've got me beat by a little," Will acknowledged, pumping gently on Jimmy's cock.

Man, that felt good! The GI laid back and spread his legs as far as they would go. Will picked up a rhythm.

"I saw a bigger one once," the kid panted. "But this is... the biggest cock... I ever jacked off!" Jimmy opened his eyes and saw that Will was jerking them both, one in each hand. Must be ambidextrous because he sure as hell seemed to be doing a great job. Movement out of the corner of his eye startled Jimmy, but when he twisted around in the seat no one was there.

"Can you feel it?" Will wheezed.

"Man, do I ever! I'm getting that feeling... right down in my balls!" the soldier acknowledged breathily. Geez, the kid was doing a whale of a job. His forefinger and thumb opened and closed around Jimmy's cock like the lips of a woman's vagina. Shit he was good!

"I'm coming, kid!" Jimmy whispered urgently, fighting to get his handkerchief out of his back pocket. He didn't quite make it. The first contraction hit, paralyzing him. His jism shot up on his shirt. He caught the next glob in the white linen and felt the kid's legs spasm as he hit his own orgasm. Shit! He didn't know a hand job could feel like this!

It took a minute or so for the two of them to come back to Earth. Jimmy had stowed himself away, and the kid was about halfway covered when the door to the john opened and the college kid emerged.

Shit! Had he seen anything? Didn't act like it. And if he did, so fucking what?

Like the GI knew he would, the kid wanted to talk about it now. That was the last thing Jimmy wanted. He felt sorta creepy and wanted to be left alone.

"Did I do it okay?"

"Great, kid. Great."

"You ever had anybody do it better?"

Naw. That was the best... hand job ever," he added inanely.

"One of these days I'm gonna learn to do the other. You know, with my mouth. Wish we had some more time; I might try it on you. I really do like your cock. It's really great!"

"Yeah, well, it likes your fist, Will. Maybe we can try it again tomorrow night."

"Can't. I get off up the road a ways. Wish I could. Man, do I ever."

As if on cue, the outlying lights of an approaching town glowed ahead of them. Despite feeling a little ashamed, Jimmy took a good look at the kid. Pug-nosed, good-looking. A guy you'd figure was scheming on some girl. Instead, he hit on a lonely GI.

They said awkward goodbyes as the bus stopped briefly. Jimmy took the opportunity to hit the onboard head and wash off his shirt. When it dried, the cum wouldn't show. That was the plan anyway.

Jimmy slept the remainder of the night, waking when the driver announced a breakfast stop. He shaved and took a spit bath in the sink of the men's room at the station before changing into a clean uniform from his carryall. As he claimed a table, the college boy slid his cereal and fruit bowls alongside Jimmy's scrambled eggs and sausage.

"Mind if I join you?"

"What happened to your girlfriend," Jimmy asked.

"Got off at the same stop as your boyfriend last night." Jimmy sat up straight, his hackles rising. "Don't get all bent out of shape. At least you got something besides talk out of him."

"What the hell are you talking about?"

"About what I saw when I went to the restroom last night. He was whanging your big dong pretty good. Hell, he was beating both of them and didn't miss a stroke."

Deciding he was caught fair and square, Jimmy simply shrugged. "Hell, I just got out of eight weeks of training. Haven't fucked a woman in over two months."

"So any port in a storm, huh?"

"I can't believe we're sitting here talking about this shit." Jimmy didn't understand why he wasn't pissed. He gave college boy a closer look. Good-looking, jock type, but older than he first thought. This guy was at the upper end of the college experience, probably a couple of years older than he was.

"The kid do a decent job?"

Enough was enough, Jimmy decided. He leaned forward and lowered his voice. "If it's any of your business, he did a damned decent job."

"My name's Doug. Yours is Jimmy. I heard the kid call you that. Anyway, Jimmy, I'll show you what good *really* is if you're still on the bus tonight. You know what's better than a hand job?"

"Yeah," Jimmy sought to contain his delayed anger. "A good piece of poontang about five-four, hundred and twenty pounds with at least twenty of them in the boobs."

The college boy smiled. "No. You just think so. What's really good is my mouth sliding up and down your cock. Unless you've got the biggest one in the country I can take the whole thing down my throat. I can suck cum out of your nuts you didn't even know you had."

Jimmy sneered. "You've sucked lots of cocks, have you?"

"Just one. My college roommate's... for the last four years. His cum was strong and musky. I can hardly wait to see what yours is like."

"Be a cold day in hell," Jimmy snarled.

The college guy smiled serenely as he rose from the table. "We'll see. Until tonight."

Jimmy returned to the bus mentally shaking his head. Within five miles, he allowed the quiet drone of the motor to put him to sleep without once looking at what's his name, Doug, two rows up and across the aisle. When he woke, the territory outside the windows had turned bleak and dramatic, so he figured they were into Arizona now. The air conditioner was struggling a little to keep things comfortable. Shit, they'd be halfway to Tennessee if they didn't stop at every Podunk town with a water tower. The bus was rarely on the interstate, but it seemed to find every back road in the country.

Doug left him alone at the lunch stop and the dinner layover, and as night fell, Jimmy figured everything was copasetic. The number of passengers continued to dwindle. At nine o'clock when College Man went to the head, Jimmy pretended to be dozing. A few minutes later, Doug claimed the seat beside him.

"Is GI's little Joe ready?"

"Fuck no! Get out of here."

"It must be a big sucker. When you walk off the bus your groin leads your nose by... a nose." Jimmy squirmed, but he didn't know if it was from discomfort or excitement. "Rick's—that's my roommate—was eight inches long. Yours beat that?"

"How the hell do I know?"

"Who else would ... besides the kid last night?"

"A couple of girls in Tennessee."

"No guys?"

"Shit, no! What you think I am, a queer?"

Doug shrugged. "I don't know. Didn't even know I was until I swallowed Rick's cum the first time."

Jimmy heard himself asking. "How'd that happen?"

Double-dated. Struck out. Went back to the dorm with a hard-on. I saw his; he saw mine. We started doing what you and that kid were doing, but it wasn't enough. Next thing I knew, I was sucking it down my throat."

"That's disgusting!"

"No, man: that was *wonderful*. He wasn't much interested in girls after that. The night before graduation he begged me to do it one last time."

"And you haven't done it to anybody since then?"

"Nope. Haven't wanted to until I saw what that kid was stroking. Almost threw him out of the seat and took over myself. But I didn't, and been hoping ever since that you'd still be on the bus tonight. Can I feel?"

"Fuck, why not!" Jimmy sighed, spreading his legs once again.

Doug wasn't as eager as Will, but he was a lot more thorough. He stroked the GI's legs and groin and belly until the cock threatened to burst through the khaki. Without asking, the college boy loosened Jimmy's clothing and tugged his trousers down his thighs.

"Shit, man! Somebody might see!"

Doug gave a smile. "Not if you'll do a better job of keeping an eye out. It's up to you. I'll be busy." With that, the slender blonde slid out of his seat and knelt on the floor. His tongue brushed the slit, picking up a small drop of pre-cum. The boy opened his mouth and admitted the entire glans. Jimmy's whole body reacted with a twitch. Doug up came to the end; then swallowed it down again, taking a little more each time. Giving his head a curious twist as he rode up and down the shaft, the college boy kept at it until his lips finally touched the black, curly hair of the soldier's pubic bush.

'Man, that's great!" Doug said, coming up for air. "Gotta be at least as big as Rick's! And thick! Can't really take it all. Feel good?"

"It feels okay," Jimmy lied. It felt fucking great!

"You've never had a blowjob before?"

"Not from a guy. This girl did it to me at school, but she couldn't take much more than the head," the GI replied, resisting an urge to push the boy back down on his cock. Doug smiled like he understood, and bent to lick the soldier's balls.

Before it was over, Jimmy's pants were down around his ankles and Doug was licking and stroking everything he could reach. He even had one hand between Jimmy's legs teasing his sphincter. Jimmy though he'd go crazy.

Then the build-up began in his balls. It radiated up into his belly. Even his nipples got into the act, standing up and tingling like mad. The soldier emitted a sound something like "ghnnnh!" and let loose.

Doug didn't break his rhythm when the GI exploded, flooding his mouth and throat and nasal passages with milky, sweet cum. The college boy rode him all the way through the orgasm, sucking and swallowing, tasting and enjoying. When the last drop had been pulled from Jimmy's body, the GI lay back against his seat exhausted. Doug came up and grinned at him.

"Better than a hand job?"

"Uh, yeah… b… better," Jimmy stammered.

Doug continued to stare at him until Jimmy realized he was still exposed. If anybody started for the head, he'd never get himself covered in time. Yet it seemed like a hell of an effort to move. Doug took it for an invitation and bent back to him. But Jimmy was finished. The college boy couldn't even get a pulse out of GI's little Joe.

Jimmy pushed him away, but was moved to offer his thanks. Wearily, he pulled his boxers and khakis into place, trying not to make too much noise fastening the freaking brass belt buckle.

Doug watched it all with interest. "You wanta know how you taste?"

"You're gonna tell me anyway, aren't you?"

"Yeah," Doug beamed. "Wish it was yours I'd been sucking for four years. You taste sorta sweet, not musky like Rick's. I like the taste of it. And I like your cock, too. It's a beauty."

"Never heard anybody's cock described that way."

"Well believe me, it is. I'll suck you anytime, soldier boy."

"Fine, next time I'm in fucking Nowheresville, I'll look you up."

The college boy was smart enough not to wear out his welcome. Within a few minutes he moved back to his own seat, leaving Jimmy to wonder about what the hell was happening to him.

The college boy disembarked at the next stop, and Jimmy was sufficiently motivated to write down the name of the place although he didn't even know the guy's name except for 'Doug'.

Strangely stimulated by more action that he'd seen since his teenage years, Jimmy had trouble settling down for the remainder of the ride. He slept off and on the rest of the night, and alternated between dozing and sightseeing most of the next day. The bleakness of desert and plain was behind them now, so he figured they must be in eastern Oklahoma or even Arkansas. He'd have to pay more attention to the towns they passed through. One more frigging night on this mechanical monster and he'd be home. He smiled a secret smile. It hadn't all been bad. Like the guy said, a busfuckingride! The smile disappeared. Shit! It had all been with guys. Well, no more of that bullfucking crap! Soft curves, billowy bosoms, and wet, hungry cunt from now on for Jimmy B. Mackey, Private Second Class, US Army Infantry.

They threw him off the bus some place in western Arkansas. Nothing personal, they were merely retiring the old one and putting him aboard a new steed. He made a beeline for the men's room and began the not-so-satisfactory process of washing out of a basin again. He shaved, brushed his teeth, took off his shirt and washed his torso the best he could. In the middle of it, some guy came in, paused for a second to look at him, and locked himself into a stall.

Out of the corner of his eye, Jimmy saw that the guy had worn some sort of uniform, but that was about all except that he was a small man. Finished with the major part of his toilet, the soldier went to the urinal to empty his bladder. Still sensitive to male attention, he noticed that there was a hole in the wall between the urinal and the shit stall. Not only that, there was an eye glued to the hole. Damned if he didn't swell up a little when he pumped his cock to make sure the last drop had fallen. He stood a moment longer than necessary, allowing it to grow a little more before opening his trousers to arrange himself comfortably and smooth his shirttail inside his trousers. He almost laughed at the show he was giving the pervert. Now he'd leave the guy panting for more. Back at the basin to wash his hands, all he could see of the guy in the stall through the mirror was a gray walking shoe and an equally gray pant leg.

Jimmy was tempted to hang around outside the men's room to see the fairy when he came out, but decided getting a good seat was a better use of his time. As soon as he stood in front of the door, other riders began lining up behind him. He laughed. Just like the fucking army. Get in line and wait! The bus driver finally showed up to open the door and allow those transferring from the other bus to board first. He took the same seat, but noticed that the seatbacks weren't nearly so high. What the hell! All that stuff was behind him now.

When the last of the passengers had boarded, Jimmy noted that the bus was half empty. The driver announced that they'd have a new jockey for the next stretch. With that, the overweight, balding man left and the new driver took over. He made a no-nonsense headcount, announced the next five stops, and claimed his seat to guide the bus out of the depot and onto a busy commercial street.

This driver was much younger, and Jimmy didn't know if that was of concern or not. If the army had taught him one thing, it was that inexperience was not to be trusted. Every time a hotshot shave tail led the platoon on an exercise shooting an azimuth, everybody knew they were in for a long haul. The grizzled NCOs could walk the compass in their sleep; but the damned second lieutenants couldn't find their way to the mess hall. Worse, the sergeants wouldn't tell the officers when they were heading in the wrong direction.

This driver looked to be about twenty-five. Not only that, he was Mex or Indian or something. At least he was dark complexioned. Black hair, probably black eyes. Jimmy watched him carefully until the man had expertly maneuvered the bus through the city streets and picked up yet another two-lane highway. This driver was different in another way, too. He constantly studied his charges in the rear-view mirror. Jimmy smiled as he wondered if the high school kid and the college boy would have gotten away with what they'd done with this guy in charge.

Most of the other riders were short-term travelers. As evening approached, Jimmy was the only one left, all the others having exited the bus along country roads somewhere. Within five minutes, the driver was eyeing Jimmy.

"Come on up and keep me awake."

Jesus! He was kidding, wasn't he? About the awake part, anyway. Nonetheless, the soldier made his way up the aisle and took a seat on the right almost opposite the driver.

"This is usually a lonely stretch," the driver said in a pleasant baritone. "Name's Steve," he added, indicating his driver ID that read Steven Larkson.

Shit, that didn't sound Mexican or Indian. Jimmy took a better look: still dark, still something exotic about the guy, mixture of bloods probably—Cajun, Red, Spic, Anglo. Whatever, it blended in this guy to make one good-looking dude. Jimmy soon learned Steve was a vet, had gotten out the previous year. Marines, but still considered the army a semi-legitimate branch of the military... but just barely. Before long, they were talking like buddies from the trenches. Of course, some of Steve's trenches had blood in them, but that didn't seem to make any difference.

As they entered the outskirts of yet another town, Steve warned him there'd be a half-hour layover. Since the soldier had been on the bus for better than three days, he offered the use of the driver's private shower in the back of the combination truck-stop/bus depot. Jimmy jumped on the offer, glad that he hadn't changed into his last clean Class A.

The shower was the finest thing he'd experienced since he jumped Mary May's bones last year when he was saying goodbye. In fact, the shower might have had a slight edge. He applied the razor again to take off the little bit of stubble that had accumulated in the past few hours and the toothbrush to take off the double cheeseburger he'd devoured a few minutes earlier. Man, he looked like a million dollars even if he said so himself!

The bus was already filling with new passengers by the time he joined the line, and as he gave Steve a thumbs-up over the shower, he noticed the driver's shoes. Gray walking shoes. Gray uniform. He almost stumbled over the step. Shit! Didn't mean a thing, did it? Lotsa guys wore gray shoes. Still, he remembered thinking the guy in the stall had worn some sort of uniform?

Once out of town, it was too dark to be certain, but damned if it didn't seem like Steve's eyes stayed on him in the rear-view. Naw! He had to be wrong. He was one macho ex-marine.

Jimmy tried to sleep, but the damned bus kept starting and stopping. A lot of times, they were halting out in the countryside. Who in the hell were these people getting off in the middle of fucking nowhere in the middle of the fucking night? Must be a bunch of farmers going home. By midnight, the bus was empty again except for the driver and him. He thought Steve would call him up, but he didn't. After a mile or so, Jimmy hesitantly got up and made his way to the front. The first thing he noticed were those damned shoes. Then he saw how fucking small Steve was. The guy in the stall had been small. Shit!

"What's the matter?" Steve asked.

Jimmy hadn't realized that it showed. "Uh, nothing. Just thinking back to the first time I saw you."

"In the men's room, you mean? Didn't think you saw me."

"Just a glimpse. Wasn't sure."

"So now I'm busted, huh?" the ex-gyrene said with a smile.

"Maybe. Yeah. Guess so. What…"

"What was I thinking? I was thinking 'Jeez, what a fucking hunk! Like to get my hands on that!'"

Jim shook his head. "Crap I don't believe this!"

"Sorry if I offended you."

"Shit! That's not what I mean! It's this fucking bus ride!" Steve shot him a look. "I mean, the first night, some high school kid jerked me off. The second, a college boy sucked my cock. And now my driver wants a piece of me! I don't believe it!"

"Believe it. I want that big cock so bad I can taste it. I want to strip you buck-naked and suck on everything you've got. Then I want you to crawl on top of me and fuck me blind!"

"*Fuck* you!" Jimmy roared. "I don't fuck *guys*!"

"Don't know what you're missing."

"Then I won't miss it, will I? Rest of it sounds okay, but I don't know about the fucking part. Hell, you were a damned marine! How come you like to fuck guys?"

"Got the first cock up my ass *in* the marines," Steve replied. "We were on a field exercise; it was in the winter, and this Lance Corporal and me crawled up in a deuce half-loaded with fart bags. We bored down in the middle to get warm. Wasn't long before that wasn't all I was getting. Good-looking fucker screwed me half to death. That was *a marine* fucking! Wonder how an army fucking compares?"

"So I'm supposed to uphold the honor of the Army by fucking your ass?"

"You'll see worse duty," Steve smiled.

"The fuck I will!"

"Exactly." We were quiet for a mile or so before he checked his watch. "Look, Jimmy, we're running about 20 minutes ahead of schedule. There's a rest stop a mile ahead. We can park and try it out… you know, see what happens. I really would like to fool around, even if you don't want to fuck me."

"Can you just park like that? Won't the cops check you out?"

Steve flashed a smile. Even bus drivers need to hit the head sometime. Nobody's gonna bother us. How about it?"

"Shit, I'm game! At least for the sucking part."

The rest area was deserted and poorly lighted. Steve pulled in behind the men's room and shut down the lights although he kept the motor running. Grabbing Jimmy's crotch, he led him to the back of the bus by the cock, which firmed up rather nicely beneath his hand.

"Now I wanta see!" he said, turning to the soldier. They undressed like military men, taking care to preserve the creases in trousers and to spread shirts over chair backs. The underwear got thrown aside.

"Man, oh man!" Steve sighed, fingering the big cock. "You could send me to heaven with that thing."

"Yeah, well, send me *somewhere*, will you?"

"You bet! Lie down, soldier boy."

It was a little weird, feeling Steve's naked flesh on his own as the guy knelt in front of Jimmy, who was sprawled on the bench seat along the back of the bus. The bus jockey couldn't take as much of the hot, throbbing cock as the college boy had, but he knew what to do with the part he could swallow. His tongue was amazing! Before Jimmy knew it he was lying on his spine with his legs across Steve's naked shoulders while the guy applied that magic tongue to his balls, behind the balls, and then his buns. Gradually, he permitted his legs to bend until Steve's tongue stroked his sphincter. The soldier jumped about a half a foot at the contact. Shit! Man! Fucking A! Then Steve pulled him over on top of him in the aisle.

"Touch me, man!" the driver whispered.

"*Wait* a minute..."

"Just touch it! Please!"

So Jimmy sat on his knees and stroked the guy's small, shapely cock a couple of times. Then Steve pulled him on top of his body. The guy's legs folded up, and Jimmy found his cockhead throbbing against the gyrene's butt hole. What the fuck! Jimmy shoved his hips forward. His cock slid into place. The sphincter gave; his glans eased inside.

"Shit!" Steve exclaimed.

"Oh, fuck!" Jimmy exhaled.

The two of them went crazy. Jimmy quickly discovered what a turn-on this man-fucking thing was, and the ex-marine learned what an army fucking was. Jimmy drove his cock so far into the smaller man that he expected to see it come out his mouth. Steve merely sighed in delight. The soldier experimented, went slow and easy for a while before slamming Steve so hard he felt he was going to come. Then he rested while Steve squirmed around doing all the work.

Shit! He'd never experienced *anything* like this, not even Mary May in the back of his pickup! Jimmy tried to hurt the other man, but his effort was in vain. Steve took everything he could dish out and begged for more! Near the end, Jimmy jerked completely out of the man, flipped him over on all fours, and rammed himself in the hole up to his balls. The guy just yelled for more! Oh, shit... Oh, *shit*... Jimmy thought as his lower half went haywire with more weird sensations than he could handle. He grunted like an animal and came and came and came—shooting more juice into that ex-gyrene than he had in his last two orgasms combined! Meanwhile, Steve was moaning for more and more.

Jimmy soon realized that the guy was coming. As Steve shot his load, his ass massaged Jimmy back to life for second round. When it was all over, they both had to crawl to the inboard head and wash one another off. It was another five minutes before Steve was able to drive the fucking bus.

The only thing the dark, good-looking driver said was, "Marines 50; Army 100!"

All Jimmy could do was sit with his eyes glazed over and marvel that this whole goddamned thing had indeed turned into a fuckingbusfuckingride for *real*!

CONTRIBUTORS
(Other Than the Editor, John Patrick)

"Semenshed of Boys"
Antler

The poet lives in Milwaukee when not traveling to perform his poems or wildernessing. His epic poem *Factory* was published by City Lights. His collection of poems *Last Words* was published by Ballantine. Winner of the Whitman Award from the Walt Whitman Society of Camden, New Jersey, and the Witter Bynner prize from the Academy and Institute of Arts & Letters in New York, his poetry has appeared in many periodicals (including *Utne Reader, Whole Earth Review* and *American Poetry Review)* and anthologies (including *Gay Roots, Erotic by Nature,* and *Gay and Lesbian Poetry of Our Time).*

"Me & the Colonel" , "Soldiers Reunion" and "The Star Recruit"
William Cozad

The author is a regular contributor to gay magazines and his startling memoirs were published by STARbooks Press in *Lover Boys* and Boys of the Night. Another of his books,"The Preacher's Boy," appeared in *Secret Passions.*

"The Draft"
Peter Gilbert

"Semi-retired" after a long career with the British Armed Forces, the author now lives in Germany but is contemplating a return to England. A frequent contributor to various periodicals, he also writes for television. He enjoys walking, photography and reading. His stories have swiftly become favorites by readers of STARbooks' anthologies.

"Military Maneuvers"
Rick Jackson, USMC

The oft-published author specializes in jarhead stories. When not travelling, he is based in Hawaii.

"Sailor Boy" and "Raw Recruits"
Ken Smith

The author, who lives in Brighton, England, started life as a simple country lad. At the tender age of 15, he joined the Royal Navy, and says he has "ridden some big ones whilst at sea. Waves mostly." A story by Ken was included in *Queer View Mirror II*, published in Canada, and he has had several of his stories published in the London-based magazines *Vulcan, Mister,* and *Zipper.*

"Deja Vu"
Ken Anderson
The author is awaiting publication of his novel, *Someone Bought the House on the Island*. A book of his poems, *The Intense Lover*, was published by STARbooks Press. The author lives in Georgia.

"Seaman's Reunion"
Peter Eros
The author is a frequent contributor to STARbooks's anthologies.

"My Boy"
Jack Ricardo
The author, who lives in Florida, is a novelist and frequent contributor to various gay magazines. His latest novel is *Last Dance at Studio 54*.

"Looking for It"
Mario Solano
This is the first of this author's short and sweet stories to be published by STARbooks Press. It will not be the last.

"The Stuff of Mystery"
Christopher Thomas
The poet has had his work published in many literary journals including *Deviance, The James White Review,* and *RFD*. He makes his living as a Gentleman Farmer.

"Busfuckingride"
Mark Wildyr:
Born and raised an Okie, Mr. Wildyr graduated Texas Christian University in Fort Worth, Texas with a degree in Government and History. Following service in the US Army, he worked in banking, finance, and administration. Mr. Wildyr has authored several novels, most with contemporary settings in his adopted state of New Mexico. Multi-cultural interactions are of particular interest to him. More recently, he has turned his attention to writing short stories exploring personal development and sexual discovery. Companion Press has purchased twelve such stories, and Alyson Publications is including one in an anthology to be published in January 2003. After making his STARbooks debut in *Wild and Willing,* Wildyr contributed the novella, "The Hawk Takes Flight" to *Fantasies Made Flesh.* Mark. Wildyr is married with two adult children and resides in Albuquerque, New Mexico.

ACKNOWLEDGEMENTS AND SOURCES

Main cover illustration courtesy
of Bacchus Releasing, famous for
Black Forest and Filmco videos.
Address: 9718 Glenoaks Blvd., Unit B,
Sun Valley, CA 91352.
Phone 800-768-9101 for free catalogue.

Secondary illustration courtesy
New Age Pictures and Gino Colbert.
Address: P.O. Box 1234, Hollywood CA 90078.

ABOUT THE EDITOR

John Patrick was a prolific, prize-winning author of fiction and non-fiction. One of his short stories, "The Well," was honored by PEN American Center as one of the best of 1987. His novels and anthologies, as well as his non-fiction works, including *Legends* and *The Best of the Superstars* series, continue to gain him new fans every day. One of his most famous short stories appears in the Badboy collection *Southern Comfort* and another appears in the collection *The Mammoth Book of Gay Short Stories*.

A divorced father of two, the author was a longtime member of the American Booksellers Association, the Florida Publishers' Association, American Civil Liberties Union, and the Adult Video Association. He resides in Florida. JP passed away in October 2001.